verse is shaking.the universe is shaking.the univ
ing.the uNiverse is shaking.the univeRse is shaki
s shaking.the universe is s   is
.the universe is shaKing.th   ng.
ing.the universe is shaking   laki
s Shaking.the universe is s   is
e is shaking.the uNiverse is shaking.   eRse
verse is shaking.the universe iS shaking.the univ
 universe is shaking.the universe is shaking.tHe
.the universe is shAking.the universe is shaking.
ing.the universe is shaking.the universe is shaki
s shaking.the uNiverse is shaking.the univeRse is
e is shaking.tHe universe is shaking.the univErse
verse is shaking.the universe is shaking.the univ
 universe is shaking.the universe is shaking.the
.the universe is shaking.the universe is shaKing.
ing.the uNiverse is shaking.the universe is shaki
s shaking. the universe iS shaking.the universe i
e is shaking.the universe is shaking.the univeRse
verse is shaking.thE universe is shaking.the univ
 universe is shaking.the univErse is shaking.tHe
.the uNiverse is shaking.the univeRse is shaking.
ing.the universe iS shaking.the universe is shaki
s shaking.thE universe is shaking.the universe is
e is shaking.the uniVerse is shaking.the uNiverse
verse is sHaking.the universe is shaking.tHe univ
e uNiverse is shaking.the univeRse is shaking.the
.the universe is shaking.the universe Is shaking.
ing.the uNiverse is shaking.the universe is shaki
s shaking.the universe is shaking.the uniVerse is
e is shaking.the unIverse is shaking.tHe universe
iverse is shaking.the univeRse is shaking.the univ
 univeRse is shaking.the universe is shaking.tHe
g.the universe is shaking.thE universe is shaking.
ing.the uNiverse is shaking.the universe is shaki
s shaking.the uniVerse is shaking.tHe uNiverse is
e is shaking.the univeRse is shaking.the universe
iverse is shaking.the universe is shaking.the univ

FIRE
IN
THE
UNNAMEABLE
COUNTRY

FIRE
IN
THE
UNNAMEABLE
COUNTRY

GHALIB ISLAM

HAMISH HAMILTON
an imprint of Penguin Canada Books Inc.

Published by the Penguin Group
Penguin Canada Books Inc.
90 Eglinton Avenue East, Suite 700, Toronto, Ontario, Canada M4P 2Y3

Penguin Group (USA) Inc., 375 Hudson Street, New York, New York 10014, U.S.A.
Penguin Books Ltd, 80 Strand, London WC2R 0RL, England
Penguin Ireland, 25 St Stephen's Green, Dublin 2, Ireland
(a division of Penguin Books Ltd)
Penguin Group (Australia), 707 Collins Street, Melbourne, Victoria 3008, Australia
(a division of Pearson Australia Group Pty Ltd)
Penguin Books India Pvt Ltd, 11 Community Centre, Panchsheel Park,
New Delhi – 110 017, India
Penguin Group (NZ), 67 Apollo Drive, Rosedale, Auckland 0632, New Zealand
(a division of Pearson New Zealand Ltd)
Penguin Books (South Africa) (Pty) Ltd, 24 Sturdee Avenue, Rosebank,
Johannesburg 2196, South Africa

Penguin Books Ltd, Registered Offices: 80 Strand, London WC2R 0RL, England

First published 2014

1 2 3 4 5 6 7 8 9 10 (RRD)

Manufactured in the U.S.A.

LIBRARY AND ARCHIVES CANADA CATALOGUING IN PUBLICATION

Islam, Ghalib, author
Fire in the unnameable country / Ghalib Islam.

ISBN 978-0-670-06700-8 (bound)

I. Title.

PS8617.S54F57 2014   C813'.6   C2013-908156-9

Visit the Penguin Canada website at www.penguin.ca

Special and corporate bulk purchase rates available; please see
www.penguin.ca/corporatesales or call 1-800-810-3104, ext. 2477.

CONTENTS

IN CONFECTIONARAYAN'S
CANDY STORE

ALAUDDIN'S
RUG

Literally, for Hed, but also, perhaps, because he will shake it so

The universe is shaking. All the light enters the world in a great breath and I am asleep. What a shame. What a shame, yells my mother in the shattered night. She howls at the air-raid sirens' spray of glass as light smashes windows and the sound rattles homes hospitals offices of our city in an unnameable country.

My mother crouches in her pitch-black living room, hand at her balloon belly, hoping she won't go into labour at this inauspicious hour, muttering her fears surely these are my final fears. She wonders the whereabouts of her husband, of course he's at Xasan Sierra's cigarette shop, the lout, no doubt doing adda, nada, yada yada, talking talk as usual from evening till dawn. She takes it out on the transistor radio minding its own business, catching fire talk with rabbit ears. Shame, she shakes her head at the reporter informing how all the city's communication facilities, telephone switchboards, television and satellite stations are bursting flames as sky rubbish keeps falling in the worst aerial bombing campaign conducted by the occupation army.

The city, my metropolitan mother, drifts with her eyes ears lips

3

sewn shut, in total darkness not unlike yours truly, Hedayatesque, still swimming in her wombwater, still corded to Shukriah Ben Jaloun, anxious, agitated, passing endocrine signals to mother wanna get born now. When the loud sounds diminish for a moment of eerie calm, Shukriah confuses the tumult inside her with the messed-up world, convinced it's sucking out the air in her lungs with all the racket. She lies down on the living room couch, not entirely convinced she isn't dead.

My mother awakes to a wail in distant streets at dawn, realizes her home is intact and that she's been chattering teeth biting lips, drawing blood while sleeping. Her venture outside proves local pharmacies have run out of painkillers, and, as Hamza the shop owner informs after getting off the phone to answer the crowd gathered in his store, the entire city has been sucked clean of antidepressants. She leaves them bickering and licks her wound. She has her own shop to attend to.

Another fire in our unnameable country. Why, asks my mother as she walks the movie-set streets to her shop while people swirl around her talking hurriedly about what the latest bombing expedition has done. She passes the cracked mirror alleyways broken homes walls floors and edifices. She sees brother offer brother half a loaf of consolation and, pity for pity, promise to help the other rebuild.

When her husband wanders wide-eyed up to her with bloodied palms/ but a scratch, he swears, insists it's only encrusted blood/ she is horrified at the sight and remembers instantly the psychological horror that felled him bedrest for years. She kisses him and forgets cursing his absence when the falling bombs last night. She orders him upstairs and insists she will open her hosiery shop as usual.

Time passes. Morning drags hours into the afternoon sun. Shukriah rubs her pregnant balloon belly before waddling to the front of her hosiery shop where neighbourhood ladies sit eating sharing shelled peanuts talking damages and a magical escape from the occupation army. Then someone mentions the arrival of a certain Alauddin, a

Disney reference — with a twist

magician, and his rug. Who is Alauddin and what do they say about Alauddin's magic carpet. Shukriah is curious and retrieves a stool from inside the shop to sit for the chatter, though she has heard them speak of him many times.

It was said that a certain Alauddin, a magician who had made a modest income once upon a time in English music halls performing sleight-of-hand routines, who had served in Alexandria in the British *He is a legend, an impossible being* Army during the Second World War, who had died two inglorious deaths, first by dysentery and then murdered after quarrelling with an army sergeant over a woman before returning to life while floating down the Suez Canal, who had been picked up by a merchant marine vessel, migrated by the luck of his toothskin to California where he began to play small parts in Hollywood, who had wound up years later in Iraq from where he had just fled the Baathist regime for tax evasion, this selfsame Alauddin with a single name had flown to our unname-able country in the dead of night about a month earlier by flying carpet and was now offering rides daily on his fabled machine.

To prove the verity of his craft, the magician described to citizens their country from the air exactly as it was, claiming he had seen it only while flying on his patterned peagreen carpet, which seemed more old than majestic, is actually ancient, he declared, from the century of Haroun al-Rashid, and which he claimed worked only by his direction. All this was true: he hovered several feet off the ground, rose twelve feet in the air, and when others tried to operate it similarly, the rug was unresponsive until Alauddin uttered some inscrutable open-sesame words which were once commonly understood, and clapped twice.

Nasiruddin Khan, enthused by descriptions of Alauddin by the nameless rebels positioned against the occupying American troops/ Nasiruddin who: Nasiruddin son of Joshimuddin Khan, owner of the largest spidersilk fields in our country in the early 1900s, Nasiruddin owner of spidersilk factories that produced soft cloth light to lift but

5

impenetrable to arrows, beautiful spidersilk that drove a century of fashion and brought the late-slaving British and later invaders, the Americans who still remain, Nasiruddin who later added pop manufacture—Capsicum Cola, Valampuri Coke, Mirror Water—to his productions, was the primary advocate of rebellion against *The Mirror*, the Hollywood enterprise that began before Hedayat was even seed-egg and swept up the entire country in a maze of scaffolding and unfinished construction and two-dimensional houses, your nation for a movie set, would you have this, Nasiruddin Khan ridiculed, as we watched the region turn to mist.

Nasiruddin Khan, enthused by the information that among the magician's past exploits was his disappearance of Alexandria during the Second World War, thereby saving it from bomb attacks, thought of Alauddin as potentially useful to the rebellion but wanted to wait until proven he was not an American operative. ↘against Americans

Watch him for now, he told his men. So for several months, Alauddin's rug becomes a household name, and his success invites other, less talented magicians, some capable of twisting wooden staffs into snakes, others lesser talented and repeating old rabbit-and-hat tricks, as the miracle of flight remains in Alauddin's grasp alone, since only he is able, with the magic carpet, to recreate the scintillating effect of the Maroon slave Amun's flight from the unnameable country and his perforation of the atmosphere through his calculated eviction by the colonial authorities at the dawn of our story elaborated elsewhere.

It's like a Hollywood gone wrong, filled with crazy characters and movie sets. At street level, our city La Maga has become the ruins of a movie set, so Alauddin sets to work at sundown on the rooftop of the hotel where he stays, and watch watch: already they're stretching from outside hotel doors through first-level corridors up five flights of stairs to the rooftop where waiters serve patrons lined up to raised platform for rug-and-flight show.

For the price of an intracity bus fare, he takes up grown women,

If you get far enough away from anything, it's hard to really understand it → living in Hollywood is about as far from real life as you can possibly get

men, screaming children who cover their eyes as they climb above the clouds and dare not look as the ground becomes an encyclopedia map. How high, he asks each person, informing that after a certain distance from the earth you feel no fear because it no longer seems real.

Given his natural charisma as well as the fact that his carpet is potentially capable of freeing people from the checkpoints of La Maga and throughout the unnameable country, he quickly becomes a threat to the occupying army, under whose hire it becomes clear Alauddin is not serving. At first they try poisoning him, which fails, since his first death from dysentery inoculated him against all attacks on the gastro-intestinal. The sniper's bullet fired from a higher rooftop at dusk when Alauddin is taking customers up into the sky misses the mark not once but four times as if the projectiles simply disappear before reaching their target. The operative responsible for strangulating the magician while he is bathing slips on a slight pool of water and lands badly on his neck, remains paralyzed for life, and Nasiruddin Khan denies the coincidental possibility of all these events and realizes Alauddin the Magician is meant to serve the cause of resistance.

In the small flat above the hosiery shop, the news of the flying rug excites even my worldweary aunt Chaya, who has cut all ties with the world in permanent convalescence and decided to remain bitter against her sister, though Reshma has no interest in her German heart palpitation/ her romantic interest, I mean, and as I will later reveal fully. Alauddin briefly unites the sisters before Reshma's scheduled departure to Berlin to study at an art academy. Our whole family, including yours truly, Hedayatesque, swimming fetal, shuttles to the hotel and lines up to test-fly the rug.

Evening, folks, only three at a time, Alauddin's young assistant directs my mother and sisters forward, leaving my father grounded. I don't mind, he shrugs under the shawl he has brought for chills, latest symptom of his curious illness.

Are you sure, my mother takes a step back, but Reshma grabs her arm. We'll only be a minute, Mamun, says my aunt.

The signal of my arrival can be described this way: high high in the air, my mother is narrating aloud with eyes closed as her sisters shout, hold hands, as Alauddin directs the sights from the distant horizon Gulf of Eden backward, and my mother tells the story already once upon a time in her mind though not yet distant past, once upon a time, your father and I met in a cemetery crowded with cirrus clouds, she tells, as the thrill of flight pushes me curious toward the world, down through the birth canal as the carpet rises, and in my mother's shock a scream flies eyes like butterfly wings flutter. I am almost here. Like death, birth is unexpected.

Afterward, we are home and an experienced neighbour serves as midwife. My head is appearing and the tension is everywhere along Shukriah's uterine walls her thighs abdomen vulva as the pale green walls breathe in and out in time to her hard labour breaths in-exhalations.

My father: I understand, Shukriah, it hurts, darling, but please just breathe. And my mother's roar: Just tell me how you understand fifty-three hours seventeen minutes of constrict relax constrict relax/ a scream interruption/ my mother resets her huffing-puffing, swiftly regains rhythm/ broken water, muscles seizing, tissues distending, she continues yelling, surely torn now, and then maybe push out a miscarriage, because like you can empathize, you man. Recall, as if you have overheard, their loving words to each other just several hours prior, but can we judge, are we in any position to judge.

Meanwhile, I am caught in the midst, who is paying attention to me, where is the doctor/man, lowly cretin man whose hot breaths populated microscopic insects inside, my mother continues cursing, as another big push and something greymucus and pink is emerges emerging from inside her until finally my owl's screech ear-rending howl.

Out of the womb and into the sky: our neighbours still report to Shukriah that first wail of Hedayat Awwal Ben Jaloun, or Owl as they would call him in his life, that cry they had waited years of slow gestation in wombwater to hear, the sound that entered their homes bustled furniture rushed window into the streets to rustle branches and tremble birds, thump hearts in chests for one what the hell moment.

Everything is monochrome. There are some nearshapes. Wet light splashes everywhere onto objects in the room. Some items are near, others farther away. Correction: this is uncertain. A pungent odour. Is it from the elongated masses waving near me. (Myself. Limbs, I would later learn, and digits. Fragments of and little control over these. But myself nevertheless.) Or is the smell over there. Other smells, but these are more nuanced, indescribable. The smells go away when the elongated masses near me disappear and then a warm shape, bright, soft, singular, a clothshape, I would learn to feel.

Hark unto the sounds. Little sounds and the bigger sounds; the bigger sounds come closer and their shapes and movements become ordered: a wholething, a face, I will come to know, of either the one or the other, mother or father. I am frightened but no one is crying. Cover him more with the blanket, my mother says as my father carries me around the room, and his smell is heavy, weighs hasha hasha from the nose, and then a yellow tinkle.

Ooh, he has soiled himself.

At least we know that works, Shukriah is laughing, gleaming. Bring him to me, please. Her smell means something like before, long ago. I am lifted closer, and then the smell is closer.

Then the dark but not so much. Like a wholething though not quite. A shadow. The universe disappears; to say it another way, sleep divides time, though I know neither word. In the beginning, the world seems dislocated from my mother's stories while I waited in the red-lit darkness of her womb, in its lub-lub comfort mother heart, its swimming sense of already and always. (Later, I would conclude that even in these earliest times, I had realized the continuity with some distant past, but knew no origin could be deduced by this feeling, and that one could not conflate it with any notion of eternity; rather, tick-tocking on and on: only a vague sensation of existing, having existed, and persisting in time.)

What others observed in Hedayat was that he didn't speak a word after his introductory howl, went dumb, and scared his parents who thought he was deaf. He waited until his second year to take his first steps, then climbed out of his perambulator without warning one day and broke into a trot in a crowded marketplace covered with glass shards and husks of rifle shots, eggplant vendors and sweet sellers until Shukriah caught up with him, surprised by the deftness and surety of his steps.

When my mother's sister Reshma returned for holidays from her studies in Berlin, he was already four years old and she swore she could hear all the answers to her questions, and later verified that the quality of his voice was the same on these earlier occasions, though at that time he did not move his lips and was still in the habit of pointing to indicate this or that thing. He showed no prodigious insight in these early years, exactly dumb, but projected endless curiosity with his eyes and the hidden desire to match the world with what he had imagined it to be before he was born.

Recall, as if I have told you, in those days Mamun M had not worked for a long time, and it was only through Shukriah's indefatigable and successful efforts to unfreeze his savings account from his playback singing days that the family managed to survive, even to pay Reshma's tuition and living expenses abroad. No one could locate his sickness anymore because he did not shit florid, was no longer wasting thin away, displayed a healthy appetite, and had re-formed talkative friendships with Xasan Sierra, the cigarette vendor, as well as Confectionarayan Babu, the candy seller, among other neighbourhood staples. Mrs. Henry, meanwhile, my parents' downstairs neighbour who owned a hosiery shop where my mother began working soon after my parents moved to La Maga, had grown arthritic and suffered from chronic diarrhea, which she blamed on the equatorial climate and infested drinking water that grew no better if boiled, she claimed, and returned to England. Before she left, Shukriah convinced her to mortgage the shop to her, allowing the old woman to add to her pension and for the family to acquire a means of supporting itself for the foreseeable future.

———————

After numerous trips to the local doctor, who was not an oncologist but who managed through conversation to prove (without actually proving) that Mamun M's illness was imaginary, my father decided he had let years of his life slip away into fabulism as he lay in bed regurgitating the past, and began to impose upon the house strict notions of reality, cutting strings of remembrance and loosening events that seemed no longer plausible, including his discovery of his father's thoughtreel rubbish, he would say, that they can read thoughts with the shortwave, another way of controlling the public imagination with fear, and that jazz orchestra blowing about a windy hallway and the pressing of the body against the wall like a carpet beetle: true to an extent, but remembering the nightmare, my father would say before casting a gaze elsewhere in time.

Hedayat remains curious of his father's thoughts those days on the magician Alauddin's sudden rise to prominence, his opinions of his wife and wife's sisters' flight on the magic rug, but at that time infant Hedayat's vow of silence was absolute, and he would not have revealed his clairaudience and grown-up thoughts for all the curiosity in the world.

Grip, Mamun M would declare, placing his thumbs and forefingers on his son's cheeks and pinching paining invoking evolution, is what *"grip" keeps us in control*

distinguishes our ability, our opposable digits, God bless, to manipulate the world and to make it human.

Shukriah, he would instruct with wagging finger: Tell this boy no funny stories beyond the grip of normality, and you too, Chaya, same-same, I am warning.

As an act of protest against the strict conditions of reality and human behaviour set down by his father's newly stentorian, masculinist voice, Hedayat briefly returned to a non-ambulatory state and acted as if he had forgotten how to walk, and when his mother yelled, see what you have done, Mamun, he showed preference for scuttling sideways, his back arched, on his hands and feet like a crab, or for crawling about like a barbaric example of the canine tribe, until his mother cajoled him to return to his original silent, ambulatory state. Recall from press reports how at that time there lay strange fruit scattered everywhere in La Maga, which would explode out your raspberry insides and reveal the true colour of your hidden organs, you know what I mean: clusters of little fruits on the treebranches and lying fallen on the dusty streets, which they told you in school to avoid at all cost.

Come along, Niramish tells one lunch hour, his mixed vegetal odour a constant warning to others to stay away, but a friend to Hedayat since at school he is the only one who will tolerate his silence. Niramish's own two problems: first the smell of mixed curry vegetables stuck to yellow turmeric fingertips, effusing from clothing, detectable from a hundred feet away. Niramish Khaja, loyal companion, smelly child: it never bothered little Hedayat the slightest, and, in fact, he interpreted the constant smell as an augury of the future, as if it were an odour destined to grow thicker in time. Niramish's second problem: narcolepsy. In a stumbling sentence, halfway through his response to the teacher's question, sitting or standing up, even poised in his characteristic loping gait, in the schoolyard or in the cracked-mirror streets, anywhere without warning, he would fall into a stertorous nod, his head would slip and his double chin would quadruple, before the snoring sound came out and came out and out until someone pinched his nostrils, wake up, Niramish, wake up, smelly child.

Hai, did it happen again, he would re-emerge with a loud snort.

Niramish, good-natured Niramish, a nutritious and well-meaning friend, would one day provide Hedayat with the perfect excuse. See him: running running toward the prize. Look, he shakes the tree, they fall to the ground, and he lifts them up out of the dust mound to see. And then the fire and the howling at these strange clusters of nectarines. A mere ten steps away, Hedayat is thrown back by an unnameable force and aside from a minor bruise on his forehead appears uninjured at first. You might say it was in consolation for his friend Niramish, who loses his right eye as well as three fingers of his right hand, pointer middle ring, and/or for the added reason of rebellion against father and father-prescribed humanity; whatever the case, Hedayat finds his hands curled up into hardened talons, unable to bend his thumbs and besotted by the added difficulty of fully working the digits of both right and left hands.

Doctors who probe observe take samples of the tendons bones nerves interstitial tissues conclude, nothing wrong, Shukriah Ma'am, seems altogether like a psychological matter.

The psychos, meanwhile, suggest all manner of cures, from hypno to shock therapy to antidepressant medication, all of which my mother refuses what we need is gently to pry open his mouth, she insists, this and nothing more, doctors sirs. Whether the loss is a rational decision or an effect of the blast no one can decide until Hedayat, too, forgets, content to take multiple-choice examinations since his writing appears to teachers like a private hieroglyphics, and not altogether worried about the future.

Eyeless-fingerless-eyepatched and the other finger-gnarled, Niramish and Hedayat form quite the pair. During trips to Confectionarayan Babu's

Hedayat chooses to be different. Niramish just is.

13

candy shop, they stand in the shadows of the crowding children, the fat smelly pirate and his friend with talons and twisted hands, crackling laughter, whoops and hollering: they are the butt of all the mobile playground's jokes. Narayan Khandakar, meanwhile, or Confectionarayan Babu, as he is known to everyone, is a gentle creature, and when the cete of badgering children leave after making purchases or get caught up in lights and buttons of arcade games, he invites, psst come on, you two, not out of pity or even to favour the son of one of his closest friends, Mamun M, but out of a spontaneous fatherly love, and pulls the string of the incandescent bulb in the cellar stairwell, and from dark corners the light spreads into bright shapes, the yellow fruits that break apart spilling candied seeds, the blue sugar packets that make you froth rabid at the mouth, the sweet toothpaste meant for eating, Confectionarayan Babu's many succoured potables, his bars and candies of all shapes.

That box over there, he never bestows a favour without first requesting they lend a nominal hand: please push it to this here.

Though Hedayat is more or less crippled at such tasks, he leans with his weight against his elbows against the box.

Here, let me do it, his friend remains better equipped despite the damage of the exploded nectarines.

Never are they allowed more than one bowl or handful of candied almonds, but none of the other children are allowed to drink from the gushing fountain that feeds the vending receptacle for iced drinks or to try the newest American chocolate bars; just being in that wonderworld is tantalizing enough.

Most important for Hedayat, he provided foil to his father/ there couldn't be two individuals more dissimilar; Mamun M was perennially preceded by a sorrowful tune while Confectionarayan, with his round ball body and insatiable sweet tooth, was every chocolatier's test subject and never had a sad word to say about anything. Confectionarayan added questions to the son's mind: Don't be so hard on your old man, he would say, he's not a bad man, and if you only knew, boy, what subterranean hallways he's seen, what a thoughtreel looks like.

Narayan Khandakar and my father would chatterbox in Xasan Sierra's cigarette shop, talking talk and playing cards in enclosed urban tin hut eat Saturday night meets Sunday morning, and Hedayat knew he knew the man and trusted the sweet seller's judgment.

Only on one occasion did Hedayat and Niramish doubt Narayan Khandakar. Psst, come here, you two, he invited us one day with a whisper into a corner of his shop we had never visited, where the light fell crooked onto boxes vessels jars of sweets whose brands we didn't recognize. With a stepladder, he climbed to the top of a candy shelf and walked gingerly along its edge. He threw an errant candy bar at us, which Niramish caught. Then he reached into a region of piled confectioneries that ate his hands, and from that dark place, brought out a metal container before declaring aha, descending steps reappearing before his adopted nephews.

Niramish and I, who had seen El Dorado in Narayan Khandakar's candy shop, were underwhelmed by what looked like an oversized tuna can. What's this, Niramish touched its smooth reflective hull. What's that, he pointed. Boys, Confectionarayan Babu beamed, I present to you my most prized possession, my greatest asset in all the world, a thoughtreel.

A thoughtreel, Niramish said, incredulously, as Hedayat moaned softly, alone, wondered what Confectionarayan Babu would do next; our uncle opened the canister and showed us its contents, a magnetic reel like the kind in cassettes and videotapes. A thoughtreel, he repeated, though alas, I have no way to listen to it.

No thoughtplayer, Niramish mocked, no thought stereo.

No, Confectionarayan said crossly, simply, now if you will excuse me, he began shooing us with a nearby broom. Niramish and I were astonished because Narayan had never behaved that way with us, and eventually, Niramish, at Hedayat's sullen insistence, changed his tone how much did you pay for it, Uncle. Boys, Narayan Khandakar sighed, I'm sorry I can't answer your questions. I merely wanted to show you an heirloom I will order buried with me one day; hopefully by then I will have had a chance to listen to a human mind on magnetic reel.

Thoughts, Niramish touched the metal hull, can you really tape a human mind.

If you can record a voice, an image, Confectionarayan shrugged.

Niramish and I wrestled with the notion of thoughts encased in metal skin, and we remained skeptical, agitated for so long Confectionarayan added that we ourselves could be mere flickers in someone's mind. What do you mean, Niramish pointed around us at the ground, the ceiling and walls, mentioned the warmer than average temperature for this time of year. Confectionarayan caught his drift the material world, and nodded, yes, but isn't your grandfather a thought if he's that much, he asked, your great-grandfather but a moment of consideration if we remember him at all. Niramish and I stared and waited for him to continue, mesmerised: Poof, Confectionarayan Babu snapped, laughed the way grown-ups do when they think children don't understand. Time turns you into space, he said without exaggerating, into two yards of earth, children.

With his words, I leapt from Confectionarayan's candy store backward in time to the Archives, to row upon row of receptacles of magnetic reels storing recorded thoughts where my father's wear and tear unto madness, though I knew nothing of that nightmare until that moment. Without asking us to, our uncle told us we began long before ourselves, and Hedayat moaned his displeasure as he stared at a dot in the farthest corner of the world, as he travelled endlessly toward that point, which he knew was Niramish and Confectionarayan Babu, his mother in her spidersilk dress, which was his grandmother's slouch and

In the end, we are all merely thoughts, memories.

16

steps, his father's cynicism, and the soft five whispers of his sisters who were yet to be born, everything he had ever known and suddenly far away and ephemeral. He hovered above the floor, vertiginous.

Narayan Khandakar retained his joyous welcoming character despite the incident, and the pair continued seeking refuge from the playground in the air and sights of the sweet cellar in their single-digit years, their mothers never quite at ease with their lingering hours, but Confectionarayan Babu always insistent they remain under his strict supervision and that a code of good behaviour always applied. It would be there that Hedayat would speak for the first time. This monumental change, however, would not have been possible had a stranger not come to town.

The appearance of Mamun M's mother and Hedayat's grandmother Gita would be Hedayat's benediction; her first revelation would be that it was the scent of her cooking he had detected on Niramish's skin as augury.

She arrived not like a survivor of torture or the perpetual contemplator of suicide, but donning a dark orange pair of sunglasses, which framed her cheekbones, and a silk neckerchief, which hid her still-exquisite collarbones, like the mother of a film star or playback singer. She had followed her son's career alongside millions without knowing he was the selfsame Mamun, and had recognized him only many years later, changed by age, deflated by illness, in a surreptitious documentary that had been featured at Cannes but banned at home because its director was supposed to be dead, a recent Badsha Abd production she had watched at an underground film club in Victoria.

It was your face for an instant as the camera panned the mirror streets, she told. I was absolutely certain and I kept the intersection in mind; in fact, it was not too far at all from where you live. I don't know, Mamun shrugged, there are so many godforsaken movie productions in this town. Twice now, the past had shown up unannounced at his

17

doorstep, undeterred by the viper's nest of |imperial| occupation, and on this second occasion he acted as if he had been interrupted in the middle of his morning victuals by the paperboy.

Shukriah, for her part, was as enthusiastic as she had been when Nur al-Din arrived with his basketful of crabs and his knapsack of melodies and his wanderlust, though this guest, she was sure, would rend no one's heart. She also realized that, despite the old woman's polished appearance, before her stood someone in search of a home.

Quietly, she suggested the extension of her visit from three days to a week, from two weeks to a month: Why not help me took-taak in the hosiery shop, Amma, and Gita never refused these kind offerings.

Over time, Shukriah was able to learn the reason for her visitation and the story of her life. It turned out that while Zachariah Ben Jaloun and his wife had not seen each other in almost twenty years, his records at the Ministry of Radio and Communications still stated Gita as his primary contact, since recall, as you may have heard, he had neither remarried nor found any stable friendships since coming back to that labyrinth of names. Two days after he put a bullet in the back of his head, my grandmother found thin meat slices in a duffle bag that had arrived without address of origin or deliveryman, in the shape of her estranged husband, with a knock on her front door one Thursday at lunchtime just as she was sipping her first spoonful of turkey broth. As his sallow chainsmoker's face disintegrated in her hands, she realized she had been smelling onions since the moment she woke up that morning, and had found him in her sheets, in the clothing hamper, in the smell of every man's sweat or cologne while shopping for the day's eats. Gita realized she hadn't distrusted the premonition for a moment, and rightfully so, so well had she and Zachariah known each other in life.

Gita was so shocked by his return that she could not help but ask him the questions she had been muttering to herself for years.

And our boy is lost now, she told him, perhaps dead, all grown up if he is alive, but probably a dacoit or a motorcycle pirate. Oh we failed, Zachariah, we utterly failed at love.

After a simple burial attended only by two or three people who still remembered him, she began to feel a lightness on her feet, as if she had regained lost years by sending some furtive mass, which had weighed unseen on her Atlas shoulders, to the grave. She quit her freelance needlework and took a job as an operator for the national telephone company.

And after many years there I thought it was high time for a living reunion with my only remaining family. How glad I am to know my son is alive and sharing a home with such a joyous woman and that he has a delightful son of his own.

Shukriah did not press her mother-in-law to fill in the gaps of her narrative right away, presuming that time would complete that task, and told her only the best parts of her own life's recent history, such as their early days in the small flat above the hosiery shop, the funny stories she would tell fetal Hedayat during her very long pregnancy.

Eight years, my God, Gita exclaimed, you would expect him to be as large as a whale.

8 year pregnancy! The events are like a movie within a movie.
Everyone is an actor - even Hedayat's dad.
→ Hed defies normality, presumptions

This is around the time our head of state Anwar the Great reunites with Dulcinea, his love mare. My father insists on attending the magisterial funeral.

Hurry up, he ushers the family into a waiting downstairs van. Labial flashes smiles energetic words pour, so hard with a whole family to travel, I hear him say, as the rise and fall of the driver's hum of understanding, acceptance.

The hum of the motor opiates me, summons sleep, and in between that time and the following scene, they encounter a rupture, an argument that would not heal for a long time. What I hear when I woke up: in front of his own mother, Shukriah shouts, and from that day onward, she refers to Mamun only by the self-reflexive pronoun himself: son, tell Himself to come now, that the table is set/ Himself is not the only eating member of the household what will Himself do about this outrageous gas bill, the old days money is not going to last forever/ is Himself ever considering another job, and so forth. When, out of habit, the more personal marker, you, falls, Shukriah's lips replace the mistake immediately with Himself. Mamun M's contrition is evenly matched by his stubbornness and his inability to utter the truth: he cannot stand the presence of his mother, as if her quiet footsteps throughout the house shake the cobwebs of older memories and return him to previous lives wrapped in spiderthread.

What was Mamun M's fantasy illness. His self-diagnosis of colon cancer had been proven otherwise by every sound individual of the medical profession except those keen on fleecing him for pharmaceutical expenses. Did he still believe he was mortally ill. Was he of the opinion that his mother would set back whatever recovery he had made. If so, why. The longer Gita stayed in their apartment, meanwhile, the more she began to feel as if her son had betrayed his spine. What was he doing all day while his wife ordered women's linen from catalogues and managed a complex credit system that kept in mind all the customers who could not pay and others who paid partially and continued to haggle or to barter for even the smallest items, while she expanded the store's inventory to include women's and children's clothing because times were so bad that one could not sustain oneself on the business of selling only hosiery.

One day, while whipping cockroaches out of their hiding spots with a long black leather strap she had brought with her, Gita tried disabusing her son of his laziness. At first the lashes only reached the corner of the bed, and Mamun felt safe by the thought that a woman who had regained a son after missing him for nearly two decades would not could not. Nevertheless, he moved his body from out of the way of the attacks just to be sure. When the following lash discovered his neck, he leapt out of bed, shrieking with indignation.

Attack me, then, strike your dear mother who bore you, she said as he shook with rage. And who wishes only the best, she lashed out again, this time catching him on a concha, the outer shell of his right ear bursting with red; note that the whip was bona fide cowhide and fashioned to injure work animals.

Shukriah found her spouse curled into a hermit crab's shell, his head shielded with his hands, weeping like a child. She felt only pity at that moment and placed her own body between him and the instrument of torture, encircling him with her arms and drawing to his level on the floor.

Enough, Amma.

I was trying to, Gita lowered the whip, ashamed.

I know, Shukriah forgave, and returned to calling Mamun by you. From that day forth, no one demanded that Mamun M work, but fate would have in store for him to return to the Archives one final time. For the moment, he busied himself at Xasan Sierra's shop, where he idly filled cigarette papers with loose tobacco for smokes and adda; the enterprising youth who had forged a career as an aleatory songsmith had grown into a bloodless middle age, drained of all his vital energies. Not even his mother's whip could salvage his former zeal.

All this occurred around the same time the great Grenadier Lhereux abandoned his lifelong desire to return to Mother France and decided to remain in the unnameable country to nurse the President back to health so the latter could summon his previous cruel strength and push all the new rats and parvenus of the judiciary and governing council into the ocean. True to his style, the grenadier said nothing to anyone about his plans and instead sought out the most beautiful and willing

21

horses in New Jerusalem to replace Dulcinea, the love mare. But he discovered that rather than improving the President's condition, Anwar sank deeper into the swamp of melancholia, weeping and singing in a private language into the manes of the beautiful thoroughbreds he would send away after exhausting his equine desires for each animal, and more strangely, that he began to assume certain pathologies of the criminal minds he had grown acquainted with over the years due to his long association with the National Security Service, such as the covering of his face with a mask made of spidersilk gossamer a suspected terrorist reportedly wore, designed to vibrate at the exact frequency of Black Organs telecommunication.

To an extent, these techniques brought him closer to Lhereux's hopes for a return to the Golden Era of false socialism, since Anwar would speak of even the earliest past as if they were the events of yesterday morning: Recall, Grenadier, when we were young men and we took blue steel to the throats of the British, or when they fired fifty-nine shots at me while I was on the podium and not one found my body and then I unbuttoned my shirt and bared my naked chest, come kill me if you will, kill your president and the saviour of New Jerusalem.

Lhereux would smile on these occasions, mutter certainly, yes, I too remember, and at night he would sit by Anwar's bed stroking an old Smith & Wesson pistol of the same variety that he had gifted to Zachariah Ben Jaloun for the purposes of the latter's suicide, because he did not trust even the guards to protect the life of his only true friend in the world.

They're going to make you prime minister, said the grenadier sadly one day, as the light of his body flickered like a cinematic superimposition onto the hard wooden reality of that bedroom.

Anwar had awakened from confounding dreams in which he was racing through the vast corridors of the Presidential Palace with a message whose content he forgot; as he ran he could not decide whether to return to the origin of things or race onward, and he did not recognize that ancient figure of the soldier who sat in the lamplight, garbed in the faded uniform of another era.

Who the hell are you, he grabbed for the closest weapon the statuette of a Hindu goddess with many arms tongue unfurled blackened face, and when the ebony wood swung through his body Lhereux found himself uninjured and realized he was in trouble.

The diaphanous illness that took hold of Grenadier Lhereux was as slow to take form and as mysterious as my father's colon cancer. The grenadier realized that his time was limited and took to appealing to the President's former obsession, the embalmed figure of Caroline Margarita Quincy, as he secretly hired looksees to find doubles of her image. He conducted a quick and thorough interview process because he felt the cobwebs of rumour shaking and saw another danger approaching. The woman who agreed to play the part for two thousand dollars a week looked exactly like Caroline Margarita at the age she abandoned her husband to join the Maroons, and danced like Salome for a few days. But because the President had conducted such thorough structural analysis of her bones and musculature in his youth, Anwar detected flaws in the seductress's movements, differences in the bending of the wrist and the twisting of the spine that Caroline Margarita's body could never have allowed, and the grenadier found himself humiliated by his efforts, gazing into the half-smiling face of his friend one day, a face that looked as though it had broken from a fever. Neither had time to recollect recent events because Xamid Sultan, the acting head of state, entered the chamber at that instant with three armed soldiers and a stack of papers.

He bowed deeply and spoke in an official language that filled the air with camphor, and by that odour Anwar awoke to a funereal political ceremony: We are offering you the venerable seat of prime minister, sign here, which will allow you to retain leadership while recovering from the death of your beloved horse, and which will allow the governing council as well as myself, Xamid Sultan, sign on this sheet, the opportunity to guide the country to the other side of this power vacuum.

It was the moment Lhereux had feared and one for which he had tried through all means of trickery to prepare Anwar, but in vain, because the President signed every sheet without a word, without even reading a page. Xamid Sultan inhaled deeply and bowed again, the soldiers relaxed the poses they had maintained during those long anxious minutes, because to enter the chamber of the President was to make one's way into a viper's nest, with cold hidden slither. The enemies exhaled bitter breaths, their clothes breathing scared camphor, and retreated with Xamid Sultan.

It took less than twenty-four hours for the scandal to echo throughout the governing order: the pages did not show Anwar's signature, and, in fact, it could not be agreed whose writing they bore, most likely one of the other members of the governing council. Xamid Sultan, whose hold on Parliament was delicate, was eaten alive by wild accusations of you forged the signatures, while those who defended him took the wrong argumentative line; in this time of crisis one cannot but take such an executive turn as so-called forgery or perjury, since they could not argue the names bore zero resemblance to the famous scrawl they had grown up with and witnessed on all official documents since the start of their careers. He himself had not noticed anything unusual about the sheets as he had walked the vestibules toward the parliamentary hall, which, recall, as everyone knows, had been built right into the Presidential Palace, and it had only filled him with a giddy excitement he could remember from celebrating his mother's second wedding with little capsicum firecrackers as a boy. He had not imagined the President would retain enough of his wiles following the strychnine loss of Dulcinea to effect such a feat as the slow-acting transformation of his signature. He had been certain he and the entire council

24

had thoroughly constrained him to the bathroom, the dining chamber, and to the bedside company of Grenadier Lhereux, that old toothless. Lhereux, he chewed over his name, but by then it was too late. Blood vessels had begun to contract and the body politic grew aware of the indecision in the highest organs of power. In the confusion, the nameless rebels, who had bided their time and honed their skills fighting in the movie sets of La Maga, but who had in the past several years extended their reach throughout the country and garnered wide popular support, broke through the defences of the Presidential Palace. → *like a movie channel*

Nasiruddin Khan, wearing a hunter's vest, wielding a shotgun he would never have to fire, and chewing on a lit cigar, stayed back while Russian-trained commandos sniped guards, cut fences, scaled walls, and netted the Presidential Palace. For a week, intense fighting flooded the whole country and the rebels managed to kidnap three out of the eight members of the Privy Council, including Grenadier Lhereux and President Anwar. The American military lost fourteen soldiers during their brave attempt to defend against the siege of Victoria, which took them totally by surprise, and the whole of the United States erupted into mourning as moral debates weeded up the television broadcasts whether we should be in this godforsaken part of the world, how many decades has it been, is it about the Gulf of Eden and natural gas resources or defending against the global communist scourge.

Occupation is kind of like living in a movie, where your actions are watched and controlled, and you walk around on a stage set for action and conflict.

As the negotiations between the nameless rebels and the governing party began, Shukriah discovered she was pregnant again. I hope to God this one doesn't talk in the womb; if I hear so much as a peep I'll abort. Mamun M could not agree more; in fact he was uneasy with the prospect of raising another child, especially since the experience with one—while raising two others who were not his by blood but more or less nevertheless—had exhausted them. Gita wished quiet congratulations, but trenches dug up her forehead.

So dense was the atmosphere and so wrapped up was the family with the world out there that they totally missed the fact that Chaya would quietly vomit in the bathrooms in the earlymorning and bubbling inside her was another great force of multiplication. Like her sister Shukriah, she was able to perceive the slow knotting of cells, to predict their answers, though the outcome of that story, which now is her tears cried onto shouldercloth, I will tell you later.

Unless I tell you now about Chaya and her child. Should I. What you are reading is less a confessional history than a tale of only the necessary portions (of which there happen to be many); besides, Chaya my dear aunt Chaya: what would she think if I. Should I. The question of her child shall hang in the balance of necessity. At the moment I abstain, your honour, dear reader, whomever whatever the hell, from revealing, I shall seven-year-old mum/ look: there the shapes take up their residence, they console, they hide, and in the gloaming, the hundred candlelight of our little home, under the air-raid sirens there arise new suspicions, silences, new sadness, which bears the weight of unrevealed pain, the pleasures of a bow-legged Archives employee who sprang nimbly onto my father's shoulders and perched there one day while Mamun Ben Jaloun was shelving metal receptacles whose contents he himself never revealed to his children, and about which Hedayat has learned with Niramish in Confectionarayan Babu's candy store.

Let me say plainly that for years, my father would bear the weight of another man on his back by himself until a telephone conversation with Ministry of Records and Sources officials would verify the existence of a hunchback on my back, turning me hunched also, he won't let go, he would say, while Shukriah Gita Chaya would suppress laughter, What man father son dear. This man, he would point, here, he would show

26

them an arm, Gita Shukriah Chaya do you not see, but they would only giggle. But even this story is taking us away from another tale, the one I started with.

Realize that to hold onto his thinashair miraculous lead over the American army through the capture of the highest individuals of the governing council, Nasiruddin Khan would have no choice but to call upon the favour of Alauddin the war magician, who was handcuffed before he was brought secretly to the Presidential Palace through an old subterranean hallway because they were unsure of whether he would be willing to lend his services, or, even if he said he would, whether he would not simply disappear, because they knew so little about him and could not trust him.

In those days, the magician wore a sharp-ended moustache he spent a long time sculpting each morning, and Nasiruddin Khan remarked to himself how ageless was his skin, how anachronistic his whole appearance/ look at those loose pantaloons and the brightly coloured shirts that went out of style centuries ago/ but first he uncuffed, apologized for the necessity of the restraining appliances, and told him what he wanted: within twenty-four hours they will bomb Victoria and the Presidential Palace; we need you, please, to repeat the Miracle of Alexandria: make us disappear from the sight of the American pilots.

Nasiruddin Khan stated his offer, which was so exorbitant it made Alauddin's throat bob up and down, and after an instant's submersion into deep thought, they became partners.

Then Alauddin the Magician immediately got to work on the greatest disappearing trick of his life. For twenty hours, he dictated they gather the most absurd items: ten thousand tons of aluminum foil, eighteen hundred fluorescent lights, Noh theatre masks all bearing the same emotion, forty-two caftans, an ancient sandalwood palanquin. They did not bother asking for a plan when they started canvassing the rooftops with metal sheets or even stop to think when he requested seventeen thousand kilograms of rancid coconut water and an equal quantity of camel shit. Then he disappeared. Though they had posted two guards outside the door of the room in which he paced from wall to wall and from where he gave orders, the guards were found sleeping, drugged, and they could not find a trace of him anywhere. In fact, Alauddin had actually fled seventeen hours prior and had them believe by the use of a double, who constantly shadowed him and who was the greatest disguise artist on the continent, that the magician was engaged in the task for which he had been advanced half his pay in platinum bars. He realized how doomed was Nasiruddin Khan when he observed the way the cola emperor suspired when he uttered the desperate sum, a fifth of his kingdom's worth, as noted in publications, and in the instant before he said yes, the war magician had already formulated his escape.

In the darkened city that cowered in fear of fire and of the talons that would rend it irreparably, no one noticed a solitary flying rug recede into the distant sky, weighted with enough riches to last the escapee forever. That was how Nasiruddin Khan realized that he had no hope in the world of retaining Victoria. They captured him when he tried to flee to the Karkaars, and his body was sliced into thin vertical steaks and all the pieces sent to the various centres of the nameless rebels, which were by then known. His tenure in the Presidential Palace lasted a grand total of forty-two hours.

CAPSICUM
CANDIES

The nameless rebels continued to explode various government outposts, harassed American positions throughout the country, left smashed mirrors everywhere as signs of their continuing resistance. But Xamid Sultan, head of National Security at that time, declared victory against them at a press conference in which he warned neighbouring nations not to harbour the criminal elements that had fled the unnameable country and would no doubt begin to destabilize their own states if not captured and eliminated. Though he insisted the nation was sailing in peaceful weather, it continued to rain metal and combustibles, and a British medical journal placed the loss of life in the last five years due to war at one hundred thousand. Several of the country's institutions survived the changeover in power, most importantly the Ministries of Radio and Telecommunications and Records and Sources, though these would be brought under the folds of a new organization simply entitled National Security Service, located in a submerged building accessible only by various secret doorways known only to its members. The most observant people understood the significance of what the national media framed as the forward momentum of the country to be something much viler when they began to pitch forward in mid-step, or when each of the only fifteen surgeons of the country were discovered, one by one, to be snoring in the operating theatre.

A new breed of tsetse fly had been aroused by the persecution of the rebels in an infected region of the plains in the northwest of the unnameable country, and the soldiers had brought back with them a sleeping disease that spread with the promptness of a fairy-tale spell. For the strongest among the afflicted, life continued after drifting off into a sleep from which they could not awake: they were able to carry on conversations as somnambulists, to continue working; some children took their lessons at school, though much more slowly; adults contributed to only a slight increase in road accidents; but sooner or later everyone succumbed to a deeper slumber. Vegetable vendors in the markets slept unaware of thefts committed by mongrel curs, who had, during their slumber, developed a taste for zucchini and eggplant.

Recognize our flat has been transformed into somnolent castle chambers of the old tale: father fast asleep in his chair, newspaper in hand, despoiled teacup still in hand, raided by drosophilae; the grandmother with a finger frozen raised lecture high, in the midst of a story that goes on and on in dreams, facing her grandson, who stands before her with head bowed, eyes closed in respectful attention; and then the two sisters of mercy and goodwill, of course, sleeping beauties to coronate the scene, in their respective positions.

Outside, the world falls comatose, as if dictated by the laws of a hidden nervous system so we might forget the ravages of civil war. Recall from endless talk and reports of the illness since its occurrence that some people, however, were spared longer than others. Xasan Sierra, for instance, who ordinarily slept on a cot in his shop, remained awake long enough to smoke twelve cartons of cigarettes. He continued to smoke as he dreamed: he saw himself sitting in the rain outside his shop, looking up at the endless downpour that didn't even moisten his cigarettes, and as he stared he wanted to call out to this other Xasan Sierra because his lungs were burning with the desire to smoke, but he could neither move nor speak, and he watched in anguish as the doppelgänger lit one stick of tobacco after the other until he heard the cocorocoroc of the roosters and it was time to wake up.

Xamid Sultan managed to avoid the illness for quite some time by staying awake with the help of coffee and meth, and during his time awake, noted everything and added it to the government's files. Sultan was a hypochondriac who had grown up in a home with a mother nurse who sprayed insecticide from morning to dusk and who begged her household please wash hands wash hands wash hands; Sultan had been certain his excessive cleanliness would save him from the fate of his countrymen. It was he who, among four others, cruised in a Jeep bursting his lungs through a megaphone declaring a state of national emergency, though no one was awake to listen, and he who sent a message to the adjacent countries, to the World Health Organization and to the United Nations before succumbing to the illness himself one exhausted red afternoon.

When word got out, and a thousand foreign doctors arrived wearing astronaut uniforms and travelled throughout the country trying unsuccessfully to administer treatment, they detected the barnyard odours of cow and goat flesh emanating from the mouths of the sleepers and concluded that some inner metamorphoses had occurred, and that those affected by the sickness were no longer human. Would-be looters and pirates thought they had found the prize of the century and fell asleep soon after they landed ashore or crossed our borders. The plague spread to the outer limits of the country, but remained exactly within its political boundaries so that the Bedouin who crossed into the unname-able country fell off their donkeys and camels and curled into sleep in the desert sands, but those who had managed through somnambular

31

Everything happening in the unnameable country is happening somewhere in reality

wherewithal to plot a method of escape returned to a regular life of day and night.

For us, all seemed lost, and for some time the world sent condolences via unanswered letters and telexes, while there spread images of a sleeping country too dangerous to enter. So strange was our conundrum that it pushed us even further from the maps of the world, since no one believed a whole nation could fall into incurable sleep.

Then one day, after the foreign doctors came and went, neither curing nor burying, a gentle shower of fireflies descended as if it was time, like the clatter of rice on rooftops of concrete or corrugated tin. The roosters awoke first, then the hens and the mongrel curs, the camels and horses and donkeys, the rust faded from the exhaust pipes of cars and metal poles, and the walls stood up straighter. Finally, when the people began to reawaken at seven-thirty in the evening, they could not understand why the whole earth glowed green or how centuries had passed and the same ruination stood everywhere: gutted buildings, cracked mirror streets, everywhere the same stench of squalor and putrefaction. Some had dreamed all this to expiration and wanted to return to the paradisiacal blue mist through which they had hitherto been walking and which held no memories, only a soft music without source and which was listened to by all the organs; others had been capable of dreaming only what was their daily retinue, and awoke believing that if they were unable to imagine a better existence, no change was possible in so-called real life.

Sadly, we swept away the firefly corpses from the streets, but their phosphorescent odour stuck to everything: clothing, cars, our conversations, the sheets, to every grain of rice we ate; we pulled it out in glowing clumps of our hair. For a year afterward we breathed only that incurable sadness that no prayer could heal, and it was rumoured that no one made love anymore. All the plants in the region where the illness had originated were deracinated, the wells destroyed so no flies could breed, and whole villages and towns left to the same fate as the Abd not so long ago.

At that time, for the first time, Hedayat wanted to speak, since while he dreamed he had gathered ideas that necessitated a more complex language than merely pointing. That was also when he and Niramish began visiting Narayan Khandakar's chocolate shop after school, and for free, because he was my father's adda friend, we were able to wander that neighbourhood foundation of childhood dreams unattended, and to consume at will.

Owner babu offered, take, Hedayat, anything you like, and Hedayat chose the most grown-up kind of candy he could see: rum candy. The candy tickled at first, iced his tongue, then shot metal nasal, clouds of invisible smoke, moved throat to lungs and came out in coughs. The first sounds Hedayat made were guttural, from a region deeper than his stomach, which were not the intestines had no name, from hidden organs.

What did you chew, son, Confectionarayan was confounded by the effects of an eating thing in his shop.

Hedayat's first words were babble in tongue in fluid indiscernible language that Confectionarayan knew was not the result of goo candy, which you chewed before placing in your parents' paths, which stuck their shoes to the asphalt, or the Amoon brand of gum, whose packages advertised in playful colours to shoot you out of the atmosphere, fly you to the moon if you blew a bubble larger than your head, or the capsicum candies called recallrecall®, a doublenegative brand of sweets so strong they made you forget you, and which sold best and was the latest bubblegum craze. Confectionarayan made me take water, ran to get milk when the symptoms continued.

Hedayat first did ow ow ow ow ow because his tongue had fallen asleep and he couldn't spit out the rum candy. Niramish and Confectionarayan were so worried they ignored any potential deeper

33

meanings of the event and interpreted the miracle only as a body in danger: the owner of the shop finally managed to reach into my throat and removed the obstacle, and Hedayat choked and spat out his first words, a whole comprehensible sentence, without angelic aid: Thank you.

As with my leap from the horizontal to the walking vertical, I shot from mum to full speech and fire so fast, dizzy among multiplied faces of Niramish and Narayan Babu in the shadows of candy boxes, shelves of bubblegum sugar buttons sour keys Turkish delights butter tarts lemon squares myriad sweet celebrations, I nearly missed my uncle's warning, words so many first words, babu, but watch out: most grown-ups aren't like me; if you talk too much they'll wash your mouth out with blood.

But it's difficult for him to follow such rules. Keep in mind: Hedayat is almost a glossolalist.

At first, I chirp incessantly, identify my surrounding environment methodically, overhead is a warbling swift, *Chaetura pelagica*, a common enough avian, liable to fly into a chimney now and again, turn a Roman arch three-hundred-sixty and you have over there, I point, a mosque oniondome, or churchtops of certain denominations, defining, explaining, raising such a clatter that Niramish, who at first is joyous to have acquired a speaking Hedayat for a friend, becomes exasperated. So I try and include him in conversation. What do the cameras film, I ask him as we walk nightingale streets where caged birds for sale shriek into microphones placed to hang from balconies overhead, as we unknowingly trace the gangster-steps of our forebears in tin pan alleys where cameras watch blind howling beggars considered some of the best unrecognized singers in the business, who separate gold from toilet water in plates and dishes and bowls along veins of open-air sewage canals. Movies, he points to posters of abundant Hollywood films. I look at the ominous omnipresence of cameras on top of traffic lights, street signs, newspaper boxes, at cameras peering car windows, through trucks, huge honking cameras ported by beastly types, more cameras than there were yesterday, and I don't believe him. I think there's more to the story, I say, and as I begin to/ Would you shut up shut up already, please, you're making it worse, this headache is made worse by your endless. I am leaving, going gone bye-bye gone home now, screams the exasperated Niramish before leaving me in a labyrinth. Neither he nor his friend suspected that the tsetse fly disease, which had officially been eradicated, was responsible for Hedayat's unending talk methodizing the world. _A rebirth of sorts?

The sound of my voice astounds me so much that I drive the family to earplugging at night, unable to quit even while sleeping, when, perhaps due to some lingering effects of the tsetse fly disease, I dream night after night of encyclopedic landscapes that feature your humble narrator roaming as boy prince, naked as Adam. Hedayat waves his hand with regal flair as he presides, heresiarch, over an animal kingdom of the mind inhabited by imaginary flora and fauna finned feathered petals. Mixed-up animals leap treebranches appearing as tusks. He turns his head one moment to the serpents shed lightning skin in the thick copse within which floats a stream. One million effervescent frogs swim through the ventricles of a beating heart floating disembodied, below the clear water.

I begin assigning names: You are a pumasticate, I call the feline mouth roar jungles into savannas during dream hours while searching bloody bite, the mouth known to devour children in their sleep, the pumasticate who travels with his friend behemadillo, a giant armoured reptile that shakes mountains with steps, who ferries the pumasticate on his hard outer shell as he sucks the air for insects like the murmuring elephantickles my right ear at night hot words lagian whisper. Irrelephants, you shoo, I usually slap my ear and say: onward ho, go now, I tell them, toward life or some measure of it. Animalia, mammalia, chordata, dividing and subdividing hallucination until one day, the kingdom turns unexpectedly into tsetse fly nightmare, into a vast antiseptic room where employees peer shortwave radios through headphones. I tiptoe through that strange scene of cubicles wide-eyes soft decibels, learning the crafts of assembly and collection, muttering excitedly when I realize, horrified, how first the thoughts are heard on wireless radio before they're stored on magnetic tape. I pace jittery across the linoleum floor, talking louder, explaining to myself how then the tapes are cut and assembled according to the specifications of the Department 6119 inspector handling the terror case until the scene disintegrates and I discover my father, astounded by my words, raising me horrified up into the air, dangling legs oaken arms holding me up. I see him through stillglued eyes, babbling sleep. See him lifting me into mid-air: child of clay and of clotted blood, he names me, born of woman, he indicts me of childhood silliness excess, faults the strength and burst of my language my play. He roars and thunders against my dangerous words. When he sets me down on the floor he hugs me so deep all the air leaves my lungs. Enough, he says, but the tsetse fly illness does something to me: from then on, I begin muttering goongooning nasal mmm and Illiquids, my blood leaping mouth onto floor. I would froth from the mouth, I shit you not; these early glossolalia scenarios were truly frightening to me and for others around me. Desperate for a cure, my mother dragged me doctor to doctor, convinced the cause was microbial and could be quelled with the right antibiotic, but they disagreed with her after a handful of failed medicinal attempts, arguing they had difficulty diagnosing the illness, they had decided glossolalia couldn't exactly be termed an infection and therefore couldn't stop it so simply.

Glossolalia. What is glossolalia and what do they say of glossolalia. You may know it as panting keening raise-the-roof kind of God talk, but my automatic tongue was different. I didn't pray for glossolalia and I fasted because I was hungry, as disobedient children do when they can't find what they want to eat. And though I'd like to eschew all presence of the characteristic diagnostic signals church fever flushed face and tears observable in the few Pentecostal establishments in our unnameable country, I must recall that my father found me one day flapping arms in T-shirt, arms with budding vanes barbs barbules, stirring the fetid air in my room with hairy forearms that looked like feathered wings, muttering the story of once upon a time a father imprisoned his son in a wardrobe.

Who are you talking to, I heard a voice behind me and turned my neck one hundred eighty degrees wide-eyed right around like an owl to find Mamun Ben Jaloun's astonished face staring at me. From then on, I tried to be quieter about my heedless iterations, but they emerged without warning like Niramish's narcoleptic sleep sessions. I would fly fantastical lines without consideration or worry for my surrounding listeners. I had become a glossolalist, an inexplicable condemnation, lifetime commitment. Hed cannot stop speaking, spewing somewhat religious fanatical tales.

The only individual who had not dreamed a thing and who passed the entire plague year as if it were a single night's dead stone rest was Mamun M. With a yawn, he returned to his idle life in Xasan Sierra's shop, which congregated with the motley neighbourhood jobless crowd, who recounted how they had passed that long time, and some wondered whether such a plague was so bad after all if it had allowed them to see so many splendorous things and if the bad things all vanished like mist at the end. Not unlike life, Mamun M shrugged, drawing heavily on an unfiltered.

He smoked almost as much as Xasan these days and had acquired a deep phlegmatic cough typical of men who gambol from one to another topic of the political, who make nada, talk on talk all day, just doing adda, he would employ the Indian term if asked, before resuming talking late into night after pulling down the steel grating over the shopfront and wandering over to one of the illegal garage bars all known and being shut down onebyone daily.

One day, while sleeping into the mid-afternoon, Hedayat, blind owl from birth because he was born from having swum clairaudient in mother waters for years while listening to her stories, learning to understand the world without seeing, who was blind enough to get his hands fruitexploded become talons from dangling cluster bombs on boughs near the schoolyard, bursts into his chamber hooting squawking chitti chitti chitti chitti chitti chitti, flapping arms and holding a black envelope that would forever break Mamun M's life of leisure.

You are hereby ordered to report at once to the Archives Department of the Ministry of Records and Sources, sincerely, Supervisor, reads the letter.

For years, Mamun Ben Jaloun has been on extended leave from the Department on grounds of medical invalidity after going mad following the discovery of his father's recorded thoughts, horrified by the implications of wandering dark hallways and corridors of the Archives, of shelving and reshelving metal receptacles of human minds, and he considers claiming sickness as continuing reason for which to forgo the injunction. After the whipping incident, neither Shukriah nor Gita complains about his idle existence, and it would be perfect for saving his life if he is capable of sensing what lies ahead; but as he watches Shukriah waddle up the stairs from the clothing store to the apartment, back down again, weighted more each day with their second child, and he feels nostalgia for his desires in those early years when, while apart, each would cross halfacity's distance to know the other's thoughts. He recalls trying, one day recently, to imagine her mind, shocked to find a haze like telephone static and a labyrinth of endless identical empty rooms guarding the vast arena that separated them, and his steps growing heavier, his breathing more laborious with the sadness of that discovery.

Mamun M realizes his time at Xasan Sierra's cigarette shop and the concomitant daily routine he has repeated for several years now is nothing but a way to avoid expiating for nearly fifteen years of joblessness. He tries helping Shukriah and Gita in the shop, as he had attempted years ago right after he left the ministry, and they don't protest his presence, in fact welcome it with warm smiles, but when he realizes he's only tripping over feet, his own and theirs, and when a second, more strongly worded letter arrives from the Ministry of Records and Sources, he begins to worry about knocks on the door in the middle of the night.

Nevertheless, I will always claim that when my father returned to the Archives, it was more as self-administered punishment than any other reason. Recall from all reports on the government at that time, Xamid Sultan's hold on the government was tenuous, and while the fate of many interim leaders of our continent is to graduate to an interminable persistent rule, his weaknesses of being a nationalist at heart yet too weak with the cudgel to tribal demands were exposed soon after he assumed the helm. One day he swore it was Friday because he saw it reflected in the mirror eyes of so many of his comrades when he went to address the Parliament about the latest American offer of building permanent navy bases on the coast of the Indian Ocean, the Gulf of Eden, and an air force landing strip in the hinterland plains that he almost. How to say it: recall video replays of the moment of pure fear experienced by the Governor during his mock execution, though he himself had designed the event from start to end. For several months after, Xamid Sultan shuffled from office to office, conducting his affairs like a man with an incubating fever inside and unsure of seeking out a physician's counsel; the slightest whispers pulled him closer into his shadow, and when the appropriate Friday actually came around, he was almost relieved to see the angel of death turn the corner in front of him and address him by his familiar name, which was known only to his mother and brother, and some would later declare he even smiled when the Mauser was raised to his already bleeding skull.

In the next three months, our unnameable currency, which had been nailed to the British pound for as long as anyone could remember, tumbled to near devaluation, and the presidency exchanged hands five times: Samir Gallili, a Chicago Boy inculcated into the black arts of global finance by the tutelage of Milton Friedman/ no stopping the tenebrous palsy of his hands/ at dinner circus legislature mornings/ lend voice to a crumpled shaky paper/ shot by unknown assailants in his sleep/ Samater Adel-Yaqub, a personal friend of Julius Neyere whom he met while attending the University of Edinburgh, but not the same brand of socialist, more the variety Big Baba liked, as he himself would say/ hoven off his hinges by whispers madness machinations/ given: the tapes were discovered later and the small player also/ possible impossible/ slow measured speech of the Manchurian candidate/ thought of as restitution for the death of the previous by opponent party members; two elections in three weeks/ voter turnout sixty-seven and seventy-three percent respectively/ names of the candidates wind-skewed into oblivion, no one will recall/ vanished from even the records of the Archives.

Finally, there rose that steely woman who would inspire the whole country with her cruelty and the imaginative ways with which she would interpret the laws prescribed to her from above. Why was the Madam aside from her flatiron hair fixated by gel and hairspray. What were the days of the Madam, which were also endless but conscribed within a more limited infinity than Anwar's. Who was she to be able to usher an angry God to the unnameable country. Recall that in the Governor's days, Allah had been present in politics, no ceremony began without a bismillah and none ended without a munazaat, but everyone thought of this as nothing more than the continuation of life, and while people such as Shukriah and Mamun were the exception, they were not ostracized or defeated into submission for living outside matrimonial bounds. Recall, since you may have heard, no woman in my family wore the hijab before 1990, let alone the niqab. No one was stoned barbaric drowned for witchcraft crazy. Remember that the cruelties that followed were different.

It was Maxwell who had wanted it: this much is clear. No one knew when he had arrived and some even claimed that he had disguised himself as a member of Parliament for years, but they surely noticed him one day during a desperate meal when what remained of the original Privy Council was trying to plan what to do now after ek dum fut-a-fut, hosanna, everything down the Thomas Crapper. Then the screeching sound came and they could not help but plug ears with fingers against that offence of metal scraping Pyrex plates: an ox-large man was dividing an omelette into so many delicate little pieces and they watched him and watched him while awaiting his first bite. Eventually, someone gathered the nerve to ask him, astonished, what the hell, to leave, and with the world's longest sigh, which scattered their papers and rattled the windowpanes, without a word he extracted a figurine of Ronald Reagan from his person and drew the string on its back.

The presidential doll began to speak. It informed that before them sat a man who had been granted moral authority by the American government to supervise all affairs within reason in the unnameable country at this time of great crisis, my friends, please bestow upon him all the love you would upon me.

They couldn't get rid of him after that. Recall, as you may have heard, Maxwell was the one who transferred briefcases stuffed with American currency to the smaller religious parties to bolster dishar-mony and disunity, and years later, would be accused by historians of concatenating the region into an archipelago. It was he who went around the Parliament with calipers and a ruler, measuring various anatomical parts, looking aah into mouths, insisting that members stand on one foot for as long as their balance held, trying to determine the most eligible leader by means hitherto unknown to us. At last, after insisting on a screaming test of who can voice-shatter tossed Pyrex plates the loudest and the most, he set aside three junior members, out of whom he chose a woman, Wafaa Ifreet, otherwise known as the Madam, to claim the seat of power though Anwar would always rule from afar.

It was widely known among Uncle's Associates that Wafaa Ifreet had marched in support of the first American invasion as well as the continuous bombing of La Maga and Benediction, among other cities, was a more willing supporter of Uncle's strategies than any Manchurian candidate, and had supported the Suppression of Speech Act, which had been used against more than just communists, as had been advertised. It was not surprising to anyone, therefore, that she won Maxwell's throatskill election to lead the unnameable country.

Meanwhile, my father descended into the Archives, whose transformation was immediate to notice: all the sound markers had been displaced due to the Archives' rearrangement. The shelves were being torn up into planks of wood to rot in warehouses, the once vast empty spaces were filled with workmen and their powered instruments, all wielding red lights in their hands and pointing to, barking orders, packing up the thoughtreels in large crates. Years ago, the dumb waiter in Supervisor's office had been replaced with a large service elevator located in a centralized area, and the ventilation system of the long hallway had been fixed and a motorized horizontal walkway added for ease of transport, while bright eggshell lights now shone overhead and innocuous jazz played through tinny speakers. Supervisor not only recognized Mamun M but even remembered details about his family and personal life, and claimed he and his wife still listened to those old filmi tracks, though no longer on vinyl but on tape.

So what's new, my father asked, anxious to get to the bottom of the mystery of why he was being recalled to this haunted house.

This, Supervisor held up a small two-dimensional object that looked as if it had been created by the most observant watchmaker: the microchip. We are transferring all the old files from magnetic tape to digital.

That was when my father got to experience the sulphurous hum and to see the skeleton of the largest supercomputer in the world, painstakingly being built for the purpose of safekeeping the souls that had until then rested independently in their own magnetic sepulchres but were now about to be stored, for the first time, in a single location.

There would be no reason for the vast space of the Archives, which would be converted into subterranean office space for the new government, and your job, Supervisor turned on his heel and rested. In front of a fountain of welders' sparks, his eyes shone luminescent coals: Your job will be to find a resting spot for the thoughtreels once we have transferred them to the computer server, but in the meantime

For six months my father descended into the Archives with colleagues who also wore wide-brimmed hats, the style of Archives employees, who also carried notebooks, cushions, bagged meals, and suffered from urinary tract disorders caused by the chemicals in the magnetic reels that sometimes caused them to piss in the vestibules because the bathrooms were far away. He travelled to addresses assigned tasks deeper and deeper in the Archives, places where bats roosted overhead and where one day he discovered what appeared by penlight to be the large wings of an unidentifiable prehistoric bird. He traced the light across its imbricated piscine feathers and wondered whether to gift the fossil wings to his son to complement his talons, but the thought saddened him and he stifled laughter. Who was Hedayat.

Substrata oblivion minds: Mamun Ben Jaloun breathed the sad air summoned by his cart of gathered thought receptacles metal shine in darkness, the dichromate gasoline blaze wafting under the door of the furnace room that was of Archives professionals burning souls. He pushed his cart toward the strangehue.

The blast of light as Mamun Ben Jaloun entered the furnace room always made him cringe. He turned his head away from the guttural negative engine pumping fire onto magnetic tape as his hands opening metal popping containers reached into cranial cavity scooped out magnetic dead brains to fling into burning. Abd, an Incinerator of the Archives with a singular slave's name, would generally dispense the reels into fire, but my father liked to stay and sometimes pass words on Abd's sick daughter pleurisy or whooping cough couldn't quite recall, on their respective jobs of burning human minds. Ask Abd, father: how many dead souls destined for incineration that day dozens scores hundreds always growing.

When the daily incinerated reels rose to a thousand-count in his quadrant, Mamun Ben Jaloun began a mental inventory because any written calculation would obviously be seized as he exited the Archives. His simple calculation multiplied estimated incinerated souls per quadrant with number of quadrants, though he was unsure of either figure.

At that time, computers were replacing tapereels in the Archives and replacing shortwave radios of the National Security Service in tasks of absorbing suspect minds, and Mamun Ben Jaloun justified his job's murderous implications with the thought that the minds he encountered had already been deleted or submitted to jailcell blackness by the time he encountered them as thoughtreels, by saying to himself he was

44

just a functionary, by claiming on cloudless days that there were no minds on the thoughtreels, only impressions, ideations.

I think they are real minds, actual souls, Abd admitted one day to my father in the furnace room in full view of a blinking camera and microphone, and I think all Department employees are shit. How much did Mamun Ben Jaloun know about the Department's overhaul and translation of the whole enterprise of surveilling and storing human minds by newer machines.

All around my father, the same fires burned in all the quadrants of the Archives: magnetic and actual fires burned as Archives employees followed orders, doused themselves with Department cologne before exiting the compound to bathe against tongues of light fire dance and smoke seeping for hours into clothes, leaving porcine or human flesh smells.

Fire in the unnameable country: what happened to the thoughtreels. All through the night, nights in a row, for days dragged weeks fits and starts until entire tombstone truckloads, load-bearing vehicles finally delivered clean, erased tapereels, forklifted metal receptacles to *The Mirror*'s warehouse storehouse. Fuck: as if they could hide the lugubrious odour, the Director sighed, making rounds of the inventory and giving the day's recording tapes a good inhale.

Ever the skeptic, Abd's surety only increased my father's doubts of actual minds on the thoughtreels though the question nagged and lingered and led him to follow whims of a secret compass whose bearings only pointed nightmare. One day, Mamun Ben Jaloun wanted to turn back except he could not decide whether behind him extended the path he had followed or what way lay ahead. Around him rested broken compartments of shelves, sinews of magnetic tapes exposed to the environment, the memories of dead smells dead thoughts, flashes of light and crimson dark, as well as other evidence of shipwreck and ruin. But it was not like the old days when one could not expect to find anyone in the labyrinth, Archives employees were always collecting reels, so he yelled hello. The echo reverberated for centuries, redoubling every few seconds and coming back and back again as a louder cry than the one he had sent out, until he became confused as to whether what he heard was his own voice or another's. When, long after, it grew silent again, he heard the stirring.

He saw a man shake his head and rise from the ashes and filth, his legs bowed and his body covered profusely with hair. The stranger babbled for a long time, incomprehensible, before finally managing to spit out, Who are you very angry, it seemed, to have been disturbed.

My father, discomfited by the other's presence, explained himself and hoped to avoid a conflict. He explained with his hands outstretched, gesturing in the energetic way to which he had grown accustomed from spending so much time with Xasan Sierra and the smoking-shop crowd.

I can pluck them for you, the stranger spoke clearly, saying he knew precisely where were the reels my father was searching for, if you allow me to ride on your shoulders, since, as you can see, he pointed to his bowed legs, I am not entirely ambulant.

And before Mamun M could consider the strange offer, the man raced around behind him, leapt nimbly simian up his back, and seated himself on his shoulders.

What in the, my father tried to unbalance the trespasser and stepped this way and that, but the greater his efforts the more the vagabond increased his weight and enwrapped his legs around Mamun's neck and shoulders, while letting fly shrieks of perverse pleasure.

The pressure was so great Mamun M felt colours throughout his body flowing from other corners of the universe and just when he thought the pain could get no worse the hairy man's fists thumped against the sides of his head and he heard such loud shouts of joy that it returned him to a functional state and invoked in Mamun M the greatest desire to inflict physical pain on his assailant, a desire he had never before experienced. But all his attempts would be set against him as, exhausted by his efforts, my father dropped to the floor, which only allowed the vagabond's feet to wrap around him even tighter.

Mamun awoke to the hairy stranger's shouts and his tugging on his ears, Get up, onward yaa. Some transformation seemed to have occurred, and as if under a spell, my father slowly rose and began galloping through the wilderness of that subterranean maze, turning and accelerating, whoa there, avoiding debris and volleying over obstacles strewn across their path until they arrived in a place where the ground shifted with every step and everything, including the weak light that drizzled onto them from above, was suffused with a dampness. By now, my father had grown somewhat accustomed to the stranger's weight and the dampness penetrated through clothing through skin, and the air was sad because it reminded him of the times he and Shukriah would attract crustaceans of the Gulf of Eden with the humidity of their love-making. My father snorted like a horse and tried to keep his balance on the shifty ground as the hairy man directed him to a spot where the spines of the shelves had not yet dissolved, and, one by one, he began to toss the correct roundmetal containers to the floor.

———————

It was impossible to remove the vagabond from Mamun's shoulders. He had the property of screaming in several languages and hissing in a dangerous way whenever he felt threatened, or to asphyxiate Mamun by pressing against my father's neck with his thighs. Supervisor had no time to consider yet another medical claim from a man who had extended his last one for nearly three thousand days, and by then, Gita, Shukriah, and Chaya were so busy with the hosiery shop that they thought of Mamun's problem as purely a social accident, the result of a petty conflict between him and one of the tatterdemalion vagabonds of the cigarette shop. At dinner, they provided the stranger his own plate of food, which he took in his raised seat, and he would apologize when he spilled the contents onto my father's head while eating.

Since Mamun M could not stand the wretched odour of the man-sized parasite, he was forced to bathe him, and I will not try to relate the acrobatic difficulties of going to toilet for two. While it is true that since the year of the sleeping plague no one in the unnameable country had fornicated, the utter lack of privacy and inability even to lie down next to Shukriah at night was an added reason for his despair. In the evenings, while my father tried desperately to read the paper or to pass the time in some other idle silent way—since he was ashamed of his condition and no longer visited his friends at Xasan Sierra's—the bow-legged stranger would babble endlessly, and switched between languages so often that only Hedayat had the patience and the time to sit at their feet and listen.

At that time, because my father thought I would be able somehow through my silence-strangespeech to pry the unseemly weight off his shoulders, he tried to understand me a little, even to get to know Niramish. My friend, meanwhile, had begun to gain the added problem of adolescent sweat glands on top of the odour of curried vegetables for which he was universally known, but even he felt sated by the know-ledge that Mamun M's difficulties outweighed most people's. And he who had been laughed at all his life could not help giggling at that odd sight of a hairy man picking nits off the head of a perfect image of gentility/ middle-aged father starched collar rolled sleeves, reading.

Ask him, baba, Mamun would insist, and I would try, but to zero avail. For months I was incapable of coaxing the minotaur to reveal his history, where from you are, why in the labyrinth, and so forth. We have noticed that the hairy stranger is no Caliban and can speak perfectly comprehensible phrases, so why the roundabout and foreign. Another way to ask: glossolalia: what provokes it. Another still: does it always work. As we have witnessed, its origin is usually the confluence of several hidden organs, historical individual spontaneous illogical-unusual to name a few. How came this stranger to possess this strange ability, and why the unnameable country. Does this trick of the tongue exist elsewhere in the world, I mean. Since it would be many months until the days of the Ranas, Q and Masoud, linked to whose life stories Hedayat's own glossolalist abilities would mature, cajoling the stranger off my father's back would have to take another route.

At that time, my friend and I were too busy wandering alleys glass bottle or cataract marijuana gaze, watching crowd actors in one camera shot or another in our city-turned-movie-set, snickering young boots, kicking dust at all their shit. I must note that I have never seen a single moment of *The Mirror* because they were manufactured for export but I know its various feature-length scenes have been shown at film festivals around the world and become hit Hollywood action flicks. Through my conversations with Niramish, I was developing my own understanding of the movie studio whose presence had increased exponentially since my father's youth. Meanwhile, the glossolalist stranger remained affixed to my father's shoulders.

My grandmother mother aunt were too busy running a business which by then was blossoming: they couldn't take down the clothes they put up on the racks fast enough to sell, to customers who now not only came from around the city but from throughout the country. Chaya had begun to design her own line of trousers-shirts; with a keen eye for style, she would grow to influence a generation of designers. Except know this: at the end of the day, when they looked in the cash register, there would be nothing but a few crumpled bills and small change. At first they cried thief, but who could have, it was only they three who ran things, and the air of mutual suspicion that was created only served to ensure that none of them were responsible. They updated books three times a day, and the figures never lied: despite having moved more stock than ever, they were hemorrhaging capital at a rate that would put them out of business very soon. But it was like that all over the unnameable country: no matter how hard people tried to make a living, they found themselves sucked bloodless, as if a mysterious source were filling its coffers with their hardearned.

THE
ANNUNCIATION
OF
NIRAMISH

At that time, many things were beginning to reveal their secret characters. A team of American archaeologists and geographers, who had come with the first staff of *The Mirror*, had spent a decade and a half wandering the hinterland plains, penned between the Karkaars, an invisible southern border, and the Gulf of Eden by a swarming dustbowl, which did not give them a moment's respite and followed them everywhere they turned, one morning stumbled upon a bubbling alcove of ash, where the air unexpectedly cleared. Anthony Sentinel, the leader of the group, later said he had seen a photograph of hell exactly like it in an encyclopedia series he used to look at as a child, and the measurements they took with their instruments, which had not suffered despite all the years of dusty wandering, confirmed it was an asphalt bay almost as ancient as the earth itself. Within it, they found strange flagellant insects and amino acid series that existed nowhere else on the planet, not to mention microorganisms that were subsisting on heavy metals and toxic chemicals.

I am inclined to believe, Sentinel reported to the BBC, that the unnameable country still contains traces of the globe at its youngest stage, and is therefore the oldest country on earth, though his comments did not result in an upgrade of our observer status in the United Nations. It is important to note the crewmen came back to America and found that no trace of their lives remained the same; several of them committed suicide.

At home, meanwhile, it turned out my aunt Chaya was not pregnant after all.

Don't want a baby, it looks like that; he don't want a baby, it looks like that, she said as a way of explaining when I asked her why she had her arms clasped around me, why she was saying take good care of yourself, Hedayat/ who was the man that also didn't want a baby, Chaya Khala/ why neither my mother nor my father would talk about Aunt Shadow/ why are you crying, Khala/ by name after her departure, but at that time there were other disappearances as well in my life.

Most important is the topic I wish I could avoid, the continued diaphanous transformation of Niramish, as if by laying down vast tracts of silence I would be able to change the reality of that time or the course of events that followed. The matter remains, however, that Niramish did die, and at the height of his powers as the Electrician.

Take it to One Arm, they would say, when the stylus of their record player broke, or when they wanted to catch American channels on their television set, and while laden with tasks so secret he could not even mention them to me, he never said no and rarely charged a fee for such pedestrian jobs. No one spoke anymore about his constant odour of curried vegetables, not even as a joke, since these days they would touch even the hem of his ermine cape. I tried to retain the fluidity of our original conversations, but found myself swept back by the lucidity of his thoughts and the surety with which he asserted his place in the world as a fixer and maker of machines.

I hope you will not take my words to mean jealousy, for understand I had no wish to achieve a popularity equal to that of my friend; in the unnameable country, one stays alive by avoiding being spoken of, hunted after. I wished for Niramish to live another thousand years. And yet. And then. Alas, once upon a time, I had a friend named Niramish. And then the first bombing at which I paid scant attention, because everything explodes eventually in this fissile country. Once upon a time, and this is true, the story of my friend Niramish coincides with the story of the first suicide bombing in the unnameable country.

How so: at that time, it had grown fashionable to wear football bags slung over one shoulder, so much that it served at once as a symbol of youthful taste as well as the utilitarian purposes of carrying and storing all manner of items, most of them not at all affiliated with sports. And also: while excluded from most international affairs, the unnameable country had nevertheless participated in its second African Cup football tournament two years earlier, in which, if you care to recall, we placed fourth, and over whose joyous occasion people erupted into the streets, celebrating with confetti and handfuls of rice dropping from overhead and sweetmeats free for all, hear ye and marhabbah. I myself held no interest in sporting events, but Niramish and I shouted and danced the steps with them while disappearing into the three A.M. haze until the coppers called us halt. Somewhere in the distance there was a thud like the falling of a large animal from the sky. Then there sang an MP's car alarm, but the subsequent cries of horror folded so neatly into those of joy all around us that we did not realize what had happened until late in the morning.

Ten days later, hours before a major financial conference in the capital Victoria, a twenty-year-old commerce student from the nation's biggest university walked into the Sheraton Hotel. He seated himself in the lobby, as a guest would, casually with arms splayed on a couch, ordered lemonade and today's *International Herald Tribune*, the staff came to inquire whether he would have/ they disappeared and then they returned.

Will you be having lunch with us, sir.

Depends on the soup, he replied without glancing up, and unfurled the business section. A single droplet of sweat emerged, unnoticed, on his left temple. He inquired of the soup menu. Then they went away and the light became peaceful in the room.

When the grey clotted plumage of the dining room blast cleared and its effects could be measured, observers were bewildered by its sheer destructive force, which had collapsed several floors above and below the first, and they had trouble believing its cause was a single bomb, though no other evidence but that which was presumed to originate from just one football bag could be found. The Belgian financial ambassador, two World Bank representatives, a high-level oldster from the Chase banking group, five or six interns, American university students on the trip of their lives, and local businessmen numbered among the seventy-six dead. More than three hundred people were injured, some of whom would later die in hospital.

Soon after, Niramish began to birbirbirbirbirbirbirbir to himself while pacing back and forth behind the screen where he soldered and joined wires in Uncleboy's father's garage. I asked him to explain the nature of his retreat from everyone in recent days, including me, and he gave me actual electrical sparks from the mouth; but the work of wires was overwhelming him, and, in fact, he wondered from time to time if doctors unhinged his head whether they would not discover his brain replaced with a nest of circuitry.

Disconcerted by the way he was hedging, I pressed him, and asked him for the first time whether he was taking contracts from the Islamic Youth Party or any of the other parties that had been hiring engineering students for their military wings. These matters were not yet well publicized, and in fact I knew of them only after overhearing one or two conversations between Grandfather and Uncleboy, a pair of diehard oldsters who had survived the years now peaking bones expanded motorcycle jumps, had thrived: garage after garage of bikes and nervy boys to motor them, hard sunlight on their hot-pepper-pouch street deals near alleyways, who had raised Niramish and me from scooters to full-power Hondas though we preferred the Warren tunnels, who could augur death in a pin-drop a hundred metres away. My owl's intuition concurred as I peered into Niramish's sign and the way his hulk bent forward at the accusation. I saw it in the twitch of his lame arm, in the laboured anger of his response, which I will not allow to grace the page so soon before his death.

Years later, it would grow apparent that I was, in fact, the last of the mastans to know. That actually, Niramish's bombs were feared and had exploded as far away as Mogadishu, where another state, another civil war, as you will recall. In fact, I found out long after all the national broadcasts began to speak of the Football Bang Electrician, whose signature explosives had garnered him the greatest notoriety of any terrorist figure in the country. He was featured as the subject of talk-show debates about the effectiveness of the new regime's counterterror measures, was bequeathed bouquets of grudging respect for his perpetual evasion of the authorities, and continued practice of his deadly art. They even echoed rumours of the Electrician's refusal to accept payment for his services, a detail that should have alerted Hedayat immediately to the truth. But I believed nothing for certain while my friend turned into a minor celebrity of sorts.

However, the wider public would not know what he looked like until he died. Internal staff of the Ministry of Records and Sources swore at each other for not being able to tune in to his head with the shortwave radio, while the Black Organs invited Shin Beit for tips on tracing this destructive character. After our confrontation, Niramish no longer trusted my insights, and for the hours I would sit by his side while he rearranged flux capacitors and hold his voltage meter, I tried my best not to irk him. Understand that while owls are solitude's signatories and live best alone as undisturbed units, they also possess the capacity to build deep friendships, whose losses tear their confidence in the whole animal kingdom. The Madam's regime had chosen the Electrician as a symbol, its greatest pariah, and I saw him reflected everywhere in the mirror streets, because who didn't wear a football bag those days. I myself had several, although Gita urged me to abandon them and even purchased a rather expensive knapsack for me in hopes I would replace them. Even the fact that the cameras craned down from above and focused on their subjects through fisheye lenses, even the fact of armoured insect riot police descending on a crowd of youths without warning, open up, let us see now, of greedy eyes and amorous tongues licking chops for a crumb of so-called evidence: none of these facts could hinder their magnetic draw. In fact, the Electrician's notoriety only increased their presence everywhere. The only person who didn't wear one was Niramish, because, as he explained, the strap would ruin his ermine cape.

One knows/one does not know/one cannot believe: all these contradictions flowed seamlessly through me as my friend drifted into an irretrievable loneliness. I awoke one night after having fallen head-down asleep on the coldmetal table of the garage where Niramish worked and could not see him anywhere.

I yelled his name and he returned loudly, I'm here, from two or three feet away, but I couldn't see him. I blinked-unblinked, called him again, and then his image flickered and readjusted to the reality of that dust-invaded space.

He shook me by my shoulders, held me aloft half as well as my father did once to rid me of the habit of presiding as heresiarch over an imaginary kingdom. Then he became fully visible.

After that incident, Niramish fashioned a pair of glasses for me because he said I was losing my sight, but their purpose was quite the opposite, for Niramish understood my gift-curse of insight and wanted to prevent me from seeing deeper. The glasses seemed altogether ordinary but they disallowed me from understanding any more than the average person when I put them on. It was a kindly gesture to protect his friend from a reality to which he had already adjusted. It was a nervous, selfish act for which I never forgave him.

What do you believe. Did Niramish and others like him whistle into the abyss to draw out an angry God. Know this: at that time the politics of the country—the banshee competitions of throatskill orchestrated by the gourmandizing Maxwell of the Reagan administration which resulted in the election of our head of state, or the back-and-forth braying by the mullahs, who traded insults after Friday prayers—failed utterly to synchronize with the spirit of the youth. In fact, we laughed at them all and recalled the theatre of the cows on the minarets as staged by the Americans, though some of us, like Hedayat, were not born when that incident occurred.

No, we could not love the Americans because they had imprisoned us with mirror-streets and spied on us with everywhere cameras of a counterfeit movie set; they had burned us with a deceptive phosphorescent fire, which resisted water, and had deprived us of the ability to earn an honest living and driven us to hidden organs of income. But we loved the symbol nevertheless: which politician, secular religious pseudo-socialist, or whateverelse, was not a dumb roan bull at the pulpit's height. What was politics if not the moocall to assembly at an odd time in the sun's route across the firmament.

No; understand: whoever committed themselves to combustible politics in those days did so strictly for money, which could not be earned another way, or for some inexplicable personal reason. Ah, if not politics then surely the monetary; yet know Niramish destroyed our hashish networks and did irreparable damage to our connections with dealers of snow, as well as all manner of opiates, when he decided to switch professions. At that time, we were making enough to purchase dozens of ermine capes, and I have already told of his aversion to accepting remunerations for his electrical work. Saint Niramish then, ascetic sadhu dervish Jesuit ideologue and knee-bending prayerer, you do snide, is this.

Yet my responsibility is not to convince you of another emotion but to relate the life of my friend as he lived it. If you must know, a large reason behind his metamorphosis into the Electrician lay in the thrill of craftsmanship. It is difficult to describe the energy that radiated from his body as he disassembled an alarm clock with only four fingers and a thumb, let alone when rewiring a complex circuitboard. But to return to the story, who betrayed Niramish and what was the cause of his death. I could not confirm how they did it until years later, but it was obvious that the failure and capture of the last bomber, incidentally also named Hedayat—widely reported in the press and the cause of tighter closures and the instalment of even more complex mirror-walls in La Maga— and his requisite torture by the Department had something to do with what happened next.

Know that Niramish rarely slept in a single place for more than a week after that, moving from one safehouse to another, harboured by Uncleboy's associates and taken out to the further reaches of the organization until he disappeared beyond the boughs of the baobab, so to speak, and none of the mastans would report to me even whether he remained alive. One day, I heard a soft hail of pebbles against my window and recognized the imp mastan standing below, Hasan or Hussein, I don't recall which of the twins. Whichever, he bugled with his empty fingers and I wished I had sprouted wings enough to drop softly down to the ground, but I was forced to sneak out via the conventional route as the household slumbered.

I shuddered though the night was warm, I felt it then and I should have/ we strode through one and the next deserted street and passed through known mirrors and appeared at the other end of the city. There was Niramish, translucent, paler than ever and seated on a bed, separated from Grandfather by the mere distance of a chess set. They were just beginning a game, but Grandfather rose at once with a nod, he departed and left the two of us to talk, but we did not talk for a long time.

In time, the air grew foul and I complained to Niramish, There are no, but where are the windows in this room, friend.

That is because they are suffocating us, yaar.

Niramish was moving pieces around the Queen's Gambit and replacing the pawns to Staunton Harold/ he was doing this and replacing them. He said, they're suffocating us, yaar, a phrase he repeated many times, They're suffocating us, he said while moving pawns to the start. But since he became angry while speaking and returned to fully visible flesh and blood, not at all diaphanous anymore, I was contented. Then he began to sob and became confused about his size. He shrank to my knee's height and began clutching at my trousers, sobbing.

I said to him, Niramish, this too shall pass, rise up, Niramish, and when he began to fade again and to flicker dangerously, I scooped him up onto my shoulder like a toddler and coddled him. It's all right, Niramish, there are others in the world and surely this misery is not the world.

He did not believe me then, and in strode Uncleboy, Telephone for Niramish, at which time my glasses fell off my face on their own accord.

Niramish descended from my shoulders because he was shy for his sobbing and his shrinking act and reached down to lift my glasses since he was closer, and as he leaned them up to me he began sobbing again because they had fallen down and broken.

I knew then, I could have said it, I felt everything but others knew absolutely.

This one is important, Uncleboy tugged on my shirt, and we left Niramish.

In the other room they came and went, and the voices jostled me between the apparitions, which spoke. They were hard drinking and a hand extended toward me, and the decanter was there. I smelled it but I had no wish for that. The smell was of whiskey and I worried for Niramish, but the air was not foul in this room and I was glad for that. I could not call the silence by name and it was not silence, for they were talking, and the voices that. A hidden organ heralded its bloody existence inside me and I doubled over in pain. The source of the pain was elusive and I began to run somewhere and to gasp because my throat or my. I waited for the pain but mostly the anxiety to pass and for Niramish's conversation to be over. When we heard the noise and smelled the smoke I felt the other. Then I ran and I realized in fact I was clutching the decanter.

I splashed the whiskey onto Niramish's face. Rise, Niramish, I pleaded, but the hole was too large and around his head there was that, and when he was lying like that. I discovered I was sobbing. I thought it was I who with my sobs was making the whole house shake, but probably it was the air outside that was moving like a furious dustbowl that had gathered for a purpose. When all the confusion was over, it was simple to understand: they had inserted a miniature explosive inside the mobile, and when we felt the house shake it was the shudder of a hidden organ, a Black Hawk helicopter that was rising now and from which the bomb had been triggered.

News of the Electrician's death rippled across the continent, and the whole world knew very soon. It was reported in the newspapers and jumped media into radios and television screens, and there was jubilation like we had never known. They tried to bury him that very day due to public health concerns. His body would not stop issuing blood and we couldn't understand, though he had been a fat adolescent, why there issued from his body blood equal to that of thirty people or more, and why the bleeding had no end, though they had bandaged his mortal head wound with wound-tight layers of cotton cloth. We would have drowned in the house where Niramish died had they not located a large tumbrel soon after to carry him to the nearest cemetery. On the way there, as respectful silent as a murder of funereal crows, they gathered behind in fours and fives at first before the dozens began streaming and then whole hundreds shorn from their lives in that horsebeaten noonlight, in the flythickened air that clotted in all lungs, drawn by the look of that sad spilling blood, which was overflowing from the tumbrel and spilling brown already for putrefaction, but which continued to drip drip drip drip. Some estimates quoted a number of nearly two hundred thousand, though I was alone that day and cannot verify.

In my grief I tore the budding feathers from my arms and the sunlight burned my skin raw. Know this, however: there were other birds, of the flighted variety unlike your narrator, crows mostly, but magpies and curlews also, as I could tell, which hovered above us like a ragged canopy, or just another convoy of Niramish's close associates and admirers. At the cemetery, they were burying an uncle who had died of lung disease or an infarction of the pulmonary valve, and some of the mastans and nameless rebels, whose faces were shielded from the cameras by scarves, asked them please, will you not give us this spot, for as you can: they pointed to the still bleeding Niramish in the barrow and then to the crowd. But they would not. The whole crowd was ready to give him, to tear up the very earth on which it stood, but still there was no ground that would accept Niramish.

The birds disappeared for lost hope and then not a wisp of cirrus overhead, no shade from even one palmate branch: the crowd swayed like a single unit, vast millipede which this side that sided out of thirst and various other discomforts. For sixteen days it wandered from cemetery to cemetery looking for a place to bury the Electrician, for that was how he had died, not as my friend who took refuge with me from the teasing afterschool crowd, not Niramish and me eating capsicum candies in Confectionarayan Babu's sweet shop or who had suffered through the bitter alienation due to his indelible odour of curried vegetables as I had for my talons or for my slow metamorphosis into an owl, not as One Arm, Quiet Talker, but the Electrician who had designed explosives that warranted conversations across borders and who now could not stop bleeding even after death.

Some thousand or more people relayed their condolences for my loss. Among them was a man weaved toward me through crowd and criers, stood gregarious with a smile and a sun-gleaming pate. He addressed me by name. In the funeral crowd, I had met Niramish's relatives, of course, but none so determined to know me and about my gangster-steps with him. Though I avoided the man, no doubt a Black Organ, I was convinced, he persisted, and finally found me pressed against the farthest cemetery wall from the entrance. Hedayat, he called, snapped a pocket mirror to light between thumb and index, showed my face in sunlight before declaring the mirror was magic, a magic gift for my dead nephew's friend, he snapped fingers. Take it, he handed me the mirror, which reflects the future, he instructed, before facing it in view of a toddler withered suck at his mother's teat.

Charlatan's tricks, I waved him away, leave me to my misery, old man, I yelled.

I am Niramish's uncle Dhikr, he insisted, followed me around, I'm his father's brother, he said before snapping again, this time bringing a small velveteen packet to appear. He showed me shoelaces, explained the contents of the package once upon a time a fabled Zachariah, your grandfather, boot-hopped across the Mediterranean into European

Plains lit by thousand-watt bulbs of the Director's choice, across papier-mâché Ural Mountains into Asia until the Chukchi Sea: you must believe in my gift of flight your grandfather's bootlaces, he instructed, in their ability to lift you out of the darkest place. May you never need them, but if you were my nephew's friend, I suggest you keep them near.

Still slighted by this stranger interrupted my sadness, amused because it was my father, the playback singer Mamun BenJaloun, who had boot-hopped the world, not my grandfather, suspicious whether the stranger had known Niramish, knew his relatives, let alone mine, and before I could say thank you, I saw his bald pate weave dense funeral crowd under the midday sun. What sorcery had he given me, this Niramish's uncle, I wondered as I pocketed the velveteen package in my shirt's secret compartment. I wouldn't recall the existence of the bootlaces or find use for them until months later, when I would find myself in the darkest place, in an Archives abyss among animals.

A thousand people extended their condolences the day they buried Niramish, yet I didn't know them. In the heat and discomfort, the teeming mass lost sense of whose memories, whose emotions belonged to whom. I caught the name of Niramish's first cigarette and echo of his coughing as recalled by a young man to the right of me who didn't speak a word the whole funeral march, his first easy sums in primary class remembered in full by his gradeschool teacher walked in the crowd silently. I drank a homemade lemonade image from a motherfriend he neglected to mention to me, saw moving picture of a curious Niramish asking about petals and petioles in her garden as soft touches of her apron to lemon-dribble cheeks. I saw her years older, hunched, sad, whipped whisper-thin to her neighbour how many more times this back and forth between the military and our boys in secret barracks, she was saying.

I was afraid of being associated with my friend and with his uncle and his uncle's gift, which bulged in my shirt's secret compartment. I denied to everyone no, I did not know him. I tore from the ridges of the crowd's belly to one moving leg and another of the crowd, to one part and the next of that singular insect made of so many tired grieving people, but they could all identify me as Niramish's friend. The people moved as one suffering animal gave up its legs and portions of its body as its constituents began to disperse, leaving Niramish still lying above the earth and still bleeding. The people were replaced by the avian convoy, which fluttered back and descended silently and remained with us until Niramish was buried.

Years later, I became aware that the Library of Congress had preserved a recording of the sixteen days it took us to find a resting place for Niramish, one that bears the title *The Annunciation of a Terrorist*. It is possible to review the verity of the events as I have described them. Truth be told, certain mysteries remain, and I am not sure I have related the correct quantity of blood that spilled from Niramish's head wound, for instance, or whether it continued spilling for as many days as I indicated or drew as many people by the sight of its unending drip-drip. But everyone knows the legend of Niramish flowed through so many hidden arteries afterward and in such gushing volume there erupted out of the many whispers-wounds certain copycat electricians who tried but failed to repeat Niramish; they were all arrested or died before.

The world spoke ill of him or well of him, they spoke of him all over the world, but no speech, nothing at all, could return Niramish to the sainthood of his simple presence. For months afterward in La Maga, the Black Organs arrested anyone cooking curried vegetables, since they identified the odour of frying mustard seeds and cauliflower as incense-symbols of the vigil act, while the mastans moved me from safehouse to safehouse to ensure I was not arrested. However, now that I no longer wore the blind glasses Niramish had fashioned for me, I could see the shadows of the mastans falling differently. The categories of friend and foe were reluctant to demarcate themselves clearly just yet, but I could tell Black Organs was not ready for Hedayat.

THE
BANQUET

Ten days later, Grandfather and associates, higherups and henchmen, visited me at the trogloscene little saferoom where they were hiding me, dusting sweet hands falling jilapi crumbs before spilling bloody talk over Niramish's death. They frowned who would play my replacement business partner. Despite my grief, I bit my tongue: silence is necessary for mastanism/mastani, language to language the same cutthroat ideology. The black economy also has its slavers and supplicants and an owl learns grip and talons over street mice gang little furballs and when to give a hoot.

But for all the braggadocio and machismo promise of the Underground Unnameable Country, the point, friends and enemies, is that Hedayat would be expected to play pawn or at most run the bishop's moves in a long game in our gang's piratical accumulations. Recall, as the story goes: in the beginning Niramish and I paid tithes regularly and easily since we had secured one of the best divisions in the city for dealing black pepper, but we stopped altogether when Niramish began lip-dribbling stones of incomprehensible, when the Electrician started talking alonethoughts of combustion and exchange belonging to his new associates.

And now Niramish was dead and Grandfather was opening a coffin little box, offering me a cigarillo: a lungful of sweet, second breath harder, and then the room pankha, spin-spin. My temples blood-hardened. Words mounted words in the smoke. Someone dragged a very large covered wagon into the room. The meaning of it all escaped me until they flung back cloth and there sat an elephantine subject, much fatter than Niramish and unlike Niramish because he possessed two well-functioning upper limbs. He sat there twiddling thumbs, awaiting his turn.

Then merdre and kingpsshit, drumroll circus introduction in the midst of mourning: Grandfather bade me shake hands with my new business partner, and I shook hands because what could I/ Grandfather offered me the devilish handshake deal of nothing at all to start with but two marijuana bricks. And my bambacino new psshitgrinning partner merely emitted a contented whine while twiddling thumbs under cloth until they rolled him away. Then, because they respected that I had been Niramish's shadow and knew I was tired of the world, they left me alone to think things over.

At first I didn't like Masoud Rana. No serious-minded goonda I knew carried a flask of Canadian rye wherever he went, while his '66 Datsun, destined to become my street career's ashes to phoenix, emitted the odour of leaded gasoline left me head-throb pull over the car, man, nauseous on green grass side of the road. We started with near-nothing.

The higherups were redrawing La Maga to account for the camps of hackneyed snuffpeddlers who couldn't keep out of jail and had to be replaced every few months. Give me more, I pleaded, and Grandfather allowed Masoud and me to seed fallow land in a high-density mirror district, a neighbourhood crowded with fire-besieged spidersilk factories where homes had become accessible only through tunnels.

What we didn't know was that there were residents in the tunnels, and that they were animals.

During one of our trips through the underground passages, Masoud Rana and I were nearly buried with a collection of goats and a young woman who was quietly, poor thing, with Eurydice-steps just behind us, with a hand on her tethered barnyard collection through the tunnels on the other side. As American bulldozers pounded above, the sarcophagus pathway rumbled behind us, the ceiling flung mud in our faces; my lungs then/ a trickle odour of urea and the faint sensation of disappear/ suffocation asphyxiation/ Hedayat began crawling.

Eventually, after a long dark time, after the tunnel behind us became dust, we found the open air breath after sweet breath. The girl gave a livid fucking scream for falling rocks and their bulldozers when we finally surfaced through a hole. So happy was she to be alive she offered us a milk goat, which Masoud and I thankfully added to our meagre assets. What began strictly as a drug trade ended up encompassing and eventually replacing/ we ended up becoming, let us say, crate porters of bread and cigarettes, cakes, baked goods, lettuce, cauliflowers, squash and legumes, pineapples, oranges, whole orchards it seemed some days, to the great disdain of Grandfather and the higherups, who saw no gains in moving away from narcotics.

The goat was the first sign of a good several months, almost as productive as in the days of Niramish; for this reason and because at that time changes were occurring quickly in Hedayat's house, he preferred to hide from them in the Warren entrails. Aunt Shadow's ballooning belly lifted her to soft nest with Samir, curious lover of both punk and disco, to his wall-to-wall emporium where lived a collection of feedback guitar recordings and Euro club hits, which featured a hammock swayed two bodies to single motion sweet melody nightly. Her departure from the apartment above the hosiery shop signalled the arrival of my sisters, the Yea and Nay Quintuplets, whose condition was bastardy, my fever-sick father decided, who originated from five loins from five fathers make one gravid female, he would mutter, frustrated, out of work until he would meet Imran, otherwise known as Gorbachev, whom he knew as a Screen of the Screens, their motorcycle gang from way back in the day. Gorbachev was now a cop and would one day employ my father in the police force as an archivist due to his knowledge of thoughtreels, which would turn our home into a prison.

Why. Let it be known Gorbachev had struck a deal with the Ministry of Records and Sources to save my father's ass, because thoughtreel theft, though the crime had no precise jurisprudential citation, was governed by Black Organs in the darkest corners of the unnameable country. He's harmless, Gorbachev had argued, see for yourselves.

One day, Department officers appeared at our front door, breezy, talkative, and seated themselves on high chairs at the entrance, before our bedroom doors, and in front of the bathroom. That was when they began demanding identification to travel between rooms in our home, to inspect our belongings, to beep and tell all the metallic items on our persons, from keys to paper clips and pens and bric-a-brac. They arbitrarily arrested my mother, consigned her to the bedroom, suspicious of her true intentions even after she swore for shit's sake, I always do the shop's inventory on Saturdays. They forbade my father from lathering his beard, made him shave with water and salt. When asked why all the regulation, they pointed to departmental procedures until otherwise specified.

My visits home at that time were becoming more and more infrequent. I missed my five sisters' births, the Yea and Nay Quintuplets' nursery hours in my mother's spidersilk hosiery shop suspended in hammocks with juicebottles, their first steps, I missed them crying their rhyme and tell exercises to hearts' content while my mother sold stockings while my father paced the store front to back or paced our home, frustrated with being reduced to a baker of bread in the kitchen for family meals though he couldn't bear the thought of returning to work in an archive of dead souls. Recall the yet untold past: an unaccountable voice in the wilderness of tape receptacles sings out to my father without warning one day and though he is used to ghosts on magnetic reels on shelves in rows of endless shelves in the Archives his workplace, its insistence I am the dead falls him bedrest down and shivering.

Ghar and bahir: despite/because of great changes in my family and in our house, I was more interested in making a courier's living sufficient income delivering fruit trees and barrels of eats to busted building neighbourhoods full of fire-refugees. One day, Masoud Rana and I received a package with a paintbrush and tunnel map from a friend of a friend of a cousin-associate of Uncleboy. The maze drawing located our subterranean destination with a dot and the inscription sweep aside the fog to find a porthole painted in air. Confused by what was obviously a poetic allusion in a strict literal line of work, we took the task for pay, and curious to observe the underground animals we had heard so much about.

Who are the Warren animals. And what do they claim of the Warren animals. Animals displaced underground by spontaneous fires on the surface is one way to say it. Once upon a time, a bombed and burning spidersilk field fills a hinterland region where men and women run from fire with bags and carryalls as dilated pupils and brown grass growth of fur on human skin; pollen noses twitch lagomorphosis, the sudden appearance of hopping refugees. Or barking order through megaphone raises greymetal glint of gun, turns scared stooping people into newly formed Pomeranians and poodles when the bright lights shine on the grassy knoll. We hear about these things as new animals fill the largest urban centres of the unnameable country fill hospitals without X-ray or ultrasound machines, with only basic surgical equipment, gauze and gloves.

Who were the Warren animals that we saw documented on television, read about in newspapers and magazines. Why the Warren animals. Once upon a time after the annunciation of Niramish, Masoud Rana and I began making a fair living running deliveries through the tunnels beneath the Palisades, the fortified neighbourhoods of La Maga governed by gangs. One day, while delivering two vegetable crates to a place they called the Ghost Hospice/

One sharp turn and deep fall later the world wasn't the same. For one thing, we were rising up the granite steps; clearly we were walking up the steps. But we felt our stomachs rise, saw ourselves descend saw other side of room staring camera and wires empty film canisters cinematic articles of production twisting inverting us with their gaze. We walked the path under its stone arch, its dust and odour in our lungs at our senses until an oblong light in the distance became a man whose face encrusted in flour, who sat on a wooden chair with a donkey's head fresh drip-drip on his lap.

At that time, it was well known Black Organs traversed the Warrens, planted scare-signs, blasted loud music always wafted up through manholes and drainage pipes, so Masoud Rana and I were unsurprised at the donkey's head on a dead man's lap, its drip-drip collecting conical amber sap on floor. We were more concerned with the fog descended over each fallen step behind us, the features of the stairway we had just crossed blotted into mist, as dark outlines of paths we didn't travel drove impossible angles.

In a place of impossible roads and thick vapour, Masoud Rana stopped, map in hand before a door. When we knocked, a rabbit woman stood there nose-a-twitch-twitch, wearing a house-frock, wide-eyed and obviously frightened of Hedayat's beaking lips gnarled hands like talons/ which rabbit doesn't fear an owl. Coasters glasses spoons and books floated out through the door as come in, inside quick quick. The contents of her home settled soft crash when she closed the entrance behind us as animals found their places again around a table; Masoud Rana and I displayed our bags' contents: carrots mould asparagus for two rabbits gleaming, meatscraps and bones for the dogs in chairs beside them, and grubs for the fish with Fu Manchu moustaches as our hostess disappeared into a kitchen interior of that burrow.

They had been speaking in the interim between raw and cooked foods. Meeting adjourned, cried a rabbit before being corrected other way, madam, by her canine compatriot. Right, she said; class dismissed then, which was of course the other and equally incorrect thing to say. The fish with Fu Manchus broke into raucous guffaw, and I joined them quietly, politely. It was Masoud Rana, with all his anthropocentric prejudice, who asked: So are you all escapees of the zoo.

That's when they emerged as if to a hidden schedule. Hard-hat construction workers dragged planar surfaces into the room, began assembling them loud shouts. Dust rose with their hammering and nailing, shelves grew wall by wall around us with lifted from boxes to stored metal receptacles along rows. We started coughing for all the dust and change; it became difficult to move for all the new occlusions.

Chief Dog, Head of Table, growled piss pus metempsychosis, waved Masoud's question aside with a hand. Today's issue, he said, is rebirth: what to do, he pointed at a pair of grey-dismal spaniels seated near us on the floor, with our fellow metamorphs.

Little Rabbit in Frock who greeted us at the porthole argued the underground conference should continue its regular scheduled program. We've given our floor companions teat to suckle, meat for sup, and bones for grind their demands, she listed. The table has its members already and to make room/

Objection, shouted a tiny poison arrow frog with a booming voice who leapt onto table ex nihilo just in time; each of us need make the slightest space

Bah humbug, interrupted the second rabbit, as dinner wait dissolved into a well-practised cacophony.

After much hard labour, continued Frog, iridescent despite the dim light, brighter than her peers, the spaniels have managed to gather chairs to sit, they demand no more food than the rest of us, and to make room for them would require the slightest shift on each of our parts.

That's when the construction clouds puffed and bulldozers rumbled heavy. The earth shook as new thoughtreel shelves rose so high so suddenly around the table they blocked the artificial lights of the Archives where the animals lived. Once upon a time, fire-fleeing residents of an unnameable country became animals driven underground. Masoud and I would have liked to continue to the conversation on the animals' origins, their previous human lives, to ask why the Archives, with its moth-eaten light, its magnetic reels on shelves, the guns and soldiers that hinted their importance. A thick-armed guard with both hands on rifle-stock lifted his eyes and fired Hedayat a warning glance.

Masoud Rana and I rarely sat at guests' tables after deliveries, we were merely waiting remuneration, and worried for exit as the construction crew enclosed us thoughtreel shelves clanging lot. I became doubly scared when the guards searched Rabbit in Frock's cauldron filled to brim with hot air. Regulation kitchen equipment, she argued, and they tasted a dollop of vapour made from the food we brought.

Fear rose to my throat and I patted the lump in my shirt's secret compartment. I passed Masoud a lace. What is it, he whispered. My grandfather's bootlace. What the hell. They're magic. Are you out of your mind, he lifted his head and looked at the guards creeping closer. Just tie it to your ankle, asshole.

It would have been simpler, I argue, if he had just done as I had asked because mere whispers more were enough to bring them uniforms and breathing down our shirts.

Two guards found Masoud and me sitting strangers, human faces among animals. They pointed bawdy tough, snickered, separated us, lifted me, turned me upside down by my ankles. Loose change, a gram packet of black pepper for personal consumption dropped to the floor. Masoud Rana removed all the couriers' items on his person at firm request, all bags and clips and clasps, all hidden cavities of his backpack found and searched and itemized while we were only trying to deliver foodstuffs to the animals, I argued.

The guards would have none of it, however, and pointed guns: march.

At first, Niramish's uncle's bootlaces fluttered silently behind our shoes, and he's a parlour magician after all, I thought as we remained captured as if without them. The guards kept their guns focused laser-sights and forced us walk one dark corridor before the next turn onto another passage of thoughtreel shelves. We passed a figure of a man whole body contorting slow silent scream before reaching an area where the sky breathed into the open underground. In that place they were still mere feet behind us. Then a long, narrow flight of stairs appeared, extended upward for miles.

Masoud Rana's heavy gait and horse exhalations kept rhythm for the march. Time passed and I felt exhausted in the midday heat, so hungry I brought the taste of the steamed air, on which the animals subsisted, to my lips. I thought too bad Masoud and I were handsup and empty your pockets whisked away before eating. While I chewed the thought, Masoud tapped my shoulder look: I turned my gaze to the improbable sight: the guards had been thwarted by our climb though courier friend and I thought we were making casual captured pace. They were miles behind us, running, and their bullets made a racket if you listened carefully. Above us rose easy steps into a hole of sky. That was when I realized the promised flight of Niramish's uncle's gift, its magic beguiling to both wearer and warder.

Masoud and I hugged and cheered our luck and wished the animals well in absentia, Dog and Rabbit Woman and the Fish with Fu Manchus. We bounded up the final steps of the stairway with festive hearts, aided by a gust of good wind. Masoud gave a shout when he reached the surface of the cavity entrance of the Archives and leapt so high he almost snagged the power lines, touched ground with an imp's glee ribald laugh, your grandfather's bootlaces, he yelled: good shit. He jumped again and again and careful, I shouted as he bounded across the moving car road with ease before bouncing in place on the sidewalk for an instant, calling me come on, man, and then leaping loud over houses and rooftops and away.

THE
CENTIMETRE
PATCH

Masoud Rana became a flea-leaping dot bounced far from Hedayat's urgent cries. They landed in opposite ends of the city. Masoud fell close enough to an old drug-runner associate's pad to dig in for respite from weightlessness and the assurance of a sweet drink. Hedayat landed in recognizable street turns and found the alleyway of grey soot and lead exhaust fumes where the motorcycle gang the Taints once conferred in a garage a generation earlier, close to his parents' home. His last brief visit was in the interim between heist partners months earlier, and he felt compelled to say hello.

Recall: our hero hugged the streetlight for warmth on an equatorial summer eve at the sight of changes. How long had I been underground, I wondered, that the world could become flickering pixelations whole walls full, ads for stadium stage acts on Game Nights of lottery and organs, of stylized billboard images of previous numbers and their associated operations, pictures announcing championing what I would soon learn was the grizzly lottery. He wanted to confer with Masoud but his colleague had travelled so fast, so far with each leap away from

Hedayat, yours truly decided on other streets, to jump instead into familiar territory of people cars noises, a neighbourhood he recognized.

Hedayat's visit home was one of respite and recovery like Masoud Rana's pitstop at a grime-associate's, far from the shit and premonition of rattraps or gunblasts of the Warren tunnels. The next day, he fell buzzing out of bed late afternoon and walked into the kitchen rolling his animal tongue sour, searching for something to eat, and was assailed by five answers to a question Gita asked: Does anyone want raisins in her bowl of wheat germ, spoken in five voices he did not recognize. Four replied yes, and one said no. His mind fluttered and the memories realigned with the last of the voices, which spoke in a loud, assured manner unlike the others.

Hedayat was able to reconcile that he actually knew all the speakers, and that he was listening to none other than the Yea and Nay Quintuplets, who were born in his absence but about whom his father had sent word via motorcycle messenger just prior to an important drug run while the son was more concerned with building a successful courier service in the Warren tunnels. It was Nehi who had spoken loudest. The others, Ha, Hum, Ji, and Achha, were quieter, less raucous insistent of what they wanted, though they accepted their grandmother's offer. Today they wanted to go to the Chance Executions, and spoke of it with as much enthusiasm as their aunts had talked of disco and punk music many years before, though the four girls hadn't yet lost their milk teeth and were very far from reaching the threshold of adolescence.

Psst, bhaiya, Nehi called me.

You're not going with the others.

No, it's no fun with them, she said, and directed follow me with a finger.

Where are we going, I pushed aside the cobwebs in her room made by the spiders she kept as pets, exhibits, she called their soft cottonlight. I peered at a latch on the floor she lifted up after pushing aside an area rug.

What's this, I picked up your hull and metal shine as I held you. I pried apart your receptacle pieces and ash exploded into my mouth and nose. They stared at me from the metal box then: fragments, tape remains amidst the dust. Is this what I think it is, I poked the ash with a finger, raised it delicately to nostrils.

That's when it happened again, this time as grey lights asphalt bursting on my tongue. I inhaled the dust a thoughtmetal taste in my mouth; then fire along my skin in all my senses. Are you okay, bhaiya, Nehi called me from behind, and that's when it happened again. Again I turned my neck one hundred and eighty degrees like an owl, like the time Niramish showed me strange fruits hanging boughs in the playground, when we shared an exploded eye and busted hands, when my hands turned talons, recall.

I saw Nehi when I turned my head owl around. She was right there of course, but I saw something else too, a faraway sight that was more than the rectangle smears mere lines I saw when Niramish and I and the exploded playground scene. It appeared clearer to me this time, as a roomful of workers in cubicles wearing headphones who seemed more palpable, realer than Nehi or Hedayat. I reached out to touch an image that seemed living, threatened to become my world as Nehi's voice swirled around me. I couldn't see her and the oldmetal grating fell from my hands when I saw what I saw with owl eyes. What, Hedayat, what did you see. But I also heard it and felt it too is the thing. What did you feel, what was it you heard. This, I thought to myself: I understood that/ tell me, bhai, Nehi tugged my sleeve, but I ignored her entreaties, threw open the bedroom window for quick breaths. I gathered myself, reassembled the moments and wondered how I had managed, once again, to turn my head a hundred and eighty. And what the hell was the office image that suddenly assaulted me, I thought; what was the fear it made inside me.

I gasped at Nehi's kind touch on my arm reminded me of the material world. After four moments, I pointed to all the shit and caboodle visible through our window. What is all this, I asked, oblivious suddenly of the meaning of the wood metal plastic construction crews everywhere. It's been happening in our street for months, don't you remember, she said patiently, don't you remember when they brought everything in a convoy of trucks. It's been happening all over the country for years, she reminded as if I had never been born. What, I asked, and she didn't say anything because everyone knew about *The Mirror*, because she was waiting for the past to return to me and for everything to make sense again. She fixed her chin on the window ledge and watched the scaffolds affixed to scaffolds with me. We talked of bones and the largest movie set in the world.

I had to peel back from the window when I lost my breath trying to follow all the wires hugging walls, travelling neighbourhood to neighbourhood, each constellation of lights camera action forming its own universe, movie sets, I mean, whose dimensions and moods were regulated precisely to indicate year and event, history and motif. What is *The Mirror* and what do they say of *The Mirror*. Recall *The Mirror* arrived, guns blazing, with the fanfare of coup d'état. It shattered the windows of the Presidential Palace and found all the doors, entered rooms without knocking. Unknown unknowns found throats, hearts bled in beds of men with hands on wives' cheeks as film crew personnel excuse me pardon me ma'am quite politely, in the cases of political personnel useful to the new regime to keep alive, threaded wires around beds, hung bright halogen lamps and situated tripods, as politicians is it truly necessary yelled come back at a better hour, while their less than lucky peers found barrels pointed faces/

60 Minutes would later reveal that Anwar, whose father had been John Quincy's personal bodyguard in youth and later rose ranks in Parliament, had contacted the Director of the CIA personally mere hours before the event, which felled Baltazar, the preceding ass in power, and several of his closest advisers, who had been informed the invasion would take place later that month and that they would be spared. From the palace to the streets: *The Mirror* spread wildly, scripted to evade climate and terrain, geography and culture, and we heard that other countries with difficult names and obscure locations had also featured similar shifts in power and certain cinematic historical developments.

Bhaiya, I felt Nehi's hand, Bhaiya, are you okay.

I reeled vertiginous as I thought about all that crap and related some of it to Nehi from documentaries and school texts. I lost track of my office vision as I watched them reinvent the world.

At that time, the apartment above the hosiery shop had become very crowded. The old linen room where Shukriah and Gita used to store odds and ends for the shop was first transformed into a nursery before it became study and play area for the Quintuplets. Hammocks were now spread out all over to house them sleeping suspended through the night or humid afternoons. In the rare occasions he found himself at home, Hedayat taught his sisters how to read, though Nehi the auto-didact taught herself. One day, he listened to her fantastical first written sentences: I found your telltale thoughts under my floor, Nehi wrote, but I don't know how to hear them beat, she sighed on the page.

The only time Hedayat found peace in the house was when he gave his sisters time; on all other occasions he was forced to wear cotton earplugs to suppress the sound of his mother's endless when will you, will you ever, is it not time, and this one: when will it have been that you, all of her entreaties on finishing school, at least secondary school, and then a college education, why not, with your owlish brains, some-thing better at least than an ass's post, until he could no longer tolerate the turbid perspiring walls or the sense that all the abscesses of her disappointment would burst at once.

Gita, meanwhile, older, slower, and wiser than her daughter-in-law, didn't care for the fact that her grandson had little formal education. Rather, her crooked finger beckoned him come hither, you, beckoned hear her worries of those tunnels you traverse, Hedayat. She spoke of her worries of those people, her worries of busting bulldozers dividing the country into movie-set fragments, of the sheer geological weight pressing for decades for centuries millennia eons millions of years on the tunnels on the country from above.

At that time, the crate-porter lives of Masoud Rana and Hedayatin the Warren tunnels, suppliers of canned meats and relatively fresh vegetables and fruits, cigarettes and the like, came to an abrupt end, as we were informed by the higherups immediately to make the switch and to begin transporting goods of higher yield: Carl Gustav rifles, ammonium nitrate, locally manufactured grenades, hardly a charity now.

What do you think, Uncleboy informed one day, picking his teeth with a switchblade. Besides, the people will eat better with less of *The Mirror* and the Madam. How could we then. Totally impossible to resist when the pure rationality: which is to indicate the metalglinting threat of a higherup. The high-density mirrors and asphyxiating security in the region of La Maga, we heard now what we didn't from Gita. The purchasers, of course, were the usual suspects: the People's Rifle Brigade and other parties the Madam tried to destroy but whose guns she could not take away from making the air hotter more humid or from harassing the Madam's regime and *The Mirror*.

Despite what you might think, the first crowd was not all gloomy characters. Some of them told sad jokes in uplifting voices and delivered joyous lines with frowning faces. They had the habit of wearing ballet slippers like the nameless rebels, were also swift-footed like their predecessors, who had splintered into five thousand factions throughout the city and regrouped into mostly religious dissident parties, which pulled up the world's eyebrows and over time heaped scorn on the unnameable country. Furthermore, they had the habit of razoring their beards thin, of peppering their words with English phrases, using back-slang like all the youths, and talking excitedly about the latest American mobile gadgetry. In one breath they would curse *The Mirror*, and in the following bless the latest L.A. blockbuster and all its minutiae. Also, they possessed the habit of disappearing like the wind in the middle of a conversation, and left you wondering whether you had been speaking to yourself the whole time.

On the one hand, such groups did not exist. The Madam's regime tried for years to deny their very reality and surreptitiously to send sharpshooters to appear out of that grey mass of smouldered bricks or the greyorange dusklight before a chessplaying crowd/ suddenly human and gun in hand, oh look at that, or for the clouds to part and to allow there/ surprise, a young Black Hawk pilot, leap now or the endless: they found it difficult sometimes to deny that members of the People's Rifle Brigade died, is what I mean to say, or that the people in their homes died in droves during targeted assassinations, or that the funereal cries of their survivors were often as large as when Niramish had passed. Because sometimes the dead jumped mirrors into the vast electronic world and could not be silenced in their coffins.

In such moments the Madam would respond in her swaggerspeech, which grew so recognizable it nearly drove out the caramelized timbre of Anwar the Memory from our earholes: There are some intransigent classes of individuals, she would say, and it is true they are a threat to the stability of our/ but not for long, hear now, what are the numbers to the Chance Executions this week, because at that time everyone was talking about the Chance Executions.

What were the Chance Executions. And how will they speak of the Chance Executions in years to come. Recall, for it is common knowledge, at first the Chance Executions were just games of luck, not unlike those that had always existed in the unnameable country since anyone could remember, and that began with the everyday sale of tokens and the plucking of four lucky numbers at dusk by its inventor, Maxwell's friend, the entrepreneur Octavio. He would draw them out of a motorized spinning cage in Victoria's Circle Point, amidst the shawl sellers, the stacks of overblown movie posters, and the vendors of bottled piquant peppers, where the crowd gathered at the end of each day, young and old alike, whether to play or to gawk, and he dispensed prizes and they were all predictable and cash at that time. Let it be known, however, that even in the earliest days the Games drew a sizeable following, since the spinning cage was bejewelled with a set of blinking lights and the display above it would announce the numbers with a whirring sound that was pleasing, and also because Octavio had an open-hearted way of speaking that was known by all since he lived in a mixed neighbourhood rather than a gated Euro-American community.

It was sheer drunken folly at first, when a singularly important effect was introduced to the Games. We can blame chance: a man, a whoever man, nameless and an irrelevant regular of the cage lottery with pinpricked skin on his vermilion cheeks, was accused in Octavio's presence at a garage bar in the capital by some of his friends of having been favoured in the last draw. While the owner sipped his spiked lemonade and tried to take no notice, Vermilion Cheeks walked over and slung his arm over the lottery baron before offering thusly: Give them what they want, boss. Let there be a little cutting if I lose tomorrow. I say the removal of a patch of my arm skin one centimetre squared.

At that moment, a musician with the unlikely name of Elvis was detuning his guitar because he was about to play a bolero, and his instrument drooped the very air. This churned the pit of Octavio's stomach as it laboured to adjust to the atmospheric difference. He replied he had no intention of changing the simple principle of a game of zero or small fortune. But then he saw the whole bar fall to raucous enthusiasm with desire for Vermilion Cheeks' potential maiming, and he reluctantly agreed for the price of his night's revelries that the wagerer should be removed of his patch of arm skin tomorrow if he did not draw the winning numbers.

The companions of Vermilion Cheeks, who had goaded and entreated him to cast the negative lot, bought more tickets than usual and convinced others to do the same. In fact, more tickets were sold the following day than ever, and out of luck or fear the unnameable individual managed to save his skin by winning a small sixth-place prize of one hundred dollars, which drew cheers and many jeers from the crowd. He won again the next day, the fourth-place prize, and on this occasion he had been persuaded to increase the potential risk to a four cubic centimetre patch and two millimetres deeper into skin.

Soon, superstitious people certain that somehow offering one's body to the draw increased chances of victory began to wager half a head of hair pulled up by the roots, the tip of his nose, the peacock lashes of a young woman, her second chin, a former athlete's chunk of calf muscle, an eyebrow, and later, when distinguished surgeons were also drawn into the fare, an ovary, a testicle, a whole cheek, a fragment of liver, a whole kidney, the fat of one's heart, and worse, far worse. Thus began the long and gory road to the Chance Executions, whose news spread like a disease as intense as the tsetse fly sickness, and which grew in pathological popularity across the classes and walks of life in the unnameable country. Eventually, Octavio appointed an internal committee to decide and regulate the damages, though as a committed democrat he argued that the audience should have a say in the nature of the dispensation of harm, and rented a banquet hall every Friday afternoon so that a privileged number could assemble there and determine the following week's grotesquery.

Things went on like this until the winnings were so large but the losses so much greater, and understand it was the bloodletting that interested people most. A community theatre donated its stage, and there the daily theme of crimson relit the hearts of the young and old alike. They laughed at the ugly man with matted hair like a dog's, whose ear was torn with a yelping cry from his very head by a former torturer of the Black Organs, and who regretted everything at the point of great pain as they all did, they cheered at the fool who had bet his left eyeball to sweeten the pot some one hundred thousand dollars more, and so on.

Things got much worse after a half-dozen men arrived at Victoria with their eyes firmly shut, who did not open their eyes for a moment, arrived dressed in stiff collars and dark suits, and held hands together like children. Without tripping once over their own feet or anyone else's, they navigated by some preternatural instinct, which somehow allowed them to augur potholes in advance and to avoid the dips in the sidewalk and the worst construction areas. They spoke to no one until they came upon the gates of the Presidential Palace. They spoke some words to the guards, which convinced him to/ but that isn't quite right: a cloud of bees coincided with their arrival, yes more like it, and while the men droned on, the guard noticed that the bees were edging ever closer and seemed to be growing angrier and swarming in a larger crowd the longer he tarried: All right, sirs, the guard nervously passed them through.

There were other gatekeepers afterward, as we can expect, and whether this trick was repeated I cannot know, but understand that even while speaking to the Madam in the Hecatomb Office, the six eyeless men did not let go of each other's hands or open their eyes once. The Madam listened politely, and sipped politely the tea from her saucer: half of them were from a multinational cell phone company, the other half belonged to a public relations firm, and together they were ready to invest billions into the lottery. They had already contacted Maxwell, who had been dumbfounded by the offer, was too goodhearted to be a shrewd businessman and capitulated early in negotiations, they said, and agreed to share power with the government and the sightless strategists in what was to be the greatest experiment in human history since *The Mirror*. After less than an hour's conversation, they convinced the Madam's regime to fertilize this great money plant, to water it wisely, as it would grow inestimable shoots with every cutting gesture.

As the fatal ritual spread everywhere, the six eyeless men worked tirelessly out of hotel rooms and briefcases, and within weeks formed a powerful lobby group with other businessmen that convinced the government to lower the legal gambling age to sixteen, though everyone knew it was possible for even junior high school children to buy tickets. It was a doubly useless manoeuvre since it would soon be impossible for anyone not to buy tickets.

All this occurred around the time I was bewitched by the most beautiful pair of ankles. Whose ankles, Hedayat. Who was Q. Why her ankles, which did nothing but join legs to feet, lower leg bones affixed to talus, articulated with tibia fibula, to form anklejoints that allowed her to hop here and there, to pass across the room in two or three bounds with a perfectly balanced bottle of blood on her head, two in each hand, and several more under each armpit, and a final bottle stowed neatly on the flat of a foot leaving one free foot for hopping.

But you understand: how could Hedayat not notice ankles in the bouncing swift thankless task of rushing about while feeding vampirical ghosts, of simultaneity refraction of time, one Q diaphanous tending to their pillows and another lucid dreaming by the linen closet, finger at her chin, which sheets to gather now and spread them across the floor, another guiding a ghost patient, a doddering dead Alzheimer man, by the elbow to the right spot, and another image of her elsewhere in the room, hush now, with finger to lips, pouring from the bottle to quiet a flickering woman's bloodlust, her whimpering want for company and conversation before the ashen glow of the television set. What a din they raise, incomprehensible maatal, pagal, crazy for trading the ace of spades for king of hearts or rook for a knight in shining armour smash dominoes down on the sidetable, do this why not, while comparing memories of life or one another's spectral pains, which continue life after death. But who.

Introduce us, Hedayat. How about that one: a once-mirrorwalker you call Fissures, who busted bloody through tain, the metal back of mirror and glass, his face and hands dripping red while travelling from image to undead, nice to meet you sitting quietly on a plastic sheet, sipping a glass of blood, blood like the kind that flows through shard-wounds on his body, which only worsen with time. Like the others, he is waiting for his second death. And elsewhere in the room, the name is Rafiq, whose story is simpler: the loneliness of the coffin unsuited him, and he wept for days before clawing digging to make it out. Then some thirty others more, believe it, and Q alone to care for them all. What is the Ghost Hospice. Why the glow of the Ghost Hospice now, excavated out of the desert like a prehistoric whale skeleton, and the beautiful living bones of Q, ankles and all, returned to us.

Have you, Q raises her eyebrows.

Yes, says Hedayat, and removes from his bag the half-kilo of hashish.

Not for me, she gives him a smile.

Oh I never, he swears with a hand at his heart, I didn't. May I, he offers after she sets the package aside, pays him with cash already at hand, before she can return to her fold of tasks.

Bemused, she allows him to take the end of the longest bedsheet in the world. Then, with fingers at each corner, a preliminary arrière-leap by both dancers as time caramelizes, and all the ghosts are watching, slowly, cameras drop slowly from the ceiling to scatter these moving images out into the universe because *The Mirror* knows how to suck the blood out of any spontaneous movement. (Years later, we would claim the Director himself was there to oversee the proceedings.) A flutter and the sheet spreads its wings. Two dancers' leap assemblé to distant music, and Hedayat unwinds the cloth fold after fold, revealing light laughter, the costume beneath. Thus begins their one-act dance whose theme is conversation.

If the two dancers were moving to music in this scene, I forget the name of the piece, I forget the colour of the bedsheets, I remember very little except their movements. Of course, it did not happen this way. Relate the facts, Hedayat. The Secret Trial prefers no embellishments. And yet it was this way, exactly this way; how else to tell a life of many moments except by relating whether one remembers them as beautiful or not.

To tell the truth, I was alone that night, and Masoud was on a delivery. Though he was scheduled for a brief trip, I knew I wouldn't see him for a long time. He had tried to convince me to accompany him, come with me, bhai, on a delivery of powdered milk and bread to a fire-besieged neighbourhood, and truly, when we got to a grimacing street of teeth and armour, of guns, guards in tanks, I thought for a moment about Niramish's uncle's bootlaces in their velveteen packet, thought of saying let's fly this shit.

Go home, he said in the face of my silence, and though at that time we were still living at our respective family residences, I knew what he meant by home. I insisted weakly, let me come, I have all my papers/ No, man, I know this guy, he pointed to the closest uniformed mustachioed guard ahead of us as the line edged closer to the check-point, and he pushed me back against soft silk cloth against bodies in the heat. The crowd enveloped me. From light years away, amidst shapes and sweat, through a hole in an auntie's earlobe, I watched Masoud Rana negotiate passage, bargain skilfully, offer cigarettes, accept a light, buffet interrogation search with twist and swivel words at the guard station, and it was when the mustachioed officer Masoud said he knew started cursing loud and searching indefatigable, where is he, when he started craning neck, pushing people aside with his arms, surveying the congregation of sounds and smells for a Hedayat, that I slipped hands into pockets and whistled quietly away from that barrier between shadow and shadow spaces of the unnameable country. Years later, I would find myself imprisoned and blame Masoud for my entrapment. On occasion, I would think about that time when I should have gone with my friend who did, through his wiles and great fortune, manage to negotiate passage to deliver a miserable package of powdered milk and bread to a school in a neighbourhood whose local grocery store had spontaneously combusted. Masoud Rana went away for a long time while delivering basic amenities to the region, and I didn't accompany him because it was necessary to spend my days with others.

I, meanwhile, went to the Ghost Hospice, also known as the Halfway House, to see the girl I was already falling in love with though I had danced with her only a few times during black-pepper deliveries. On the second occasion she allowed me to fold bedsheets with her, and this time, she greeted me with her spirited embrace, before hours passed as we made the bed, watched ghosts. I asked her of their origins. Many were from the lottery, she said, others poisoned by the lottery, still others had slipped and lost legs on American bananapeel landmines, though truth be told some ghosts belonged to the common aneurysm and cancer variety of undead. How many ways to die in the unnameable country, Q sighed.

Because life continued all around her, Q, the operator of the Ghost Hospice, didn't believe in the sanctity of death, because she knew about other deaths more devastating than the first. The rope of her hair tossed as she worked, and the whole Hospice echoed her hum and song. Why do they go on living, I asked her. Others remember them or they remember being remembered, and thusly, the living enliven the dead, she shrugged. On occasion, she said, it's jor or jeed that persists beyond life, the sheer strength of will, and some of them say to me they would prefer even the worst parts they were denied when death hissed out in army uniform or exploded suddenly around them: the decay and vanishing of old age they never got to experience. Those were some of her answers as we folded sheets bobbing, humming goongooning fly you to the moon as Sinatra crooned vinyl, our fluttering feet never descending from above the floor as filmic reconstructions, *Mirror* sequences, have no doubt narrated. How beautiful Q's ankles were.

I spent that night at the Ghost Hospice as I had done before, but on this occasion, without Masoud's company. I slept in the storage room with cleaning supplies and shelves full of blood bottles, in a hammock. I lay awake all night listening to the sound of spiders knitting clouds from floor to door to ceiling.

When Masoud was away, I began to neglect my business and to spend all my time with Q. There was simply too much work at the Ghost Hospice, too many words. Q and I funnelled blood into bottles, which arrived in vats off the backs of vans once a week.

What kind of blood.

Human.

Really.

She wouldn't verify and smiled mischievous. I lifted her chin up to the light and her smile overflowed.

There was much to do: drugs and palliative care to provide, liquid meals to prepare, we had to endure the peregrinations through hell that every ghost, no matter how well adjusted to a second life, disappeared into, foulmouthed and overflowing. And then one day, to deal with the inevitable: an errant touch or a sheet of sunlight too heavy, and burst into ash with a slight rotten odour, which meant one had to sweep up ghost ashes and perform the rites appropriate for a second passing. But time passed as we did these things and watched these things together, and the Ghost Hospice filled with our love.

Then one day, a fee fi swing of the front doors and a giant interruption in the form of a business partner and friend, Masoud Rana swinging arms, knocking over this and spilling that, pissed is what, why weren't you there, hear him asking me, forgetting he was the one who told me not to follow him, yet remembering correctly, however, that I should have protested rather than assented to his request. Why didn't you help me, he empties the refrigerator to find a cold soda. Where were you when I descended the longest line of stairs with a barrel at my back, a uniformed Uncle trailing, forcing me to traverse corridors where radio antennae swoop silently and suck up the tiniest particles of thoughts.

How was it, I grinned all bhai-bhai and shit, did you deliver the milk.

Yes, he said soberly, milk and bread both, he said, and sipped his soda, heaving, sobbing. Before narrating his return trip across the checkpoint he told me another story first, this one about how last night, he slept on the floor of a classroom next to a teacher who let me into her abode, he said, after long wander in brick and pothole streets with dinner supplies in my backpack. I arrived after a night's interrogation in the early-evening sunlight still so incendiary you had to gambol across hot hot sands after congested minivan ride that left you staring at houses converging streets, wondering which was the house with the ram's head knocker that had ordered powdered milk. I asked this person that person, touched invisible coins with fingers, I paid a man that sold iced drinks who told me where, and there she was, I finally saw her through a mouth-open front door, there she was nesting hungry students, infants spread out on the floor around what turned out to be her bed, a thin central mattress and sheet, while older pupils slept in a column of hammocks suspended from the ceiling, each level accessible by stepladder. Since I brought bread and powdered milk, she was able to provide a rudimentary meal for the kids, some of whom had to be awakened for the occasion, and with the remainder of the milk and bread, she began hatching a dessert using eggs and sugar she had on hand, which she said would make a tasty breakfast on the hotplate near the back of the classroom. What is the name of this place, I asked her while she cooked. It used to be called Epsilante, she said, home of traditional spider harvest. And now, I asked her. Ask the Director or Xamid Sultan, head of National Security, she said, or the Americans, she laughed a little too loudly, looked around to catch waking eyes, put a hand up to her mouth.

Masoud told the tale with his usual swagger, in real time so moments weighed life's minutes, and we listened as we ate after our day's work. At a pause on fork and plate, with a cough, Q left came back with a shine tilting right left right left in hand, sat beside us and what's that, I asked. I took the winning lottery ticket from her, an old kind like the ones you could buy a long time ago, and looked at the holographic image of New York City skyscrapers pawing clouds in three-dimension photograph above date and time of flight, gasped, you're shitting me, I said. Many years later, I would shiver thin T-shirt in air-conditioned airport with face pressed to fog window glass, weeping blood from stomach wound while watching Q depart forever, but this time we talked tongues, as here, she mumbled here, onto my mouth in damp light. I didn't argue with her as, hand in hand, we departed Masoud's company/ where the hell are you two/ never mind, she told him as she pulled me toward the interior of the Hospice.

Time passed and Masoud Rana and I saw less of each other. He knocked now before entering the Halfway House, while recently, he would have burst door heaving rabbithaul by scruff of its neck: See what I bring you, he would have announced, before throwing a pound bag of herb on kitchen table or a thousand-dollar catch of bills. Q and I had become inseparable and he remained incorrigible in his bahir and black-pepper ways. Although she and I lived grant to NGO grant, cans of tuna, two pita bread meals a day, her sheer determination and ebullience was food enough for me.

———————

Time passed and one day, the television told us the Americans were adding a vast prison facility to the old tapereel Archives of the Ministry of Records and Sources, which had been replaced by newer techno-logical surveillance facilities, to house accused terrorists outside the jurisdiction of sunlight and beyond even the sight of God, and that this act of the central government had aroused in the people a desire for rebellion unknown since the first days of *The Mirror*. One hundred thousand people had taken to the streets and Victoria University and La Maga Technical Institute had once again become heated centres of resistance.

Recall at that time, however, we were all much weaker than when the Director first arrived. By continuously watching and recording us in filmed instalments, *The Mirror* demoralized and weakened the spirit of the whole population; it made us wish shadows could be exchanged between people, or that the art of ventriloquism had developed to a point where one could throw one's voice beyond reach of the microphones.

The Chance Games, meanwhile, as they were also called, had reduced all our focus to the immediate present, destroyed most links with the past and nearly all understanding of a future beyond the petty goals of the Cola prize or the avoidance of glass shards in an unfortunate can of coffee crystals, and which led at most to winning more cans and therefore to more tickets and, more than anything, to an infinite increase in the discourse of cars and houses, which could also be won, and which we were all supposed to want.

The public removal of body parts still played a large role in the lottery, but since everyone now played the game, winnings and losses needed to be democratized, by which I mean distributed to all possible products, especially those eaten or imbibed. Cancer rates surged, infant mortality grew up into a bigger crisis, tumescent hidden organs burst one day; some people died and others hid in living death as more and more ghosts wandered the mirrors of Victoria and Benediction, Conception, and La Maga. No one blamed the Games because every day someone won, we were always winning, and no one noticed when it was no longer voluntary to have a centimetre patch of skin or a hidden organ removed from inside you. The maniacal jingles of the lottery sang into our very bones from television commercials, the talons of the billboard ads for consume victory enjoy removed your eyeballs well before the assigned date for the operation, and the carnival was spinning round and round and round its own ashes. The people of the unnameable country retained enough sense to understand the greatest prize was meant to be the perpetual lottery itself, to whose vast amphitheatrical sacrificial stage dutifully followed those whose numbers bespoke gallbladder removal, or give us a twisted rib lest you wish to be hounded by the Gaming Commission or the constabulary.

Yet we could do nothing because what wasn't the Chance Games. What went beyond it. Even its founder, Octavio, who had previously had the softest of demeanours, grew hardened by his experiment with wealth. He had never imagined success in the manner of everywhere tentacles, and the scaffold-stage of great violence, which, it was true, he had encouraged at the start, but only because he had trusted the people and confused the perverse rule of the gladiator mob for democracy. He no longer frequented the capital's garage bars for fear of being thronged, either kissed endlessly by women who could never turn his heart or strangulated by his enemies, though he still preferred his lemonade spiked and to drink alone. All his old friends deserted him at the unbreathable upper atmosphere of exorbitant wealth, and his only remaining companion, Maxwell, was by then an altogether different person also: thin and the wearer of a wiry moustache and speaker of fluent Arabic and Somali, a member of Parliament, who went by the name Abu Yusuf, though he had remained a grey eminence hidden organ and still as influential as ever. His hair had rapidly greyed from encountering all the hatred in the unnameable country, but he tirelessly dyed it black every morning and retained his indefatigable spirit by convincing himself that he was still young.

I'm sad, friend, Octavio said to him one day.

Maxwell, however, as if he were merely reading contemporary events like they had been written many years ago, performed the rite of exegesis and claimed to Octavio, You have no reason to be sad, why you're the owner of the greatest Mammon temple overflowing with riches and blood.

You can take all that shit if you want, friend, but I know the lottery is a cancer that neither I nor anyone could stop if we tried.

Maxwell sighed, recalling it was what others had said of *The Mirror* many years earlier. Many years earlier, in my father's time, our country began becoming a movie set. At that time, when the Director came, the streets were knitted labyrinths through which motorcycle goondas with swift ballet slippers leapt onto Honda seats. In smoke and growl wall and gravel landscapes, National Security Service battled communists the way we fight terrorists today, pored minds by shortwave to understand who might be responsible for the latest inexplicable fires.

GANGSTER-STEPS

BACKSLANG

Hedayat's bustle and trade happens in such streets. Dense with movie cameras and mirrors, they make you wonder how an owl with eyes and ears so knowledgeable could be so clueless about the exact stuff of the movie's construction. What is *The Mirror*, Hedayat, and what do they say of *The Mirror*. When did the movie that caught us in lenses on film stock on feed and take-up in magazines whirring mile after magnetic mile: when did it all begin.

Was it *The Mirror* when my father and the Screens and their thousand and one flights on motorbike.

Recall, as the story goes, they were hustling, glossolating, talking talk betting organs in the unnameable country before the lottery, even before mirror-walls in the streets began multiplying spontaneous fires in front of movie cameras. Son to father isn't the usual journey in a family history, but the unnameable country necessitates gangster-leaps backward. To know Hedayat requires us to know his father, to understand the father means we travel labyrinth streets to the grandfather, to understand whom requires us to move back still to great-grandfather unto mist and the origin of things: to once upon a time.

After saying one or two things about the son, let's learn about his father.

While Ben Jaloun the son prefers to cart his toxicological vegetable wares through the Warren tunnels by foot, the father survived an era when death was dynast on the back of a motorbike.

How could you remember chiaroscuro: the play of line and shadow, figures in the lamplight. Why. How. Who dares cross these Stygian waters. A sickbed. An ill woman. What about her. A common scene. For a week this poor woman has been unable to rise from the horizontal or to take anything but small sips of water. The doctor has blockaded himself in his clinic with all the relevant drugs, suddenly afraid of being afflicted by the influenza epidemic that rages throughout the unnameable country. Neighbours from the same tenement have identified death's rattle, and gathered around arguing hissing about which religion's last rites should be deployed. The Hindus claim her as one of theirs; her father was Muslim, reminds the camphor-wielding wife of a huzoor; she lived with a Christian and bore a child by him, declares another correctly. Thusly they debate her passing as she rattles on, and as someone watches by the corner, surrounded by a crush of older adolescents.

Come, he is nudged by the elbow and drawn out of the atmosphere of suffering into the hallway where they wait in their torn tees, arms folded, their black skin-hugging jeans folded up to the shins. A hot pestilential draught kicks up his hair, and in the neardarkness a moth kisses the wall.

Outside, Qismis shakes her hanging locks and turns up a sad smile, makes room on the 250 cc handmedown Honda.

Giddyup, calls Imran, and they make dust, as the maw of the night widens to swallow them whole. Two other swarming motorbikes and one scooter follow closely. Though he is four to six years younger, his desires are like theirs. Recall the characteristic male bravado of that time: shattering beer glasses two-tone grey suits and a spidersilk fedora, the high dawn windows screaming glass with kids in the air who would soon nurse in bed their blood and wounds grey mucus mornings swimming cigarettes in cognac vase, the quiet masculinity of tempered rage, drunken sophistry drawn from a few sacred passed-along volumes of literature, the hooting along and recapitulating every line of every villain, perfectly accented, from American cinema, fighting with the ushers and drawing a blade at the earliest incitement, cutting class, spitting on arresting cops, rolling over geezers, forgetting or mispronouncing the names of their fathers.

Victoria, 1968: the youthful restless hodgepodge capital of a country that either cannot be found on the maps of the world or is referred to as the nameless country, or the British Protectorate of His Majesty George the Mad, Quinceystan in jokes; though in all seriousness it is the unnameable country, though, declared independence from Motherengland a decade ago already. Here, the boy revels in the endless days and makes sacrifice at night to the god of neon-lit brothels and leaded gasoline. His Sisyphus stone is a mother who is still learning the dying art.

The first time, in the scattering dusklight one May, she walked weighed down with boulders in her pockets, rattling them like mountains with her hands buried deep in each side of her dress, into the waves of the Gulf of Eden. The shoreline had been overrun by so many crabs then, not even the call of come all ye and harvest by the Ministry of Natural Resources could help diminish their number. He covered the distance from the carousel to the shoreline with the patter of little feet as fast as his kid's stride could carry him. She smelled like the sea as she lay there, grey and defeated. He helped pick crabs off her dress while someone kissed her and teased her to come out, so deeply had she buried inside herself; and when she finally gasped, she cried like a newborn and the boy thought it would never happen again.

This heat never gives up the ghost, he thinks as he extends his grip tighter around Qismis. Always the heat or the equatorial rain in the unnameable country, which is not like the heat, but falls like a photograph. It's always already a memory. Disappears into the dust faster than you get a chance to soak your nose in it.

Many years from now, he screams over the hum of two hundred and fifty cubic centimetres, I will die far from this place.

I will die here, his mother had declared one day after they had finished painting their flat pale banana yellow, a year or so after Zachariah had disappeared without even a note or a word, with only the air of his unfilled clothes and camouflage uniform left behind as reminders of his existence. His mother never mentioned him again, but the surface never reveals the full extent of an injury. He stopped asking about his whereabouts or hunting for him aimlessly in the streets. Rumours flew that he had been snagged by the Ministry of Radio and Communications, and he had been either eliminated or secreted so deep in its intestines he would never have contact again with non-ministry members. His mother, too, had once worked for them, people said, though she herself denied everything, rejected the whole of her past.

Things begin now, she had said.

Do you mean now, he asked.

Now, she had said.

What about now.

And now, she waited a moment, then cut the air with her hand. and now. and now. and now, endlessly now, she kept beginning again and again.

Until, he had asked her oblivion eyes.

The second time his mother had tried, it had been the noose, a small fragment of which still remained hanging on the metal hook in the ceiling of the living room slash kitchen. Rejected by the sea, she grew convinced the air, or lack thereof, the imitation of fruit, could salvage misery.

Through the classroom window, the boy watched a branch twist in the breeze, lost in a reverie as it extended through the wall and into the room. Asphyxiated, he ran out of the room through the recognizable narrow streets. He cut her down from the ceiling with his blade, but the five minutes' suffocation slowed her, dealt irreparable damage, left her shrivelled up inside herself.

The kind of mother you have, the matronly upstairs woman Zora had taken him into her home one day to tell, rattling the good china-ware. Her kind of woman is common in our country but still not ordinary. You can never know the reasons she keeps trying.

Do you know.

No, I do not. But the shadow of a lie crossed her face and he persisted as she sipped her tea. Drink yours before it gets cold, she instructed. I don't know if your mother was ever happy, boy, she told on. But maybe once upon a time, one day long ago, when she and your father were young and they were eating oranges near the souks.

The boy tried through intuition to find that place, and near a bridge that bore the name of the executed last governor, he discovered a dampness and an ancient depression in the grass and a seat of orange blossoms, which seemed to verify the old woman's story. On the presumption they were going to market, he showed his mother these things and asked her if they meant anything, but she could honestly not recall their importance.

————————

They came to an alleyway where the boy's back hairs bristled. He envisioned the blade where it always was, in the sock-holster above his right ankle. Qismis put her hands over his eyes and though it was his protocol never to allow anyone to block his vision, they were her hands. The swish as Imran pulled back the sheet and his sight returned.

Now, my malenky boy genius, behold what I give to you.

They all gazed, and everyone, especially the newer members of the gang, salivated as before them stood a refurbished 170 cc Honda, glistening red, painted new.

Is it not protocol, Imran, asked Abdi, who had recently finished scooter and picked up his first Honda, isn't it true initiates must drive scooters before passing onto the motorbike.

To hell with all that. No scooters for our little guy. A full motor-cycle. When they did not immediately assent, he continued: For fuck's sake, his mother is rattling animal from the throat, his father is beastly dead, we have before us a near orphan, more or less, who, if he cannot make a home on a leather seat, will be nothing but a homeless, is it not.

I won't allow it, Imran cut the air with his right hand. He saw a shadow cross the faces of his companions, but it was a silent and momentary lapse of faith in his leadership. He knew they understood: the boy was quiet but useful when he spoke. What strange words he invented when incensed or enervated, when suddenly with his tongue he could leap up from a weak posture with the strength to take on a goonda or a whole group of them. The Dushman, rival motorcyclists, were felled one evening when there swarmed locust around them a chorus of voices ex nihilo.

The verbatim report afterward from a nameless Dushman: It sounded like twenty madmen were howling, what am I saying, forget menwomen, at least fifty of what were ghosts apparitions without shape, howling in all kinds of languages, though the source, I swear, if I recall accurately, though do not quote: it was a boy, no older than thirteenfourteen, if you'll hear me, beinchuts, sisterfuckers if you don't understand me. He was standing off to the side of those motorcycle cunts, with a hand at his throat, speaking furiously with probably, looking, anyway, like fifty tongues.

Thus was born the myth of the boy whose identity to enemies was as precise as the wind, nameless, I mean. (Know that glossolalia is the term Hedayat has prescribed to a host of phenomena throughout the unnameable country's past, because the gift of the future—and its arrogance—is the ability to cull the past and call it anything it likes.) And thus the Screens, the formal title of the so-called motorcycle cunts we have been following, cast an honorific distant chill in enemies and friends alike.

The boy became more of a curiosity than a legend, and the group worked hard to veil his unique contribution, which allowed them to demand higher payment for security for businesses and individuals, and to rob without implementing actual violence. What use is there for hard metal if the tongue suffices.

Three or four years passed during which they challenged all the adolescent gangs of Victoria, leaving alone only the top-dog elders, who watched nervously and debated among themselves whether to assimilate or exterminate. They looted tourists, they shot, they jooked up and held up five-o'clockers. They stored wealth in an open-sesame cellar down the cold hatch of a butchery adjacent to the largest kebab house in Victoria: British pounds, American greens, diamond studs and lapis lazuli, gold watches stuffed into the hook-hanging slaughter: innards of sheep and goat and cow. They evaded the police in open chases, though by movement they were tracked and identified all and sundry.

They met with disaster, like when a young scooter, no more than sixteen, a recent who had always wanted to be like the older toughs, and who wanted to prove something when they were robbing one day. A circle around him and little jabs to the ego, initiative invisible daggers, you see: so he drank a whole vase of homemade rice liquor in one swipe. He faltered his steps and just when they were teasing that he would sick now, entire gulf of eden, you'll see, any moment now, like pankha, spin-spinning like a fan, yaars, and a high rising bleating laughter out of one of the older throats, watch this kid, he's got the hero, as another steadied him and let me see aahed into his mouth, when something happened. And what did.

Hai, Imran said, and the others drew closer. Down his throat and blue like a pilot light, he said.

Yes, there, Qismis pointed.

Then instead of bile remnant alcohol or undigested, a fire emerged, unrelenting and huge, and that is how half of Imran's scalp became scorched and how years later, when mediating between the Fraternal Order of Victoria Police and the unyielding kleptocrats and street gangs of the late 1980s, amusingly, he would be known as Gorbachev. The young scooter emitted black flames and that charcoal smell emerged when an animal has turned to meat. Some fragments of cloth remained and perhaps the digits extending from his palms. They forgot his goodname and Hedayat cannot raise it from the hecatombs of their memories. Also. And then. While the Screens gained prominence, the boy, who shall not remain nameless forever, whose name you already know think hard, grew up wanting for nothing, though I prevaricate. Since all stories eventually cross the Rubicon of the love tale, we might as well begin immediately in the name of, beyond good and evil, I mean.

Do you recall the touch of Qismis the night the boy left his mother to die a natural death, thinking she is certain to go sooner than later and it is better this way. Do you remember the raisinscent of her right hand as it gently covered his nose while meaning only to shade his eyes. Of course not, for I did not care for details, but they grow important to the story.

A caveat before we leap: he is guarded, believe me, understands that to craft a life on the leatherseat of a Honda means to give up certainty, to trade ghar for bahir, home for the outofdoors, and to forget the notion of a repeating woman unless one takes on a brothelmate and makes with her a usually short-lived and generally dissatisfying romance. Unless one is as lucky as Imran. But who is Qismis. And why does she roam with the nervy boys and return in the early mornings with Paris cologne effusing from neck and wrist, with hundreds in her purse, to faceslaps and eye-gouges bishalo jaat, poisoned female of a poisoned family, her mother's guaranteed gaali, and to her father's weak protests she says she is working, leave aside the broom-handle and let her earn a factory income if she can, wife, times are hard.

Qismis is not a fatale kind of girl. She is, believe me, tough, but in discrete, quite inscrutable ways, which: it was she, for example, who spearheaded the burial of Scooter's blackened corpse and she who scrubbed their garage headquarters with lye and then detergent. Half the ideas for robberies or engagements with rival gangs are hers, though whispered lagian into Imran's ears. So perhaps Hedayat was wrong about his non-fatale judgment, and she does in fact carry several qualities of the stolid movie females she watches with as much intent to emulate as the boys do their cinema villains.

But with Mamun: she watches him curiously, another way, his mouth especially, for that is where his strangeness lies. Not an especially uncharacteristic jaw, not a set of Eastwood or Gable lips, nothing reptilian or psittaciform about the tongue, but watch out when his back is against the wall, and, more often these days, when he concentrates with the intention to dissimulate or argue ten points at once.

No doubt, in turn, Imran follows her gaze and tracks the seconds and microseconds, every error of eyes and breath. As the brother of a three-bullets skull and wasted Owl, of the Owls, possibly the most notorious drug runners and cultivators of opium and cane in the entire continent, he expects perfection, and relates tales of the grand days of Victoria's goondas as if he himself had taken part, though let us leave his elaborate details out for the moment. The boy hesitates at even the thought of that something unnameable because he has greater worries.

Twelve days from his eighteenth, his mother is perpetually inventing elaborate ways of suiciding, and, unfortunately, none of them works. Electricity has been her latest; she has successfully rewired the whole house in an attempt to find the perfect charge that would deliver an instant passing. The boy wonders whether all the years of wanting to die have in fact backfired: that his mother now thinks of herself, in a demonstrable way, quite impenetrable to death. She has tried, how I have tried, she will shake her head, and still the last does not come, beta, Azarael is allergic to my soul. Perhaps her reason for living, he has thought many times, has become to prove she cannot die. Impenetrable to love, forgetful of details of all but the immediate past, her only pleasure seems to be in her work, in bordering curtains for Zora's small needlecraft business, of fashioning little socks for infants, in threading the needle eye a hundred times a day.

I did not even die in the Epidemic (which we had no time for mention), she says to her son when he makes an appearance, though the keloid scars around her neck from her noose-attempt flared up during the fever from, and she began to throat-rattle, as we heard in the beginning of this. Such is his mother, edging always toward the unknown, impossible to predict, but. Three times she has taken poison, it should be added, arsenic rat poison included, the efforts of which turned her skin blue, as if she had imbibed universal sins and survived despite. For all that was said of her ceaseless death and dying, her hidden organs continued to pump fluids through her body's beleaguered channels, and her brain passed and received signals and composed the world anew.

Learn: the mother woman to whom we have been referring is none other than Gita, as you might have guessed, and it is only for the purpose of indulging in mystery that we have withheld her name for the past few pages. Know also: just as glossolalia was her unbeknownst creation, the Server Backslang can be traced to her also. Nowadays, the youths claim Server was born on the motorbike. Mamun Ben Jaloun would later say he was its progenitor, its first cadence-rhymester, and hold a grudge against the world for never being recognized as such.

But what is the Server Backslang. And tell us, Hedayat, how it came to be. Is it located in a robust elephant-thread for Gita's failing eyes, for the several hundred coasters to make before her son's birthday, in the nonsense melody: a backwards Caliban on a tempest island who makes merry, speaks Abol Tabol. Gita's mind isn't what it used to be. In any case, a new vernacular soon appears in the garage, which is no laughing matter. The practical street applications of such a language are self-evident to a young enterprising youth like Mamun, and the Screens begin to forge collegial code-words with colleagues and customers. It comes into play during their robbery of a shipment of cane, where a few backwords cue the hijack, and Pestilent B, a swift, small rodent-like man, drives a motorcycle alongside the vehicle as his brother, a sidecar aptly called Pestilent A, climbs aboard.

Excuse me, sirs, but do you know the way to: and then the bullet, as confusion scatters the ranks of driver and shipper, and there is blood too.

For the Screens it is their first large-scale heist of a larger drug enterprise, and the only question becomes where to store and how to sell doublequick. For the first time there is no more room in the butchery and they must contemplate holding companies and crooked banks, of which there is no shortage in the unnameable country.

Like a king of the chessboard, Imran's actual role in the gang's everyday transactions is limited to single-steps, though theoretically he has freedom to move in any direction he likes. To make longer movements, he needs to utilize knights and bishops. Or, if you would care to envision the Screens as a basilica: Qismis is the chancel near the front,

Imran watches from the rear as its narthex, Mamun is now the nave, flanked by the scooters and other Hondas in the aisles; but we needn't be so formalist about it, god does not live here. Things are changing, in any case, dynamism is the key to their success, and a church is too static a metaphor.

On Mamun's eighteenth, Imran imbibes more spirits than the stock exchange gambler, otherwise remembered as merely the red-nosed Theodore Quincy, father of John Quincy the pirate-emperor. Imran stumbles out of the Pepperpot and disappears with only his assistant, one of the Pestilent brothers, after him with his bad accident leg. The rest of them tarry, voices lowered, with quiet intermittent laughter, though their hereandthere caresses make it plain that Qismis and Mamun would like to be left alone. Respectfully, though a little curious about how the night will change the dynamics of the Screens, they follow out of doors. Dissolve the scene of bar stools, guitar music, and spilled booze mixing with the occasional fist.

Come, she takes him by the hand and they pass a high-walled corridor and the sound of a key turning a lock. A small animal rushes at Qismis's knee and shivers there awaiting a caress or a cudgelling. Scoundrel, she pets, and Mamun notices it is a little girl, after all, aged two or three perhaps, but who moves with astonishing speed, one minute on top of what is probably a table, but the darkness, and in the next moment on the countertop, rushing around and spilling marbles or rocks from her mouth, one by one by one.

Your sister.

Yes, Qismis says, and orders her to bed. The girl opens her mouth and at first Mamun hears nothing, but then he catches a note on the highest register, and he realizes the girl's protest is one meant for the bats. There she remains, standing on the countertop, rubbing her eyes and crying in a language few can hear, and for a moment Mamun wonders where the irresponsible parents might be to allow a small child to remain awake at such an hour. Something stirs around his foot, and he realizes he is stepping on a blanket, and a shape objects to being awakened with a murmel, and then another murmel murmel, and suddenly the room is overflowing with a cauliflower garden of infants and slightly older.

You are the eldest, Mamun again, as Qismis stifles her laughter. The front room is the nursery, she explains, and begins shushing and suckling from the bottle and trying obviously to prevent the parents from waking.

How many.

She lights a lamp and the sight overwhelms: blankets and cushions, toys, crumpled newspaper beds and plastic bottles half-full of milk. Seventeen, but they are not all siblings.

Hedayat will explain: Some are cousins, the children of disappeared neighbours, many reasons all packed into this room. Since Mamun feels ashamed to have his hands empty while she is beleaguered by the score, he tries bidding one or two of them to sleep, inventing nursery rhymes under his breath, bunlets and carrots, songs for the marmots, how many ducks do you have, and so forth. At four-thirty, after a head count, they finally manage to have them fed and succoured, cooing before retiring to her room, but the task for which they came here seems no longer appropriate. She changes the sheets and informs a little tersely this is an old-fashioned swansdown mattress, has he ever slept on such a thing, one must be careful. They lie down none too gently and all the white feathers waft out from under their bodies and turn up into cirrus clouds before spreading all across the room. (It would be this that would break them, a single feather of evidence would be enough.)

Their bodies are too tired then and sleep finds them before, but the morning is different, and the rest of the day is pleasure after pleasure after their ravenous hunger. Somewhere in its midst, though she knows

111

otherwise because they all go to the brothels, she smiles when he says, I've never known the touch of a woman before you.

———————————

Now it just so happens that not all the Screens would prefer a changing of the guards, including Mamun, not that our hero has it in his mind to lead the group; if offered the chance he would reel back, since he is actually incapable of the task due to a lack of desire and strength of conviction; to add to his bad credentials, he has fallen in love. A furtive discussion occurs anyway and divides the crowd.

They all know Nikhil, who was initially unsure of Mamun Ben Jaloun's leap-frogging over scooter onto a privileged status, has great respect for glossolalia and Backslang, among attributes that have resulted in the Screens' recent cull. Others are not so sure. The effect of glossolalia is no magic, a trickster's sleight of tongue whose effect cannot be fully measured since it has been used only several times, and then only to sow confusion among the ranks of enemies, such as the Dushman, as we have witnessed, and which could easily have been produced by weapons or by other means. Backslang, meanwhile, is a code language, which has come in handy on one major occasion, and like all codes, if understood by enemies, it could become a detriment greater than its boon.

Nikhil, however, points out possible glossolalist uses in negotiating contracts and formulating trade relations, while besides, and here the ad hominem lowdown begins: Imran is a drunk, a cheater, lout, how many of us have been promised full cuts of the flank and been tossed neck bones instead. Beneath our feet hangs a whole open-sesame cellar, whose secret password only he knows, overflowing with so many riches that, and how much of all this is yours, he points, or yours, he points. I am more Screen than he, Nikhil does not say.

In the darkness of the garage, emptied of its three top members, he has taken temporary control and the sound of his own voice is inebriating. There are, of course, protests.

If insurrection is what he proposes, one of the Pestilent brothers hisses, then the devil himself should take the poison instead of passing the chalice.

He plays with a yo-yo, not looking directly with even the one cross eye that sees, the other staring glassily into the future, which, as everyone knows, it has some weak power to augur; he cat's-cradles, walks the dog, snakes the plastic yellow around the world. He does not ask where is, nor do any of the others notice the sound of a rodent-man scurrying; no one wonders where goes his brother, Pestilent B, who played, if you will recall from all the stories since the incident, a major role in the heroin heist that forever changed the fortunes of the Screens.

And so, through the dark mewling alleyways travels Pestilent B, kicking cats and scratching flea bites and swearing at his misfortune of having to play spy while the master drinks away yet another evening, composing spitting foaming the right words at the mouth as he heads across town to find Imran.

The conversation finds Qismis and Mamun the following day, and neither is enthused by the idea, but the die has been cast. After a full week's absence, the leader walks shipwrecked and dripping back to the garage, claiming to have undertaken the longest sea-journey across the highways of the state in order to secure a major investment. What investment, let me tell you.

Here, you: Qismis is awed by his state. Give me your, she removes his shredded denim jacket. She has never seen him so wolf-bitten, so excitable.

Imran lets, but doesn't stop for a breath or a word edgewise against him: I went to meet a member of the Taints, good first-class goondas who normally do middle jobs/ tain't cocks, tain't assholes, he joked, just carryalls that mule drugs across border passings or on airplanes/ who need help with an odd job, he explained, during perhaps the largest political function of the century, involving some of the most famous international dignitaries.

Of course I agreed, and on my way back, he relates by way of an explanation for his withered appearance: There was a crowd of marchers, protesting this and that, as they are apt to do in our age, not just here in the unnameable country but all around the world. All I did was merely: will you not give me passage on this hellish hot hot day, and they took me to be an enemy of their political cause, will you believe. I am not a politico, to hell with your cause, I said, which made them only madder, and they began with their banners and placards and fists and some with even britvas, and so here I am, one backstab away from death herself. But I have come to deliver the good news, he was on a roll, they could not protest, the plan was too complete, he had gone to great lengths, they would not only let him down if they spoke out but also the opportunity to increase the group's status.

Imran flew over the details, spun on his heels as he spoke, leapt and pirouetted, on the night of suchandsuch, he announced the greatest opportunity bankers, politicians, a whole vault of whoknowswhat, not to mention pastries, gooseberry wine: to get inside is the hardest trick, and some of us must up up up through the sewage pipes carrying our good suits in polythene sacks, others must sneak in days in advance and secrete ourselves in various locations throughout the building, while still others should be hidden in beer vats, such as you, you, and you: he pointed to Nikhil, Qismis, and Mamun. The first obeyed, the latter two did not.

For all his recent rebel talk, Nikhil is more the archangel Gibreel, closer to God than the damned Iblis, a follower of directions more than a rebel. He hears the nozzle hooked onto the aperture and then there is a muffled scream, could have been the beer through the pipes. In the autopsy weeks later, all his organs are discovered drowned, alcohol poisoned, though many had leaked out through skin and poking bones into the pressurized liquids. After that horrid affair, published in all the major papers as a macabre oddity, there were no more rebellions in the Screens.

Dignitaries from around the world—well, a handful of KUBARK information officers from PD Prime, or in everyday language, Uncle Sam's nephews disguised as Eastern European dignitaries—were at the important conference at which the Screens were helping the Taints. The question of the evening: should the unnameable country join the Eastern bloc. It was famous and fateful and would bring the United States into the equation and trigger a twenty-year-long proxy war that threatened to destabilize the whole region, the whole of which begins with a most eccentric speech, reported the world over, in some cases as an exacting example of Communist madness, characterized by others as exciting and inventive. In the beginning, however, it is quite clear Nikita Khrushchev has caught stage fright after realizing on the podium he has misplaced his speech. His chief adviser pleaded sick and refused to accompany him to such a godforsaken corner of the world, and now the great leader of the Soviet republic finds himself without words and suddenly without official manners or the ability to improvise. (Recall that from time to time it will occur to even the most experienced actors, and politicians are no different.)

From under the podium, Mamun cannot know any of these things, he is merely hiding, and the first kick he receives is not meant as anything but an expression of Khrushchev's frustrations. But the leader

realizes lengthening his foot releases a parcel of words out of nothingness, let us not ask by what means divine or otherwise, in a quiet
whisper: Ladies and gentlemen of these United Nations.

He looks around the room. No one else seems to have heard them.
What dwarf or miracle homunculus was hidden here, but Khrushchev
dares not search the podium. A miracle is a miracle unrevealed, and
loses all power to bring the people to their reverential knees when the
tearing Christ is demonstrated to be a fraud. Nikita Khrushchev invents
this justification and continues. The words seem like a right fit for the
occasion, so the great leader, sweating underarm boulders and not from
the equatorial heat, repeats them as if they were his. Kick kick, another
little kick. The last one a little too close to the head. And the words: We
have gathered here to discuss the possibility of the unnameable country's role in the greater family of socialist nations of the world.

Surprised, and a little indignant, like a mule realizing for the
first time he must be put to work, Mamun Ben Jaloun cannot remove
himself from the role of spindoctor and correspondingly supplies words
to kicks. Another kick.

The question, of course, is not so simple since the Soviet family
must take into account the distinct history and cultures of the people in
this region, as must the unnameable country consider our differences.

A pause and a wince. A kick further, though softer, more
encouraging.

And: if it is possible for Cuba, Tanzania, it is possible et cetera,
and we must declare it would be a great caltilp pahsim, Mamun Ben
Jaloun recites, to lose the unnameable country to the capitalist mode
of production. It would be a pahsim, Khrushchev repeats, having lost
the ability to invent or speak agentially, as bound to the underpodium
speech supplier as today's teleprompter politicians are to theirs, a
great caltilp pahsim, he says, to which the audience laughs heartily
at the neologism, comprehending it to mean an animal of failure, as

newspapers for years afterward would refer to the next government boondoggle as a great possum or walloping marsupial of a mistake out of whose pouch many appended problems would emerge. The last part of the address is rollicking backtongue, which few besides the Screens in the room understood, but within the style of the whole document, it seemed quite fitting. Governor Anwar rises to applaud and the whole room follows. There are hoots and whistles from Imran, which gives him away as an outsider.

———————

The KUBARK agents are the first to dive into the stuffed pastries before taking flight to Washington. Two days later, the newly elected Richard Nixon, having campaigned on the escalation of the Vietnam War to certain victory, sends three lonely Phantoms over Victoria: a school, a mosque, and a hospital are destroyed. The Governor, who, it's true, was edging closer to an official alliance with the U.S.S.R. and was indeed swayed by Khrushchev's speech, but had not yet dove, immediately raised the receiver for the Kremlin. Four hundred and thirty-one people perished, over a thousand were seriously injured, including Zora's niece, her husband, and a baby daughter, while Imran's brother died, as did sixty-four teachers, a roomful of worshippers gathered for Friday prayer, fifty-seven dialysis patients, and so on; but none of our chief characters was lost in that first raid, so the story may continue more or less unabated.

The broader details: The Taints, it turns out, among other street gangs, were posties, mocksters, howdoyoucallit, agents provocateurs, whose purpose was to draw the Screens into a trap. This was no international business conference, and true, the government risked losing face if some major act of violence was to have broken out during the delegates' speeches or the reception afterward, but they benefited from having taken the risk: Imran was arrested for Nikhil's murder near the roasted crabs, and for the attempted murders of Mamun and Qismis. Some of the others caught wind of Pestilent A's warnings, took heed sometime during the speeches and fled, but most were caught. The last of the three was removed from her beer vat where she silently awaited her signal and was released to a nursery internment, under her mother's watchful gaze, before disappearing three years later after acquiring a false passport. The first, the leader of the gang, was interrogated and tortured for seventy-two days by the vilest means until he revealed the password to the open-sesame cellar. There, all the gang's precious booty was removed, Imran was stripped of his clothing, his mouth stuffed with wool, and left hook-hanging among the eviscerated animals in zero degrees for forty hours before being transferred, hypothermic, hardly shivering anymore, to a holding cell. Luckily, Imran's condition improved, as the police decided instead of wasting him to treat him at the best hospitals our country had to offer, and when recovered, to fashion new clothes, to salary him; most importantly, they gave him title and the respectful position of inspector, to turn him into a spy for them. Thusly, they converted him from gangster-steps to dancing jive at police ballroom events. He would return to save my father's life many years in the future, just you wait.

The fate of Mamun Ben Jaloun, however, is the most interesting. After security forces hauled him out of the underpodium, Nikita Khrushchev himself intervened in his case, stating that he knew of the boy's presence while delivering his speech and could not help but marvel at such a deep interest in politics that would drive a person to such depths. Embarrassed, the Governor quietly transferred him to the care of Grenadier Lhereux, who whisked him out of the reception hall and labelled him an unnameable trespasser to be kept under close watch. Mamun Ben Jaloun was bounced from department to department until several weeks later he found himself in a large room situated with many desks behind which there lay piled many folders and papers pushed and pencilled and hemmed and hawed over by innumerable employees. They were too busy, or pretending to be too busy, to notice his presence at first, and only near lunchtime did someone look up, pss-hmm, yes, pss-pss, another pair of hawkish eyes, and another, these ones bespectacled, until suddenly the whole room was pss-pssing about the shackled stranger who had been in their midst for who knew how long.

State your name, someone said.

Our hero did as asked.

What do you want, another asked.

Stunned by the question's absurdity, Mamun Ben Jaloun stayed silent.

Ask him if he has had lunch.

No, that's irrelevant, another voice piped up, ask his name again, I've forgotten it.

My name is Mamun Ben Jaloun and I am here because.

Because what, asked the bespectacled man.

Because I'm not certain, I think one of you is supposed to know.

But how are we to know why you are here if you won't tell us.

Because, Mamun faltered, because you're officials, it's your jobs.

The whole room sprang up in a laughter that began and ended exactly together.

Can someone undo my shackles, they've been eating my shins. The pss-pss began again and a collective decision as iterated once more by the bespectacled man, who might have been a higher official: we're not certain, we'll have to confer. And they did not, they remained still.

Just then, a bell sounded and like salivating puppies, they ran over one another's feet out of the single door, bounding left and right through the hallway outside. Mamun Ben Jaloun, whose shackles were too heavy and who was too exhausted by the previous weeks to do anything, remained where he stood.

THE
WARDROBE
ORDERLY

Difficult to know what a man does unless we watch his exact movements. Today, for instance, we find Zachariah Ben Jaloun trying to scratch his nose by manipulating his moustache, walking with his arms by his side, hardly moving them at all as he strides down the hall of the great and same cathedral-edifice he entered more than two decades ago as an error, where he was tortured, released, from which he departed with his original name, and to which, it is true, he returned by choice or otherwise, and whose staves he has climbed to assume a directorial position.

Today, Zachariah Ben Jaloun removes his handkerchief and sneezes as he passes an interrogation room, and the sound drowns a howling yelping no don't, though the horrors he can suppress by this spontaneous effusion would have stuck needles deep in his conscience many years ago. Or is this Zachariah Ben Jaloun at all. Which is to ask, is this the same man we were following not too long ago, who would read the poems of E.E. Cummings and bite into raw onions for a good cry. The surname is not too uncommon in the continent, though we must admit it is found more often in its western corner than in its eastern corridors, while there are innumerable Zachariahs everywhere in the world.

What did this Zachariah Ben Jaloun do when informed one day by a peon, sir, there is an eighteen-year-old assigned to the status of unnameable by Grenadier Lhereux himself, captured in the Assembly Hall after the Khrushchev talk, and now floating around the system, drifting from one department to the next. Sir, he says he doesn't know where to go, that he feels quite like a ghost in shackles, sir.

Bring him in, Zachariah Ben Jaloun says, lighting an unfiltered tar-black cigarette. Yes, what can I do for you.

Sir, I have asked several hundred people to undo my shackles but no one will abide by my request. As well, for the past four months I have been eating the scraps that fall from the desks of the employees in the central room, and sometimes I am able to find soda in the refrigerator in the staff lounge, but otherwise I have been starving.

Yes, it is bound to happen. However, none of us has the authority to free your bonds until you have been cleared of all charges.

But sir, I have met with no magistrate or lawyer, there has been no hearing, no case presented against me, and no charges, sir.

That is your problem exactly then. Zachariah Ben Jaloun smokes nonchalantly. You must discover the nature of the charges against you.

Surely we can surmise from these words that before us sits another Zachariah than the one who kept certain human features bound up within the nutshell of his soul, guarded against the arid corridors of Ministry of Records and Sources, against the dead air of shortwave radios peering into trespassing on unsuspecting minds. But twenty years plus is a long time for a man to encounter many changes, to lose and gain many shadows. Let us continue wrestling with the possibility.

May I ask a question, Mamun Ben Jaloun says, and continues,

though the man neither agrees nor disagrees: What is your position in this company.

I am director of internal communications.

And what is your name.

What business is it of yours. Zachariah blows smoke into the boy's face.

May I have one.

The director of internal communications slides his mother-of-pearl cigarette case across the table and even offers his own lit cigarette as fire.

Because, the boy says, smoking, feeling much better after the first few draws, I feel mirrored in your features, and I have heard stories, though my mother will not verify them and one cannot rely on rumours, that my father works in the Ministry of Radio and Communications. Is that not where we are.

Yes, Zachariah Ben Jaloun says.

After this exchange, which does not culminate in ecstatic reunion, the bureaucratic procedure flies more smoothly. Though it is still not discovered what the boy's charges are, and since it will take several months yet for the offices to confer and compare files from investigations to date, and to create these if they did not yet exist, Zachariah Ben Jaloun allows Mamun Ben Jaloun to sit in a corner of his office beside the door, to reside there during the day, and to curl up and sleep there at night, sit quietly while people come and go during daytime appointments, or to leaf through the senseless bureaucratic manuals, though many of these are censored in black. At lunchtime Zachariah forces him not to eat the scraps of not any and all employees, but only from his plate. This second arrangement is less than suitable, for it regulates Mamun's diet in unappealing ways: Zachariah Ben Jaloun prefers cooked onions in just about everything, including in his rice pudding as well as his black coffee. Eventually, since Grenadier Lhereux's office and even certain lower departments are backlogged and will be so for the foreseeable future, Zachariah Ben Jaloun offers Mamun a job.

A job, what kind.

Judging from the nature of your arrest, your youth, and your keenness with words, you can be a wardrobe orderly.

The claustrophobic sound of the title brings back memories of Khrushchev's kicks to his shoulders and back, and Mamun isn't thrilled by the prospect.

I will pay you a salary, which will be credited against your consumption of foodstuffs, go toward compensating us for your boarding in my office, and even toward the systemic expenses any citizen incurs from being processed as an unnameable for an extended length of time.

I didn't know of such costs.

There are. So what do you say to, and Zachariah Ben Jaloun stated a paltry sum unworthy of mention.

I don't seem to have much of a choice, the boy casts his eyes downward.

One always has choice. Here is the most intolerable assertion to Mamun, which flies against the face of all veritable logic, and by which he feels crushed.

———————

When he first started in the wardrobe, it was difficult to breathe or to see anything, but slowly, Mamun Ben Jaloun grew accustomed to the cracks of light that flittered in, and when the Director was not looking, it was even possible to hold the doors slightly ajar, just as long as no one was able to tell he was keeping post inside the furniture. The job of an orderly was custodial and secretarial, to provide general assistance, whether to leap out of the armoire at the exact moment and serve tea to interviewees, as you will recall from Zachariah Ben Jaloun's first trip to the Department, to mop up blood and other effluvia from pre-interrogational tortures, or to retain whole memoranda inside the skull and supply the odd forgotten word or even large chunks of memorized text during the course of institutional transactions that occurred in the room.

Every day, they come and go and speak of this interned, that interned; due to the high costs of internment in even a wardrobe, the organization's goal is to intern the subject in his own home at his own expense and to defer the responsibility of internment to many organizations and individuals.

After three months of good labour, Zachariah presents Mamun a tailcoat and a crisp pair of black trousers, which, he informs, is uniform for his trade.

Is it possible to have a light in there, not a candle, because that might lead to fire, but maybe an electric lamp.

Zachariah is stunned by the question. No orderly has ever asked for such a, in fact most prefer the darkness because it offers the correct shade to remember the details of the work and in which to nap during the long horary spans of inaction. But I will inquire with others, he nods slowly with a knitted forehead.

No no no no, Mamun takes back his request, he does not wish to cause a fuss, especially when he feels he is edging closer to some judgment on his purgatorial condition. Nothing for sure, of course, but he has heard things. Sometimes, when Zachariah Ben Jaloun is away on business on another floor for hours at a time, he visits the officials of the central room, where they cluck away at typewriters and to each other and forget whose thoughts are whose, so that some memoranda will be filled with another individual's invoice figures. And what strange names they have. Calamity A through to M, and then the letters take off from N onward, but beginning with some other prefix, such as

Filibuster, Mylar, or Nanaimo, before the alphabet starts again in other equally strange way. They are nicknames, surely, since what mother would call her son Mylar, no matter how thin or strong he was. Mamun Ben Jaloun cannot say he has become friends with any of the officials, since they still do not always remember who he is, but once, one of the Calamities, a woman called Calamity L, mentions that things are pushing along, the grenadier's office has been reviewing a transcript of Khrushchev's speech and is cross-referencing it with eyewitness reports as well as police documents that describe a member of the Screens matching Mamun's description.

After the initial bout of fear, our hero is relieved. Even a guilty verdict would be a grateful change. Prison would be worse, surely, in many respects than the life of a wardrobe orderly, but at least his meals would be his, and perhaps there would be no shackles.

And what of Qismis, he asks, though he realizes that he is lucky enough to have received any information at all about his own case.

A grumble passes through the office just then, though he is not sure if it is just thunder from the daily stress or a response to his question.

I am sorry, Calamity L pushes up her glasses, that information is not ready for release or has been classified by higher authorities.

The months pass, and his longing for the aimless backspeech of his mother, those few errant caresses from Qismis, and much else belonging to his everyday life with the Screens drowns him with memories of the future, which will not, with frustration and hatred for all the hallways and offices and wardrobes of the world, as his case disappears into the annals of institutional memory—a polite way of saying its movements are unnoticeable if they occur at all. And that no knowledge leaks out. The system is porous, Mamun realizes from his conversations with the bureaucrats, but like a cell membrane that selectively allows certain materials to exit its perimeter and not others.

Flight: a new beginning. The possibility exists, he thinks. The window in Zachariah Ben Jaloun's office is only three floors above the ground. Outside, there is a courtyard and the gate is guarded, but the darwan is a drowsy guard who may respond well to the sleight of throat. Near the northwest corner of the wall grows a baobab tree with a waterswollen trunk, palmate leaves, and long hanging fruits. On one of the higher branches is situated a large white beehive, and sometimes a man, like an apparition, garbed in loose-fitting all-white clothing, his face covered with a handkerchief, will bring a high high stepladder, which he will climb to inspect the hive. He wonders if. But the lock on the window is too difficult, and who knows whether the beekeeper would help with his very high stepladder.

Time passes. Two months or perhaps only a day that drags on sixty times as long. Housed in his usual darkness, Mamun provides the whole copy of an interrogation transcript in whispers gauged to travel exactly as far as Zachariah Ben Jaloun's ears and not to reach those belonging to the deputy chief of Inspections sitting across the desk, complete with every ow ow ow ow ow ow, every wince and hyperventilation and scream, though ask the boy whether he remembers the nature of the case and he will be unable to respond.

One day, based on his exemplary service, Mamun is offered a reward: Anything you like, young man, call it by name and it shall appear.

Our hero's request is simple: A sewing needle, he says.

When asked why such a trifling object, be bold in your asking, anything I said anything, Mamun Ben Jaloun replies, There are two reasons, sir: the first is sentimental, a sewing needle would remind me of my ailing mother, whom I have not seen for nearly a year, while the second is practical: my trousers have many tears, as is plain to the eye, he shows, and I feel embarrassed to walk about in their condition, though I pass through these halls like a clinking ghost and no one takes notice of me.

A day later, Mamun receives a small velvet box with a silver needle and black thread to match the colour of his pants. And after a week to the day—he bides his time for the exact moment and to provide himself sufficient occasion to ward off bubbling fears—he visits the central office and makes his usual rounds, asking all the natural questions, asking the young ones what are your evening plans, though he knows these are shut-ins, not the bottle smashing motorcycle driving late-show cinema types, how is your mother's health, has your sister married yet, oh she has eloped what an extraordinary turn of events, while to the older ones he inquires what are your aches, would an echinacea pastille not clear up that unsightly skin irritation, the lower back, yes, even for a youngster like myself, quite a vulnerable place on the body, agreed.

Eventually, he comes around to Calamity L, who is quieter than the others and hides behind a mountain of papers, who is more forward with her responses and unlike most in the office, remembers Mamun Ben Jaloun's name.

How now, she greets, nodding up down up down at the sight of his arrival like a pecking hen.

Just fine, Calamity L, although I have been itching madly at the ears.

Then scratch, why not, she nods vigorously.

But I have not explained: the itch resides deeper inside the ear canal.

Oh, a more difficult issue, then, to do away with.

Yes, for exactly that reason I was wondering if you could lend me one of your hairpins.

My hairpin, whyever for, she is suspicious.

But to scratch with.

She looks me up and down up and down.

You know, anything, a twig, a pencil, a pencap, would suffice.

Her voice rises in pitch-volume and the office cabal cranes its many necks, have they all nothing better to do—Mamun's palms clam up with sweat, his heart races for this is no ordinary request, but he tries to brighten the occasion with a smile, a shuffle, a jingle of his chains.

Eventually, after a lengthy description of the merits of exactly the hairpin she wears at digging into reservoirs of cerumen, The wax you see is less likely to come out, he gestures with a finger in the ear, and then the scoop in the back of your pin would be perfect for so forth.

Calamity L removes a single hairpin from her chignon and tweezes it into his hands.

I'll remember you by this, he kisses it and bows with grand romantic gesture, drawing winks and knowing glances from all the men, now we see the true nature of the exchange, nods and laughter, as Calamity L flushes and removes her foggy glasses to give them a good wipe-down.

————————————

Before we go further, for the story of the wardrobe orderly is a swift chapter in the life of Mamun Ben Jaloun, and before we realize it will come to a close, we must at least try to decipher the nature of Zachariah's flight from family and home and his relocation in the labyrinth. But the fact remains, there is less to know than we would imagine; that he is hollow is clearly observable. In the past twenty years, the spongiform tissue of Zachariah Ben Jaloun's lungs has depleted due to a rare, slow, wasting consumptive illness assisted by his tobacco addiction. In appearance, he is gaunt and his eyes have lost the permanent reflection of the Victoria dusklight that was once his favourite food besides raw onions. Today, Zachariah Ben Jaloun labours over the arrest of eight hundred youths in connection to a treason case, whose thoughtreels are so many, papers so haphazardly stored, and whose trial will so obviously never see the light of day that the matter has leaked even into the international press due especially to the accidental capture of a foreign dignitary's son vacationing ratpack a whole bunch of them. He was plucked for questions, the mid-level functionary reported to Lhereux. And now, the grenadier asked. The functionary fidgeted for the right words, and made the sign of blackness with his hands.

As director of internal communications, Zachariah's job is to cast blame and to localize the problem so that neither the ministry nor the Department nor the Governor's office falls into disrepute. Bring them out, he orders, and there they appear in the central courtyard one by one like ants or some other colony insect, some clutching their lost teeth, their shrunken bodies enchained to the one before and behind him, stabbed in the eyes by the sunlight, stinking putrefaction or the devil, accustomed to a life of prison cannibalism and every one perplexed by the sudden whiteness of the clouds, the red of the earth, and even by what they are in the clear light of day: a shapeless mass that heaves and sighs and groans together as if its suffering is collective and no individual among the eight hundred remains after the centuries.

Zachariah observes them and cannot tell them apart. Who is the dignitary's son, he asks, and no one raises his hand. Has he died, he asks, and they cannot respond. Who here retains the power of speech, he asks, and some noises that might be language appear from somewhere. It may be necessary to eliminate all of them.

Zachariah Ben Jaloun lights another filterless nasty tar-black cigarette. Once upon a time, it would have been possible to consult in private with an insightful spirit like Gita on such matters, how to weigh one's conscience against the tasks of pure evil, but with Gita gone and now. He lets fall a sigh. No, he does not regret, no such fragile emotion remains inside his hollow chest, but the images, due to the remnants of his once-writer's memory, appear now and again to plague or to ask mute questions. With Gita gone. But now wait. What if.

At exactly that moment, Mamun Ben Jaloun has solved the problem of the difficult lock; one says solved when one means nearly, the devil reveals his details but the execution is another matter: the internal mechanism's design is as he predicted and a hairpin and needle were the right tools, but the lock itself is old, rusted, jammed. Noises. Not just Zachariah Ben Jaloun down the hall, but others as well. With all his might, Ben Jaloun the son jostles the needle while holding apart with the hairpin the two connective elements that spring shut, and though he has been trying for hours, deus ex machina and a divine click. Hurriedly he pushes up the window, and for the first time in months he breathes the open air. He does not see the apiarist of the baobab tree or the high high stepladder, and while recall his original plan was to unlock his shackles after the window/ but no time now. Our confidence man leaps.

It takes a very long time for him to reach the ground, for three stories are higher than one thinks when planning escape. As well, a gust of strong wind pushes him up so that it feels for several seconds that he is rising, not falling, and so curious is his descent that even a bee pauses near him in mid-flight to take better notice.

The pain is greater than any sense of relief or freedom since we should remember Mamun Ben Jaloun is wearing steel leggings and chains, which add to his weight. The hobbling distance to the wall is also vast, and he remains halfway there, looks behind over his shoulders, stops, rests, stares ahead, another halfway to overcome.

When Zachariah Ben Jaloun returned to his office and found his window unlocked and his son missing, he knew the inevitable had occurred and it would be impossible to take back his mistakes. He stared through the window and watched the back of the limping, full-grown Mamun Ben Jaloun edging closer to freedom, and drew the curtains shut before directing the captain and major of the armed forces, who had accompanied him to gather the boy for the purpose of utilizing his glossolalist tongue, of whose existence the whole Department, whole unnameable country knew, to unlock the mouths of the silent prisoners so Ben Jaloun the father might be able to identify and extract the dignitary's son and not have to order the execution of all eight hundred prisoners.

Check the floor below, Zachariah orders. He likes to hide sometimes in the central room and quack with the menial employees; as well, he was in the Assembly Room when arrested and may have gone there since criminals and dogs are apt to return to their own vomit.

The newspapers demand answers, as does the Belgian government. Fearing an international fall from grace, the Governor publicly orders an internal investigation, which means, more or less, be diligent when burning all relevant files and invent a believable story, the evidence and plausible alibis for the disappearance of hundreds of people, including a foreigner. He designates a committee of twelve, headed by himself, in which the director of internal communications is to play a major role.

The Governor's approach to the situation is simple: allude to the constant American bombings and agitation propaganda and declare the necessity to be vigilant against all foreigners, due to their potential role as spies. In the meantime, locate the foreign dignitary's son or someone of a similar appearance and present his pictures to the press as a captured member of a U.S.-aided contra group. Even his closest advisers are astonished.

If you will excuse me, Governor, interrupts Grenadier Lhereux, perhaps the only individual with the confidence to speak the truth: it will fly as well as a mountain of cow shit.

Never in the history of international politics has there existed such a leader, who was placed in power by the Americans, who rejected the West and turned to the Eastern bloc, and who would be ousted and replaced by a democratically elected socialist doctor who would keep a roan heifer in his office capable of supplying nearly all the country's poor with their daily intake of milk before being replaced by the woman forever known as the Madam. Nevertheless, things proceed according to plan and each committee member is assigned a task: whether to locate the ambassador's son, destroy the records, begin a public relations war, manufacture the proper lies, or gather consent for the regime's continued rule. During the meeting, Zachariah Ben Jaloun has smoked nearly a whole pack of cigarettes. In his twenty years' service to the organization whose front is the Ministry of Radio and Communications but whose true task lies in the total comprehension and control of the populace by brutal precision, he has learned to suppress his own volition to the extent that to ask what is the nature of freedom and how might I be accountable to such a question has ceased to occur to him. But having witnessed the vigilance of his son—no doubt he is my son, the same broad forehead, high cheekbones, deep-seated, thoughtful eyes, his extraordinary efforts to be free—Zachariah feels energized, capable finally of the task he has put off for many years.

And Ben Jaloun, the Governor says, I have received your report on the missing unnameable. Any word on his whereabouts.

We are conducting a search, sir, I will keep you abreast of all developments. Afterward, at around midday, Zachariah Ben Jaloun walks the two flights of stairs to his office, and for the first time in many years he contemplates his slim volume of poetry, *Orange Blossoms*, his epic poem that was never published, his life with Gita, the birth of his son, his return to the Department and his quiet rise up its ranks, his thoughtless rooster romances with twenty or more nameless women, which led to the birth of at least one other child, a daughter Ananya, whom he also abandoned with as much thought as his son.

They wanted me back and I came, he realizes, not because I had to, but then, what could I have done. Power breaks, and power makes. He thinks of the past. When he reaches his office, he looks into the wardrobe and remembers the months his indentured son whispered to him all the memorized secrets of the documents he was allowed to read and many more he should not have touched, of the precision of his voice, which he inherited from his mother. Gita, he shudders, as the name triggers a small earthquake in his room.

Recall the unnameable history, alternative possibility you cannot know: it is Zachariah Ben Jaloun, who in ten years' time would have decided the storage of the thoughtreels in the hulking interior of the SS *Nothingatall* in the Museum of Cultural History, which would allow for an alternative infamous first encounter by Hedayat and Q with the unnameable country's past. Instead now. And this, finally. Zachariah Ben Jaloun removes a small Smith & Wesson black revolver, which Grenadier Lhereux presented to him on the fifth anniversary of Anwar's rule, from the lowest drawer of his desk and raises it up to the roof of his mouth. Outside, all the bees scatter at the sound of the single shot.

IN
THE
ENDLESS
MOVIE
STUDIO

What were raw onions for Zachariah Ben Jaloun would be raisins for his son.

Outside the asphyxiating borders of the Ministry of Radio and Communications, my father realized that captivity had compressed all the sad things in the world inside a wardrobe, and at the sheer relief of release from internment, he started crying uncontrollably. In fact, as soon as he got past its gates, which were ajar, and whose darwan could have been a large sack of rice, slumped over like one as he slept, his eyes closed on the job, his right hand around a smooth rifle butt, Zachariah Ben Jaloun paused for a second before the rusty gate, pushed it open as he held his breath. Luckily, the guard continued sleeping, and with a sniffle that nearly betrayed him, my father disappeared into the crowded streets.

How he managed to unlock his shackles while weeping, fiddling lock and chain with eyes smudged camera lenses, how he avoided re-arrest by the constabulary, to search for and fail to discover even a single member of the Screens or a word of their existence from anyone in the old neighbourhood, why he didn't revisit his mother and clambered instead, weeping quietly, onto the storage space of the bus that would take him out of the capital and south along the coast of the Indian Ocean to a city called La Maga, to slither out and crawl, all the while sobbing, snotting, wiping his nose on his shirt when it became unbearably suffused with snot, still weeping as he crossed into the dreaming city and the city of expensive taste, so much so that residents complained about the prices of common goods, why does a kilogram of sorghum run three times as high as it does in Victoria, or how come a crate of oranges costs half a week's salary for the average worker: all these things we can't know. But the luck of a former Screen should not be doubted.

Let us follow him to La Maga, where his weeping turns inevitably to hiccupping: what can one say about that blinding city without first mentioning its sister, Benediction, whose blessings from international investors as a model for the whole continent and whose economic success can be measured by the litre and a single word: oil. While we were entrapped in the labyrinth with Zachariah Ben Jaloun and Gita Nothingatall, there were more enterprising young people in the unnameable country, materials engineers, systems designers, architects, and technocrats who were planning on gouging the earth for black gold. Whatever they earned in Benediction, which was, and remains today, hollow, save for its off-coast refineries and saltwater flats housing their employees and the children and wives of their employees, they would come to throw into the confusing glitter of La Maga.

There had been changes since my father's internment as a wardrobe orderly, and he wondered about them as they wandered the streets, the pups wearing plastic dolls' faces that children dragged on shoelace leashes, the dishevelled fountains cracked hairlines along their granite basins where bums bathed in homeless water, the pipes extending out of velocity wounded buildings still smoking the last rocket, not far from expansive flats advertised with faces of the rich and famous. Mamun Ben Jaloun noted signs from last month that alerted residents of future firebombs and walked scorched streets and through burnt houses whose skeletons, indefeasible, featured fresh scaffolds and ladders. Lights and sliders rose out of the twisted road amidst a plinth and rubble. A boy, half a metre high, emerged from a destroyed interior with a bowl in one hand, and he held his other hand up to his face with a murmur a quizzical gaze. Mamun, who himself had just escaped prison, rifled through his pockets, ashamed and searching for a morsel or coins. Suddenly, an older boy came out from inside holding a pistol, and he shouted to Mamun Ben Jaloun, demanding identification. My father, who could produce none and didn't know whether the gun was real but didn't for a moment doubt the seriousness of the situation lifted arms in a pose of surrender and insisted over and over he was just a traveller. What is this place, he asked finally after overturning a thousand pockets on his person, managing to convince the guard he was innocent. He wiped common snot from his nose, inquired why is it like this. You mean why is it all burned and stuff, replied the older boy. Yes, why the ruins. They told us we were in a movie and we thought all the guns were fake. Who was fighting.

The Americans are always fighting.

The boy laughed and the sound arrived at my father's ears two seconds after the child produced it, though he stood right next to my father.

The sky turned a different colour suddenly, and there arose another laugh, faint laughter, distant firecracker burst with a burnt smell that confused Mamun Ben Jaloun and made it hard to recall whether it was night or day. When he remembered it was in the afternoon, he was lower to the ground than he thought, and he got up from his crouch and saw the older boy clutching his ear, defeated. Sonofabitch, the boy swore, and surveyed his bloody ear, and the wounded streets. He shouted names of friends or demons, though, as my father observed, no one else was around except the infant child who had lifted his fists in a defensive posture in a nearby corner. I heard the Director himself was coming today, mumbled the older boy. My father didn't understand. So much had changed since he had been interned. What's the name of the movie, he asked, but the kid was distracted now and swore vengeance in harsh tones before disappearing forever into the shadows.

My father waited a long time before continuing along his way. His original sadness returned and he started hiccupping Qismis again. Time passed and he took no notice of the twenty-four workmen's hours a day each day on beams extending skyscrapers overhead, the sight of employees labouring exposed to high winds on the eighty-eighth floor or higher.

He didn't understand exactly why the pavement gave way to polished concrete floors situating desks, open front and combo desks, desks whose lips rose open mouths soiled notebooks pens pencils remainder lunches in schools whose classrooms principals and super-intendents could enter and observe on a whim because the walls were blown wide open and lizards now peered and cockroaches scurried out of incisions punctures penetrated walls.

Why did a parched lips hospital appear at a street corner without warning. With broken bread in one hand and a pitcher in the other, a nurse watered a long-suffering resident under natural lighting condi-tions. Cloudburst, she said as she held up a palm to feel the rain, before slipping under a tarp shielding machines measuring heart rate, blood pressure, brain waves, beeping talking among themselves.

Sunlight, she muttered; she smiled as she stared at the combina-tion sky. Why were scaffolds affixed to incomplete buildings, scaffolds buttressing wooden platforms attached to scaffolds holding scaffolds, why here and there a ladder, perhaps four stories high, leaning against a wall, left without regard for future or former use, why had ditches and holes been dug by private army contractors about whom my father didn't know, their actual stories hidden by the march and constant growth of *The Mirror*.

Night fell. Mamun Ben Jaloun walked with snail tracks of dried mucus on his face and saltwater streaming from all the unnatural light attacking the retina. He cried and walked sadly along the cluttered walkways of hawkers and bric-a-brac salesmen and little boys selling tea out of thermoses with their female counterparts braided flowers in their hair and with vegetable baskets rested on padded cloths on their heads. High streetlamps and added halogen lanterns provided hardlighting, and in the city centre at night there congregated movable feasts of grilled mutton, dancing girls, village theatre among other rural delicacies imported for the urban and international crowds. Within this mess, my father (or the man I claim is my father) wandered-hic for a long time, watching-hic-hic the ladies fanning themselves while the wind moved their blue dresses of mousseline de soie, as they gazed strangely at the wounded young man with a spasmodic diaphragm. Perhaps he offered his services to a small restaurant that served mouthbreeders to tourists and sold them as delicacies, but Mamun Ben Jaloun's nose was always keen to recognize the smell of the goondas of any new place, and it is likely he soon found a spot behind a bread truck waiting for jettisoned baked goods to land in his outstretched hands whether by chance or the zeal of an accomplice, here, you glottal-strange bastard, catch. And where did he sleep. The streets have their resting places and, if not, one can always claim a spot in a mosque and rest from prayer to prayer.

After a certain length of time—and note that it was not at all uncommon for vagabonds of that era to end up there—Mamun Ben Jaloun realized he had found himself in the district of La Maga where the movie studios were in full swing, and he realized he didn't know when they had started, when a camera here a microphone there or a region of scaffolds had multiplied into certainty, what compass his feet

138

had followed to this place of shadows without origin. He couldn't tell when the world had begun.

My father hummed softy, and when a syllable burst somewhere behind him, a sound without warning that surprised him/ frightened, he hummed louder, lost his step, stumbled, then started defiantly singing all the notes he knew in order to overcome his fear of these unknown streets, of walking dark streets in his freed prisoner outfit, its longstanding wear and tear, and he thought of what he could be in this movie studio city, actor singer or what, and what name he would call himself. He addressed the second problem first, and decided since movie personnel never used their real names, he would invent an alternative. Shikari, he thought of choosing, or maybe Mamun Shikkok/ too didactic, old fashioned, they would surely say/ Mamun Mamun, then, he thought of keeping it simple/ you're almosting it, he thought/ Mamun M, he decided finally, Mamun M, he said aloud, louder, he said it again, leaped up and clicked his heels, sure of

So my father wanted to be a singer. Did he do it. What did he do. And then. And yet. Hedayat thinks. He remembers. Recall, though I hadn't told you that when he was younger, Hedayat would lie on the family room couch after school and read old magazines featuring his father.

With his glossolalist tongue, yours truly would prater away in a low voice to find all the missing notes in-between entertainment journalism. He would hum, sometimes he would sing juicy lyrics claiming the strangest of things. On one occasion he landed the jackpot, discovered that all of Mamun M's studio performances needed raisins for some reason.

Raisins, why the hell for. Raisins, raisins alone and at every meal: raisins imbedded in rice or as the passive ingredients of a chicken dish or khir or dahi, Mamun would find raisins intolerable: wrinkled palms and fingertips, their ancient, manymonthsearlier touch, the face of Qismis, the smell of her clothing, her hair, would rise up ghostly from the plate, a sense of longing, raisins, absolutely necessary. The literary force of raisins would seize Mamun's throat, and he would discover early in his career as a playback singer his incapacity to perform without a fistful of raisins first, like a saltpetre gargle for the throat or a kerosene wick to some saccharine gunblast first line of a song. A hit. Which is not to say that for Mamun Ben Jaloun/ Mamun M, I mean/ song stood equated with nostalgia, and the brief memory of his romance with Qismis needed to be rekindled each time he opened his throat to sing. Eventually, the face of Qismis disappeared so that he could no longer recall its contours or its cleft chin, its sharpness which collected prominently at the nose: as if they had been dried out and put to mortar and pestle, she turned into powdered sound, and the flight of one thousand verses he would pen on such diverse topics as the names of the cities of the unnameable country, the open veins of La Maga La Maga, a thief's despair at being forced to rob his beloved's home, the contemplations of a blind vicar, the elegy for a man who turned into a thousand billboards, who performed in English, Quinceyenglish, Somali, and some later translated by Manna Dei into Bengali and Hindi, within the short span of eight or nine years, had nothing at all to do with her.

Then total khatam before thirty: his voice and fame would be reduced to cinders, and after a few failed attempts at rising up the rungs of La Maga Studios as a songwriter, he would be flattened into the impecunious inarticulate role of boom-mike operator: hold it higher, MM, still in the shot, bhai, what a duffer this one. His heart was never in it, and until he would meet my mother.

But we're getting ahead of ourselves, too far ahead. Let's back to the right instant. There is work to be done. How did it all begin. Don't you want to know how my father got his big break. He was not discovered in a chic café in the artists' quarters of La Maga and celebrated for his jawline or the shape of his eyes, dragged into the frame of a shot, stand next to her, beta, let us see how the light falls on your ruddy hair. He never possessed the face of an actor. Neither did he stand in line with all the wretched art school graduates of the unnameable country at the gates of a new production, thronging like an infestation of carpet beetles, waiting to be handed out some minor role in order to be able to place their feet onto the rickety staircase of La Maga Studios while brazen balusters came undone by their collective weight. Know this: they heard him only. In fact, it was only his voice they ever saw. Once imprisoned, always in prison: this guard would not let him pass. He waited all day, however, and as a motorcade carrying the Director made its way inside, took a second chance.

He introduced himself unintentionally with a hiccup, and the hiccups continued. Sir-hic, I am hic-hic to have been hic-cluded in the cavalry, but I was late hicka for my shoe, you see this, he takes off a shoe and removes a bent hobnail holding together some fragments of unstitched leather, and therefore. But this guard was not a sleepy sack of potatoes; he was as large as Pantagruel and a suspicious fellow besides, with halitosis one could sniff-source a hundred metres away.

You are either included, he boomed with his badsmelling tongue, as part of the Director's inner staff or you go to hell.

And yet. Aha: underneath the ogee of his pants flies my father, laughing gleeful, already intoxicated though he has not yet had a spot to drink. The guard does not know whether to follow or stand awaiting the next part of the motorcade. Finally, he waves off the error: where will he go, he thinks, there are many others like me inside, only stronger and larger, he cannot get very far.

The guards inside were indeed larger, each one taller than the previous, but that was their precise weakness, and my father manages to swoop under all their legs and to pass onward. He cranes his neck as he arrives upon an oriel window, oooh aaah, how beauteous, he gawks, not real of course, painted on, papier-mâchéd and cardboarded together last Thursday, but it looks fitting for a grand whereforeart-thou Romeo scene. Meanwhile, the hullabaloo is spreading, some guards are even venturing to leave their posts and running running my father disappears into one of the actors' living-sleeping quarters, dodging a hanging lamp and burying underneath garments that wrap around themselves and the entire room in miles of silk and velvet. Know that he is inside an actress's dressing room and hiding with his fist around a bottle of rum brandy, or what he thinks is, pinched from her furtive collection, drinking gleeful, burping, hiccupping laughing alone about nothing at all and without fear. The fire burns away everything hard palate uvula and tongue to mush, soft palate lips all of it, and only by probing with two fingers is he able to reassure his speaking organs remain intact. By the third sip, the fire opiates, and by the fourth, he is fast asleep, though still hiccupping twice a minute or so.

Fee fi, the actress Sharmilla returns with a tattooed giant, presumably her lover or perhaps a handler, why not both. Whipping her purse into the sea of ochre and azure costumes, she begins to plant kisses on Handler Lover.

Normally acquiescent to her affections, this time he wrinkles his brow, pushes her back lightly, fee fi, and begins to sniff the cloth and pulling at it, uncovering chairs, a bed, among other items of furniture.

Don't hiccup, Mamun Ben Jaloun, or do so: perform only according to the story's needs. Hic-hic.

Wait, I smell something as well, she surveys the air and treads across the folds. What she smells is an opened bottle of austerlitz, her father's gift before graduating into the endless studio, now do not open this, bibi, before twenty-six minimum, and she has managed thus far, and would have kept the promise had not.

Got him, the giant shouts: little rabbit by the scruff of his neck, punching kicking air, awakened rudely and hic-hiccupping, and now to be sent flying out of the film studio boundaries. Loafer from somewhere, the giant gnashes his teeth and lifts Mamun up to eye level.

And without a thought—since all manifestations of glossolalia, as we have noticed, are aleatory if anything, subconscious and prior to thinking—my father launches into a song about floating on the vaulted wind, the seductive weather brought me here and I have turned into a reed, he sings, forgetting to fear the giant's reprisal, leg-dangling above ground, looking the actress sharp in the eyes, but now the storm gathers, so sweetly he sings, do not deracinate, batting eyelashes and hands together pleading please spare me a return on darkening clouds, O beholder of my misfortunes, that Sharmilla raises her hand and touches my father's forehead.

I will take no action against or on your behalf, she says, but you cannot stay here.

Th-hic you, he says, and he bows and bids them goodbye. The giant, he notices, is not so tall after all, since he fits in the studio room with inches to spare above his head, though he is indeed broad as a barrel, and with indecipherable scripture painted all across his body. The actress, if we are to cast in her direction a few meagre words that will no doubt fail to capture her beauty in human presence: no, let us refrain, for already he is outside and walking quickly.

Mamun Ben Jaloun threads the alleyways and passes movie sets and wires and lights strewn about, of simulated rooms in houses blending with fake courtrooms and schools, hospitals and prisons, painted backdrop landscapes under which there lie other landscapes that can be rolled over to reveal still more scenery, and he wonders in which of these places he may house himself for a night's rest.

Is that him: a loud cry from under a streetlamp: a crowd of flashlights, latis or sticks, lathis or kicks, stones for added measure, and my father must take to the wind once again to avoid attack. There he goes: gambolling across the Mediterranean, flying around the world, now in Constantinople, if that is a real place, dangling next from the chandelier of a Central Asiatic palace belonging to a Tartar emperor, boot-hopping across the Chukchi Sea, knocking over boom mikes and papier-mâché mountains, whole forests and ravines, skyscrapers and monorails. They chase and chase him. And he runs or flies, all the while singing. He sings, which may have helped him travel faster and faster until they were so far in the past he could not see even a single pair of chasing feet or hear a crying throat, no lathis or mobs or Pantagruel guards anywhere.

Exhausted, he fell into the ample lap of a woman with wide parted thighs, sitting on the bare floor of an emptied warehouse containing a single camera situated on a dolly track and on whose rear wall was a blank canvas framed by a white plaster parget border. She was minding her own business, stroking several young dogs, which fled upon his rude entrance. She had a kindly laugh, however, and did not mind the intrusion.

She held my father tightly until he cried like a baby: Tell me your name. She would not let him go until he complied.

And yourself, he twisted in her grasp, held her to the question indignantly by clogging her nostrils with two fingers.

Me, she cried with a snort and a piggish squeal at his mirror inquiry: Who am I. Why I'm Lady Jerusalem, everybody knows me.

My father removed his fingers from her nose and wanted to relax in Lady Jerusalem's strong fleshy arms, which held him so tightly he nearly fell choking asleep, and perhaps he did, for a minute or an hour, but a din woke him too soon.

The young dogs had returned. Oh it's time for their milk, she said, and got up onto her feet, yet from where in this wilderness would she find such a thing as milk.

Upon her release all the blood readjusted to its proper places in Mamun Ben Jaloun's body. He saw now that on the back wall there was a switch that Lady Jerusalem touched before stepping gingerly out of the way. The floor over there began to move as if to the whims of a controlled minor earthquake. And Mamun realized that part of the ground on which he sat belonged to the outer section of a circle, while the parget-framed white canvas at the rear belonged to its inner remainder, on which was situated a panorama of two halves, the first of which was the hitherto described warehouse space, exchangeable at the flick of a switch with a second a domestic exhibit, furnished lightly but still outfitted with a gas stove, a cot, a small bookshelf half-stocked with volumes whose titles were unreadable, and a refrigerator.

Come on, sweeties, Lady Jerusalem said as the six or seven dogs crowded around her. She shut the fridge door and poured milk straight into their throats from the height of her ear and they caught its stream, rarely missing, and licking up the few errant spilled drops. Then she rustled up some greens and fried up a few fish steaks in olive oil with garlic on the gas stove before adding vinaigrette: A salad, she offered, as if she often entertained guests this way.

It seemed natural that they should share her cot, and when the contents of the fridge thinned, a grocer boy arrived ringing his bicycle bell and produced a rye loaf from his front basket, dried apricots and figs, fresh lobster caught just yesterday in the Indian Ocean, ma'am.

How does she procure the necessary income, he wondered, but knew it would be rude to ask.

I am allotted a stipend by the studio, she explained on her own as they supped on a lamb and mint dish. I shadow an actress, Sharmilla, you may have heard of her, I have been performing her dance routines for years; we cut a similar enough figure, though our faces differ, you might have noticed if you have seen even one of her films—our films, she corrected. I am waiting for the Director to shoot the next scene. It's a musical, of course, and a domestic scene, and I don't mind rehearsing the role, she glanced at him sharply.

Mamun Ben Jaloun assented with a nod: having been chased by guards and then a stick-wielding mob across what seemed like the whole world, the company of a kindly shadow dancer was a welcome change. And, in a way, they were free: surrounded by only three walls, not by the regular four that construct every domicile and prison, and while passersby could come and go and watch as they pleased, Mamun Ben Jaloun adjusted even to the idea that secretaries and clipboard holders would arrive from time to time in the most intimate moments to count down the hours before filming, signalling makeup artists who, with garrulous chatter, would improve Lady Jerusalem's appearance with a few dabs of colour, and lighting staff who would shine thousands of volts onto their living quarters and exchange any hour for high noon.

The fulfilling event, however, never occurred: the makeup artists and members of the film crew always disappeared, the scene was never filmed, and for two or three days afterward, Lady Jerusalem sulked and ate tinned mussels one can after another until, bloated, she would lie moaning and begging to be administered an emetic.

Mamun did not mind caring for her on these occasions, and did so tenderly, kissing her eyelids and midriff: Sleep, it will pass.

One night American bombs fell onto the studios some miles away, and the microcosmos burned, whole countries disappeared; the moon, cardboard and two-dimensional palaces were ruined, thousands of costumes and characters turned to cinder. On that night, Lady Jerusalem's kisses tasted of explosive jetsam, ash, she was a baker, or worse yet, the oven, and he was the smouldering bread. As they huddled together under the cover of the kitchen table, he felt shrunken, as if held by the walls of a deep furnace. He longed to make blinding steps, let loose a song and hurry from this place. But he stayed. Thereafter, her embraces and kisses, every extended contact, in fact, asphyxiated him.

While it was true her physical presence was not overwhelming in sight and she remained what he considered attractive by her hair and her smells and so forth, her mouth became like a vacuum that threatened to suck away his very life with each kiss. For hours afterward, he would sit at the edge of the cot while she smacked his back with a flat palm, as he tried to recover his voice and the wind in his lungs. When he recovered, he related his difficulties to her while she assumed her prior problems, which this time were so crippling that for the first time he thought of calling paramedics, but where could they be found in this part of the studio when the fires were still going on elsewhere. Thankfully, the crisis passed and they lived together for several months more, though in chaste circumstances, during which time the young dogs visited more often, and sometimes displayed great animosity toward him.

Know at that age, Mamun Ben Jaloun had no ambitions to become a playback singer, and we can imagine he would never have done so had he stationed himself indefinitely with Lady Jerusalem. Luckily, he was arrested not too long after.

One day there arrived a man garbed in exceedingly wide-legged bells, which were the style of the era. Above his shoulders he had thrown a long grey shawl, more like a cloak, and he stood at the open wall, smartly saluted to no one before letting loose a scroll that dragged along the ground like the longest lie. He read from that indecipherable document with its many since-therefores and notwith-standings, which apparently justified what happened next: eight or nine trolls, or little children, drew from under his loose pants and from the folds of his cloak and climbed all over Mamun Ben Jaloun and overwhelmed him, held his eyes shut and dragged him away from the screaming Lady Jerusalem, rendered helpless and held in place by the remainder of the document, which named her and kept her there.

The dolly track, it would appear, also serves as an internal rail line, as indicated by the small engine comes into view, pulling behind it a dozen or so bathtub gondola cars, and our hero soon finds himself transported jhigjhig-takrtakr, jhigjhig-takrtakr, across green fields of sorghum and gilded paintings of fonio and wheat, or perhaps the latter too are real, as he leaves behind Lady Jerusalem, who seems deeply affected by his sudden capture.

Look: she runs along the dolly track until all the cars have disappeared, dispirited weeping as she waves, though we cannot be sure this is not another part she has been rehearsing and with which she is familiar, regard the twists and entrechats, no doubt expressions of a trained shadow dancer.

The journey is long, and eventually Mamun Ben Jaloun falls asleep to the rhythm of the miniature train, whose tight quarters force him to pull his knees up to his chest, and which moves across the dolly tracks jhigjhig-takrtakr, jhigjhig-takrtakr. (Note that the engine car is sufficiently larger even for a grown individual with very large pants and nine or eight munchkins hiding in his clothing, enough to fit all and with ample room to spare.) A jar of marmalade and thin, tasteless wafers, some nearly rotten tomatoes, a jerrycan of water: these proffered in a bag are to last him one week, at the end of which he finds his legs so weakened from their constrained unmitigated pose that up with you, his captor with the wide-legged pants drags him into the right place: Mamun Ben Jaloun finds himself sitting in an enormous wooden chair in a room with many photographs of heroes of the silver screens and pillars not unlike those in a courthouse.

My name is Soni Aadam. I am the staff sergeant of studio security, the light falls on a man's face as he introduces himself. I am also a notable producer, he lists over one hundred short films, documentaries and features, few of which we would be acquainted with. Why have you come here.

I was brought here, my father replied.

Who brought you into the studio, the man thundered.

Please, Mamun Ben Jaloun responded, with shivering knocking feet that pressed against each other underneath the desk separating the two characters: I have no wish to bother anyone.

And yet there is the remaining charge of your illicit drunkenness in Sharmilla's dressing room, the theft of her father's gifted bottle of austerlitz, beiman bettomiz, where from you are, and then khattash: a thappar-slap across the face after all the gaalis. The staff sergeant and producer chewed on the cigar on which he puffed in between words, and Mamun Ben Jaloun noticed flecks of paan had collected around his mouth from some earlier bout of mastication. The ceiling fan overhead sucked up all the smoke in swirls. For three moments the official appeared to be engulfed in a tornado.

Then two frail characters, a very old man and a hunching and equally senescent woman, gained our hero's attention; they appeared from the open door leading out to a dark vestibule, bearing two trays, one with a steaming cup of tea with milk and another bearing the contents of a dinner: hot rice, several curries in tiffin containers, and a decanter filled with daal.

The woman surveyed Mamun Ben Jaloun with her left eye, which roamed while the right eye was focused on serving. With her left hand she held the tray while also pouring the tea. With her right she poked my father's shoulder, What do you mean, she asked.

Excuse me, Mamun replied, but I haven't said anything.

The hag mumbled something with the left side of her mouth while with the right side she clearly asked the producer whether she should bring out the dessert now or wait.

My father was confused by her multiplicity, her ability to speak to two people at once with a single mouth, and he was about to ask how she performed her trick, was it an act of ventriloquism, but before he had a chance, she yessirred the staff sergeant producer, picked up the empty containers, and departed.

Meanwhile, the second character, the very old man, was combing the official's hair with his fingers, possibly scanning for nits, while the producer ate. With every bite he seemed to grow more self-assured, and in the light he seemed indefeasible.

Tell me, what class of individual are you: dancer, singer, key grip, or what, cinematographer, et cetera and so forth, do you practise a meaningful trade.

Singer, my father said, since out of the options provided it seemed most reasonable to choose.

And what do you sing.

My own songs mostly, or just fragments, melodies that seemingly appear and disappear at their own will.

So a composer, the staff sergeant producer grew interested, which is probably why Lady Jerusalem took an interest in you. Generally, I would have a trespasser thrown out of the studio at once or force him to take a charwoman's role if you truly wanted to work, but seeing that your manners aren't so bad, he looked my father up and down, and you are not so terribly groomed—which is important, as you can tell I have an assistant make sure I am always presentable, he indicated with his brow to the old man who had finished combing the official's hair and had now moved on to closely inspect his shirt—I will allow you an audition. Mmm, a singer, he continued, raising a drumstick from his plate, biting through flesh and into the bone crac-crac, we'll see about that. My father was about to ask a question about the nature of the audition but the staff sergeant producer waved it off and kicked the small old man, who had begun purring and nuzzling up against his legs under the table.

My clipboard, Ben Jaloun, he kicked him again, and the little man leapt three feet into the air, screaming incomprehensibly. My father laughed into his shirt-collar while the secretary stared down his frail employee from a great height.

Midget, you listen, he began.

I am neither midget, excusesir, nor a dwarf, the man winced, rubbing his back and shoulders, my stature is the result of advanced age only.

Ben Jaloun, I am weary of your constant amendments to my speech; and if you will, please, unless you wish to suffer several more kicks, retrieve my clipboard from there over there. He pointed off into the distant reaches of the office, which appeared difficult to navigate, replete with an obstacle course of filing cabinets and stacks of paper that reached the height of two grown men, and that were covered all over by knotted and ancient cobwebs.

Retrieving a kerosene lamp from a table close at reach, little Ben Jaloun looked pensively into the darkness.

Just what are you waiting for, the official thundered.

Please, my lord, the little man begged, it's just that this particular corner is quite resistant to light.

And this was true. The little flame from the lamp trembled as if daunted by the sheer opacity of the items that lay ahead or out of fear that some unaccountable evil would emerge at any moment. And when it went out altogether, the old man had no matches.

You'll have to see with your hands, now, won't you, oh ho, said the official, laughing.

For the next hour, while my father's stomach grumbled and he sat in place without a complaint, while the official licked the bowl of daal round and round, picked every grain of rice off the table, even stealing one back from an ant, the old fragile man could be heard rummaging through the endless pile of corrugated boxes, opening and shutting filing cabinets, and rifling through papers and folders.

And let not a single item be disturbed, the staff sergeant warned, ringing for Ben Jaloun's counterpart, the two-faced old woman who had served him earlier. She lurched out from behind the door as if she had been waiting there all the while.

Take him to the green room, Sangeeta, he ordered. I'll mark it down on the clipboard when that idiot returns from there over there, but you know the way: it's a day's journey by dolly-car, so make sure to pack enough provisions; tell Omar Omar I sent him.

In fact, the journey stretched on for a day more than expected, and while for a withered old woman a gondola car is the perfect size, Mamun Ben Jaloun feared that this time the contortions would deal his body lasting damage. (In fact, they wouldn't, but in a strange twist of fate, his son, your humble narrator Hedayat, would for the first six years of his life be afflicted by nightmarish rides on a tiny toy train and would awake from them limping.) The lunar terrain was unchanging all the way there, every leaf of grass, stalk of foliage removed for miles to make way for the filming of a science fiction film by Satyajit Ray rejected by Universal Pictures, a lifeless landscape except for the glistening koi moving about in a man-made pond on which the alien first lands.

Once again he would have to be removed from the gondola car and hauled to the appropriate location. This time he found himself in a pitch-black room that sizzled for a moment before being lit up by a single prick of light: someone was smoking. Another pinprick of fire somewhere nearby. Something like a bodiless head bobbing. The shadows on the walls confused my father, for in the dim light they seemed not at all correspondent to possible objects in an enclosed space: there appeared silhouettes of gnarled boughs, or perhaps these were only very long fingers.

Sing, someone commanded. Mamun Ben Jaloun found it absurd that some people had gathered at the exact moment of his arrival in a darkened room to hear him sing, that singing for any reason except to sing from one's heart and for no one's pleasure but one's own held any meaning. He found it equally absurd that he would probably abide by their request, only he could not think of even one song. Meanwhile, all the cigarette smoke was choking him. More and more little pricks of light gathered in the room, they revealed little nimbus clouds while he was choking and coughing. He unbuttoned his shirt to the middle and this helped to a degree, but he continued to cough; requesting that they did not smoke would probably do nothing, but he asked anyway. As if they had not heard, they demanded to know what he would perform.

So as to ease the tension, perhaps, some lights turned on from above, and by their aid he saw a woman who appeared like Lady Jerusalem but who was probably Sharmilla or another of her shadow dancers, who stood watching while stroking a small grinning animal. There were others, but he could not tell how many. My father recognized he was standing on a raised platform, which was probably a stage but which felt like the gallows.

Sing, shouted the man who must have been the music director, and merrily, he commanded, but nothing emerged from my father's throat.

If I hiccup now, he began wishing against the inevitable, but when he opened his lips a sweet warble emerged instead, the notes wafted up his throat smoothly, uninterrupted by the smoke. He sang as does a picaresque troubadour, of his own story, what else: I vaulted here on a miscreant wind, he sang, I turned into a reed in the fleshy arms of a baker woman whose dogs bit me, he exaggerated, a woman who never sang but turned on her toes so lovely. There were other verses, of course, to fill out the details, including descriptions of the two-throated old lady who brought him here and had disappeared, and at the end of which everything was still. Finally, it was they who began to cough, one after another, and finally in unison, as if the coughing was substitute for applause.

He may be awarded a room in a flat in the songwriters' district, Apartment 1-B on St. Cathcrine's, said the man who must have been Omar Omar, the double-name giver of apartments in those parts of the studio at that time. Rent is free for the first month but he must produce consistently to stay subsequent months. Next, he cried loudly, as a door opened and fresh air poured in and Mamun Ben Jaloun could finally breathe. He looked where the light was abundant. From behind the door it was plain to see the beginning of a long winding animal stretching possibly for miles, constituting no doubt others who too wanted to be playback singers.

My father's shyness exceeds his desire to impress or to earn his keep, and producers realize he can only introduce or record his ideas in pitch-blackness; note that in La Maga Studios, auditions are traditionally held in the dark, but recordings require the sound engineer to see the appropriate dials and switches, and as a compromise someone suggests he wear a pair of blinding dark shades, which simulates the total absence of objects and people.

For the rest of Mamun Ben Jaloun's singing career, he would be known as Blind Man Mamun, a cognomen he rejects until realizing years later many women interpreted his handicap as a mysterious and attractive condition. He does not prefer the moniker of Mamun M either, mind you, he simply stumbled hiccupping onto it the first time he was asked and never had the heart to correct the studio heads after the cheques began to arrive correctly under that name.

At first, my father's output is slight, and he manages barely to write one song per month, belaboured forced creations that lyrically and structurally reflect his inexperience, and only several of which are admitted into films. These hardly dragnet enough to pay for the room in the cramped flat in the songwriters' district of the studio, which he shares with six others also attempting the same craft, each with his own failings: one young man is too didactic with his melodies, another so avant-garde he usually loses the thread of his songs, others with limited ranges, and all of them raising a caterwaul to high hell night and day with the intention of writing the one song whose payback would be the tenure singer's role in which Mamun M found himself so easily.

But shhhh listen carefully, as my father eventually learns to do: realize that since the walls are thin, the compositions of all seven musicians are in fact tethered inseparable, fragments and rehearsals of one and the same song, and it is possible, by choosing the rhythmical shift from one attempt and the major-minor change from another, to sew together a track that stands up much better than any single attempt. Thusly, he manages by bricoleur's feat to write his first winning tracks and to gather the confidence to shut out the cacophony of his peers and housemates, to move into a small flat of his own and finally to open up his own vault of melodies.

His matured style impresses Soni Aadam, the chief of security we met earlier, who is also the producer of a dozen films simultaneously, and who therefore requires a perpetual supply of songs to develop their scores. He prefers my father over other songsters and gives him ample opportunity to develop his craft, and the pictures prove it. A photograph of my father in front of a large ribbon microphone, large shades preventing us from seeing the expression in his eyes when he hits a G over middle C, a photograph in front of a piano with three fingers poised over white keys black keys, a photograph where he shakes hands with Mohammed Rafi, another one while recording with a hundred-man Wall of Sound string and woodwind orchestra. A song about the clinking of chains in a nameless ministry of arid corridors and dusty offices, or of working in the potash mines or labouring in the citrus groves: the nature of my father's songs changes drastically over his career. Like his father, he tries to avoid politics and would desperately edit his lyrics, but the melodies would always return the words to their original course.

Sometime around his third year in the trade as a songwriter, he discovered the hidden strength of raisins and things began to fall apart.

It is arguable what part the Black Organs had to play, whether they introduced the drug slowly and habituated him to its daily use; such machinations were not uncommon in La Maga Studios. (Understand that all the vital fluids of his memory of Qismis had by then been dried and sucked out by Lady Jerusalem's embraces and her vacuum-incinerating kisses, so the memory of raisin wrinkled fingertips and palms, the past, cannot be blamed.) The change, in any case, was immediate and absolute. Observe: it was always a fistful in the morning and then another at mid-morning before recording, some more along-side the afternoon coffee; nobody suspected a thing, you see, who cares how many raisins a man eats on a given day, who has ever become sick or overdosed on raisins, how many friends would insist on rehabilita-tion or therapy if one is a raisin addict.

Still more and more raisins, in the cakes and the rice, the salads and meat dishes, with the food, but more often as a standalone drug. People differ in their capacity to handle chemical substances. And raisins for Mamun M proved to be highly addictive. Past their initial impact on the nervous system as an upper, they dragged him into a two-kilogram-a-day habit of dried gutrot and grape, paroxysm high epileptic flashes, come synesthesia ochre rotted flutes, come rot ejacu-late fainting slumber, and raisins raisins your pockets full, sell your mother for a sack of raisins. And with the raisins came the accom-panying symptoms of decay: mix it with the butter: a too-tall pair of naked legs moves past, like this, a female voice asks amidst the sound of mortar and pestle, the rustle of hands on cloth, her skirt slips and our camera-eye moves to reveal another naked body in the room, two more behind her on top. His lyrics at that time grew so junky-drenched and his voice so shaky, aged so far beyond his twenty-six years, that Soni Aadam gave him an ultimatum: replace your life or we will replace you. Secretly, he began employing Mimic Mamuns, trying to pass these off as the original himself in screenplays, but the audience would not have it. My father's populist observations in song were inimitable.

There were riots, believe it or not: we will not tolerate, shouted the placards and the crowd. Can't fool won't fool all the people, they chorused. Soni Aadam was forced to apologize publicly and even compensated the real Mamun for the songs he did not sing in efforts to cajole him into resuming his ordinary rate of production, but Mamun Ben Jaloun would not budge from his sandlot. He had the finest silica brought to him in bags and became a connoisseur of the stuff. He loved letting it trickle through his fingers, perhaps as much as he loved women or that wrinkled saccharine familiar.

Eventually, Soni Aadam brought the mountain to Muhammad: a full studio outfit arrived in several trucks along with a top-notch roundtheclock producer, just in case Mamun awoke from a succour binge with an idea. For several years, it worked. Lying on his back, with a microphone suspended from the ceiling, my father would sing, somehow capable in the horizontal of accomplishing what he could no longer manage vertically, the notes rising, pausing, before resuming their climb up the scales; never had his voice been sweeter, more melancholic. Audiences were satisfied once again though the famous playback singer never appeared in public, and the only stories of his personal life were so rancid they must have been concocted by enemy publicists.

Mamun M never agreed to interviews, remained barricaded in the large flaking plaster-walled mansion he purchased in his second year as a songwriter, whose servants roamed the halls busy with unassigned tasks, and which once filled in the nighttime with the youthful rebels of that generation but now remained silent as Mamun M, who was altogether silent except in song, where his observations of the lives of ordinary people remained accurate enough that the public wondered whether, like certain sultans in the Arabian Nights, he would visit the orchards, graveyards, factories, herders' plains, mines, and oil refineries of his lyrics, disguised as a plebe. Regard: a crowd gathers around a niqabi woman, they tear her veil at the black cloth because, secretly, Mamun M is hidden underneath. Denuded horrified, the woman cries and throws dust onto her forehead. The crowd is ashamed and several of the perpetrators are severely beaten. Such scenes were not uncommon at that time.

What else did the sultan survey that Hedayat's owl eyes summon, that his automatic tongue can hoot and chitter about: nothing at all. Mamun Ben Jaloun didn't for a moment see the hard-callused hands of the oil worker or natural-gas plant labourer making all the stuff the unnameable country was known to the world for. Rather, my father wandered set to film set, laying a track here another song there, his feet always following some distant melody, and, as others around him noticed, always trying to dig out some actual story swimming under the skin: why the endless movie studio, he always wondered. Mamun Ben Jaloun, restless, young, inquisitive, always inquiring, why do they burn every movie set after they're done filming. But no one told him. No one seemed to know.

Then, without warning, he gave it all up. Just shy of his thirtieth birthday, Mamun M received a call from a documentarian Badsha Abd that in these hottest months, or jilaal, an artificial drought was brewing in the burning pastoral reaches of the unnameable country. Recall, for it is said at that time Mamun M received countless offers to serve as assistant director, producer, even to act, though we have noted he has no camera face; whatever provoked him, then, to accept such a lowly, nominal role aside from the fact that one grows tired of the senseless roaming across paved granite walkways, smooth to the naked soles of the feet, drinking cup after cup of aniseed liquor and eating raisins, as we know, by the fisted kilograms. As well, if you must know: the curiosity of leaving the constant threat of fiction was there, of fleeing the prison of the studio (which was contrasted only with the prison of his large home with its repeating rooms of ottomans and plush cushions, and lonely eyes of some woman who had called for him and would not leave until he saw her, and who would no doubt assent to the silent call of just one finger come hither) to pursue an actual story once again. Perhaps more than anything, a fulfilling existence requires struggle, and this is what my father wished for at that age.

So: not yet thirty, Mamun M expended his last breath as the sole singer and composer of the score for the spaghetti western *The Fall Guy*, a most disappointing production, before departing with a crew of documentarians as its boom-mike operator to distant burning plains. Two weeks later, Soni Aadam's outer bell rang and the postman called urgently from beyond the gate. He thrust into the producer's hand a package in the shape of a book supposedly from his friend Mamun M and scooted away on the back of a 150 cc Honda.

Soni Aadam wasted no time tearing the wrapping; he had never received a written communiqué from Mamun M, nor any gift in the mail, and he knew the message was urgent. A bookmark fell to the ground. Before he could bend all the way to the floor, the five-hundred-gram bomb exploded, leaving nothing but teeth shards limb fragments.

Two other producers and one director were killed by similar means within twenty-four hours. Five Ilyushin fighter jets firebombed La Maga Studios; the Governor's defence was that in an era of imperialist domination, one had to fight the enemy within with perhaps greater furor, and there was no bigger enemy than an endless studio involved in the ceaseless production of anti-socialist propaganda.

The rest of his life, my father would attest to his innocence; he would shed genuine tears over Soni Aadam's death and for the demise of the golden era of La Maga Studios (which would be rebuilt but in another image). By the time the news discovered him, however, he would be deep into another existence, secluded and examining other deaths with documentary filmmaker Badsha Abd. We can observe, however, that for the second time, my father predicted demise on the horizon and absconded from an ostensible high ground for the ditch. Never again would he be able to tolerate the taste of raisins or sing another note. Ashes to ashes, powdered sound to desert sands: Qismis, his mother, the Screens all to dust and a deeper forgetting, to the sands of the unnameable country. Many years later, crowds would gather at playback bars around the unnameable country and along to the backing tracks of the old La Maga Studio hits, and they would try to warble and coo like Mamun M in the movies. So ritualized did these events become that aggravated five-o'clockers would binge on malt liquor and start fisticuffs at the first cracked note; one was allowed no mistakes or personal renditions that strayed too far from the original.

La Maga Studios, meanwhile, survived the American bombs but would not survive the Governor's wrath. The entire world a movie set burned. Airplane missiles combined with self-administered gasoline blazes used commonly in the city to clear space for the next film segment. Firehoses malfunctioned and people leapt into an artificial canal that they were building to facilitate joy, and for a moment while riding a camel outside city lines, my father turned his head over his shoulder and caught sight of a region of mist.

THIRSTY
GHOSTS

For all the records of flash and song, recall my father escapes the film studio's fires of disrepute and its actual fires by fleeing into the burning hinterland plains of the unnameable country. He has heard reports of artificial drought, of the Governor's poison deposits sunk into town wells, Anwar's explosions burst granite walls descending tumult, his disrupted irrigation systems wilted whole communities destitute flesh and mouths yawning up into sky, and he wants to see the landscape himself.

Famine and drought invite related torments: Mamun Ben Jaloun the boom-mike man, Badsha Abd the director of production, Gibreel the cameraman, and Abdel-Aziz the cinematographer, find footage in wreckage, in the labour of millions of insect heartbeats beating wings mandibles chewed away all leaves of mangroves and acacia, every corn kernel and all the grains of sorghum. Children have been scouring for substitute dinner portions, reports indicate, catching unnameable acaudate rodents that peer cautiously out of parched earth, ceaseless animals multiplying ad infinitum, eating all the leftover crops, and capable of surviving, they say, even on bare soil.

All the doors of all the houses are unlocked, all the rooms sawdust walls unkempt beds scattered cutlery broken television sets. Does anyone live here, my father asks, picks up a burning stone in the front yard of a house and holds it in his right palm, unable to think of whatisit in the heat. He swallows thick and throws the stone very far.

They walk until nightfall, they set up camp. They shoot some reels of thirty-five millimetres. All the Governor's Jeeps and all the Governor's men have dealt irreparable: whole destroyed villages without a breathing plant or man in some areas. They wander in the dust that lifts up onto clothes in hair under fingernails, the dust they eat in their meals despite all efforts, dust in their water mud in stomachs intestines in their piss, their brains feel dusty from thought to thought.

They find a watch with a leather strap in the sands, and Mamun Ben Jaloun puts it on. Then the days begin to change shape as the watch tells desert time. They notice the sites of the dynamited wells appear in different locations than on maps, places where the air tastes of hurried figs, dried apples. Haunted memories saturate the landscape Governor's Jeeps blades of dust in the eyes and loose shadow flickering behind lanky man, child screaming grown-up hand he was holding becomes translucent, a pulmonary sky pumping to far blinking lights they're coming, pack you all into the car now and escape into near road venal motion onto highway to Benediction or La Maga.

They wander in the dust until the heat renders Abdel-Aziz, their cinematographer, delirious and unable to continue, laughing crying glossolating fluent incomprehensible, incapable of walking eating. They are forced to tie him to the back of a donkey. The mountains beside in front behind them reach into the unblemished sky as their path finds new sands without reprieve, and Abdel-Aziz has taken violently ill.

Then a sand scuttling sound, a wheel and movement: an animal or man emerges suddenly out of nearby rocks. The strange meaning becomes apparent: a fat dwarf situated nimbly along the inner lip of a metal hoop has come rolling down the path, and smashes against a rock. The film crew is too astonished in the stifling heat with concerns of sickness and death/ what will they do without a cinematographer/ to say anything and watches the creature lean its hoop against their tarpaulin sicktent, bend low to whisper thick clotted sounds through the open door into the cinematographer's ear.

Mamun Ben Jaloun has taken to a nearby rock constellation but before he can return with a sizeable stick to shoo away the strange intruder, the metal hoop is already rolling path into grey-azure horizon. What did he say, my father shakes the cinematographer ashen forehead parched lips limbs barely moving under bedsheet.

But the blood parasites infecting Abdel-Aziz have already taken their toll, it seems. The aid of saline solution and nutrient broth, litres of water coaxing hours of conversation, produces a sleepless lull. Just as my father and the film crew are measuring cigarettes until the next town, having given the cinematographer up to ghosts, laughter emerges from inside the sicktent.

My father gets there first, feeds water to dying lips bids speak, friend. Whispers, inaudible syllables: father bends closer, tell me of the dwarf, of your illness, speak words, any words, words about death even, against death. The cinematographer's first skittering sentences fight wind at the tent rasping throat tosses prophecy, his lucid mind peaks through emaciated flesh, he beckons come closer:

A city, he says, high above the Karkaars with houses built onto the sides of mountain passes, bridges of spiderthread, a city of thirsty ghosts, the Governor's men slit spidersacs to collect rain no water dynamited wells.

The dwarf told you, my father asks.

A loud yellow braying donkey sound, a guffaw from the cracked lips of Abdel-Aziz. The cinematographer died laughing not too long, several days later, a gruesome demise, if you will recall from stories commonly told, paroxysms and frothing at the sides of the mouth. His corpse mixed with sand easy, however, and then they were relieved. The event was a turning point in my father's career as a documentarian, for he suddenly found himself promoted to replace Abdel-Aziz, though he had no experience with such a job.

You'll do fine, Badsha Abd pats him on the back and gives him a quick lesson on the laconic art of cinema: a lonely crow plus deserted bough equals desolation, moving hand to moving head and sudden sound makes slap, you can cause blue metal tang and a guitar all cubes and fretboard pickups heavy distortion twingtwang strings, and know a slaughter goat can give a man's eyeball as thin stream atmosphere slices moonlight.

And all this how, my father asked.

Cinema and showbiz, Badsha Abd replied with a shrug.

Then it got nightfall. And then a sound. Hark unto the cry: Shidane Shidane, the ghost of Shidane. Hear his howl a moan a half-slaughtered animal. But that would not be the Americans' doing or the Governor's. Not exactly. And yet. A question, nevertheless: can a ghost haunt you before bodyandsoul has gone, before a life has even arrowed concep- tion gestation. A pre-emptive haunting perhaps, a warning, if we are superstitious. But our party moves on, leaving the sound for the coyotes to claim as theirs. The theme of the locusts is not accompanied by rivers of blood, or diadem of burning bush.

If God walks alongside this crowd then he is like a djinn's shadow: lux, pure light, invisible. How long did they wander thusly. How many dynamited ruined wells did they find and film in silence. And what of a train's skeleton half-buried in the dust, beyond the realm of railway tracks for miles in any direction: look there a string of excoriated boxcars. Recall from newspaper reminders that somewhere else they are still excavating the skeleton of the largest prehistoric whale ever documented. Time enough to ask: who are the Abd, since you may be wondering about Badsha and before him. And why are they, since we're all about them suddenly and a great deal.

Historically, much of the land directly south of the Gulf of Eden has belonged to the Abd, and they have enjoyed strong historical ties to the governing elite despite the governments' overtime changing heads and diadem doctrines, throughout which the Abd remained strong nevertheless. Picture for yourself the long history of KUBARK funding when it needed Uncle: CIA moolah, in short, to well-water the lawns and to high-rise strong walls of better-defended estates of necessary individuals. Badsha of the bunch, the chief Abd of our story, was born to a Queen Bulbul without a crown, much beloved for her humming of popular radio tunes, which she hummed in the courtyard of her home while watering flowers, but which people supposedly heard for miles around because it was said she had the gift of humming directly into ears.

Things began to go wrong when the KUBARK sounded up a big tree-rustle about pan-Arab nationalism and the wider global threat of International Communism, to which the Abd lifted eyebrows, who hell and did we ever, and it was around or exactly this time Badsha Abd cried into the world for the first time. Suddenly, the Abd, unfunded unchained by the CIA, had to fend for themselves, which they managed by buying their way into the film industry.

Badsha grew up in the cracked splendour of the Abd family's wealth, the ceilings and walls of which served as the backdrop of his first documentary productions. Quieter than his relatives and few friends, he amused himself by trailing miles of black glossy out of his pockets, though impossible, that would have ruined the tapes, so this way instead: with his thumbs always triggered on the Super 8 pointed in the wrong direction: reels of tape documenting the attempts of polio children to stagger after years of illness, or of a man lying along a harbour while speaking to the fleas on his shoulder.

Badsha Abd spent his adolescence disappeared into underground places of heat, noise, foul air, and confusion, so it's no surprise we find him followed by the sound of Shidane Shidane, the ghost of Shidane, or threading village after village of blackened parched corpses unburied, shrunken, untouched even by scavenger dogs. The walls of wells collapsed imploded inward, the water buried under stones thirty metres below the earth. Sometimes the stone-baked bodies of women and men frozen in their efforts to scrape with their hands to lift the stones.

In the towns, the documentarians manage to broach water from the reluctant, and to replace their donkeys with less exhausted, sturdier asses of burden. The towns give way to the plains, another village, but this one has a few survivors, a wheezing woman in the grave dimensions of a small hut, behind a courtyard effusing the sweet stench of corpses, newly rotting, side by side. They shoot thirty-five millimetres as she expires. No one offers water, though the thought crosses Mamun Ben Jaloun's mind.

Husks of rifle shells and the odd Jeep drives in from far sands with the oblivion question: you. Do you know, the insignia-heavy man asks, this region is a war zone, but we are a film crew, we have permits, as the air stews Badsha Abd's skin under beige polyester shirt for minutes seconds decades as the crew swims or stands, sits, probably, with hands behind their skulls as directed, on the thirsty ground, under the slicing sky. Murray's men, the crew whispers, just as transistors flare voices make dust electric wiring, they're talking from far.

Who is Murray, no one asks, because legends speak long before him.

Walk, says a man to the reedy man to a man with a nervous jitter until a gun pushes up Badsha of the group and he walks, with others behind him, into a large truck with a weather-beaten tarpaulin cover.

The film crew occupies the truck's perimeter benches gasoline odour old cola can food smells, one occupying soldier per two or three or four crew members. Darkness finds my father and his friends save a dangling light above for the bumpy ride. The ground gives way to reaches of sky or sleep as motorsounds surround them. When my father awakes, the back door is a mouth opening brighter light than even in the unnameable desert of their recent crossing. Then single-file through a two-dimensional hallway through which they have to pass sideways to a high vaulted room guided by fear of the gun barrel at the back of every two or three or four men.

Seat yourselves, commands a voice. Time passes. The air grows foul and full of the smell of bodies in close proximity, as thoughts contracting translucent jellyfish axons in phosphorescent water and whole tribe of grey-bodied young thirsty ghosts of dynamited wells rasping requesting.

A young girl enters with a vase of water floating flower petals, without glasses, and Gibreel, the first recipient, is unsure of what just make with your hands, she instructs, before pouring stream after stream from the vessel to the bowl of his hands cool water, strength, all the marine animals return to thoughts, stifling world of strange bodies become thirsty fellow travellers in a cavernous echo chamber where no new characters enter for so long their gun-toting keepers begin playing cards, laughing, smoking, exchanging sordid details seated around a table near the large doors about their mothers, daughters, sons, girl-friends. Sand begins to fill the room from a hole in the ceiling high above.

Gibreel raises the question first, but must wait until the guards' exchange of insults, throwing hands onto the table, trading cards, comes to a reasonable pause, at which point they are evasive: this time of year in this part of the country makes dustbowls its common feature, they claim. The sand keeps falling, rises to the height of their ankles and the guards secure their guns on the table under towels clean away from the dust, lift their chairs, whose legs descend to the floor, and lift the table of their game by similar extensions, before continuing to converse and curse several metres higher up than the documentary crew.

Just as Badsha Abd et al are trying to devise a method of rotating the lowest man on a potential human pyramid to compete against racing suffocation, simultaneously declaring futility, defeat, as well as screaming at the guards look at us help us, the sandstorm ceases and the front door opens to reveal an enormous carnivore in desert military costume, whose heaving breaths move the room's dust in swirls and who seems more fearful than being buried alive.

Although his great shadow hides his face, they know him from television, magazines, radio, newspapers as the man that governs the ungovernable interior of the unnameable country, from mere sugges-tion of his figure, his characteristic war limp, his plodding steps and immense appetite. He sits on a chair that barely supports his weight, at the wide dinner table that just reaches his knees, and on which the girl who served the film crew prisoners water from a vase produces six dozen eggs, a whole head of lamb, whose brains he prepares to consume by making a careful circumference incision of the skull with garden shears, a large bucket of pilaf rice, ten kilograms of alfalfa sprouts, steamed landlorn shellfish resistant to all manoeuvres of cutlery, a pot of chickpea salad with tomatoes and finely chopped cucumbers.

In between the khir and dahi, he notices the diminutive film crew inching closer to the crumbs and remainder shells of his escargot dinner contents that now grace the knee-high sands on the floor of the eating chamber.

The giant watches, bemused by the cautious steps of the starved, parched film crew prisoners whose guards are lost to card hands in their isolated revelry. Harsh bidis and strong drink follow dessert as Mamun Ben Jaloun discovers a forgotten whole mutton roast at the edge of the table, and then booming laughter, vibration into marrow as the crew asks again, Mr. Giant, if you are listening, some food, if you may. The giant, who hadn't heard the first request due to damaged ears years of exploded cartridge yells in desert sunshine see the faintest scurry in the horizon, fire in the hole, said nothing and watched the crew make a pyramid with knees on backs on knees to the table surface. Then his hardest laughter at the toppled sight of splayed bodies on sand as success after all: they have the mutton.

Tell me, who are you, little men that eat of my table, and why do you molest Epsilante, my home and county.

No one asks his name in turn because they know the man of the many metal lapels on his costume, this Murray whose face is so blinding they are forced to look at his boots under the table or at his pants, the same pair he wore when he cooked all the earlobes, fingers, toenails, gallbladder and viscera of an enemy with sea salt over a gas stove. They fear to look at the mouth of the man who once spoke with it the decree to bring to him the cooked bodies of all the people on the street that had refused to grant him his specially designed, universally acknowledged salute, which required all the limbs of one's body to perform when he passed, and so many limbs and ounces of indeterminable flesh had gathered in his audience at a dinner table with silverware, candelabras, and serving coffins that he had supposedly wept into the collar of his ring-hand man General Gargantua, my one true companion in the world because only you understand my feeling that despite all the moral ignominy and United Nations inquisitions good food should not go to waste/ the film crew already knew Murray.

We are travellers, Mamun Ben Jaloun answers, filmmakers, who have permits, he says as sand falls through the hole in the ceiling and rises higher every moment.

As the film crew eats on the floor, the girl with the water vase with floating petals returns to pour into their hands one by one. She sits next to my father, who out of the desire to repay her hospitality offers her a bite of his dinner portion. She obliges his request, and asks why the film crew has arrived at this viper's nest, since her giant master is known to have watched others buried by descending sands while he ate meal after meal seated higher above. My father would be frightened if it wasn't for the girl's murmurs like a cat intoxicating preening sounds mewling and soft pawing at his face and hair, the server suddenly soft before him as lips touch lips a key to more urgent caresses, her whispers now, before the giant awakens, before the guards turn their heads from their endless prattle of cards, she says as she points to a corner of the room a mile away.

My father looks up at the towering source of snoring sounds head-down fast asleep on a table far larger than its last appearance, and astonished, he notices the gun-toting guards have turned into hunched-over boulders at the corner of the table, their lifeless guns now also granite, their cards whoosh into the wind through the ceiling has begun again to scatter the sands and the cards, a windstorm in the room and a mile to walk in the desert at your eyelids in your lungs, you worry about the camera equipment as much as your health.

When Mamun Ben Jaloun and the film crew discovered the ladder against the wall that led up to the ceiling hatch, they turn around just in time to see the overturning table, the bellow of the great beast their captor realizing his alcoholic error, the listless boulder guards whose card-playing carelessness has turned them into rocks against better judgment, his underestimation of this Mamun Ben Jaloun and his film crew who are now almost at the ceiling hatch out of his subterranean lair.

The giant is blinded by drunken rage, by the windstorm of a room designed for fearful mystery, and forced to drag feet through sands difficult for even his long strides. The ceiling hatch gives problems for the first few attempts as ants in a line up a ladder to the prize it finally opens with an ambitious howl into the greater dustbowl than in the room.

Through the ceiling hatch: my father and the film crew fly far from one another in the ragged dust, and against the stronger winds outside at their eyes and senses than in the giant's lair they strive to gather themselves. When Mamun Ben Jaloun finds a wall a lee against the storm, he rests a moment inside his heartbeat.

Love, you ask. We are not at the cemetery of spiderclouds yet, just its premonition: Mamun Ben Jaloun looks around him and sees cirrus wisps cover the wall, the street, sees webs thread the road ahead; my mother and father haven't met yet but the fated spiders of their first encounter have already laid the groundwork.

Mamun the boom-mike operator follows the gossamer threads to the first shopkeep that obliges him a glass of water. The film crew, he describes their equipment and adventure-beaten hide and wear, and of course the bric-a-brac salesman knows, they're leaving the first day of the coming month, staying currently at Sural's hotel, he provides address and direction.

At the hotel, a lot of camera equipment and professional opinions have gathered in the foyer. Abd greets a filmmaker friend he knows from a previous project and the two of them talk about their current movies, which are peripheral scenes, they agree, in the gargantuan *Mirror* that is all the images and has colonized the country since a time no one can remember anymore. Abd shares his thoughts on spiderclouds, which American armaments manufacturers have been working hard to transform into antiballistics weaponry, while his colleague, Rasul, relates his filming of giants in the region. My hypothesis, he says to Badsha, is that eating human flesh makes one physically huge.

Before they part ways, he asks Badsha, where are you going next, and when he hears the response, La Maga, he claps loud, shit, man, he says, and adds that only in a few other cities in the unnameable country does the movie truly represent its title in theme and form. He talks of a place where mirrors choke streets and of an unnameable resistance exploding reflective labyrinth walls in that place. Rasul tells him that spiderthread is evermore becoming the reason for the American occupation: they want it on all army apparel, he says, from bullet-resistant vests to tank shields; it would change the shape of the soldier from heavy metal klunk to fleet feet on the ground or in the air.

Abd nods, such an inimitable resource, he says.

And so the Americans, Rasul points at the occupation army everywhere in the unnameable country.

While they converse, not too far away, my father continues taking notes of the shopkeep's description, asks what of these spiderclouds. What of them, man, quips the shopkeep. I have never seen anything like them, says Mamun Ben Jaloun. They are everywhere in Epsilante, but especially in darker places, points the seller of sunwarmed cola and sugar biscuits toward an area of gravemounds on mottled soil and serious flowers.

Mamun Ben Jaloun is curious.

SPIDERCLOUDS

Cirrus clouds cover the cemetery grounds where my mother and father first meet. A girl is collecting, basketing the clouds, which are everywhere on gravemounds, thicker between skeletal branches of the cemetery's flora. As for fauna, minnow lizards accustomed to such environments feed on spiders and insects caught in spiderwebs, dart up for quick catches before retreating into shadows. Local lore features these animals in stories; their iridescent skin means fire for short, whether flames of watchout for burn or the softer light of lust love or romance.

Light and shadow in the cemetery. Feminine silhouette against moving clouds and moon soft pulses of light against a body hunched from carrying a basket on its back. Then the girl rises and my father hears the grey sounds, her evocations: arachnids moving in the clouds their nests, spiders like the ones the camera crew has thus far encountered.

Recall the unnameable history: even before John Quincy landed on our shores and sent uniformed others like him into our nation's viscera, industrialists had appropriated spiderthread into their design and conquest, but age-old methods of spider harvesting have lingered in some communities of our nation.

Badsha Abd's records of dynamited wells are remembered today as well as his footage of traditional methods of harvesting spiderthread, which he collected at my father's insistence that we know of the spiders, but not of their close latticework, microscopic artistry, their sheer proliferation in cemeteries and gardens where people still harvest spiderwebs by hand for design work.

Her eyes haunt, serval's glisten, cat eyes in nightblackness. We needed you tonight, Badsha Abd tells Mamun Ben Jaloun after my father reunites with the film crew at Sural's hotel, takes news of their next spider destination, makes haste at the first opportunity back to the cemetery of spiderwebs to catch sight of her rare harvest. I was occupied, he says to describe his increasing absences. How so.

My father speaks briefly on the cemetery of spiderwebs as a curious scientific phenomenon but reveals few details of the girl his heart.

The camera crew begs Mamun Ben Jaloun to allow night footage of their meetings and of this region's rare methods of dealing and making with spiderthread. So adamant he is and so nervous their encounters will not culminate into even a kiss, he asks Badsha Abd for direction. The filmmaker, however, is too thirsty for footage and in no mood for love. Tell the girl to join the crew; my clothes are tatters and there are spider sanctuaries where we're going.

Night fevers, sleeplessness, biting entrails, Mamun Ben Jaloun is afflicted by involuntary summons of feline eyes by invented names because he does not know the name of the spider harvester. He stalls the crew's departure by any means, citing the importance of gossamer clouds deep in the region's dynamited wells that require filming, as he prepares for his own efforts of the heart with a demonstration. She is perplexed by his commitment to the camera's focus, its film reel and insect ardour of load, reload, his stories of its ability to catch and retell the world, by his utter devotion to a machine. What do you make, he takes her hand against all judgment. A low wind pushes the cemetery clouds and the light hesitates moonlight sunlight she is talking, touching, moving around a room in which spidersilk leotards are arranged on wax mannequins where her host of silk shirts and ballet shoes are scattered on a hard wooden floor from which rises a skeletal rack, spidersilk shawls, my own design, touch, she tells, and his fingers seem to pass through the fabric as he raises it to her cheek.

The filmmaker in my father is enthralled by the colours and objects before him, by her loom and this dressmaker's esoteric craft, this woman who invokes in him the conviction that the rhythm of all the world is flesh fingers cheek water breath eyelashes touch eyelashes, nose bumps nose, excuse me, they laugh, and hours, days pass in such cases, we will excuse them to their desires and move with Badsha Abd's words: We will move, the director says, when the search party returns with the latest news, I'm due back in the studio tomorrow.

Mist and sand, prickles of light in the distance: when my father and the girl spot the film crew caravan, they are a mile away because they had not thought before the morning's mouthfuls of patisserie they passed between lips open doors to their desires dragged morning into afternoon sun until there were no sheets on the bed anymore because they had been replaced by all the sugar in the house.

Everyone in town knew of the film crew's whereabouts, thankfully, and it was at the borders of Epsilante when they finally saw Badsha Abd's curious circus moving on horses and donkeys as if motor vehicles hadn't been invented. Then the cinematographer and the girl find feet tossing high sands smoke panting fast breaths and furious screaming, lungeing, waving arms, carrying, pushing forward. Someone notices them running and shouting and sends a man on an animal for them. Thank you, my father looks ahead at the approaching sight, then at the girl with the serval's eyes he has already begun to love.

How did you know, she asks between kisses, how did you know my name.

THE
MIRROR

The young couple employ the documentary crew's journey through desert and mountain and plain territories to understand each other's company, tirelessly conversing, kissing, grooming, cooking together, and bask in wild orchards where arachnids cast nets to catch pools of sunlight that float in their basins long after dark. They bid goodbye to Badsha Abd's caravan of cameras and rare silk only after they become dazzled enough by a place they think deserves their anchor, just as Badsha Abd departed to make ways deeper into unnameable spider sanctuaries. They decided to call La Maga, with its artificial canal recently fashioned to connect the city with the Jubba River rippling water like metal glass, home. I've been here before, my father wanted to say to my mother, but his playback singer's life seemed like another world, and La Maga had been burned and rebuilt by movie sets so many times, he could hardly recognize it.

La Maga. Here, a thirty-degree-angle man leans his whole weight on a pole. He walks the length of a ship and pushes, glides it backward through the artificial canal. Open glass elevators affixed to the outside of buildings would rise and fall according to people's needs, and it was such a bustling young city that even the President had bought a home there. He would arrive in a long motorcade without warning, and dragging a circus. He was good personal friends with the Director, who had a seat in the Privy Council and called the shots on zoning and the construction of new streets and movie sets in the country. The Director's great project, reflected in his work's title, was a madhouse of mirrors turned country into unnameable maze, which left us bewildered and frightened each time we needed to step outside for basic amenities. Luckily, the nameless rebels, who believed the film was actually a way for the national security forces to team up with the occupation Americans to contain all movement in our country to predictable reflection, broke all the mirrors near my parents' home only to find them replaced with duplicates, which they destroyed. On and on went the tit-for-tat until the time of Hedayat's birth, when the rebels managed to guard sufficient free walking space for people in our neighbourhood to do their daily business.

Recall at that time, Anwar, president of our country, governor of an unnameable region of the world, would sit at the table with his favourite horse, Dulcinea, whom he had acquired by exchanging the doll corpse of Caroline Margarita Quincy as the primary seat of his affections, having at least publicly given up all scientific experiments in necromancy; though it was said that secretly he had driven his researchers to abandon the twentieth-century laboratory in favour of the mercurial occult arts of the European medieval age in hopes of restoring the queen to life. Recall his equine love was more rewarding than the listless rooster romances he would conduct in the shadowy corners of the Presidential Palace with maids and whoever may come, and one that he defended in his mad older years as if it were the sanctified union of husband and wife. He would feed her oats from his own hand and comb her roan coat and braid her hair even in front of foreign dignitaries; he taught her to sleep curled up next to him in a vast, comfortable bed of straw mattresses. He would ride her, but never for long distances, and only for her own health, and would not allow anyone else to clean up her shit. And he still ruled the unnameable country as if he were an unruly child, with the desire to bestow upon it the order of a perfectly predictable train schedule and the eradication of simple pestilences, two things for which, after all was said and done, one could not fault him. At least during the time of Anwar the Great, people still say, men and women did not fall asleep standing up in the middle of conversations due to the plague of the tsetse fly.

But the internal dynamics of government were less than stable: the Director's encroachment on La Maga, for instance, though it brought down foreign Western investment, drench-drowned the city, was a deviance the Kremlin did not interpret lightly, and within the Privy Council and among his closest supporters, opinions were split and grumbles sounded. Anwar recognized the slow demise of the Eastern bloc; Grenadier Lhereux had been following American economists, who had been predicting it for years, and the President no longer believed in the panacea, as he did in his early years, of delinking from global capitalism. Finally a pragmatist in his autumnal years, he turned to the West, let in the termites of foreign investment and ownership, and watched the walls crumble, or, as it is more apt to say, transform into mirrors. They brought them in frigates, landed on Victoria shores with a million of them, men in uniform that planted them on the streets there, and Benediction was flooded reflective within a week. By the time they got to La Maga, American military boys were such experts at setting up labyrinth-walls they covered the city in less than a day. Though we had heard that the mirrors were no joking matter and that they were defended by the most powerful guns in the world, some people thought it was fun at first. Local goondas tried to make off with a few of them and were arrested so fast, beaten bloody pulp and stored in vacuum jailcells for so long, most people left the mirrors alone after that.

The rise of Nasiruddin Khan must be noted here, as the spoiled playboy son of a soft-drinks mogul who, after acquiring a French education, came home with a head full of 1968 ideas and wanted to take hammer and sickle to every mirror that Hollywood brought to our country. Joshimuddin Khan's continual pressing, take a job in the family multinational, please take a wife at least, fell on deaf ears, and Nasiruddin Khan, who used to spend five hours a day sculpting his hair with the exact oil combinations and treating his sensitive skin with lotions, became a guerilla. He protested the multiplication of corporate logos, the infinite Americanization of the country, by forming a mirror-breaking squad that began systematically attacking La Maga's looking glasses. The nameless Hollywood production, which quickly became known as *The Mirror* due to its reflective sets, increased its security personnel, and Governor Anwar provided added protection to its continued growth and capture of the unnameable country.

Mirror-mirrors in the streets, mirrors everywhere; mirrors reflecting growing shrinking focusing, guiding roads, walkways, our thoughts. For as long as I can remember, there was *The Mirror*. And yet. And then. Realize that for years, the nameless rebels also existed, and would silently remove obstructions in people's lives, that for decades they would remain locked in unending combat with the central government committed to allowing the occupation army. What I mean is, though in a few short years the people would make him regret it, President Anwar let the Director film everything.

In the bustling city, the young couple struggled dearly at first, and survived only because of Shukriah's sacrifices, which included pawning off the very dress she wore in Epsilante, as well as the clothes belonging to the twins, passing them off as the finest articles of damask. In a cheap flat above the hosiery store they shared with numerous families of cats, roaches, and termites, which were more ceaseless and destructive than either, she pursued a regimen of roundtheclock trampling underfoot; where is the spider when you need him.

To add to her responsibilities, Shukriah received word she would have to care for her younger sisters because her cousin, a pharmacist, could no longer support the twins' expenses due to the fact his own health was deteriorating past the point of treatment in the unnameable country. I am going to Argentina, he wrote, where I hope the people's commitment to good food will bestow upon my stomach lining its much-needed revitalization.

The twins arrived bearing gifts of antihistamines and boric acid and incurable hypochondria. In need of immediate employment, Shukriah convinced Mrs. Henry, their landlady and owner of the hosiery shop downstairs, that despite her inexperience she should be employed as a salesgirl. And although her sisters were pre-adolescents in the prime of mischief who offered no escape from their ceaseless babble that began with morning breakfast isn't as good as we used to have in Epsilante, Dada bhai would boil our eggs, Chaya doesn't like poached eggs, and continued into evening with the contest of giggles against schoolwork and television-show humour, Shukriah insisted on homeschooling them before they could afford to send them to primary school.

Meanwhile, Mamun Ben Jaloun's bank account had been frozen since the newspapers had declared his death, and while no next of kin had claimed the enclosed sum—which was not exorbitant (recall the reports of his lavish habits near the end of his playback singing career as well as the sandlot extensions to his home, which was repossessed by the President's cronies)—a complex bureaucratic procedure awaited him in his attempts at solvency.

He tried soon upon arriving at La Maga to visit the Ministry of Records and Sources to reclaim his earnings as a playback singer. Of a recent construction, the architectural influences of the ministry were clear: straight powerful lines and right angles, very few windows, and bereft of the baroque fanfare that characterized the Ministry of Radio and Communications. A Soviet architect bearing the single name of Rakitin is supposed to have designed the edifice, though the President, as usual, assumed total credit, as he did for all the important buildings throughout the unnameable country, having once taken an architecture degree at the University of Bologna.

Mamun Ben Jaloun heard not a hinge's creak but rather the crinkle of a page turning as he pushed open its front doors, and he had the distinct feeling he was entering a fantastical realm.

The receptionist, who addressed visitors, sat before a desk at the central point between two hallways verging in opposite directions, and sat enclosed in the vicissitudes of a sudoku puzzle, scrawling numbers on the page before him and tearing out clumps of hair, anxiously repeating, It can't be, it just can't, muttering and spitting.

Excuse me.

One moment.

Three hundred moments passed and the air grew heavy and began to smell foul. Out of the corner of an eye, the receptionist satisfied himself of the uninspiring dimensions of the person before him and coughed, Tell me, would you alert anyone if I used the number six twice to make this set work, he pushed the crumpled pages of last week's newspaper toward Mamun Ben Jaloun.

You have my word, Mamun swore, as it seemed like an easy way to push along.

The clerk only rejoiced in his answer, and with a few tugs on his long, thin beard returned to the puzzle in earnest.

I am merely looking for

Not yet, the clerk crossed out some figures, replaced them with new ones until satisfied with having solved a great dilemma. He directed with a hand without looking up from the puzzle: To file for sickness or matrimony, follow the hallway to the left and up the stairs to the second-floor lobby; for a minor insurance claim, also to the left, but up four flights of stairs, it will wind you, walk slowly, though that is only personal advice; for a major insurance claim, right hallway, third door, easy enough; for all other matters consult the General Information Desk on the second floor: take the right vestibule all the way to the end and go down to the basement.

The basement but also the second floor.

The clerk did not repeat himself, content with having supplied the correct information. For two moments longer, Mamun Ben Jaloun remained standing in place. But then, noticing that it was he himself who was delaying the task at hand, he walked toward his destination.

In the equatorial climate of the region one never feels cold, and yet in the important ministries it remains fashionable to run the air conditioning at blizzard settings in order to reflect the atmospheres of the northern continents. The farther Mamun walked down the hall, the colder he felt, and he swore at himself, though he could not have foreseen the circumstances, for not having brought a scarf. His chest began to hurt and he was sure icicles were forming in his lungs and that surely he would contract pneumonia, pulmonary fever, other deathly illnesses. His breaths were slow, laborious contractions, and several times he knelt to rest in the empty hallway, which filled up with cries or maybe laughter, though from where, what sources. When he reached the end, he wondered if he should turn around, the basement would surely be even colder and damper, but he had travelled so far and it had cost him perhaps nearly half a day; besides, the tender memory of his friends deserved at least a portion more of his suffering, let alone the monetary promise he had made to Shukriah.

What he discovered, however, was quite the contrary: the basement was a tropical hothouse, well lit, with colourful weeds growing seamlessly out of cracks in the floor. His destination turned out to be an expansive room with a large set of movable screens that workers shifted to make new three-coloured/four-cornered workspaces, and which looked as chaotic as a university newspaper office, with movie posters, stacks of papers, and typesetting machines growing like hallway plants out of the floor. Employees, or people one gathered were employees, rushed about fulfilling what were no doubt important tasks judging from the swiftness and surety of their movements.

Mamun Ben Jaloun wanted to test the contradictory information he had received, second floor and basement, to see whether he had arrived in the right place, and a bespectacled woman, noticing a stranger was standing around with no place to go, approached him with suspicion: Are you here for the warehouse position.

Before he could answer, someone from behind a nearby screen shouted: Tell him to fill out an application and rush it immediately to Augusto.

Recall he had come here to file, but before any full thought could be uttered, Mamun Ben Jaloun found himself led by the hand by the bespectacled woman whose feet flew faster and dragged him flying behind her, You must understand that unlike other ministries we do not tolerate tardiness, you are already several hours late for your appointment and Augusto is generally an intolerant man. While I do admit that lately he has acquired some respect for me due to my organization of the last two shipments, I cannot spend my arduously acquired professional currency on strangers. Strangers, she stopped for a second and let go of his hand, which glowed from being nearly wrenched from the socket, to whom do I have the pleasure of speaking.

Ben Jaloun, my father panted a reply, you walk very fast, quicker than most people run.

Thank you, she seemed legitimately pleased by the observation, and before giving him the chance to make her acquaintance in turn, the nameless woman grabbed his hand again and flew up a set of stairs, crossed an expansive hallway in under a minute, made some deft turns and then: they arrived at the entrails of industry.

Recall that while his parents, Gita Nothingatall and Zachariah Ben Jaloun, began their stories serving the unnameable country's brain and sympathetic nervous system, it would be my father's fate to wind up at the colon of the unnameable country. Around him, forklifts struggled desperately with shapes. The light fell crooked and smelled noxious. The sounds were those of the hidden variety to which only the average person, the factory worker, the warehouse dispatcher, the lowly street pirate, or the restaurant dishwasher, is privy, and although my father had once been a famous playback singer, he had clearly fallen underground.

What did you say.

My mouth said shudder, replied my father to Augusto.

A nearby man broke from a group of workers who were laughing loudly and unkindly. He was almost perfectly spherical and struggled to remain on his feet as he approached them.

Morgiana, what runt have you brought me, I told you I need a big man to move these mirror-walls, at least two hundred pounds.

I am sorry, Augusto, the woman genuflected, I assure you I won't fail you next time, she bowed her head as my father stared mouth agape, astounded by her sycophancy, but he was the only one who answered the call, she mumbled a barely audible excuse.

At this point, Mamun Ben Jaloun might have admitted that he was not here for a job and instead he had only come to unlock his bank account and report the deaths of three of his friends in a small town called Epsilante, but it touched him to the quick when recalling he was an unemployed man with a family to support, a beggar, in short, who had little right to be choosy about where he worked or in what conditions.

I was a, he began, about to say singer.

185

You were, were you, Augusto said, before telling him the job consisted of heavy lifting, no experience required, have you ever dealt with mirrors.

No, sir.

Be careful because they scratch easy, and because of the bad luck business when shattering.

Scandalized by his weak lungs and lack of spinal fortitude, Shukriah was put slightly at ease by Mamun Ben Jaloun's awareness that steady employment was a surer way of staying alive than by savings. Within several days, however, it grew obvious that my father, who had always been among the boniest of the Screens and had been physically weakened, as had they all by recent misadventures, dropped and cracked three mirrors while also nearly stepping in the way of a forklift.

You are not meant for this job, the spherical Augusto informed him, not unkindly, as my father pleaded with him on his way out that if there were another position, sir, elsewhere in the ministry, I should be happy to.

Probably, in fact certainly, Augusto said, though I don't know of any, try consulting General Information Services, and slammed the door behind him.

Mamun Ben Jaloun discovered the same hallway through which Morgiana had dragged him flying behind her lightning feet and he tried for several days to traverse the hallways of the ministry in hopes of returning to the office with the movable screens and the colourful plants which grew right out of cracks in the floor. People hurried by and glowered or stared right through him as if they were ghosts, some smoked thick cigars and unfurled newspapers from under their armpits. Farther along, a pair of old men played Chinese checkers while a crush of people threw change, placed bets shouting incomprehensible.

He slept in a thoroughfare and awoke with a cop's shining flashlight a retinoscope into his eyes. He heard them say not him, though no one spoke the words. He was not arrested.

Sometime later, he arrived at a snaking queue and tapped a shoulder to ask what is this here, brother.

The man sniffled, and he shifted from foot to wooden foot. Veterans' Bureau, informed the hobbling man, before mumbling something about an infection. He opened his mouth wide as if to a doctor: a swollen mouth in which there unhinged from the upper palate and from the lower jaw innumerable rows of suckers not unlike a lamprey's, and the mouth within the mouth hissed at Mamun Ben Jaloun like a prehistoric marine animal.

My father shuddered and hurried on. He had not eaten for forty hours and purchased a spicy clove and cinnamon tea from an old woman who sat on a stool in front of a cauldron, which was heated by a lonely flame underneath, powered by a canister of fuel. She asked which hallway was his destination, and he responded second floor, basement, to which she nodded with closed eyes and pursed lips before proffering directions for several minutes without stopping thiswaythat-wayrightthenleft, she kept saying until Mamun realized this ministry building was a more massive labyrinth than he had imagined or that the woman was mad or simply desired the company of a stranger on whom to unleash words, any words at all.

He walked along after passing her a few coins more than she had asked for, and came upon the first stairwell he had seen since he began his journey. Gingerly, he lowered himself down the steps, not wishing to spill the hot tea, taking sips now and then, but his care would be lost to the wind, which, once he opened the door to the belowfloor, blew with such gale force that the hot fluid flew up and scalded his face. In pain, Mamun Ben Jaloun pressed himself flat against the wall, against the wind like a cockroach, and inched along on his side until the first door, which was locked. He continued along for ten minutes until the second door, whose handle turned; he was thrown headlong into some-one's chest.

Mamun Ben Jaloun excused himself profusely but the stranger waved off the sorries, patted down his tie, none of that, there has been some malfunction of the ventilation system, you're not to.

Then a gaze of recognition from those large eyes belonging to a flat, elliptical face as the neck extended forward for closer scrutiny: You are Mamun Ben Jaloun, is this true.

My father was confused; it had been so long since anyone had recognized him by face.

The playback singer. There were one or two photos of you in maga-zines, he explained when my father said nothing.

Yes, my father smiled sheepishly, though I haven't sung a note in years.

Ah, the man lifted a finger to his lips, my wife still puts on some of your records now and then. At any rate, I was expecting to hear from you tomorrow, not today, at least as General Information Services informed; but the ventilation mishap gives me some time today and I don't mind seeing you now.

They knew that

Yes, they said it would probably take three days due to the traffic and your inexperience with this part of the ministry. Please sit, sit, please, may I offer

Mamun asked for water as the man disappeared behind a large stack of papers. Mamun looked around. The sign on the desk said Assistant Archives Supervisor, and there was no name. The room bore a musty smell and water dripped from the ceiling at various parts onto plastic buckets, and on the sides of the higher-than-human stacks of paper it was possible to see the bright orange mould growing.

Supervisor smiled as he offered water and the meeting began in earnest after a few further instantiations of smalltalk, reminiscences of what La Maga Studios was before the Great Fire, what it had become now that the President's forces had infiltrated, Sharmilla, do you know the actress.

Yes, my father said, I have worked with her and even offended her on occasion.

Supervisor leaned closer and placed a hand at one corner of his mouth, this is just a secret from a fan to a former filmi: she is an Organ, an intelligence officer.

Sharmilla, Mamun raised his voice unconsciously. He was incredulous: I didn't imagine her to be politically motivated one way or another.

That's precisely the kind of individual they look for. What one needs are eyes and ears, nothing more, just your organs without the body, because otherwise.

For a moment the assistant archives supervisor just stared; then with his hands he torqued an imaginary wrench: Imagine I am twisting your genitals, Mr. Ben Jaloun. My father's face narrowed as the assistant archives supervisor laughed a little too loudly. Anyhow, I am taking us away from the true purpose of our meeting.

Yes, my father said coolly, I am looking for work that involves no lifting.

Well, I'm sorry, Mr. Ben Jaloun, the Archives Department of the Ministry of Records and Sources cannot promise that you wouldn't have to lift the odd file or thoughtreel.

Thought what.

Thoughtreel, yes, it's best we get right to the Archives themselves and I'll show you our library. Supervisor stepped around the desk and the high various folders, he pressed a button Mamun had not noticed, and the wall to the left of them sprang apart and revealed a larger than usual but still cramped dumbwaiter. We shall have to squeeze tightly, I don't trust you to go alone since you have never been to the Archives.

My father didn't believe it could be done, perhaps they would be crushed in the attempt, and when he suggested the mortal possibility, Supervisor only repeated that he did not trust Mamun Ben Jaloun to take the dumbwaiter alone.

Come along, it's been done many times.

So they pressed body to body like cooked shrimp in an elevator fetid breaths for the ride, in a machine a tiny box whose dimensions also held Supervisor's large side-bag dug into Mamun's ribs/ the elevator jerked, it dropped two or three stories, caught its fall, before descending a long distance smoothly. When they got out it took a long time for Mamun to straighten out his spine and for his eyes to adjust to the dim light showed dark shelves as they got closer. Lines, squares, and rectangles extended upward several stories, and above them floated a black sky from which shone a track of faintly lit red obelisks.

The sounds joined one another, started and stopped at specific. On their own accord. They turned corners, which led to more of what seemed like the same. But these were no aimless peregrinations.

You can clearly hear the sounds dividing sections, Supervisor said, necessary sounds due to dim lighting in the Archives, which is also necessary in order to preserve the thoughtreels as well as certain photosensitive files, clearly demarcated by acoustic markers examinable by plugging into the headphone jack of any thoughtreel in any region of this library. He demonstrated by removing a set of headphones from his side-bag, and removed a metal receptacle from the shelves. He plugged the headphone jack into the thoughtreel, pressed play, and passed Mamun the headphones and immediate lightningflashes/ sounds climbed dendrites in my father's skull, sounds that flecks of wind, pushed words, and my father could catch them, though most jagged syntax were sliced metal to the ears as nerves grow leaf and sepals from the bones in his hand. My father nearly lost his balance as tissues moved, murmured, partial thoughts appeared, and when taken together left the sense upon removing headphones: my body, a bloody waste-land, Mamun Ben Jaloun heard someone else's thoughts say to him. You can one-by-one the minds of the 1920s when you walk along their shelf alley, Supervisor said pleasantly; catch the brass band cacophony sometime, he pointed when they got to reels from 1940 to 1950, which sometimes sing, informed Supervisor, while on other occasions you'll plug into a dead note, he continued, meaning this is what remains of my brain. Then there are times, Supervisor lowered his voice, as he kneaded a sound with his hands, kesh-kesh-kesh-kesh-kesh-kesh-kesh-kesh, he kept saying, before informing my father that Black Organs had gathered minds over decades and organized human remainders into an order that seems confusing at first, but you will get to know this system, Mamun Ben Jaloun.

My father fumbled through his own bag, I don't have a notepad, he apologized for all the lost/ But Supervisor waved, one must remember. Eventually, you will be provided with a penlight, Mamun Ben Jaloun, when you have to gather specific records and bring them upstairs for investigation.

I don't understand what these records specify exactly, and what is a thoughtreel exactly.

Have you heard of Department 6119, Supervisor used the moniker employed commonly by insiders, and which, because my father had been transferred indoors after first having served as a gun-toting government employee, a guard protecting the crown of offices and corridors against smoulder streets of the descendants of Bemis or Illium or Dictum or Amun of the Maroons, whose once upon a time is necessary to understand why the unnameable country remained a hothouse and who today still screamed as droves in outdoor voices about their respective contemporary dilemmas and grievances, should have known. Supervisor pivoted on his right foot so that he was now directly turned toward. He stood a full foot taller than my father and his shoulders were so robust and his nostrils so wide that in the strange light he appeared more minotaur than man.

Of course, my father said.

Of course, Supervisor said after a pause and a squint of areyoulying eyes. The thoughtreels are recordings of Individuals of Interest to the State, he informed my father.

Recordings of their minds, you mean.

Precisely.

I don't understand.

Supervisor cast a sidelong glance as if to indicate are you daft, have you never swung on the grapevine of rumour, what social animal are you, and explained that the process was complex and for the most part classified to employees of the Archives, even to himself. If you must know anything further, understand that we are the colon of the Ministry of Records and Sources, he continued, and after us it is only the incinerator or the sea.

They walked corridors lit by red obelisks, and as they walked, all the thoughtreels crowded incomprehensible, murmur on shelves. And though every so often a sound would ring out to inform them of which region of the Archives they were traversing, it was difficult to differentiate clime and era, the decades of thought.

Do you have any more words, Supervisor asked.

Slight hesitation, and then: when do I start.

Right; you will begin at seven-thirty sharp tomorrow.

Must we ride the dumbwaiter again, my father trailed behind.

Supervisor: Like always.

———————

Time passed and the tiny flat above old Mrs. Henry's hosiery shop grew reordered. The last residents, who, according to their remaining belongings and their briny lingering odour, were quite possibly nautical pirates, grew less dense and the new family asserted its presence. The cats were reduced to two in number, a tabby and a tortoiseshell, the rest of them given away to neighbours or rendered destruction, while the cockroaches were driven to ruin by Shukriah's introduction of jumping spiders. The old plumbing, which had been clogged for years by knotted and compressed hair, was cleared of its obstructions and no longer beleaguered them with thick gurgling sounds at night, while due to frequent nationwide power outages their home was occasionally plunged into darkness and they outlined the apartment with so many wax candles in preparation that Mrs. Henry, during a short visit upstairs, remarked that she had not laid eyes on such a collection since her father's wake in a Roman Catholic basilica.

The combined income of Mamun Ben Jaloun and his partner (let me inform that the pair were not husband and wife and would never feel the need to formalize their relationship with the weighty consecration of marriage) allowed the twins Reshma and Chaya to attend school, who both showed promise, as they focused their indefatigable lightning energy toward scholastic diligence.

At first, Mamun Ben Jaloun would tell stories about his strange job: And then I have to crush into the width of a tiny crevette, he would crouch low as the girls giggled and clapped and assailed him with questions about the specifics of the dumbwaiter, which they wanted desperately to ride and he promised them one day they would, though he always stopped short of mentioning the smells of the archives or the reels to which they were appended, and not because he himself did not exactly understand their significance.

At that time, there was no shortage of food in the house, and Shukriah and Mamun felt so much love for each other it was often impossible to restrain their fingers, like anxious anemone caressing and kneading, for they had at most a few hours in the week to themselves alone, when they sent the twins to the neighbours' with a rice pudding bribe, go play, they would pat them on their heads before diving into their sea's desires, which were no secret to anyone, and which made the neighbours laugh, since their noises could be heard all the way from Xasan Sierra's cigarette shop as well as five hundred metres in every other direction. The apartment would grow so humid with their lovemaking that snails would take up residence and crabs from the Indian Ocean would find their way inside by scuttling under the door. Then the couple would be forced to throw all the crustaceans into a boiling pot and open all the windows in a desperate attempt to aerate the rooms before the twins returned.

Their lives were so self-enclosed, so obsessed were they with their delighted repetitions, that they could not have desired anything more, and it was not altogether surprising when Shukriah announced one day that she was pregnant. Mamun Ben Jaloun had the sense and muscular composure to pull up his brows in time to forget for one moment how would the family support another child, and he feigned unfettered joy as the young family celebrated with neighbours for seven non-stop days, lighting ribbon flares and green chili firecrackers and explosive candles of coloured light, as everyone feasted on sweets until sickened.

It was around the time the unnameable country's debts could no longer be accommodated by the Soviets, and against the Kremlin's severest warnings, the President felt forced to meet with a team from the International Monetary Fund that had been hounding him for years like leprechauns that would turn up in the maid's sweepings from under the armoire, would appear out of banishment unannounced at his door with please accept this gift a block of hay and a bag of oats for the first lady Dulcinea, or would whisper pss pss suggestions from the corner of his skull even during meetings and sheepishly adjust their ties when he thundered how in the world did you manage until, finally, when their buzzbuzzing became impossible to avoid and the country's fiscal situation turned utterly unmanageable, he agreed, okay let's break bread together at the same table and draw up a Hollywood structural adjustment policy of metamorphosing La Maga into a vast film set, thereby inviting all the vultures of the world.

Recognizing his preternatural paranoia and trying to allay his concern that film types were naturally rebellious—just recall what I had to do in La Maga, Misters Brown and Golgotha as well as you others whose names I do not remember since there are so many of you but you all leach my bones the same way and speak in an identical mosquito-pitch English—the sixteen pupilless economists all shook their heads in unison and offered that, in fact, the changes they wanted would deepen the President's capacity to bestow order onto the parts of the country that were rebelling against his rule, and the money, Mr. President, as they snapped open a dozen briefcases simultaneously, just think.

Not one of them, however, could have predicted the thick resistance from the student union of La Maga Technical Institute, which began organizing rallies and circulated petitions to remove the Director from the city and shut down production of *The Mirror*, which was the name of the film. Recall that early in *The Mirror*'s invention, when its dissolution was still possible, crowds of non-unionized oil workers, unemployed graduates of the humanities and social sciences, teachers, garments workers, members of the nomadic community, all of whom had been deeply affected by its damming of the Jubba River to create a biblical flood scene, gathered by the tens of thousands before retreating, burning and bleeding from rubber-bullet wounds and tearing from the eyes from the putrescent gas hurled into their faces by the shielded exoskeletal constabulary. Firehoses and the threat of the fire next time will not be so merciful: recall the movie crew also set fire to whole neighbourhoods to dramatize the destruction of La Maga Studios by the American bombings; to be clear, *The Mirror* wanted to recreate the unnameable country from the beginning to its prophetic calamitous demise irrespective of cost, whether monetary or in corpse-form. In order to bewilder and entrap the locals, for a filmic reason was never established, old alleyways were proved without warning one day to be false, as someone (anyone, an empty word meaning many people) saw extending before him the path to his home, the one he had every day travelled for maybe twenty years, but this time his nose banged into glass and he realized the door before him was reflection, another trick of the mirrors.

From warehouses like that of Augusto's, inestimable mirror-walls travelled in coffin boxes throughout the city, and with the addition of smoke and light and the incessant camera gaze, the locals forgot the feeling of living real lives. Recall, because they remain, checkpoints were re-established throughout the city and guards patted down and searched everyone for weapons just as they did before Independence. Unemployment skyrocketed and the mirrors became more than a nuisance, grew into the means by which to restrict food supplies and flow of other necessities. Since La Maga residents could not be trusted, employees from Bangladesh, Bhutan, across the border Ethiopia, down south Somalia, from Vietnam and China arrived to take up jobs boarding up neighbourhoods with reflective walls until the city began to resemble an impassable funhouse.

Some people became incapable of understanding the differences between their moving bodies and their reflections and turned mad from looking at themselves all inverted reduced enlarged reflected every day. Still others died of natural causes, but continued living reflected lives in the mirrors, having forgotten the natural course of their bodies through time; one saw dead people walking in the souks, talking with the living, reaching out for plums through the looking glass, frustrated by their inability to touch anything in the world. Astonished, their families became confused about whether to mourn. Then several hundred cats died of a mysterious illness, and the stench of desperation could be detected even on the breaths of the most resistant of the city's intelligentsia, some of whom began to believe in the invincibility of *The Mirror* and argued that since the film was meant to be the longest ever in history, all fragments of the recorded images could prove useful to the production, even its possible defeat.

A cult of the Director sprang up and some young people claimed the resistance was a vain attempt to curb Progress, that the Soviets had directed the course of the nameless country's history for many years without significant improvement in the lives of ordinary people, so why not now the West.

But who was the Director and what did they say of the Director. To us, he had no other name but Smith; we knew he had once worked as a psychiatrist, was originally educated at Columbia University, completed a dissertation on sociopathy some twenty years earlier, and was noted early in his career to have been quite fond of the rhododendron as a flower of memory, a means of inciting yes in his patients and willing them to aleatory remembrance of any moment of their past he wished to probe.

———————

Sometime in the second year of the film, the industrialist Nasiruddin Khan, whose ownership of seventeen soda factories in the continent and whose desire to become an even more ruthless soft-drink manufacturer than Coca-Cola was known to all, began directing some of his expertise with paramilitary forces to the cause of resisting *The Mirror*. Training camps were set up in the Karkaars and our boys began to pretend they were gauchos recruited by Fidel's army while/ our boys began to revive the Battle of Algiers and disguised themselves among the urban masses, to wear women's clothing and hide missiles under dresses, to fire Kalashnikovs and garrotte with fishing lines and onehands behind backs. The Russians supplied weapons, and bombs began to explode in La Maga neighbourhoods and locals died in droves; and when cameramen also died and gaffer boys were wounded and when the film equipment caught fire.

At first the Director's security forces as well as the police and state army were taken aback; mirrors exploded and liberated forgotten streets, communication devices were stolen, so-called collaborators were interrogated and revealed the moviemaker's macabre secret designs on entrapping not only La Maga but also, in time, the whole unnameable country. The nameless militia posted their men at every street corner and travelled house to house to recruit young boys as looksees and follow-follows. While the resistance now had wide popular support in the city, few residents were happy about the escalation of violence.

This has got to stop, Shukriah said one day as the cockroaches in the apartment began warring against the daddy-long-legs in greater number, or else there will be no sugar for the pancake batter because the roaches will get to it all.

One outcome of the extended conflict was the extreme protraction of your humble narrator's gestation inside his mother's womb. Recall from schoolboy lessons pregnancy for the field mouse lasts no more than three weeks prior to the litter; in *Felis domesticus*, two months at most; in larger mammals, such as the elephant, this period extends to an average of eleven months, while the mother whale must endure it as long as two years. Doctors were baffled, neighbours and friends called hex and foul, while others debated whether the condition could bear possible boon to my health and future life. Let it be known that the shepherdess Shukriah carried me in her womb for no less than eight years, six months, fourteen days, twelve hours, and twenty-one minutes from fertilization onward; add thirty-seven hours if you wish to calculate that figure from the moment of conception.

My mother, however, for all the nauseating discomfort, the back-aches and strange dreams, inexplicable desires to eat silt or freshly blown glass, to drink the pure mucus of the snail, would lapse into bouts of laughter and hysteria during which she would swear she could hear me gurgle and speak in gestus, listen to what he says: He will not come out until this war has come to an end, can you believe it, trickster naughty boy this one.

Tell him to hurry up and get born, my father would mutter in frustration, for the girls, who were now in the early stages of puberty and somewhat slower and more cautious in their physical movements, were swiftly walling themselves into unnameable countries of their own design. They imported construction materials from faraway places, while Mamun Ben Jaloun neither understood nor wanted any part of the punk slogan no future nor the disco injunction to party off the wall, which belonged respectively to Reshma and Chaya, as they had begun to differentiate themselves by dress and hairstyle and musical ethos, and to quarrel ceaselessly about popular figures and issues of which he was totally ignorant. They raspberry-tongued at the everywhere cameras and blew pink bubblegum bubbles into the faces of the film crew, compared notes with friends on the handsome moustaches of the rebels, whose soft absurd shoes of canvas and their ability to disappear into cats' shadows, as well as the size of their rifles. They left pink bubbleballoons hanging in the walls of the flat like bloated frog throats, and it was clear they would not remain a moment longer in the tiny apartment above the hosiery shop than they had to.

All the while, Mamun wished for his wife to return to her regular prior-to-pregnancy self, before she became the garrulous whispering, laughingtoherself woman into which the fetal Hedayat had transformed her. Everything had changed. What in the old days was sure to be the sound of wedding firecrackers or the effusion of Roman candles in the celebration of a birth was now more likely the exchange of shots between the Director's security forces and the rebels or the explosion of a mirror-wall.

Years earlier, when he and Shukriah were close, she would be able to say upon his return home you were in suchandsuchasection in the Archives today, not because the odours would linger on his clothing but because they shared everything then and it was natural to be able to understand the particulars of the other's reality whenever either of them wanted to. Later, during the period of her oracular conversations with her unborn son, Mamun Ben Jaloun felt the tain of a mirror creep up between his mind and hers, as if when she gazed at him she saw only her/ and he was banished from knowing her thoughts in those long eight and a half years. Shukriah, meanwhile, honed her insights to certain prescience and would have been able to travel through the labyrinth of thoughts blindfolded if she had wanted, to distinguish ages and genders and to outline in advance whole stories of magnetized captured minds without the aid of a tape player.

It took years and much entreaty for Mamun Ben Jaloun to acquire a penlight from Supervisor, who reluctantly provided and which enabled our hero to read the names printed on the Archive reels. For many months, his job involved only to identify by the sound quality of the recorded thoughts which magnetic files were chronologically misplaced in row upon row of unending columns. While he knew, because Supervisor had informed him, and as well due to his official wanderings, that the Archives were strictly divided into quadrants, he would often discover that one section ended too soon or another started before expected. Having a penlight did not help with these broader demarcations since the effect of the instrument was deliberately weak and designed only for close inspections of individual files, and he was told repeatedly to clip his nosehairs, to habituate himself to wearing deafening headphones when not at work so as to keep a clear set of ears for Archives sounds, and, ultimately, to hone his hearing organs.

It was a hard job that started you dawn-early, made you wait outside Supervisor's office with other Archives clerks, holding dearly onto loose articles of clothing or your briefcase if you happened to carry such a piece of luggage, because the ventilation system perpetually; Supervisor had been wrong in saying the breakdown was temporary, though the force of the winds had been fixed down to thunderstorm-levels rather than gale. One could not fraternize with one's co-workers during these minutes in the hallway over tea due to the inclement weather, and spent the time instead pressed flat like a beetle against the wall to avoid being blown away. Then the door would slam open and Supervisor would yell the name of the next man and drag him by the arm into the office as one by one the day's assignments poured in from higher chains of command.

Within an hour, or at most seventy-five minutes, one found oneself curled up, lying down in a maggot shape little comma in the dumbwaiter. To discover a misplaced thoughtreel, the most common assignment for a novice, it was necessary first to recognize the wrong recording in the score: to detect the crinkle sound of that shirt earlier today doesn't belong with the thoughtreel that gives us the sound of unleaded gasoline the first year of its wide introduction in the unnameable country with the adjacent precise recording of the football match. One crept along until homing in on the precise reel until it was possible to pluck out the mistake, before placing it in the right section.

On occasion, while he handled the roundmetal containers, Mamun Ben Jaloun felt dizzy. Other times he experienced strange effects that at first he interpreted as combinations of loneliness and the red-lit darkness of that vast subterranean library. The sounds would vibrate everything, the depths of his entrails. Then an almost-voice, a wilderness cry that disappeared almost as soon as it arose and returned him to the maze of sounds. In these short moments he felt like weeping from the gut. The transition from sensation to clear sound, the synthetic formation of stories: and truly, this did happen: my father began to feel over time what his wife had always sensed from afar and what he knew rationally to be a fact, namely that living minds were stored in the thoughtreels. At the exact moment of revelation he felt only fear, and trembled under pale sheets in his bed upon hurrying feverish home the first time a thoughtreel sang out to him without the aid of headphones plugged into a magnetic player.

Hark unto me, Mamun Ben Jaloun, for, like you, I too once had life. Recall: limp-handed cluttering to the floor, he had let drop the roundmetal container.

Cover me, he said to Shukriah, as the walls shivered. And she brought him another blanket because all the blood had left his extremities.

What happened, she asked.

I heard the angel of God speaking, Mamun replied.

Shukriah said that was blasphemy and held him tightly, asked again: Tell me what happened today, but Mamun just teeth-chattered. Recall he did not submit at once to the powers of his own understanding. He had never heard voices quite this way and was troubled about his mental health.

A question: did Shukriah not know the details of what terrified Mamun, or was she, by that time, lost mirror-mirror in my head, in the looking-glass world of her own suffering and solipsistic desires to eat silt among other desires. If the latter, then where does the culprit-seeking blame-casting finger point: from the womb he would not allow their love to flow as the simple love between a man and a woman not only because he desired all his mother's love but because through her he wanted to siphon all the love in the world.

In the Pits, as the Archives were known among the clerks, there were no friends and many wanderers, like Mamun, sent to gather the errant file that had not been listened to perhaps in twenty years because some higherup inspections agent at the Ministry of Records and Sources demanded. There were also rumours that the Archives hid a priestly caste of silent ghosts, who wandered searching furtively for the one file that would contain within it all the thoughtreels, an infinite and sacred document. It was said the Archives were in fact so vast that some employees had descended below and never ridden the dumbwaiter back up to the surface. Supposedly, they had managed to cultivate edible plants in the dim light because they knew which plumbing pipes to tap for clean water and even farmed rodents for food; they lived in solitude and total custodial devotion to the Archives. Some even claimed that these rogues played mischievous tricks on clerks, that in fact they were the ones who misplaced the files and forced the work onto their shoulders, but let me make clear that no one ever verified the existence of such a cult or discovered material evidence of their occult beliefs or the slightest proof of an infinite thoughtreel that contained all the reels. More common were the whistling ghosts, ordinary clerks who by sound warned others of their presence and reminded them of their discontented solitude. Of these, my father became acquainted with one Simon, a stooping melancholic who happened on occasion to arrive in the mornings at around the same time as Mamun.

After they happened to curl up into the dumbwaiter together several times, Mamun gathered up the courage to disclose the event of the singing reel, which had never repeated but which still sang in his head time to time: Has it ever happened to you, man.

We are keepers of dead souls, Simon shrugged, I wouldn't be surprised if one of these tin cans leapt at your throat or bit you.

When my father didn't answer, Simon dropped a thoughtreel. Did you hear something, my father asked.

No, did you.

One day, Mamun M awoke gasping for breath, swimming out of a dream of Qismis, of whom he had not dreamed in many years. He dreamed that they were putting to bed a flock of children, who wandered pissing and laughing in a cauliflower patch, and that now, exhausted, they were about to retire to her bedroom and make love, but they never got beyond the first kiss, which was so long and which sucked so much air out of his lungs that Shukriah, bewildered, was forced to beat him on his back with the flat of her hand in order to restore his breathing, but still Mamun Ben Jaloun did not awaken and for several minutes spoke to her as his former lover.

At work, he wandered through the pitch markers, unable to find the reel of his search, a radio singer's magnetic iteration of middle C that just wasn't there, and not even the penlight could help him. He hummed a movie tune to reset his ears, drummed against his kneecaps, contrary to departmental regulations, which encouraged hushhushing all personal sounds, including the inadvertent gastrointestinal. Sometimes the sound of his hair growing oozed out of his forearms and scalp, while another time the sound of raisins hitting a metal bowl; the latter directed him to his restless life of women and song.

The Archives, which were generally cool due to their subterranean placement, had heated today to an unbearable degree, though it is true he had been warned by Supervisor that the boilers were malfunctioning and the whole building would be affected for the next several days. Mamun Ben Jaloun unbuttoned his shirt and took a large whiff of raw onions. He suspired the words orange blossoms without understanding their meaning. Unexpectedly, Mamun Ben Jaloun wanted nothing more than to strip nude and munch on raw onion after onion; from where did the hunger.

He arrived at a portion of the Archives where all the thoughtreels had tumbled off the shelves and lay in a pile like drying. Such disorder was so unnatural in the Archives that he forgot his assigned task and began replacing on the shelves one by one. His skin tingled as he touched the roundmetal containers. Then the dizziness again and Mamun placed his fingers into his ears for a moment and sang one pure note that resonated through the whole subterranean cavity. The dizziness passed and everything halted. Then he bent low to pick up the next reel and shone his penlight at the tag: Zachariah Ben Jaloun.

Hidden organs passed conflicting received messages inside Ben Jaloun the son. Recall he had discovered his father once earlier and had been enslaved by him. And recall Mamun Ben Jaloun had played so many roles in his life—motorcycle pirate wardrobe orderly street urchin playback singer cinematographer prisoner of a spider woman, now the husband of a former shepherdess and an Archives clerk—and had flowed from one to the next with such ease and thoughtlessness for the past, never imagining lost time as a violent break with the moving present, not forever gone and always enjoined to now by desire and memory, that, above all else, when the past returned as ghostly physical ailments he had begun to experience lately it filled him with fear, and with a greater curiosity to understand. He stiffened his back and turned behind him, then stared as far ahead as possible through the black fog, though he knew there was probably no one around for at least one hundred square metres, before hiding the thoughtreel under his shirt.

He hurried home, shivering from an elemental fever. Septillion reptilian scales and ashen hair: Mamun Ben Jaloun was drenched in his own perspiration. Cover me, he said to Shukriah through chattering teeth, and she did so.

Tell me what happened, she asked, touching his cool forehead with the back of a hand, then running her hands through his hair and rising ash up from his hair: a grey fog of ash covered the room and Shukriah began to cough and to choke. Bedridden by a fever that doctors could not detect and at the mercy of the bubblegum twins, who used the opportunity to assail him with inedible concoctions they called soup and with anecdotes and intrigues from their lives whose dramas were too complex for a feverish/even unfeverish mind to untangle, it took Shukriah three weeks to find the right magnetic tape player to play the reel, though she located it just down the street in Xasan Sierra's ciga-rette shop. The vendor was unwilling to part with what he claimed was a family heirloom.

Too many dollars to buy, he said, and would not sell, but eventu-ally agreed to rent it to her for one week.

Shukriah set up the instrument in their bedroom with the door firmly shut to block smells of the lizard soup the twins were cooking, and at first the sounds made no sense to her at all. They seemed like the effect of a voice refracted through a prism or a broken mirror. But Mamun Ben Jaloun recognized certain properties of rhythm that were not dissimilar to his own way of thinking. He played and replayed the reel until the week was over and then went shivering to Xasan Sierra himself, begging for another week's extension, which the vendor reluc-tantly granted, but only after pawning off onto Mamun a carton of clove cigarettes and demanding an increase by twenty percent on the instru-ment's rent.

So again, the squeal of the tape, let's listen: blank verses in whispers trying to hide even from his listening ownmind the here-andthere thoughts everyday worries, flight of an opening stanza before the poem puts down feet, stamps out its meter, spreads out multiplies. Suddenly the who are you and why do you do, questions and repeti-tions, the cracks of the batons and the penetrations into/the rupture and the twisted desolate, the pitter-patter reminders only. Mamun Ben Jaloun is studying hard to understand the madness and disintegration of Zachariah Ben Jaloun's mind, the transformation of the thinking person into a butcher-functionary: the thoughtreel illustrates the way each sentence of Zachariah Ben Jaloun's thoughts initially functioned not unlike a mathematical set with one of its phrases (orange blossoms, for instance) behaving as a variable that would repeat the preceding verse.

There occurred two functions of the mind simultaneously, he noticed: one directly concerned with the world at large and the other internal and secret, doing the work of poetry. As is understandable, the tape was a fragment of the untenable infinity of the blank verses of *Facsimile* that Zachariah Ben Jaloun constantly rehearsed in his younger days while working at the British Intelligence Service in the Heart of Arabia, replaying them infinitely and growing heavier each day with a series-poem like none other in history, which was never published and which he could not commit to the page owing to a mysterious ailment that eventually rendered him illiterate. As it went on to reveal, the regression formula of Zachariah Ben Jaloun's mind was disturbed through torture by the introduction of jagged rhythms white noise, until, as the second side of the thoughtreel, which Shukriah had accidentally played first, evinced, his mind would spontaneously attempt to make the same leaps, but found itself destroyed incapable; the tape stopped at around age thirty.

By the time Mamun Ben Jaloun understood the secret of his father's thoughtreel and the history of his transformation, his elemental fever had more or less subsided, though his hair continued to smell like ash and would not return to its original crow's hue but remained a smoky grey instead. He returned to the office with his furlough crumpled in his breast pocket and discovered that the wind had disappeared in the hallway, but that despite the better weather, still no one spoke while they waited in queue for their daily assignment. Supervisor accepted the slip of absence and said nothing, which indicated that he knew—though he did wrinkle his brow at his changed hair colour—and as the day proceeded, Mamun Ben Jaloun began to relax.

Is there life in the Archives. He doubted the myths of the ghosts and their search for the infinite reel. It seemed to him, forgetting for a moment the poetic specificity of Zachariah Ben Jaloun's mind, that all the reels were the same in that they were all documents of suffering. A weightlessness began to infect his steps. Like Badsha Abd, he lost his footsteps; they no longer registered on the ground, as if his record on earth was already erased. New pains assailed his gut, and Supervisor warned that any more missed days would result in his termination. In a way, Mamun Ben Jaloun wished for nothing more, though the question how would the family persist were such an event, as well as imagining the drove of vultures just waiting to seize upon an opportunity to assume his ministry post, drove him to continue taking the dumbwaiter every day into the Archives.

One day, the dizziness, fevers, mental weaknesses, hallucinations, and his smoke and ashen hair were accompanied by bloody shit in the toilet. In the bathroom mirror he pulled his drum-taut cheeks and watched the thin wreaths of smoke rise from the tip of his skull, opened his ruined mouth full of loose teeth, and realized he was not yet forty but appeared and felt like an old man. Which hidden organ was failing inside. Would he remember his marriage night with death. Would he live on in the mirrors like certain ghosts of the city which failed to recognize they were dead. He located the beginnings of his illness in time and cursed the life of Zachariah Ben Jaloun and wished he had never known his father even in the fragments he had come to know him; he cursed his curiosity and his theft of the thoughtreel and burned it without a thought or ritual inside their tiny flat while Shukriah screamed and tore out hair and mourned as if he was committing murder. He raved that his mother had loved him and he had abandoned her without a thought, did not even bother to seek her out after escaping his shackled life in his father's office wardrobe; what cobwebbed reality did she exist in he would never know.

He lamented thus, endlessly for two whole days and so self-obsessed had he become that Shukriah, who had for the last year been emerging slowly out of the solipsism of her extended pregnancy, finally returned fire and berated him for not noticing he was not a child to be thinking all the time about parentsandyourbloodypast, let me remind that I too have a history and they (meaning us, writer reader et al) don't know a damn thing about this, and in fact, Mamun Ben Jaloun, referring to him by his original and full name, there are two growing children in our home and your years of neglect have inflicted such damage that she did not have the heart to finish this sentence.

And how will it be, Allah, when the other one, she referred to Hedayatesque, slapped her forehead. I am dying, Shukriah, he said, in front of Reshma and Chaya, who had never seen them fight and were astounded by the revelation and began to weep. Not emerging for a second out of his hermit crab's shell, he retained the upper hand.

THE
STRANGER
FROM
BERLIN

Rest assured my father would live long enough to see my birth. And before leaving the world, his life would revisit him like a long ceaseless pageant. The major first return was that of Badsha Abd, who it was announced in the papers and local radio would be awarded a posthumous prize at a gala in La Maga as a hero of the nation, a martyr of the unnameable country, for spreading all throughout the world so many reasons for its unexceptionable recognition by the international community.

Somewhere between the salad course and the main course, strangers appeared with the look of worn-out jackals in a drought, with dry tongues wagging silently just have a look at these tourtières and gooseberry wine, led by a man who appeared weighted with the desire to say something. No one knew how they had got past the armed guards at the front of the Ministry of Records and Sources, but the President was speaking, so they forgot about them immediately, because, though aged, that stentorian voice still had the ability to freeze grasshoppers in mid-bounce and to stop the air from moving.

We are here to honour one of the finest minds our country has ever produced, the President was saying, and I only wish my dear friend Badsha Abd himself could be here to receive it himself.

But I am not dead, said the man whose locks were withered and forehead wizened, but who was still so modest that he did not leave footsteps when he walked.

The President continued, It is as if we can still hear his voice, testament to the truth that our country produces nothing less than immortal workers of the imagination.

Salad forks knocked against wine glasses, Hear hear, and the gentleman from the Swiss Academy of Arts and Letters extended a glance toward the three strangers, but no one else paid them mind.

Even in the middle of the speech, when Badsha Abd jumped jacks and yelled, I am here, in body, plain to see, fools, the security guards did not drag them away, and they were so thoroughly perplexed by the total disregard that the three survivors themselves began to believe their non-existence. Slideshows of their works played on as the three exited. They wandered through La Maga, silently observed the cameras that extended from cranes, assaulted people out of the ground, half-buried in the soil, and all their years of wandering had not prepared them for such a hellish interpretation of the craft of filmmaking.

My father emerged out of the pharmacy: Salauddin, he exclaimed, why Mohammed Wallia, even you, Badsha Abd.

The first of the three looked to their leader for confirmation and the third replied, Sorry, you have us mistaken for look-alikes. In La Maga, which had reproduced every image in the world, it was unsurprising that these men could be actors, so with a single glance further, my father mumbled apologies and made his way through the mirror-strewn streets.

Not too long after, a tall, thin young man with downcast eyes knocked on their door, and bestowing a wickerwork basket of live snails and crabs as a gift, he claimed to be the son of Mamun M and a woman named Qismis.

I live in Berlin, he said over dinner, and explained he was on vacation from university and had always wanted to visit the unnameable country, the birthplace of his parents, La Maga especially given its recent changes; then someone here had asked his identity and pointed him out to where the family resided.

Mamun M, who was by then taking so many different medicines that he interpreted the stranger's polyglottal abilities as glossolalia, tested him further by asking where on his mother's neck lay the square-shaped mole, as well as the year of his birth.

The stranger told him these things and added that in fact he had resided in his mother's womb for three and a half years before being born, and this evidence of Mamun M's slow, ponderous seed confirmed his son's identity.

I am Nur al-Din, he introduced.

You may stay here, Shukriah offered before Mamun M had a chance, for as long as you'd like, though as you can see, she pointed around her, the quarters are cramped.

I couldn't, he refused with many thanks, but his father and step-mother were so insistent, as were his stepsisters, who took a liking to their foreign stepbrother at once, that he had no choice but to take up a hammock in the space that served as the living-dining-kitchen area.

In the afternoons he would remove a melodica from his enormous army knapsack and play renditions of popular songs on the radio: Now guess this one, and this, the majority of which, between the two sisters, were known, but the game was inexhaustible and never failed to excite all three of them as they sat cross-legged shelling peanuts into a large blue bowl, salting them and eating and laughing until Shukriah came to bid them goodnight, not too late, and please for your father's sake, she would press a finger to her lips.

At dinner, he informed Shukriah and Mamun that the girls surprised him with their worldliness. He had imagined the unnameable country as barely existing, politically isolated from global film and pop culture, that it could be reached by only a handful of international flights, but that they had informed him the world still managed to seep in even if they put up mirror-walls so people were meant to see only themselves. When Shukriah asked if the girls had exaggerated, blown up their unnameable country into endless combustion, he laughed, took each of the sisters, seated on each side of him, by the hand. He laughed jovially, said that just today they had directed him to their favourite record shop in the city, and there, a gangly chainsmoker named Samir had explained how he ordered vinyl each month from a London distributor, though now it's every other month due to the troubles, Samir had said, and half of them don't arrive, he had lamented between puffs; nevertheless, the tween had pointed to the posters of American heroes and British idols, to the walls of records he had managed to retain: We have to make a home in the world.

But I've really come for another reason, Nur al-Din confessed to the family as he took a Super 8 camera out from his knapsack under the table. Oh, Reshma raised eyebrows. Oh, Chaya shadowed her sister. Of course, said Nur al-Din, flaring a hand to indicate the count-less tourists that came yearly for the same purpose: I wanted to film your endless film.

It seemed like such a fraternal and chaste communion that at first it only contented Shukriah, and she encouraged the siblings to grow closer, hoping that Nur al-Din's slow speech and measured movements would cast in her daughters a similar worldly temperament, and she would pack the three of them lunches to take in tote bags before they set out in La Maga's mirror-maze streets. They would laugh and play in their reflections until halted at a shatter mirror intersection by guards interested in identification and nameless rebels. He spoke of Reshma, with her song and click-up heels, her flock of violins that seemed to follow her wherever she went, who never seemed to be bothered by such intrusions, taking them as the daily trespasses of an unnameable country. Have you ever noticed, he asked Shukriah, your sister's ability to always find makeup artists ready to offer their services before situating her in the next take, matched by Chaya's nonchalance punctuated by her face pressed with white powder makeup and black eyeshadow, the second twin's abhorrence for flair and her precise knowledge of all the square miles *The Mirror* had occupied and how many homes schools hospitals factories had been burnt to crisp or become movie sets. You wonder why all the fire and revolt, Chaya had snickered. I thought it was for spidersilk, Nur al-Din retorted. Yes, it's for spidersilk, but spidersilk is also a metaphor, said Chaya; once upon a time, they used to use it to stop arrows, but they're making it so nothing can stop *The Mirror*.

During the thirty minutes of their absence, all the love Chaya ever held for her sister curdled into milk too sour for words. Remember: it was Reshma who staked claim to the heart of their stepbrother, though she did it in silence and with an overabundance of goodwill, which burned her sister and even irked Shukriah, who understood the nuances of the rift more than she let on. Both wrote furiously to Nur al-Din and counted the weeks before his replies. At first these arrived together, separated at most by one anxious day, and Chaya's heart was contented with the thought that despite the content of his words, which only spoke of the everyday passage of time and at most a short description of travel to a nearby city for some prosaic purpose, her sister seemed no better off in the struggle. Then, for no apparent reason, Reshma's letters began to arrive more frequently, and though she had never read any of their exchanges, Chaya assumed their romance was flourishing and increased her efforts. How to exit this mirror prison, she wrote, could you give a clue. In our unnameable country there are only walls and in Berlin, at least as I imagine, lies everything beyond. Nur al-Din wrote back, don't be so sure, here the cabbage is boiled until one tastes only the water, all the apples taste better in the unnameable country, and besides, we have our own explosions these days: read: Red Army Faction.

Desperate to understand her sister's communiqués with Nur al-Din, she began from the beginning and started by imagining all the possibilities of the thirty minutes during which he and Reshma had been alone. What had they exchanged. Could it even have been a kiss. Why had she not interfered. She imagined having taken his hand before she had had a chance, pretending to have been her sister if need be, despite the fact that Reshma's hair was cropped short and fashioned to rise pointed from the skull like individuated stalactites and hers fell like rain down to her hips. Perhaps, then, it would be easier to assume Reshma's identity in a letter in order to sound the depths and differences of his language and to find the truth, though the response would be addressed to her other, and so that.

Finally, incapable of bearing it any longer, she asked him directly where his heart lay, with her sister or with her. In a cruel, lengthy, comical reply only several days afterward, he declared, in fact he was bound to take up residence after his studies with a woman he had fallen deeply in love with several months after his return from the unnameable country, and, besides, he had never imagined either of them romantically since we're siblings, remember.

A day afterward, Reshma declared at dinner she had applied to an art academy in Berlin and if accepted she would move there in the following September.

Go, Chaya spat across the table, knowing in her heart the truth: he doesn't love either of us, he has someone closer at hand. Besides, she did not say, it is not easy to escape the city of mirrors let alone passport out of the country altogether.

Fool, her sister's eyes grew sharp, her jaw jutted prognathous forward, matted red fur sprouted around her chin, her teeth grew out of her gums animal sharp, and her face became that of a fox's, lean and hungry, reflecting the long months of Chaya's antipathy with a single glare. Then the light shifted, her face softened, returned to its human shape, and Reshma laughed out of pity: he's our brother, and hardly the reason I am moving.

Astonished, Chaya asked: Why, then.

Because I am tired of La Maga and because I want to learn how to paint.

Chaya swallowed deeply, she drank the curdled sour milk of her conscience and suffered from such debilitating stomach cramps that she joined her father in bed and sought his commiseration, and finding it neither here nor in the stern gaze of Shukriah, who knew the content of both of their exchanges with Nur al-Din since she had kept up communication with him separately, nor at school with her friends, who could not plumb the depths of the tragedy, she wept alone for weeks until her eyes were raw. Never again did she write to her half-brother, who was not even that in truth since they shared neither the same mother nor father, not even after he apologized for his previous curt reply and extended a letter of invitation to her as well, you were looking for a way out of La Maga, Berlin has several fine art academies, your sister has shown interest in painting, you might be able to make a home here if you want to try your hand at some other craft, but Chaya would remain in the unnameable country for the rest of her life.

As for Reshma: migration is rupture, deracination, the cruelty of incalculable loss before all else. When the migrant finds herself contented with her decision to relocate, she is usually years removed from her initial mourning. Reshma's story is beyond the scope of the unnameable country and her suffering, her total failure in the world of

art, her hungry years and later exalted joys and hagiographic annunciation may be documented elsewhere.

———————

Meanwhile, Hedayatesque is patiently awaiting the outcome of the
Director's war and the rebels' war, corded to mother and bubbling
into wombwater what she believes are words, pulling himself into
bones and new tissue skin day by day. She speaks to him in full adult
sentences, as one would do to a grown-up child of nearly ten years.
Today on the radio, she tells him while ironing, they were saying that
if the President doesn't remove Ivanovich, the Russian spy, from his
council, the Americans will resume their bombing, and the President
will then be arrested before being deported and imprisoned without
trial in Seychelles, can you imagine. She sighed, either suffocate by
gazing at your own face ten thousand times a day or die by fire. What
else can I say, she is kneading dough and talking aloud as I am listening
intently: I have no choice, after all. How can one have sympathy for
a butcher, and yet: I think our President has become too indulgent to
horses and cows and to foreigners, she declares, and he should stand
up for the people of our unnameable country.

Soon, the first wooden bomb fell onto the minaret of a La Maga
mosque and broke apart spilling one ton of paper ribbons on which
were printed more than one million obscenities. Nasiruddin Khan, who
was no observant Muslim and a shrewd capitalist at the end of the day,
detected opportunity and seized upon it. He himself performed the call
to prayer from the minaret of the assaulted mosque, and neither in the
morning nor at midday, not in the afternoon or at dusk or evening,
with his hoarse, unpractised voice at such an odd point in the sun's
progress across the sky that curious La Maga residents threaded their
way through the mirror-walls in the streets and coursed into the edifice

just to hear what was what. Then obscenity for obscenity, the cola merchant matched the heat of the dummy explosive and its one million swears until they were forced to bring out five oscillating fans, and still it was not enough, they turned up the overhead fans but these only circulated the hot air of his breath and fanned the frustration and anger of the people.

The people began to echo, we cannot allow, must defend others said, swear for a swear; and they asked is it possible, jostled shoulder to shoulder, They are resorting to bombs because the cameras are all jammed with dirt, and we have broken so many mirrors the dead have nowhere to go, are finally realizing the truth and have retreated quietly into their graves. Down with the Director, they whispered aloud as they poured into the streets, to hell with that horse's ass in the Presidential Palace, not yet confident to yell the words and mimicking the rebels who, it was known, wore ballet slippers and blended into the mirror background of La Maga and emphasized hush-hush above all else.

News of the dirty bomb exploded through the city and, fakery for fakery, Nasiruddin Khan's crew supplied the necessary ingredients and people got to work: dummy horses were built, dummy cars, dummy tanks, marionettes so lifelike that when string-pulled from second-story tenement flats they responded with the motions of actual limbs; ventriloquists found work, out-of-work magicians became useful in the war effort, classrooms took on the atmosphere of the factory, everything changed.

In the Presidential Palace, the head of state was so obsessed with personal matters he could not be reached by telephone telex letters or in person. Dulcinea had taken gravely ill, poisoned it was said, by someone close to the leader, though whom it was not known, her hind legs collapsed whenever she tried to raise herself, and she dropped to the floor each time she tried from vertigo, she could not take food and was barely capable of swallowing water. It may therefore be true that

Anwar had no idea of what horrors followed next, that he was therefore not responsible, he himself is not known to have given the orders, but no one in the unnameable country forgave him anyway for what occurred.

Recall, as we often do in the unnameable country: one Wednesday evening the sky fluttered and more than two thousand children were lured outside by a beautiful green precipitation, which fell at first like a drizzle of fireflies and which some of them tried to catch on their tongues. But soon the air grew solid, suffused with fumes so noxious that even the marionettes were knocked flat off their feet, and those who tried to rescue the children and survived later compared the experience to walking through hellfire. The children, and, at first, even some curious adults, thought the sky was just releasing the fake elements of the American theatre war and went out to inspect, to mock, perhaps even to enjoy the novelty. The wounds they suffered, however, were evidence of something purely diabolical, for pouring water onto skin made it worse, and the children screamed as the fire seeped deeper into hidden organs and fizzled for hours like the rock candies of Confectionarayan Babu (who stayed inside his candy shop and was saved and whose shop was spared only by an inscrutable miracle of small things), as it rained this way for hours and dummy houses burned and real buildings met actual demise as the city grew engulfed in a fire that had no cure.

More than five thousand people died, it was said, more than eight thousand were injured in the Night of the Green Rain, and though the General Assembly of the United Nations condemned the American targeting of civilians as well as the use of cruel and unusual instruments of destruction, the Security Council stopped short of defining the event as a war crime. Soon after, the radios broadcast the sad news that Dulcinea never recovered from her mysterious illness, had passed on and just yesterday was laid to rest in a horse-sized ivory-laden coffin on the palace grounds. Following a period of mourning the President re-emerged into public life with renewed vigour and mirthless desire to avenge the murder of his last great romance, though he did not know to what degree he had lost ground within even his Privy Council, as well as among his closest legislative and judicial supporters, for his selfish absence, and more for his failure to provide adequate words to describe the grief of the nation.

At that time, they said Grenadier Lhereux would assume the helm. Doddering, close to eighty, he carried his teeth in a velveteen box and was rumoured not to be able to perform the day's activities without first bathing several hours in a revitalizing concoction of aromatic herbs, whose exact formula only he knew and whose ingredients were imported from more than a dozen separate countries. But whoever spoke to him concluded at once his mind retained the lucidity of that day in the trenches of Vimy Ridge, where he had risen to the rank of major in an hour's exploits at age seventeen, and that he still possessed the heroic candour reserved for men of a bygone generation.

Lhereux himself would not speak of power so easily, and those plotting the coup understood this, though it was said he would have been content to remain a grey eminence, a hidden organ, invisible functionary of the unnameable country for the rest of his days irrespective of who played leader.

The time has come, Xamid Sultan patted him on the back outside the legislative house under a threatening phlegmatic sky one Friday afternoon, will you do us the honour.

Lhereux provided the response of his life after having lived in the unnameable country for more than fifty years when he said, I am here to observe, Xamid, and one day I will return to Montpellier where my mother still keeps her house and a quaint plum and cherry orchard.

Soon, it became so impossible to demarcate between what was real in La Maga and what was intended to be cinematic action that no one was certain when American soldiers appeared in every corner. They crawled from beneath the sewer gratings and stepped out of the bathroom doors of common citizens, who hadn't noticed them come in without knocking, Sorry, needed to shit pretty bad, ma'am. If asked, they claimed they had arrived only to assist the elderly to cross the street and to prevent women from being assaulted by the rebels, but so far as we are aware, the elderly of La Maga tended to retain an ambulatory spirit until the end of their days and died suddenly in bed without sickness and more out of the conviction their time had come, while no woman had asked any soldier to hold her hand since the rebels were not known to have. Besides, we were more accustomed to uncle big bad's lupine megaphone bursts—We know you are in there, asshole-terrorizers; out of that tenement flat or we will blow you out—the scuttling of soldiers distribution of wires and deposition of charges, the huff-and-puff of Major Collin Salt through the conical instrument, which transformed his orders into growling sand, which offered you the mercy of imprisonment and torture or delivered death with a count-down of two more one more minute terrorists the walls fell down on top of you in the middle of breath memory and then you were flattened like so many daddy-long-legs.

The nameless rebels were shyer than the Americans and appeared and disappeared like catless grins, hitting and running still clad in ballet slippers. It was true they died in greater number, but since the night of the phosphorescent green water-resistant fire, it had become nearly impossible to distinguish between the residents of the city and the rebels. Mother's constant reading aloud of the events to her unborn son took a turn of invention as she realized the war was giving no sign of retreat; my father's days were numbered, and that if I was not born soon I might never be introduced to my aunt Reshma before she left for the Berlin art academy to which she had been accepted. Furthermore, her own body and mind had suffered so much in the recent past she was worried she might not be able to tolerate another year of pregnancy. Thus, events that were too large were shrunk by concave mirrors of speech, while slight victories, such as a minor increase in the availability of grain in the stores, would be magnified exponentially in order to encourage; the war continued and in fact escalated but I swam contented after years of ardour and worry.

My mother coaxed me finally to be born. Having wombed me nine and one-third multiples longer than the giantess Gargamelle, and utterly exhausted by the ordeal, Shukriah wondered if my entry into the world would in any way resemble an ordinary birth or whether I would in fact emerge like Athena from her head or cast within an eggshell, in which case she would have to incubate me further like a swan-maiden. She bellytickled, she teased, she sang loving verses, and still I remained stuck in place, possibly out of nervousness like an actor prior to the first night of performance after many a long rehearsal.

One day, two hours before dawn, La Maga awoke to simultaneous bovine cries emerging from every minaret in the city. What unholy rascals like myself would laugh about many years later found interpretation in observant five-times-a-day-kneelers as the greatest insult; cows on every minaret, can you believe, trained cows who had walked up perilous steps on their own, seemingly, to call the faithful. Like the wooden bomb replete with ribbons of a million obscene messages, Nasiruddin Khan appeared out of the safety of his miniature cola empire to deliver yet another hot message, this one so incendiary one of the ceiling fans overheated and disconnected, falling with a crash and nearly lopping off several heads in the audience. Nearly overcome by the omen of misfortune, the crowd struggled for a moment with the choice of dispersing, but let me say it for why suppress the news when the news.

Nasiruddin Khan silenced the people with a hand: La Maga is not alone in this struggle, all over the world it is becoming impossible to avoid the fact that we are no longer living with airstrikes but a full-fledged invasion, the people are united and they are with you. He began to read a letter from Joe Slovo: our brothers and sisters in South Africa have extended their solidarity, he read aloud that tender document, which pacified the isolated residents of a faraway country and reminded them that there existed a world beyond their mirror-walls and that others too were struggling. Remember, however: on this occasion, the unknotters were ready; if the film cameras were not all but destroyed and the mirrors were cracking, at least the saboteurs, paid informants, spies, and plainclothes provocateurs were gaining strength, and some sources claimed at least a third of the audience that day consisted of hidden organs, eyes and ears, which saw and heard everything.

Following the death of Dulcinea, the President began to dress in garments made of camel hair and to favour eating locusts and raw honey, withdrawing his campaign to discover the perpetrator of his horse's poisoning after appeasing himself with the senseless execution of eighty random men and women hand-picked by the Department and eventually withdrawing into a babble that was less than glossolalia, inscrutable and incapable of effecting any change in the world. He became lost to all, for the first time even to Grenadier Lhereux, who had on every other occasion succeeded in tethering Anwar to the basic realities of governance and washing up every day, and the Privy Council realized it had discovered the miracle it had been searching for and suggested immediately creating for the head of state the docile, sheared-samson position of prime minister without any formal powers, and to choose a new president from the cadre of groomed politicos and military men.

Lhereux instantly regretted refusing the role of the unnameable country's leader when he realized that change was inevitable and considered his retirement and even contacted his mother to ask whether she would not allow him to bring a friend to stay in their Montpellier cottage for a short visit.

The centenarian wrote back insisting that her boy abandon his romantic forays in the dark lands where he had chosen to waste his life and that he shouldn't bother coming home if he did not arrive as he had left it: with his head bowed and as a God-fearing Catholic.

The great grenadier tried not to argue sense and to make the best of the situation. He stood in the balcony of the Presidential Palace where Anwar used to give speeches to scintillated crowds and took a whiff of the sulphurous air. The taste of ash collected on his palate and he realized that all throughout the unnameable country, the same fire burned, just as it had twenty years ago when the British were forced to leave and tried then to rule from afar. He cursed this country and its senseless multitude; he had lived here fifty years and still had not found happiness or understood what its people wanted.

SATAN AND
THE MAROONS

FABLE
OF
YESHUA

Questions push. Curiosity bids us backward in time. The tale of now is the story of every now before now meaning present time. How many strangers have arrived on our shores. Years ago, Yeshua himself came to our country, rumours tell us. My grandfather heard that story first not long after he met my grandmother in the cubicles of the office of the British Intelligence Service in the Heart of Arabia. My grandmother heard it too right after they met.

Did my grandparents go to the movies when they became sweethearts. Recall at that time there was a fire and fanfare show in town: the nameless rebels vs. *The Mirror*. Shoot to shards broken glass and alleyway scuffles erupted daily while the beginning of it all, including and especially the start of the cinema, its origin, which occurred exactly at the same time as a CIA coup placing Anwar in power, disappeared into a cinematic wonderland, the once upon a time of a movie designed for export.

By the time my grandfather and grandmother fell in love, everyone had forgotten why sharpshooters with SLRs and Technicolor film cameras shot scene after scene on sliders, on tracks, or through moving cars as dynamic microphones hung wire thin from rooftops or swung on peeled umbrella veins shading chickens for sale. Exotic lizards and belly dancers vibrated in front of thirty-five millimetres in the equatorial heat.

Zachariah Ben Jaloun goes to market one morning, and there he spots Gita. From far away he calls her name, and though she carries a bag in one hand and the other handles indiscernible fruit, she turns in the movie breeze blows hair and shines. She turns to her name called song: crap, there's that man, she puts hand up to cheek to check her makeup. She waves. Let's give them music to arm them against trepidation, reintroductions, as they share more than a handshake, less than a hug.

Then there are scenes of everyday life: they walk through the old souks where they hear the drumming of Quinceyenglish, and where children play in Server, or inverted slang, and run with birdwhistles that sound like chickadees when filled to the quarter and doves when filled halfway. Everywhere, cranes make shadows, and fluorescent lights hide in wait for when it gets dark.

They're shooting a historical docudrama, Mamun Ben Jaloun informs, pointing at a replica naval vessel from the turn of the twentieth century resting on the back of a flatbed truck. They walk along the overpass recently renamed after Governor Anwar, and share oranges on a knoll.

While they sit in aimless conversation, taste oranges, the dips and rises of the other's voice, an eyeless man comes searching for a morsel and coins. He sits beside them hastily, let me rest for a moment, he says, though not to the pair. Just behind him, as if they had been following him for a long time, two men find the knoll, and mercilessly, the first plants tripod legs and the second fixes a quick camera on top to catch the moment.

The blind man sits next to Gita and Zachariah, quivers for a moment, cataract eyes unaware. Are they gone he asks, and neither Gita nor Zachariah knows what to say because *The Mirror* is here. The two film workers place index to lips shush. Yes, says Gita, they're gone, she says, as the camera's jib arms swivel and the lens inches closer to their conversation.

Would you like a plum, Gita offers, and the beggar, who is a beggar judging by appearance, says please. Who are you, asks Zachariah Ben Jaloun, biting succour for cinematic effect. He looks at the ragged guest whose tattered clothes resist sunlight, whose shadows fall darker, thicker. In post-production, they must have delighted in the natural difference between him and the other characters.

Who am I, Yeshua's companion nods gravely as yes, who are you, Gita echoes.

Recall if you have heard the story elsewhere: this mendicant is not Yeshua, and that the fable is related by a companion of Yeshua.

Plum after plum, Gita urged him go on. She offered bread and milk from her bag's grocery stores. Tell us, she cajoled.

Who am I.

Yes, who are you.

————————————

What is the Fable of Yeshua. And what do they say of the Fable of Yeshua. When Yeshua came to the unnameable country did he not sow discord in the souks, casting lots, those against and those who believed his story. Why did he and the Amharic Jews come to decide the earth would swallow them and allow them tunnel-passage back to Jerusalem. Why were they driven from the Holy Land. In plain truth, enemies and

229

friends, when Yeshua and the Amharic Jews came to the unnameable country, drenched in brine from clothes to the marrow, stinking pesticide, blinded, hungry, shivering cold, they were mute, couldn't say a word about what had happened, who they were. That is to say, Yeshua and the six others had arrived at the shores of the unnameable country without a boat or any other visible craft, and for twenty-four hours could not explain their past.

Grenadier Lhereux, second in command to Anwar, head of state, whom the nameless rebels called Governor because our nation is a province among other unnameable countries according to their socialist claptrap, was a singularly calm man of rational persuasion, and an amateur linguist. After being the first official to take charge of the situation, Anwar found himself concluding that no human language contained so many pharyngeal stops and strange syntactical breaks, and that the strangers were glossolating in either rubbish or angelic tongue.

Yeshua regained his speech before the others and claimed that the seven had travelled from the unnameable country to Israel to make aliyah. After being told they would have to wait for security clearance, then after being sprayed by Israeli Secret Service in the face with the pungent insecticide dicholorottengas, they were shouted at in a language that was claimed to be Hebrew, which they did not understand and which proved they were not Jews and possibly spies. They were shackled together by the feet and left eyerotting in a small jail cell with other refugees, common criminals, and by the smells and sounds of it, several chickens and a goat. Most important, none of this may be true. By the grace of the she-goat's owner, they were allowed to suckle from its udder and kept alive for the week before being taken on a boat to the Red Sea.

Surely, then, Yeshua said, we were going to die. Shit sticks, they told us frightening things about picking worms off of clams as mist and cold pawed, fought our faces. Our breaths rattled. We were blind, but more out of the fear we felt at our sudden condition, for death is the greater blindness, we began to babble, all together and in a spontaneous coordinated way, which has not stopped for the others and into which I descend now and again. When they dropped us, entangled, into the water, we were carried away from them by swift current, and the sound of the motor disappeared after some minutes, which means they did not pursue us. By the grace of God we floatedon the water, south for several days, wet, hungry, exhausted, sightless, embattled by waves much of that time, through the Red Sea, Yeshua supposed, through the Gulf of Eden, before finally arriving at the shores of your unnameable country, which we thought was New Jerusalem.

But the story had its faults. Grenadier Lhereux could discover no Egyptian, Yemeni, or Israeli naval records to verify the storm on that date; the weather, in fact, had been quite clear. They said they arrived very early in the morning, and this too was incredulous. It was a youth named Abdullah who claimed he woke up to urinate in the outhouse near his fisherman's hut, his eyes pasty, still sleepy, and was astounded in early daylight by who were these men-looking flotsam. Lhereux wrote down the boy's testimony. A fisherman, Mahmud, meanwhile, claimed the strangers had in fact arrived later in the day, at around one-thirty in the afternoon, and that he himself had brought them into his hut where the Governor met them for the first time several days later, by which time a hundred other refugees had floated onto the shore. Other individuals also claimed they were the first to find the six blind, shackled men.

The Fable of Yeshua is apocryphal. Was it true they were discovered with no boat in sight, and were wet, shivering, and had no luggage, no water or food, no provisions at all. Had they huddled together for warmth for hours before being brought inside a fisherman Mahmud's shack. There, the newly blind began accustoming themselves to their blindness, to distinguishing between children and adults, females and males, the old and young, intuitively by smell and touch. They were incapable of communicating, as I have mentioned, for the first twenty-four hours, and were visited in the afternoon by the Governor, not for humanitarian purposes but out of the same perverse curiosity that afflicted half the city of La Maga. He had the strangers interned in a nearby hospital, treated until at least one of them had regained his speech.

The Governor, witnessing first-hand the poverty of the society of fishermen, the beach huts that had stood ramshackle tenuous against the gusts of the sea for as long as anyone could remember, did nothing to uplift their condition. Nor did he take up the matter of the strange visitors with anyone from the nascent Israeli government. Our unnameable country was being forced by the other Arab states to shoulder the weight of the Palestinian refugees, and in the fishermen's huts he saw a solution. He declared that Grenadier Lhereux should arrange for the provision of plastic and wood and other building supplies so that more such huts may be built on La Maga's shores, and that the arriving refugees might fish and live there until their fates could be determined.

The shipless refugees lived in a crowded hut with fishermen in the area and changes came naturally with time. Yoni stirred the heart of Abdullah, the youth who always claimed to have found the sea-drenched travellers first, who fell in love with her because he realized she saw more than the sighted, and the two were married one Saturday. The others, too, grew accustomed to their harsh lives and new circumstances. One of them climbed high school rungs to university and became a teacher. Another learned carpentry. The population of the beachside village grew from two thousand to twenty-six times that amount within a year due to Palestinian immigrants, and help was limited and the fish did not always visit nets, nor was there ample arable soil to grow what one liked. Six of the seven visitors did not wish to return to Israel, but Yeshua grew old and with age his mind began to long even more for the true Jerusalem.

Then the eyeless old man got up and left the two orange eaters on the grass. Why did we interrupt with the Fable of Yeshua when we were talking about Gita and Zachariah. While we were wading through Yeshua's tale, time has passed for the pair as well: have taken a shining to each other and many significant details have been shared—Gita's loss of time, sometimes whole hours will go by and I will realize them as minutes; Zachariah's two names, his inexplicable illiteracy, which he has been trying to treat by eating raw onions.

Gita begins teaching Zachariah Ben Janoun to read again. Excellent, she nods when he does it right, you are making progress. He feels shy to reveal the existence of his blank verses, harder to come by these days, harder to write while exhausting hours at the border or while bedded rootless soil. Night after night, Zachariah descends. Each morning, he surfaces increasingly illiterate but dug up and alive somehow with hope he'll deliver a complete manuscript to Benjamin Pasha's secretary.

Who knows whether he still remembers Zachariah, even the professor has possibly forgotten him. He received several invitations, and the most recent communiqué expressed sadness for Zachariah Ben Jaloun's lack of response; but uncomfortable with his slowness in production and his inexplicable illiteracy, Zachariah never wrote back.

What are you doing, Gita will ask as he paces sometimes from one end of the small flat to the other, staring intently at a certain corner of the ceiling, mumbling with pages in his hand.

Reading, he will say, but it is obvious his mind is elsewhere. And some earlymornings he will leave the house, which eventually has become his house as well, since he resides there more often than in his own flat (which he is renting to a university student and considering releasing altogether), and toward whose rent he now contributes, without returning for a whole day. Sorry, I was running errands he will say, and account for his absence with a kiss, a bag of vegetables, or a gift menagerie, something for the house, he will say. Slowly, however, the pages are ordering themselves and the narrative and prosody are aligning, but at the expense of Gita's accumulating suspicions.

One day she discovers herself summoned before the desk of the assistant to the vice president of Assembly, and finds it empty. Gita is unsure what to do, and from somewhere in the room there is a cough, and a voice instructs her to occupy the seat before her. With trepidation, she does so, and the meeting commences.

Your name has come up in several quarterly reports as an astute employee, the voice informs, and it is for this reason we are assigning you to an internal task force that will review a single magnetic tape.

A large disembodied eye appears for a moment above the desk and disappears after two blinks.

Sir, Gita tries not to notice, I am a collector, while this seems like the job of an assembler or investigator.

A hissing chorus, like a disenchanted film crowd at an offensive scene. A clap and the sound dissipates.

Never mind them, the voice reassures. We are certain you can complete the task, why would you have been chosen otherwise.

And now, another clap: a tall, thin man sporting coattails and a rigid curling moustache emerges from the wardrobe wielding the tapereel. Take this, he says in the voice that was just addressing her.

Why were you inside the wardrobe, Gita asks, astonished, annoyed. It seems highly suspicious; how can I trust to take this job if my supervisor cannot address me in plain sight.

Her interrogation breaks the mustachioed tall man, please believe me, he confesses behind his watery moustache, when I say I have no authority even to sit at the edge of the chair belonging to the vice president's assistant, since in fact I am not he but actually his junior secretary, and only because he has taken ill for the past six weeks that I am allowed to enter this office at all. It was his order that I was to deliver this message and all others from inside the wardrobe because he did not want to confuse employees during his absence into thinking anyone but he could play assistant to the vice president of Assembly; it would have been dishonest.

Gita rummages through her purse for a tissue: poor man, she thinks, what a beastly department, and she refrains from demanding an explanation for the disembodied eye or the chorus of hisses.

Stranger events began soon afterward. Gita began to mirror Zachariah's eggshell-tiptoeing around the issue of his blank verses, and she did not tell him of her new assignment. There was no particular reason why she said nothing, and did not think her silence an indication their affections had soured. Come find me if you can, she may have been saying. Or she may have simply forgotten because it was an unusual thoughtreel assignment.

The reel itself: lighter and thinner than any she had handled, while inside was a new style of magnetic tape, its surface argentine and perfectly reflective, smooth to the touch, though she was careful to handle it with latex gloves, as was natural to her profession. The thoughts began in the midst, so she assumed it had not been edited. There was one prominent voice that branched into a number of secondary, then even tertiary and ancillary voices, which returned to the main voice as if it were the refrain. They belonged obviously to a schizophrenic person, but she could not discover anything unusual about the content.

Musings about daily life, a certain mellifluous strain to the thoughts: the affairs of an overworked mind in middle bureaucracy was all.

Sometime early in the long two-year period she reviewed the seventeen-minute-long reel, she noted her discoveries to the visiting supervisor and added, I must not be up to the task, I find nothing of.

Nothingatall, the visiting supervisor sighed her surname, you were chosen for your capacity for seeing thoughts in thoughtreels, an unusual gift that should have led you to discover something important about the contents of this particular tape. Do not tell me you have fallen behind, that others assigned to the task have understood much more than you; the deputy chief of the Department thinks highly of your work and would be disappointed to hear.

Gita burned with frustration and shame, and returned to her desk. Meanwhile, Zachariah Ben Janoun had been sent to the far reaches of Collections, a part of the labyrinth of corridors and interlacing cubicles where the air conditioning was malfunctioning; stalactites had begun to form on the ceiling and it snowed there so often a minor ice age appeared to have graced this office space in our equatorial climate. Employees brought jackets and sweaters, which would otherwise never be worn, and blankets to work. So isolated were these individuals, and so mindless their task, to listen for certain registers of sound and to document these according to their frequency of occurrence, that when one spoke, others echoed the identical words, perhaps forgetting that in the real world one spoke for oneself alone.

Because it was so far from the major arteries of the department, Zachariah was forced to drive a small motorized buggy to the appointed location each morning and to drive back in the evening, each time shooing away the gaggle of employees who would try to hang onto his buggy or clamber onto its tarpaulin roof, why should we walk when you.

Zachariah would begin to relate these events to Gita but she seemed too preoccupied to notice his words or even his caresses. At first their physical desire for each other had been unrelenting. Then a pattern developed, and the regularity of the sexual act allowed them to enjoy the minutiae of tastes and sounds and smells of the other; but some time ago, the mist of platitude had fallen over each of their bodies, and while it was Gita who had noticed first, it hid Zachariah deeper behind himself. Flooded by guilt, he felt the immediate need to confess about the blank verses and thusly to correct the only betrayal against her he could remember; but when he tried she merely turned over and kept sleeping. True to mirror form, she did not reveal the nature of her problems with interpreting the new thoughtreel, or even of its existence.

In the bath, Zachariah brushes his skin with coarse black soap. Zachariah sings in the shower: find me as an onion, he sings/ pulled from fronds, your hair/ and peeled by your mouth and tulips. Find you, he trills minor/ and find me, he ascends major/ O you, he climbs highest falsetto, dips basso deep to deliver final gusto to the disinterred, inhabitable beloved of his song. In the kitchen Gita dances to someone else's tune while her boyfriend showers, this guy must have been a musician or something, she thinks, as the melodies in his dead head move her limbs. She dances as she listens to them on headphones. She pauses, rewinds the reel in its player, pauses, listens, starts again from the top as she discovers in its irresolute dimensions of just singing at my job, just chewing on a cud of melody, among the crowded voices that characterize many terror suspects she handles, an addictive form, repeating and won't leave her, leaves her humming, longing for it even after she peels the headphones off her head. She rubs her temples, I'm listening to someone else's thoughts, she says softly; she feels icky, as she always does when realizing again that she's violating a deeper privacy than most people imagine possible. And then. And yet.

A mysterious hum inside her. A guilt-glad feeling, excitement to be frank, thrill, to say it clearer, of touching someone through vast space and time, of handling a life became artifact. Hedayat thinks, he mutters. Could it be, he asks no one, that his grandmother Gita has become enchanted with the man on the thoughtreel whose mind she wrestles with day after day at her job.

It has been known to occur in the Ministry of Records and Sources, and prohibitive regulations generally avert such malignant events: barring special terror cases, no collector or assembler may deal with a single tape for longer than two weeks, but even then it happens.

One night, Gita wakes unexpectedly, rises to slake a parched throat, and finds the waistcoated junior secretary to the assistant of the departmental vice president, mustachioed and a mollycoddle, you will remember, rummaging through one of the deepest drawers of her collection. Appalled, she finds herself unable to speak, only to buzz or to hiss, and only garners the attention of the secretary with the combination of these sounds and the accidental knocking against her coffeetable.

The waistcoated man leaps up and puts a hand to his heart, claiming myocardial infarction you'll kill me by surprise.

What are you doing here, Gita manages to ask the moment after her own heart has stopped fluttering.

I was given a key to your apartment by your landlord when I informed him who I was in relation to your work and that it was an emergency and I needed immediately to see you.

Why didn't you simply knock, Gita whispers furiously, feeling a cicada-buzz rising to her throat. And could it not have waited until the morning.

Emergency, he reminded, and shook an index. Then he passed her a padded manila envelope, which from touch she could detect contained another reel, as he rattled off a few important memoranda in a low hiss.

Because the whole event transpired without waking Zachariah Ben Janoun, she did not bother to rouse him, and once again averted having to mention the changes in her occupation. She did not sleep for the remainder of the night. Dawn illumined the bizarre incidents characterizing the last year, and Gita realized that, unaware, a new state of expectancy had taken hold of her: surprises and violations of her privacy were to repeat so long as she did not solve the problem of the thoughtreel. A subsequent resolution, therefore: she should understand the tape at once, since there seemed no way of claiming defeat and returning to an ordinary life. She passed three fingers through Zachariah's hair and wished for the unknotting of whatever inside prevented him from speaking freely to her. As if her desire was granted, he sighed peacefully, and turned toward her hand, without waking.

Two weeks later, Gita discovered strange patterns in the second magnetic tape, which, she was informed, belonged to the same file and therefore, she assumed, to the identical mind, guided by not one rhythm but many: sometimes terza rima like the Dantean comedies, though she does not know it by that name, other times a hopscotch of dactyls troches, lub-lubbing iambic on certain occasions like a heart, not hidden within the thoughts, but comprising the thoughts themselves. The whole mind, it grows clear to her, or at least the transcribed artefact of the mind on the magnetic reel, is a work founded on rhythm.

At 3:23 P.M. that very afternoon, she is arrested.

Recall: such is the history of the unnameable country: always at the cusp one finds oneself suddenly interned.

An assignment: gather overwhelming evidence from the text and present a report to the General Assembly of the United Nations on behalf of every dead soul of the unnameable country.

Understand: in fact, it was a mortal error on part of both individuals to have kept from the other their respective secret.

Grenadier Lhereux, who would oversee their interrogations at a distance, reviewed the pair's psychological records well in advance and declared they were the types who would not speak to each other about the matter until too late, and this finding allowed the nascent Department of Special Affairs to continue with their plans.

Gita's cell is shrouded in half-light, and since she is an especially ordered person her prison-order trousers and overshirt are two sizes too large and must be held up by the straps. After the initial bout of nauseating fear, she passes through the walls of the cell unseen, walks invisible quick through the streets and returns home to the awaiting arms of Zachariah Ben Jaloun. She does not.

Zachariah, meanwhile, arrested at 5:48 P.M. the same day by seventeen Black Organs of the peace, who swoop down on Zachariah Ben Janoun/Ben Jaloun while he stands waiting for her outside the cathedral-edifice where they work, is native to the unnameable country and greater accustomed to the state of exception that has and will forever haunt its borders and corridors, and for many reasons is more resolute: already by the time he arrives at his cell he has put Gita out of his mind and is preparing for survival.

A shadow blocks all the light in the room. It belongs to a man who speaks: Zachariah Ben Jaloun.

Yes, I am he.

Zachariah Ben Janoun.

In the dark, our hero says nothing about the other Zachariah, already understanding the nature of the trap.

For four years you have been living a lie, a double identity, the nature of which has been carefully documented by the Department of Special Affairs.

Regard, something heavy falls as the shapeless man steps aside. The light moves slowly from the dangling single incandescent lightbulb at the far end of the cell across the room's dimensions as if crossing the globe. Zachariah sees a folder sitting on a table, which bends and creaks desperately under the folder's large mass of many loose sheets of paper. Our file, or your file, rather, weighs exactly as much as you do, Zachariah, sixty-four point three kilograms, am I correct.

Last time I checked, sir, though the stated figure is ten units under the actual.

Good. You have a respectful demeanour, which will help you in this place, the interrogator paces. The light shifts when he moves and the interrogator's profile changes from prognathous to concave, his arms grow longer-shorter, his hair covers his face before receding into the baldness of his scalp, his shadow bends exceedingly: his body exhibits endless change. Tell us, benjanoun benjaloun, what brought you to choose a second identity.

I was called Ben Janoun, sir, by my supervisor when offered a post at the Ministry of Radio and Communications, and since at the time I was unemployed and to correct a superior during an interview would have meant possible denial of the job, I allowed him and subsequently all others in the Ministry of Records and Sources to refer to me by an incorrect name. For this act I am wholly contrite and submit myself to rehabilitation in a correctional or psychiatric facility.

And yet what you have spoken is the grossest untruth.

Sir.

Yes, the interrogator looks closely at a sheet in the file. He has raised up the heavy folder, which must be very dense because while containing perhaps seven hundred pages it manages to weigh more than sixty kilograms, and the man carrying it, therefore, must be exceedingly powerful because he rests it on a single palm. See here, your date of birth, January suchandsuch, nineteen twenty-four.

That is correct, sir.

And the name, he brings the sheet of paper closer. Through the green faded uniform the man's flesh releases the sweet stench of attar and Zachariah is forced to breathe through his mouth.

Zachariah Ben Janoun, the captive is forced to say, since that is the name he sees.

The female warder who enters the room is wearing the same Chinese slippers as in Gita's collection, the ones she meant to sell as a final alternative, and seeing them on the feet of another drains all her confidence. Already she has fled this place several ways: she has flown through the small chink in the window, she has accompanied the scurrying rats through the unseen holes and they have led her through secret passageways, and she has also transparently moved through the walls, as we know. Always, she has returned to shed deep onion tears.

We are feeding you now, the woman declares, as if bestowing a gift. The tray contains frozen homogenous yellow in a plastic bowl and a grey bun. Wait until it cools, the warder says before exiting.

A day passes, or part of a day. The contents of the tray disappear and no subsequent meals are provided. Over the course of the next four days, however, twenty-four meals find their way to Gita's cell, some of which are inedible, many of which lie uneaten, and over the following week, these decompose without being removed. Rats arrive in swarming numbers. Gita fears rodents less than mosquitoes, fleas and the diseases they carry, as visions of ancient plague, of fever boils genital pustules tumefaction of the lymph nodes leave her hanging on the tips of her fingers upside down from the ceiling. Finally, a man arrives to interrogate her.

Under what pretext did you enter the country, Ms. Nothingatall.

To seek employment, she passes a hand across her clammy cheeks; the fever persists.

And to this effect you found the unnameable country satisfactory interrogation point

Yes, I was awarded a post at the Ministry of Radio and Telecommunications as a collector.

Ah, the man nodded, writing it all down. And there you met Zachariah Ben Janoun.

I did, yes.

I mean, you met Zachariah Ben Jaloun.

A silence akin to Zachariah's at the reminder of the double identity.

What did you think when he first revealed his second name to you; do you think of him as one or the other man when you think of him; be truthful, Gita.

The truth, sir: I think of him as Zachariah, Ben Jaloun is his birth name while Ben Janoun is his name at work.

Do you find it strange one man possesses two names. Might it not be possible you wake up in the morning next to a second man without certainty.

I don't understand the nature of the question, sir.

The interrogator slips a long thin finger deep inside his ear, so deep it disappears all the way to the knuckle. He twists it back and forth as if adjusting a hidden organ. Do you know what you actually discovered when analyzing the last magnetic reel. He effuses a spineless rumbling sound, which might be called laughter and which shakes the building to its foundations. We have so far to go, he speaks through a yawning hole in his head, and there is so much for you to learn.

The following months delivered to Gita all the discomforts one person could possibly live through: putrescence, a decomposing animal a dung-heap smell without any, sometimes faint while close on other occasions. By breathing through the mouth it was possible, but not for long. Vomit. Cloudy piss. Nowhere to urinate but an ancient overflowing toilet. The coming and going of ghostly cellmates who tarried without talking, looked at her, pointed, disappeared soon after arriving like transient fellow passengers destined for connecting flights. The isolation was difficult, but it allowed for the reordering and play of memory. For months at a time they would leave you with nothing but the walls and a low oscillating hum until shapes rose up and you floated like Yeshua across the surface of the Gulf of Eden, thinking it was the Dead Sea. What is the Fable of Yeshua. And how do they speak of the Fable of Yeshua.

The man arrived again and ordered her gently to descend from the ceiling, where she had taken to roosting, hanging from her fingertips. She crabscuttled slowly before leaping onto the floor. Please have a seat, he pointed to her cot.

She did as he requested and assumed a seated, human form. He asked her to recount the early stages of her relationship with benjaloun-benjanoun, and she related in loving detail their brief conversation in the department, quite casual, though I laughed, I recall, and he did not join me but enjoyed the sound, before speaking of their spirited encounter in the market some weeks later.

Talk to me about Yeshua.

What to say, she frowned, but an eyeless man speaking of his life, of which there are many so many maimed and disfigured living corpses.

I am not asking for a comparative demographic study, merely an account of this stranger's story.

It was apocryphal, she said, he told it several ways, forgot parts, filled in gaps, restated the beginning three times, then Zachariah told it again to me as if I wasn't there, and I remembered it back to him later and it was different.

What do you remember. That there were seven and they were accused at the Israeli border of being a danger to the nascent state, of not being Jews, of being a treasonous cete of badgers and spies, this much one could know. Did you believe it.

She thought for a moment while biting her lower lip. He was an eyeless man who claimed to have been blinded by the border guards. Zachariah, who has served as a border guard, could attest to the everyday cruelty of the profession and so.

Did you believe they were terrorists.

No.

Why not.

Because they were poor men who happened to be black and who merely wanted.

They were not terrorists, then, to you.

I cannot know for certain, but in which way does the matter relate to my imprisonment.

You visited them afterward.

Yes, Zachariah showed a curiosity about their story and wanted to see the spot where supposedly the earth opened up as a tunnel that led to a false body of water that drowned Yeshua the blind Amharic Jew.

You did what then.

We sat with Yoni, who was good, and with her small hands she made us bitter coffee in a hut not larger, Gita pointed to the cell, than this place, and after speaking a while with her and with several of Yeshua's companions, we returned home and made love.

You realize that to fraternize with members of the Brotherhood places you in a dangerous category, especially as a non-citizen of the unnameable country.

As far as I was aware, the unnameable country was not a state but a nameless British protectorate and that as a citizen of the Commonwealth I am under the protection of His Majesty King George the Mad.

You have misperceived your political status as well as ours. Only rotten tongues in the heads of certain intellectual classes or vagabonds would wag to call us an unnameable country, but soon we will be on all the maps of the world, not just the ones on which you would point and which compassed you here.

How could you know.

We know some things, he said casually.

Just as casually, the tortures mounted. Gita grew ill and her belly swelled so that it became difficult to crawl along or to hang from the wall or the ceiling, and she was forced to recline on the stinking cot for longer periods. In the mornings, she began to desire mud, leaves of raw grass, and sheep's milk straight from the udder. Soon after, there arrived men in her cell who abused her and stripped her naked, and they were also naked and they pierced her. The same questions were asked but worded slightly differently, with the intention that she should forget the order of the past, so much so that it became difficult to remember whether the swelling of her belly happened before or after the arrival of the men, who differed in their odours and the shapes of their bodies. And so we cannot know whether the father of the child born to her some months later, which she delivered howling alone in the presence of three hundred pairs of eyes with the assistance of only a midwife in that very cell, was Zachariah's or another's.

You are ill, the man returns.

My baby, she is twisting her hands into dead branches, and her words consumptive grey.

He is safe. We haven't and wouldn't harm your son. He has done nothing. As for yourself, we have analyzed your records and found you criminally negligent but psychologically incapable of accepting responsibility for your actions. You always were and remain in need of psychiatric care.

When can I go, the faint smell of a raw onion at her nostrils, when can I see him.

Zachariah, you mean.

Yes.

You shall see him upon your release.

———————

What hell finds Zachariah Ben Janoun today. And why did we take up the story of Zachariah Ben Janoun at all. As we just discovered, he may not be my grandfather, but genealogy is a knotted and ambiguous affair, and the greater reasons for telling the story reside in losing oneself to the possibility that one could be wrong about everything. Beyond genealogy, but just barely. There is a thread, I declare, and it is frayed and tenuous: Zachariah Ben Janoun loves Gita, this much is true, but to love an absence, an apparition, is different from the love of an everyday woman of arms and a tongue, of thoughts embraces and actual words. And they take advantage of his love. Who then. How. They. Anonymous skulls, a certain memory of the differentiated curvature of interrogators' snouts, but most physical details are fuzzy.

There was the first, the protean one, you will recall, who lifted the heavy file and darkened the room and changed shape in the light. Then he multiplied into others, spoke in British-accented Plainenglish sometimes, accusing him of harbouring, exactly in the bare dimensions of his cell after being forced into prison overalls, bombs inside his dress. Zachariah denied with poise until the closeness of the torturer, the hatred in his voice, his spittle disgusting mouth made Zachariah weep without an onion to aid.

Abruptly, a second man entered the room in a huff and the two passed inaudible officialdoms, really, is that so, the ruffling of papers, could it be, the Britisher examined his papers again, yes, I do believe. Sorry, chap, seems like I've got the wrong room here, I'm supposed to be examining in fourthreesixone, not room onesixfourthree. And then, like a sheepish professor late for a lecture he dashed off. Insensibly, however, though Zachariah Ben Janoun was in no position to argue, he returned several weeks later and started a more serious theatre involving Zachariah's friend, Professor, if you'll recall the unname.

Would you like to see him, the examiner held up a hanging lightbulb and pointed it to the corner where Zachariah Ben Janoun hadn't noticed for the always weak light. For the first time, Zachariah Ben Janoun realized he had a companion, as he saw before him, bundled chrysalis and slits for eyes, the sitting face and body, the face hidden by bandages, recognizable by the curly hair. The light fell away and back onto Zachariah's face but the bandaged face, accompanying body, the moan, could have been the professor.

The drama began afresh as a weighty file appeared in a wagon, pushed along by a paralytic, the one with half-a-face hanging limp and sallow, and who dragged his left leg, and whose left hand swung limply by his side. The paralytic took a long time to bring the charges to the fold. He cleared his throat and read them: numerous connections with communist academics, terrorists, and writers, a participant at weekly subversive gatherings, simultaneously a scandal in high and low societies, sometimes played a corrupt woman in yellow or red negligees at parties, a sexual pervert, as you can, heavily reprimanded for misconduct at job as a border guard.

Partway through the recitation, the paralytic fell drooling asleep. A by the way, just to ask: what were Zachariah's rights. Also the vomit: he was drugged so often the mere thought of food made him vomit. He would think of Gita. In these moments, while listening over shortwave, they took advantage.

It was she who led us to you, they would thunder, she who belonged to an internal surveillance team in the Ministry of Radio and Communications and wore the mask of affection to do so.

Such things were known to happen, Zachariah had heard stories of decade-long marriages constructed for the purpose of police entrapment, but he could not believe. She had been arrested too, after all.

He was a liar, a scoundrel, were you not suspicious of his behaviour for months before his arrest. This latter point Gita could not deny, as the interrogator paced around her. The magnetic tape you studied for years was nothing but a document of a dangerous terrorist imagination, a subversive mind belonging to a person who deceived a whole organization and his friends with a double identity. Zachariah is a very bad man, though he appeared to you sometimes to be good.

The prisoners'dilemma: if Gita confesses the correct untruth and Zachariah confesses, then their collective loss is total and insurmountable, since neither will be returned to the other. If either agrees to the Organs' reality while the other refuses to do so, then the loss is still total since the condemned will prevent reunion. If neither speaks, then the horror continues indefinitely. Gita is told that Zachariah has finally broken and admitted to her part in nationalist conspiracies against the state, of her Communist leanings, of her adultery and other deviant, what was she doing living out of wedlock with a man in the first place. Your cell is an hourglass, they tell her, we have only so much patience, terrorism is a time-sensitive issue, as sand pours in through the ventilation system, choking dust and grey ash: sand fills the cell until it buries the chair on which Gita sits, the cot on which she rests. Gita scurries up the wall and presses flat like a chinch against the ceiling, but the sand is rising, the sign of the hourglass is not a lie, and soon the dust will enter her lungs. Then it starts, perhaps the whole reason we began.

Through her lips a cry. An interruption first, a tickle in the throat: what is glossolalia; does it bear a singular point of origin or is its existence owed to multiple beginnings.

Gita feels a force seize her flattened body and it nearly wrenches out her throat: words words in Server Backslang, tracing backward into old slave Quinceyenglish, fragments somehow in Naga, in Bangla and minor languages she has never spoken, some languages she has never heard, until the sands force her to recede to the width of a millimetre or less, to the dimension of a sheet of paper against the ceiling, until she screams in Plainenglish. She screams, yes, yes I did whatever you say, I'll sign it, I'll denounce him, just don't anymore.

The snap of a latch and Gita's cell door opens, releasing the dust and the putrescent air. The ventilation shaft whirs to an end. The door remains open and she continues to hang from the ceiling. Accustomed to the darkness and the enclosure she grapples with the meaning of this change, and for two days they do not come even to feed her.

―――――――――

Finally, out of hunger, she descends from the ceiling and edges toward the door, wades through grey knee-deep lunar dust. Fluorescent white tubes in horizontal rows across the ceiling, everywhere a dull plain glow, the swift movement of nurses in uniform through a long corridor extending behind and ahead of her, custodial staff sweeping up the sand emerging out from her room, and patients wheeling about, a large nursery filled with incubators. She searches through the names and sees at the far end, written on a plain white card over a plastic casing, the words Baby Nothingatall.

The warm grasp of a stranger's hand, a smile, it must have been a difficult labour, he had some trouble with jaundice but we've contained.

As if she had only come to the hospital to give birth. She finds herself suckling her child, sharing a room with a menopausal breast cancer patient, eating cakes and listening to American jazz records over the public announcement system while enduring her neighbour's endless descriptions of a childless middle age, excoriated adipose tissue, and the virtues of morphine.

The child's forehead seems to bear a certain resemblance to

Zachariah's, and closer examination makes: children at that age don't keenly assume the faces they will wear in life. She shivers in the balmy equatorial heat. She will not release the child from her clutches, so to palliate her anxieties they place a crib next to her bed.

At night she awakens with screaming terrors and paroxysms, which they suppress with drugs. They occur so often she is connected to an intravenous. Granular residue in her lungs. Tumefaction of her vulva. No explanations or inquiries. Hasty treatment.

She asks one kind nurse, where is the child's father; but the nurse is unaware of any prior history in her case, is unaware of familial connections. She will ask, she ensures.

Months pass and Gita wonders about her flat. No doubt by now it has been seized, probably the landlord has given her up for ghost and rented it to others, no doubt sold all her drawers within drawers within drawers, her clothing furniture bric-a-brac, not to mention Zachariah Ben Janoun's. How long has she been here. Weeks, months maybe.

Not a day less than two years, she is informed by a judge advocate general, who arrives in gleaming epaulets, and behind whom stands a paralytic orderly who pulls a wagon in which is contained a fat green folder holding many loose pages. The judge advocate general motions for the orderly to find the right leaves, sign here and here, and here as well.

The sheer military presence is enough to guide her through the formalities without a moan of protest. She does not look at the pages she is signing or ask about Zachariah, the question does not seem relevant at the moment.

Due to your psychiatric and physical health, the uniformed man informs, you will be unable to perform your previous duties at the Department, but the Ministry of Radio and Communications is aware of your high performance before your decline and will ensure you are awarded some level of employment and will contact you in due time. Until then you can live from a small state stipend. Your belongings, which were under the possession of the state, will be restored in a new apartment outfitted with sufficient furnishings for yourself and the child.

At 2 P.M. on Wednesday, the Governor received a note on the interrogations of Gita Nothingatall and Zachariah Ben Jaloun. He had followed their entire story with a certain bemused curiosity and was interested to know of the results. Grenadier Lhereux himself delivered the memorandum and was about to relate its contents when the Governor hushed him and drew him down to the carpeted floor of the Hecatomb Office.

Listen, he said, as he turned a knob on the wall near the light switch and pressed his ear to the floor. Come come, he beckoned the grenadier follow suit as he listened closely to drops of grain fall on balances and scales in every marketplace of Benediction, the sounds of peeling oranges in Victoria kitchens, of the slap of sandals on Conception streets to mean the kenning bustle and economic growth, as the love-shouts of anguish and delight in La Maga bedrooms and fields and rooftops found his eardrums suddenly, the sounds in houses of La Maga of fornicating mice and ferrets, and the sounds of birds screwing in the skies above. Included was a thud, a scree of stones sliding a mountainside in the hinterland, and if you tilt your head exactly the right way, Anwar said, everything in our country vibrates inner ear to your toes.

Lhereux, who had never entered the Governor's office and knew of the acquisition and arrangement of the most sophisticated audio equipment because he belonged to a selection of the leader's closest associates, was astonished when he discovered the effects of his superior's successful campaign of bugging the country, which began before Black Organs and independently of *The Mirror*, the two forces that together would turn the nation into an infinitely surveilled movie studio.

So what'll it be, Zachariah, Ben Jaloun or Ben Janoun. The interrogator's head bends in the light and disappears in certain angles as his hands gnarl talons, shadows on the wall.

Zachariah can't bear to look directly into his face, and, besides, he does not know the right answer. They have reproduced his blank verses and have read them aloud so many times, in such perverted rhythms, have questioned and sullied every line with such vigour that he feels only disgust for the name Ben Jaloun, which was for him always the title of a minor poet. But Ben Janoun seems equally duplicitous, a name he used to obtain employment on false grounds at Department 6119, where he could never return for the shame he has no doubt heaped onto a venerable institution of the unnameable country. They do not cajole, they don't have to: he eventually understands.

When he walks cautiously out the doors of the centre and feels the seadrenched air on his face for the first time in more than two years, Zachariah Ben Jaloun rejoins the world as a mid-ranking checkpoint guard, an illiterate with no particular desires and broken in more ways than he can recognize. He is given an address and fifty dollars, taxis along the La Maga streets without particularly knowing what to expect, though he has been told the individual he meets cannot refuse him.

A host of varicose veins and atrophied leg muscles: the journey up three flights of the urine-soaked stairwell proves difficult and on the second turn he must rest. A murder of adolescent boys with long wooden swords in the darkness, wearing dark capes fashioned probably by their mothers.

Who goes, the eldest asks, extending his weapon toward Zachariah's throat.

I am Zachariah Ben Janoun, and I: he reads it out loud.

What business have you here.

No business of yours.

He receives a thrashing until the scream of a foxwhistle and the appearance of a large matronly woman who tears the boys off him, who rebukes and spanks them until they cry and scatter.

She offers him her scarf to wipe the blood off his head. Rascals, by God, she calls them between gritted teeth, miscreants, vagrants, vagabonds, illiterates, badmash haramzadas and whateverelse: please pay them no notice; true, they will one day grow up to be robber barons but one can occasionally spank their asses red until then.

Hoisting him over her arm, she carries him wheezing up to the appointed door. She is bound to be home, the woman says, poor creature, she hardly ventures out. He hears the cry of a small child from inside and wonders where he has come.

After a very long time, the door opens a crack and the sad face of a middle-aged woman appears. Yes, she seems reluctant to open farther.

You have a visitor, the matronly woman answers.

The door yawns open. Zachariah, who has not looked at his own mirrored image in a long time, is astonished by the changes that are possible to notice in hers even at a first glance. Then there is weeping, the exclamations of surprise and ululations of joy, as one can expect. The child has never known a tortured returning father and cries for all the commotion.

The matronly woman does not leave, so this is the Zachariah I have heard so much about, she says, ah.

Here, Zachariah had the opportunity to add Ben Janoun, but in an instant, the old name he had abandoned years earlier returned to him when he saw his son's face. Ben Jaloun, he concluded, my name is Zachariah Ben Jaloun. And what is your name, he bends toward the child.

Mamun, Gita says.

Mamun, Zachariah calls, as the child draws back from his outstretched arms with a start and disappears under the folds of his mother's dress. Zachariah looks at Gita finds it difficult to retain a smile;

having borne the youthful appearance of a girl not more than two years earlier, and now, though barely thirty, she appears fifteen years older.

He himself is scared of his face the first time he gazes into the bathroom mirror/ that grey emaciated hunchbacked thing, could it really be Zachariah Ben Jaloun, why with jowls hanging folds of loose leather. Could he really ring around Zachariah Ben Jaloun's calves with index finger and thumb. Why is it so difficult to lift a child into his arms, he recalls the introduction, albeit a crying, confused child that evades affection.

Many words and babble, and already, the inheritance of glossolalia is clear in Mamun Ben Jaloun's inscrutable sounds spirited speech that scare his parents. They have to remind him to use English or Bangla or Quinceyenglish, to say something they understand instead of venturing into minor languages.

Zachariah wasn't given a stipend and, forced to work, returns to the officers' den where he encounters the same supervisor, who no longer recognizes him and demands identification, Ben Jaloun, he looks at the card, says at the name, yes, I remember, he admits finally. You may ask Major Mahmoud to show you the ropes, he says, as if Zachariah has no training as a border guard.

Mahmoud himself, albeit older, remains virtually unchanged, and welcomes his old friend with the same vigour. He smokes the same black unfiltered cigarettes and still offers, though Zachariah Ben Jaloun has never accepted. Come now, we're older, Mahmoud says, what's the use anymore of denying life's pleasures. And Zachariah accepts the words and draws a thin, long, dark cigarette out of the case. He coughs, sputters and stares at the same cityscape, he remembers meeting Gita on similar streets as a border guard, of being haunted by her grey eyes. How long it's been, he blows smoke, measures the strata of geological time. And yet, he thinks, I am here.

Where am I, he wonders as he looks around at the assistants

carrying magazines for film cameras, carrying black bags for portable darkrooms. This border region has become a centre of the historical docudrama they were filming years earlier, he thinks, before he was imprisoned, even before Gita and Department 6119. Mahmoud informed him they had turned Quincy's so-called Peacock Palace, which had become the Museum of Cultural History, into a film set to record scenes for a segment of *The Mirror*. What were they filming.

Zachariah thought of his return home as miraculous, so much like the sensational stories of Yeshua, the blind Amharic Jew who said he and his companions floated on water by God's grace for days until they felt a false breeze against their faces. People argued it was possible Yeshua knew he hadn't arrived at the shores of the Mediterranean, but how could he have known he had come to the Gulf of Eden. Yoni didn't break his heart, others around him did not tell him, and others still did not believe the story.

JOURNEY
TO
THE
UNNAMEABLE
COUNTRY

Hedayat thinks. He mumbles and groans, imagines, glossolates at all hours while waking or sleeping to the great distress of friends and family, just as he did during the tsetse fly plague. With sleight of tongue, he conjures a past *The Mirror* claims to know and to have filmed in such detail, one wonders when the cameras crabbing left, trucking right through streets and sidewalks on dolly tracks, casting hard lights sharp shadows, started filming everyday life and movie scenes. Does *The Mirror* know our history. (Why does Hedayat care.)

What is history in the unnameable country when year after year the Ministry of Records and Sources comes in trucks during dark hours and cricket buzz when all the kids are in bed. They take away last year's books to burn because they no longer match today's truth. Keeners tief texts for their own play and destruction, however, and teachers are traditionally allowed to write to the Ministry of Records and Sources for permission to allow students to build personal bonfires at the end of each school year. Before I called it quits with school, they were teaching us the story of Caroline and John Quincy, slaver and rogue empress, a certain way.

They were telling us Yeshua's story is not unlike an older tale of our country, of unmitigable suffering aboard a ship of bodies baking in barrels, hundreds of doomed slaves in prison-containers. The men are destined to be field slaves, John Quincy is wooing Caroline Codite under electric lights in his manor house adjacent to heath flowers rough grass on an evening of crowned appetizers: his chefs have carefully hidden diamond studs for guests to find, meaning right bite broken teeth, indigestion, or the luckiest shit.

Quincy himself, however, is interested only in the daffodil landscape over which he and Caroline lift briefly together in each other's embrace, come with me, he grazes at her neck and ear in the warm breeze. He promises her oceans of iridescent animals, taverns in faraway lands where we will share mussels and shellfish and buttered bread, places for dictionaries to teach us to move our mouths in new ways, he holds her above the ground as the clock strikes a strange hour and the gramophone inside the house plays a heartbeat sound.

Caroline agrees to spend her days a continent away in the house her new husband strews with heath flowers to remind her of their first floating love encounter. The Peacock Palace: its hallways into hallways adjoined to hallways without rooms, but Caroline most enjoys its rooms lifting platforms grinding gears into next-level chambers, the ones with blue artwork on the walls solid shapes straight lines definitive curves latest rebellions against form and structure. Quincy's other major purchases: slaves that hew wood, draw water from the well, bake bread, pray for their masters' health and well-being at scheduled times.

Some days, Caroline rides a wooden palanquin carried on her slaves' shoulders, shaded by lace penumbra to new market catch: bodies from the hinterland of the unnameable country that with haggling and chains, yawning maws, sweat and undergarments, are to be sold men women children all into bondage. One night, she dreams of a library of metal containers on shelf after shelf, turns whispers empty hallways onto yet another collection of metal containers. An eyeless man is organizing the receptacles, and she asks him what he is doing. Separating living minds from dead minds, he says.

Caroline watches the librarian resume his task of placing metal containers from a cart onto the stacks, and assumes the employee of such a serious institution would no doubt disabuse her of opening a metal vessel to see its contents, and though blind he would hear her trespass, so she walks, wanders the labyrinth to find a vestibule free of the eyeless man, but he appears in every corridor, at times in the distance, closer on occasions, in one instance amplified so large she can see streams of black tape emerging from his skull.

That was when Caroline awoke to her husband's nearhead, the terrifying tape image a memory. We're going today, Quincy reminded her with crinkled closer sheets hand at her hair. I know, she recalled their schedule, saw in her mind their steam trip like others aboard the SS *Nothingatall* to deliver hundreds of barrels of slaves to new masters oceans away: slave children ask prior to the embrace of wooden darkness is the ocean made of metal or glass, are hurried into barrels because an irreducible night neither fog nor end of day is pressing against the body of the craft, because the notes on a lone violin on the shore are becoming faster and more frantic as the sun burns bare slave soles of feet in the harbour encampment.

Caroline shifts her weight in bed. Already, she does not want to leave the sanctuary of the Peacock Palace for yet another delivery of bondsmen to slavers like her husband, to leave her home where llamas and birds of all colour and shape wander uncaged, her castle with its sherbet fountains and rooms of artists who have taken up residence, who paint in imaginary colours stretching whole hallways, its dancers who spin on toes to the brush-rhythm of their painting compatriots.

Yet she finds her feet follow a familiar wooden incline, board Quincy's ship a lazarium of risen bodies same black faces at gunpoint as last journey, she thinks. Into the wooden casing with you, she hears her husband order, into tight container water bags food parcels, into the shipment coffins not thrown into mournful ocean spray on the last trip as coastguards spotted them trafficking human beings in the garbage manner outlawed for many years, she would remind her husband from time to time, astonished at his determination on each occasion to continue undeterred, as if unaware of the century.

She pouts mirror-mirror in their cabin room, rouging cheeks and sticking colour on dance-evening lips though they are far from appropriate functions and sociality. Her head overheats from such trips, she thinks, as she hears mealtime sounds opened wooden cases of another world, of slaves and ship journeys and soft woollen blankets as her head finds soft damp odour of bedsheets wonders nature of her illness.

One night during the see-saw ship ride, Caroline dreams a fire-image burning burning, of husband Quincy standing before a cavern crowd along a volcanic perimeter, and she awakes shivering alone, frightened of the image she is sure is situated in the country of their destination, and again she wants only the soft-follicle melodies of so many violins playing roundtheclock in every room of her Peacock Palace.

Turn around, fever says lips moving husband, man, turn around, Caroline says, frightened of her dream, future light, as she steps onto the deck to talk to Quincy, and breathes the ocean air.

SATAN
AND
THE
MAROONS

Quincy turned around at his wife's delirious behest and his bewildered crew stored his great slave ship at the riverhead near their home. Then the uxorious conqueror sat with a hot meal, lifted spoon after spoonful of revitalizing sauce and meats his slaves pre-chewed for their mistress's health, so weakened was she by her mysterious vision sickness mastication had become a heavy order.

Caroline saw a bird shivering light turn distance into wing. It flew flickering wall into room. She saw a future echo: two kids in a candy store overfilling with confectioneries, the fat kid eating chocolate, the owl one with talons for hands glossolating angelic tongue.

Caroline's health improved after visits from Bovaire, first-rate healer of the French army, whose regimen of antibiotics upon associating yellow-tinge fever illness with its microbial source lifted her out of bed finally into sitting, window-staring, before returning to a walkabout state enough to spy on the chickenhands standing around, jawing on leaves and stalks. She liked to make friendly with the slaves, to pick nits from their braids and accuse one of infecting the others with insects if discord was the game of the day, while another occasion would find her humming the same tune over and over as if lost in her own thoughts, while in reality she had left her throat on auto while her ears—nearly as keen as Moriah Mahatmama's, head servant, it should be noted—were honed into the slightest changes of tone inflection pitch of their creole Quinceyenglish.

While the Passage had infantilized native languages, the slaves found ways to keep mothertongues alive through song and nursery rhymes, and because it was hard to control their speech when they were not wearing their metal plates. The slaves, who knew they were constantly watched, made no mischief in the company of Caroline, whose husband scared, whippersnapper of the cow leather, but it was she who dealt the subtler and arguably more dangerous forms of terror.

In the days before the Maroons, the children were the bravest, and would pelt Caroline Margarita with walnuts, unseen from the canopy, alone and giggling like squirrels at the ouch-ouch scampering lady. Field slaves would eyesmile and wink, silently making fun of her prissy walk, her lips, which pursed like an asshole when she concentrated, as the soft breeze of rebellion was already in the air, and Caroline's intuition sensed this subtle shift in the narrative of power, which was plain to see in dreams and in waking life. She befriended young children with candied apples and jujubes, and while their parents tried in vain, she would pry into their dreams by sifting through their babble. All she got was nothing words bubbling phrases cut apart marron cima Cimarron, meaning nothing to her. Older subjects were evasive, would fail even to refer to the nothing words, and would point instead to some distracting bird or imitate the howl of a distant coyote.

Frustrated, Caroline brought the words marron and Cimarron back to her husband, whose backhairs bristled and whose eyes widened at their mention. He roused his officers, bade come here his overseers, before consulting the Somnambulists seated on their hard wooden chairs in their endless rest perpetual work, in their sleeptalk in a room through which moved other days of other ages, who in their waking dreams saw a future department of desk after desk in rows of thought leeches sucking the life out of unsuspecting citizens of the unnameable country, the chamber of twin chairs where minions of centipedes made love in dark corners, the room with crabs from the far shores of Masoud Rana's bleeding foot many years in the future, a room of so many spiderwebs Moriah Mahatmamagave up trying to clear them and watched as they consulted scalp to toe the landscapes of Illium and Dictum, Illium with his twisted throat that from birth made him speak slanted stones difficult words. Dictum, on the other hand, always shot straight to the point: they have already gathered outside the estate, he stared at Caroline with cataract clouds that hid the moment and allowed him to understand.

Quincy heard the news and made a big row about inventory and demanded that the numbers of sleeping and working slaves be counted and rebranded.

Mouth agape, the overseers swore on his records the problem was so recent it had escaped even Tuesday's head count.

Who and where, Quincy flogged one adolescent red back and behind, and then an old woman begging and toothless. She kept pointing while they stuck pincers into her sides and no one could understand the howling words, though Caroline kept pursing her lips and thinking hard during the proceedings.

Unpredictable explosive bunch, Quincy laughed; stick a firecracker in the behind of this one, he ordered. While fifty-odd houseslaves gathered in the courtyard, the bottom half of the old woman disappeared into fire, and then the top half one or two writhing moments later.

Throughout these evil proceedings, Caroline Quincy noted the bubbling-to-surface of her husband's bloodlust, an energy that differed so greatly from his careful and supine performances in the marital chamber where he would lie next to her for a long time also flat on back, wondering, wandering eight fingers along her ribs, under her shoulder blades, distracted, aloof, alone in his own flybuzzing mind, that she came to understand in which corners of his spirit he stored his youth. She wanted to help. And yet what could she do. In her dreams the daily inquisitions replayed and the non-discoveries—for a week had passed, letters and telegrams had been sent out to nearby estates, none of whom had counted odd figures of missing slaves—until she gathered meaning.

The assexploded woman, she began.

Yes, he was listening. The covers of the bed crinkled closer together.

She gave us a clue, Caroline brought her face so close to Quincy's face, whispered so quietly even I can't hear.

Quincy thought for a second, hawing humming as if to vibrate the dying woman's words closer, then kissed his wife and leapt out of bed like a ten-year-old. He whistled out his dogs and whistled out his right-handmen. He rushed downstairs and gathered his infantryman's helmet from decades past. He gathered up his rifles and his six-shooters, his redcoat with its gold epaulets. He shone his blackarmy boots until he could see his chin on them. Then he went out in search of the man who was planning a rebellion.

Secretly, the knot tightened as the one hundred fourteen Maroons rested their horses and reviewed quietly the remaining tasks. Cattle and sheep grazed on wheat and cereals and other sun crops, several small fires gave light, hidden behind a rocky enclosure. The encampment stood four miles south of the shores of the Gulf of Eden along the mountainous region, at a point that would be later known as Maroon Peak. And it was, in fact, Ellipses, Quincy's righthandman, who noticed the smoke first and asked if he should go up there and examine it.

No, Quincy whispered, let's make tracks.

They tethered the horses a safe distance away and treaded softly back. The encampment was high up and while there was a path, they could not risk being seen. They wanted only to hear, and craggy folds of grey mountain rock helped. They climbed into a crevasse.

Fifty metres above, on a plateau, the sentries that evening, Rudolfo and Solomon, watched the craggy moon face brighten as evening inked the sky a deeper violet. The russet soil augured no victors because there were looksees along every possible route. An hour earlier someone mentioned two separate horse pirates, fresh and dangerouslooking, but Rudolfo and Solomon who were weary from hewing firewood for the day's meal, made less of the discovery and shared a pipe. They had forgotten their original names on the Passage, though Solomon said he could remember it partially.

It was four syllables long, he could remember, and contained the sound ngua, but the memory ended there.

Rudolfo said all his memories before arriving to the unnameable country had been erased by the black milk they had been given to drink, and the lalapping strangewaters of the journey, and frankly, he didn't care.

Why not, Solomon handed him the pipe.

Because the past is a mist, friend, and the further you walk into the mist the more plain it is to see there is no way to go back where you came from.

They spoke on their disagreements as the soft sounds of hell emerged from the distance. Underneath the stage, fifty metres below their hidden crevasse, John Quincy and his righthandman listened as the scene unfolded. They could not see, but this only piqued their interest more.

What ho and who goes there, Solomon says at the ghost-pale apparition, which seems not to hear.

Stop where you are, Rudolfo lifts his rifle, and at this the old woman halts.

They approach her slowly and Solomon questions her in English and Quinceyenglish. What is a white woman doing so far from her home, alone and unguarded in these dangerous times.

She will not speak and her craggy face scares them because refracted by moonlight it looks a little too much like.

Torches and men wielding torches respond to all the shouting. The rule for intruders is immediate severe, but since this is an old woman and apparently deafanddumb, Amunji's word is necessary to make the decisions.

Amun asks them to leave the prisoner with him.

So you are the one, she says.

So you can speak.

Please untie me.

And what would I gain; the simple objective is to eliminate any intruders in this congress.

You Maroons, she laughs. That is the name others elsewhere have given such expeditions, so what's your point.

Nothing; they say you have violated the laws of the country, that you are renegades, and that you should return at once to estates and owners.

It was then Amunji noticed: her makeup had been carefully applied, so thickly that it was virtually a mask, and that her eyes shone too brightly for an old woman's face. He leaned over to examine her brow in the flickering firelight and got a faceful of mucus. Calmly, he produced a rag from somewhere in the tent, wiped his face before wetting it in bucketwater and cleaning off another time. What witch this one, he saw again the contrast of youthful skin and shock of white hair.

He knew her name also and said it now: Caroline Margarita Quincy. Ah you, bibi, he laughed, so they are sending you, he slipped into a more humorous tone. If this is the case, sky is falling and all is lost, no. So tell me, Margarita-begum, wifey of ol' Johnny boy: are you a messenger or just a plain old spy.

Neither.

Well, you've got to be one, he hopped on his left foot. Or another, he hopped on his right.

I am neither.

Well, explain then, because no doubt you have words.

I am a defector, she said straight-eyed, without a blink.

My great-grandfather laughed and laughed, he couldn't stop laughing, and then when he stopped he just started again.

Joke it up, said Caroline, but you're laughing away your opportunity to learn about Quincy's defences and his plan of attack.

We have our own plans, Caroline, and your involvement will only endanger them. Although, he stood up, you realize you have made the job a lot easier in some ways.

Is that right.

Absolutely, he came closer, lowered so that they were nearly eye-level. Your husband is a brutal man, as you know.

That's why I'm here, because brutality doesn't become me.

Amunji bit his lip to keep from laughing again. Nevertheless, he asked: Why did you disguise yourself.

Because I thought if your men recognized me they would kill me at once.

And if they saw an old woman they would have been more merciful to you.

Yes.

And that in my presence you could explain yourself.

I didn't know who you would be, so I didn't think that far ahead.

Hum.

Please, she sighed, you don't understand the meaning of living under the rule of such a dictator.

A butcher, he added.

Yes.

He had waited to call him the names, a scoundrel, a pirate. Not a pirate, Amunji shook his head, there is brotherly compassion among pirates, as far as I know.

The tent folds rustled, a stranger entered, whispers passed between him and Amunji. It seems, he returned his attention to that strange girl-woman with her smooth face gloved hands and her starched white hair, it seems your husband sent spies to follow you.

Do you know this for a fact; as far as I am aware, I stole away from home on the fastest horse on coarse rocky terrain and over water to avoid pursuit. If he is nearby, if he has followed me, it was his own doing, I didn't forewarn him.

Amunji paced, I have heard that ordinarily one sends a bloody ear or a digit of the captor's hand to alert the party in question of the serious-ness of the matter. But, bibi, since you seem genuine, he italicized, there is no need to harm. I need, however, a token of your presence, something by which to indicate to your husband you are captured and that as many of us he kills, we have the one life he values most. Because he does, or does he, I should ask, love you.

Caroline Margarita blinked. Then with a savage expression she added: That man loves nobody.

Amunji untied her hands. Please give me your wedding band, he asked.

Caroline inhaled sharply. He withdrew his machete and she did not resist, slipped it off her finger.

Thank you, he said, you're going to be a great help.

Meanwhile—recall we left them hanging—Quincy and Ellipses heard a sound. It was a question first uttered in English and repeated in Quinceyenglish. Who could it be this sound, they gesticulated and quizzed each other with eye expressions. They waited three moments longer until torchlights passed over them and they were certain of danger.

They crept deeper into the gash in the rocks and the feeling of grey sediment fossilized molluscs and million-year animal bones frightened Quincy so much he began to pray to god as Hedayat would on one occasion in futuretime, for life and whatelse. Then the others were coming from above and across and they were stepping quietly, but they could still hear them. And then they went away. The Maroons, one presumes, began looking elsewhere, and in this gap Quincy and Ellipses made haste.

From a distance it was plain to see their horses had been slaughtered and that already magpies and buzzards had descended though it was not their hour. Without a way out, they meandered through the forest, which was as difficult as the most difficult segment of the labyrinth of hedge and grass that wandered so far off the estate and whose construction he himself had ordered. At that moment, Quincy felt like plucking out his eyes and eating them for what godforsaken and how did we arrive, as he forgot the games he had instructed the architects play, all the false and emergency exits they had written down for him on a map.

For two days they wandered. They wandered until Quincy lost the map he had kept inside his head, neatly folded and stored inside a crate whose lock and key were now lost. When at last they turned a corner and found themselves at the northern edge of the cornfield, Quincy's relief forbade all questions of why and how. The face of Bijou, his

269

manservant, descending the ship's now elegant staircase, elated him. But the sodden expression on that bright crinkling face told otherwise. The price of her release: his dry words blew the news simple and high off the paper that was produced: unchain the slaves, wake the others, the Somnambulists, abolish indenture and slavery, and declare the equality of all inhabitants of the unnameable country. Signed, Caroline Margarita ~~Quincy~~. Below the signature, impressed upon the page with three drops of blood, was her plaintosee left thumbprint.

The questions abound who among the missing slaves, why did Caroline, and all the questions then. Quincy's anguish bore these added confused dimensions but he managed. Drag out the harnesses, whistle out the dogs, whistle out the men, and there were so many of them then, but Quincy had miscalculated his body because he landed assheap on his wheat stalks, confused by the lack of motion. Ellipses, Bijou, others carried him to his room where Moriah, his most trusted houseslave, prepared a goulash of tripe and barley and nightshade, which was supposed to. It slowed his breathing and his wild dreams of vengeance.

Bovaire, he identified the doctor by name when the latter entered.

The one and only, the mustachioed and so forth doctor announced.

Bovaire, Quincy coughed, medic and healer, he laughed and coughed and hurt himself further by these efforts. One of the brightest doctors of the French army once upon a time, we should add during the pneumonic tumult. Stethoscopes were removed.

Inhale, said Bovaire. Cough for me. Urinate. Do as, he ordered as men in his profession have the right. He removed a hypodermic for a painkiller.

Whatever was the illness—and there were various possibilities bandied about and not worth repeating—no one could keep Quincy from Caroline Caroline Caroline Caroline he drew strength from the refrain while stumbling searching for his redcoat with the golden epaulets. Ass and stubborn fool, Bovaire replaced the hypodermic into his case after the shot, you'll meet your death out there.

At that time out there a congress of Maroons was happening without anyone knowing. There were discussions in the crevasses and grey craggy rocks of who would play intermediary and negotiate with the slaveowners. That was when Amun modified a rifle that could spit no more for a box of empty bullets to fire buttons and rocks, suggested raids of Quincy's and surrounding landowners' estates to collect spiderthread and spiderlooms to design a tripwire system to tell them of near dangers. The Maroons amassed an inventory of blankets rope spoons pots cauldrons gourds twenty horses, and began trading with a community of neither slaves nor landowners, from whom they acquired sharper swords and heavier weapons.

They invented hymns at firelight sang questions who takes from darker races/ does he leave as good and as much from others, continued into daylight their lyrics recollecting fetid slave ship journey aboard Quincy's SS *Nothingatall*, their sudden return to the estate and field-burdens, and thus they continued, with Amun singing loudest like Satan in the conference of the one-third before overthrowing God in heaven, sowing discord and speaking of freedom as if it was too many things to be only the right fruit from the right tree.

Caroline's tent folds opened to reveal the slave that had been in congress with the others, who stood before her burning words. His words moved the lone kerosene flame lamplight tremors, and Caroline Margarita watched my great-grandfather Amun, watched the way he gestured, took a page from a book she might once have crossed, listened to his mixed metaphors stirred up a strange blood music. She noticed the words when he paused would continue humming inside her. That night, she dreamed a great walnut tree husband Quincy felled and felt every axe swing as if she were the walnut tree. She felt her feet and toes turning into its uprooted roots. She awoke amidst a blaze as

271

the walnut tree burned a fever inside her. She sat up and drank from the gourd of water by her cot, asked for water again and again.

Are you ill, asked the guard that had been posted.

What is the next stage, she asked.

I'm sorry, but I'm unauthorized to reveal any information.

A-O-I A-O-I

Quincy's men stormed the encampment and found mist and charcoal, embers and the remainder of fires, embers and not much else. Ellipses communicated via wireless radio—a monstrous new instrument that appeared to have conquered distance—from the back of a mule.

Quincy's hepatic fever had lessened, but left him weakened, incontinent, babbling brook rushing riverine words headlong over words who knew what meaning. Others took his place on the hunt for the missing slaves, three-quarters infantry and several hundred strong, with eighty dogs hot on the trail.

To disclose the name of the leader: Bemis, himself an owner of five thousand indentures and slaves, and the conjurer of elation: aha, he says at his dogs' discovery of a close trail. And yet dismay would be more proper: ambush.

A hail of stones and fire, the whizzing of combustibles. Rusty blades pounced and Bemis realized his party should not have come to this valley, where they were now encircled in turbid swampy lowlands.

Their horses' feet sunk into the clay, while gunners struggled to position their weapons, finding no solid footing.

They killed themselves, historians would later write, by friendly fire. Twenty-five Maroons also perished, but their numbers are another story. Stories of the Maroons' victory burned throughout the nameless country. As if an alarm had been sounded, deserters from numerous estates found their way miraculously to the rebel camp, with clothes on backs, with metal plates in their mouths, and what else.

Caroline by this point had been given an administrative position; she wrote it all down, their names, their names prior to arriving to the unnameable country on the SS *Nothingatall*, the names of their owners before desertion, whether they could contribute culinary, medical, or literary skills among useful attributes, and whatever else needed to be written down. She exchanges her only dress for a simple coarse cloth because it's what everyone else wears, and begins diligently to obtain the confidence of the rebels, who, aside from Amunji, who hawks over each of her decisions, see her as an administrative fulcrum necessary for the rebellion. But she is nimble, pushes deftly aside by acquiring the favours of one or another of the higherups. The pushandshove generates a strange friction between them. Rumours of lipstick and sametent night-excursions emerge, although both provide believable alternative explanations.

Then one day there is a sound. And then they all stand and point and wonder of possible sky meanings what could this cloud-dust at a single-propeller British aircraft indiscriminately showering school-age photos of Caroline posing in front of a chocolate fountain higher than a grown man and at Caroline and John Quincy younger and living together in various shades brighter than this hard earth and humble bread on which she subsists and for which she gives her solemn mysterious thanks in silence. She realizes she is famous, simultaneously a missing person and a fugitive, a curious somebody worth something ex nihilo, quite unlike the whole minuscule British protectorate, so nascent it had not yet time to be properly born, to be named or counted among the nations of the world.

Not too long after, the British prime minister rushes frigates and dreadnoughts to its shores while war is waged all across Europe and new inventions for the people's betterment are brandished reflective clean before being exploded smithereens. Aviation had begun only several years prior in an American desert, and due to some ingenious individuals had already started to benefit humanity. As the small plane flows above their heads some shots are fired, all miss, and the pilot does a dosedo once around the crowd before climbing over the clouds and into the horizon.

Hemmed against the Gulf of Eden, the Maroons realized they had grown reliant, in previous months of internal resistance, on surprise fires within the estates, on small groups of indentures or slaves driving off landowners with pitchforks and shovels, and the more recent developments: platoons were being found out, their impromptu stratagems predicted, their locations on the tiny patch of land identified.

Years later, a frightening tyrant identified for the time being only as the Governor would imprison himself in a large house known as the Peacock Palace, where he would discover and fall in love with the forever-embalmed Caroline Quincy, and whence he would order the construction of a large-scale map destined to theatreswallow all of the unnameable country, to transform the country into a map itself, a simulacrum, but that is a larger and later story whose particulars Hedayat has no time at present to recount.

More important, there is a funny, if you will consider: Quincy has become a bambacino since the gone of Caroline, a big baby who has transported all his favourites, including his gramophone and Eddie Cincinnati records, two life-sized soldiers pirated from Kublai Khan's tomb, as well as an ensouled pair of mechanical birds named Q and

A, gifted to him by a Swiss cuckoo clock maker. He babbled and bored with the figurines in time, installed actual men as the play figures of his imaginary warcraft, while there raged a real conflict just outside.

Bemis, among other generals, would visit the infantilized leader and interpret his desires from the movements of the simulation.

I'm tired of playing with cavalry, Quincy said to Bemis one day. In Europe they're doing it on the wing.

The Great War is over, his friend reminded. And we have aerial transportation in the continent, you should know.

Quincy rubbed his eyes as if emerging from under a mountain of years. He realized his amnesiac recession had turned the clock back to childhood nowhere but in his room. Take me to Admiral Mulligan of the British Navy, he ordered Bemis, who abided.

He drove Quincy in his new combustion-engine Ford with the mahogany sidings and a foghorn. They beep-beeped their way through the upanddown roads, which had not yet been paved and were strewn with ditches, some dug by Maroon saboteurs and others by counter-revolutionaries, each for the purpose of cutting the other's flow. They arrived at the estate of a fellow pirate and slaver by the name of Juan Ignacio Baltazar, who welcomed Quincy like a long-lost brother.

You look like chicken soup, Baltazar told him, and it was true: the illness had rendered the once merelythin pirate chesthollow gaunt and withered of his internal organs, out of whose eyes there issued water as if he was a feathered sufferer of fowl pox. All true, he looked like shit, but his presence in a room stuffed with British officers engendered silence and awe. They had heard stories of his travels and travails like Noah, his choices of the right flora and human animals for the new colony, and though some did not believe in the dream wars between knave and master, all had followed the stories on newspaper and radio. John Quincy received a standing ovation when he entered the room because he was famous and important. He was shown aerial photographs of the indentures' and slaves' last known whereabouts, an updated map of the still-nameless country was unfurled, for which the walls between three rooms were required to be demolished, and which created a new play-space for Quincy's man-sized figurines.

What we need, Quincy said, is a list of everybody—every slave in every estate.

How, they asked. Tell us, they implored.

Quincy responded by shrinking to a size that befit the map, which, though large, was still smaller than the unnameable country. When he rose again before the astonished crowd, he produced a single word they all agreed as the solution: Caroline.

Within hours, a plan was incubated and beaked out into the world as a quiet and assertive little bird. A young corporal sergeant named Thomas, with a long slicing jib that punctuated his ability to penetrate enemy minds, had been recruited for his heroic reconnaissance exploits in doubleyou doubleyou one, and made to wash up on the nearest shore to the Maroons' camp.

To the question who are you, I am, he began, and pretended to play wounded. The trick was to present himself as an indenture though he was clearly an imposter. He had a splint on his legs and his ow ow ow ow ow caterwauling saved him from the truth.

I believe him, said Caroline, he looks hurt.

Though he's obviously lying, said Amunji.

I believe otherwise.

Some were stunned, though others remained unsurprised, having awaited exactly such a revelation of what they believed were her turncoat true colours. In time, she had become a much-needed functionary, a channel by which the revolution—which Amunji and the other higherups had upgraded from the status of rebellion, because these days it was bloodier still—could work at all, through her hands working numbers and tables all day, digesting and dispensing data, storing whole ranks and files inside her skull. They relied on her for the facts on the ground to enable the strategies of battle. In short, her opinions mattered.

What do you believe, Amunji asked.

That he knows Quincy, and that we should drain him of all that he knows.

On this point they argued, because it was dangerous to have one untrustworthy affiliate (meaning Caroline), the revolution could not risk another. Besides, what could he know; they all turned to look at his meek eyes, which revealed only pain, and his twisted mouth, which in pain grimaced from his busted shin. They never got to grill him properly because someone entered the conference tent and informed that spies had detected her from nearby waters. The Maroons, who were afraid of the sea because it reminded them of the Passage, and because they had no navy—since they barely had an army—decided to leave camp immediately and drive farther inland. The prisoner will come with us, it was decided, and in the cover of night, in small bands more difficult to detect, they spread out across the fields descending from the mountains.

Years later, historians would document this moment as the revolution's undoing, when slave battalions scattered like a bag of winds and were caught by British sails, so to speak. More literally, they were shot to smithereens by the onshore navymen. But for the moment, they are still safe.

In the dark Caroline Margarita slips in place next to Amun the glossolalist in the tall grasses during the longest march to oblivion. He recognizes her plaintive breathing and is surprised to find her hand in his; their fingers clasp together.

I'm frightened, she says.

He has never heard her speak of fear, in fact of any part of her inner life. Her eyes are the same dark pool as the night.

We'll be home soon, he says instinctively, without thinking of the meaning of his words. But it is the right thing to say. Ahead, they see the lights of their barracks, but Rudolfo is there and the others are there, maybe one hundred of them. Rudolfo signals the first blast. There would be many fires in the unnameable country, and like all others, Quincy's attack on the Maroons made a lasting iridescence in the sky; you could trace the shots for miles, talking death's language whatever the colour, taking sounds right out of the throat.

In the darkness, Amunji finds himself screaming vowels, finds only vowels, his tongue does A-O-I in the air, A-O-I, he says again until he feels something. Maybe his arm is soaked. A-O-I, he yells without reply though she was holding his hand. Glossolalia is an unpredictable miracle, and while later, other members of my family would become overwhelmed by its unnameable, my great-grandfather would be the first to experience its limits. A-O-I, he screams in the midst of other screams and of others. He touches the pain and the red; indeed his arm.

Dawn's roseblush finds fifteen rebels remaining and all captured. Amun, son of/ first in a succession of family members to be arrested. A-O-I, meanwhile, was restored to Caroline Margarita, wife of John Quincy.

———————

When reunited after the infinite separation of a year or part of a year she seems different, her muscles more sculpted, her face and skin weather-beaten, her palms coarser, her voice more apt to rise into the imperative you must see do and so on. He, on the other hand, appears as if the iron of his bones has rusted in the meantime. He returns to her what he has been waiting to give, after removing from his pocket the wedding band she had sent in an envelope. She accepts out of pity for the prune before her who had once gallantly ordered hundreds to drag a ship across the unnameable country to the Gulf of Eden.

Flashes of the recent past return where is Amun without warning.

Who.

The indenture who spoke strange words.

Many of them do, he embraces her deeply, so closely she can hear his ribs bending with the cric-croc pressure.

She finds herself unable to speak, discovers no air in there anywhere; then what a pang at whatever he would say next.

Dear, a commanding officer of the British Navy would like to speak with you for a few moments. Do you mind if I stay in the room.

Caroline's heart/ she regrets everything, her rash flight into the thick of war, what was she doing thinking, and now without a single friend, remarried to a tyrant, and queen of the Horn of Oblivion.

Her voice shows no sign of anxiety when she asks what can I do for you, Admiral Mulligan. But before the admiral has a chance to remove his hat, she is clapping her hands Moriah, she is saying, bring us a tray will you.

Please, Quincy rises, this is not a tea party.

No no, Mulligan retorts, I'm in the mood for tea. Please, let's sit and chat awhile, Mrs. Quincy. A porcelain cat strikes six, repeats six strikes, turns its tail round, leans down its black hat and replaces it headwise; its redpainted tongue laps from a saucer of milk. Onto a teak lacquered table there appear cakes and confectioneries, tea and Ethiopian coffee, chicken and raisins, rice, and Caroline realizes she is famished.

After the pirate emperor and the admiral had doused their throats the latter spoke. He spoke and he wrote it all down. So what did she then: she says this, if you must know, she does not say anything, she laughs and laughs the way Amunji laughs at her when she is trying to deceive him, when he laughs at her until she actually does become the deserter as he asks, and sits before him denuded of her old woman's makeup, when she becomes the beginning of a revolutionary in an embryonic struggle against. (The numbers, by the way, are growing quickly against and the fire too, but you must hang on for those.) She laughs at John Quincy and Arthur Mulligan until they feel like two grains of sand in the desert of her imagination.

He tries again, explains to her that the war for the unnameable country/

You would prostitute your wife, she interrupts, for a neck of the woods that doesn't appear officially on any map of the world.

I would not; I am not asking you to do anything but continue what you yourself took the initiative to do.

To persuade him with my charms. Something of that nature. But to stop short of. What else. She thinks for three long moments. Where is he, she asks.

Somewhere.

Where.

Dungeoned, he waved off.

She didn't further; and instead: I have been corresponding with Anastasia, she said, referring to the fabled sole surviving immediate family of the deposed Romanovs.

And, he urged.

She had not, by the way. All her letters had been opened, carefully scrutinized, re-parcelled; it was known she had received no mail for the past six months. Nevertheless, she continued with the lie: she wanted to join Anastasia in Berlin, where she was hiding at the Weimar chancellor's daughter-in-law's apartment. What she wanted was safe passage.

So you're leaving me.

I'm not divorcing you, if that's what you mean, but I don't want to live anymore in this smouldering continent.

Do this for me, he pleaded, let us crush the rebellion and we'll go anywhere in the world you like.

But we'll have to come back because you haven't left and I have.

Please understand we have built a whole country together. And the heart, he concluded with more flair than he had managed in years, is an involuntary muscle; who knows why I, he stopped short. His wife appreciated his spontaneity; still, all was not well.

INSIDE
THE
GRAND
PIANO

The next day, Amun is brought shackled to an unadorned entrance of the Peacock Palace reserved for meagre guests or capture, driven underground metal gratings toward a prison cell covered in wet grey light. His hands hard worked lock and chain until the panther leapt beyond reproach or control of his guards. All the prisoners in the Peacock Palace cheer thief.

Amun weaves and wends through gaslit hallways as they chase him. They chase him as he flies flames through dark corridors, as he enters quick exits a spidersilk design room among the loom and toil of John Quincy's workshops prior to the first spidersilk factory. From thousand years' labour of woof and warp in hinterland villages of the unnameable country, of long dresses and arrow-resistant silk shirts, Quincy wanted to produce antiballistic wear for the British military.

That morning, he petted sad Caroline before leaving her a music box in her room and the unspecified promise of more. She rolled out of bed when he left. The recent churn of her heart lifted her restless wander through interior of Peacock Palace searching for an outside face indoors. The atmosphere changed from humid to high mountain wisp as she passed door after door wondered what labyrinth functions within. Since it's easier to choose an open door over a closed one, Caroline peeked into, entered a room that was wall to wall spider-clouds and mottled webs. A man paced with notebook in hand, one side of the room to the another, jotting words in a journal about an old woman seated at a loom with skin of bark and back bent hands rooted to thread and motion. In a country late growing its colonial institutions, it wasn't an absurd question: Which department are you from, she asked the official stammering at sight of wife of the owner of all the dark corridors in the world. Caroline, curious, pushed past him toward the labouring woman doesn't lift eyes from her work. For whom, she asked Notebook in Hand of the old woman's make. Where does she eat her daily bread in this room and machine, she wondered, wondered bruised nails on the old woman's hands, Caroline's pang of emotion the result, no doubt, of recent audacious adventure-run into Maroon wilds. A scratch, the crone laughed a sandpaper rasp at her stare. Meanwhile, Notebook in Hand wrote it all down. Every day they come for the silk, he said simply. Caroline looked at the young man two moments and left the room.

In the hallway, sounds of the loom room give way to a collective hum that Caroline realizes when passing the next, all the next rooms, means silk manufacture behind closed doors. Why John Quincy never informed his wife of the spider husbandry going on constantly in the Peacock Palace is a forgotten question of her mind when corridor becomes crawlspace pressing against her sides squeezing, makes her move hands drag body toward the only light around, ahead of her through barely a hole in the wall.

She lies fetal on the floor for hard breaths, catches wind on carpet until realizing where she is: an enormous room populated by plastic shrubbery and rocks and a doum palm in a sandscape shaded high ceiling. Two further accoutrements of note: a grand piano and a cry for help. What the hell.

Caroline Margarita walked toward the instrument's wooden sheen, its Cristofori design, unusual, though no more than recent crawlspaces and spiderweb workshops of her home. She reached the piano's clavier, its semicircle sweep above which rested a difficult page of music. She had taken piano lessons as a girl that allowed her slow interpret chords; she played spritz orange melodies rose citrus from the soundboard, as help. Caroline continued, stared at the inside-outside landscape around her as help, again the sound from inside the instrument, a garish cry.

She lifted the soundboard and saw instead of wires and felted hammers an impenetrable darkness, and heard the buzz of an ancient language. She brushed thick sounds aside and realized a man sat huddled in the corner, head in hands. For a moment, he cowered, but then Caroline said, Amun, it's only me. She recognized the Maroon and encouraged him to climb up the sides of the instrument.

When John Quincy entered the room with his dogs and his men, his enemy had already climbed out of the piano bunker and was embracing his wife in plain sight. What the hell.

Quincy had bought the grand piano from Spanish piano maker Roque Federico, who constructed it with a secret bunker, a beguiling interior deeper than exterior measurements showed to allow. Federico remarked in a letter correspondence with Quincy that the piano's architecture relied on a simple magic: the cubic interior was designed to make the viewer forget the trick of mirrors and, instead, climb inside for a sit. What better invention, Federico concluded, for World Wartime.

Quincy's first shot was a warning and the next whizzed above the pair's heads with pensive anxiety. The following bullets flew closer but seemed to turn in mid-air to avoid both Caroline and Amun. Who killed her is uncertain, whether the slaver or his men, but it's well known John Quincy mourned his wife's loss with greater care than he bestowed upon the living Caroline. He had them remove her brain with pincers through her nose, sew her up before bathing her for weeks in the strongest preservatives to turn her dead and simultaneously alive: he made them embalm her.

FLY
YOU
TO
THE
MOON

Quincy, with all his guns and gall, blamed Amun for Caroline's death, but knew that to do away with him minor explosion wouldn't suffice because the slaves were still loose. Rather, his demise needed to occur between seeming equals, regalia and fanfare, astronomic theatre. At exactly 5:32 A.M. the next morning, after a swift court martial under nascent military laws of the unnameable country, they brought the Maroon Amun before a dirigible, fat with helium and growling from the motor, that lorded over the crowd of slaves like a ferocious animal. Its rough canvas hide was once a violent purple but time and neglect had eroded it to a matte complexion. A thick cloud of steam effused from the balloon constructed specifically to house the sole pilot of this absurd mission to discover whether the political lines on the maps made by the landowners are inscribed within the physiognomy of the city.

Question: what was the taste of frozen on his palate like when he discovered, somewhere in the stratosphere, the true nature of his ascent. Another: did the map of the region truly resemble the political crisscross Quincy had shown him before sending him. Did Amun have a chance to look down. Curioser and curioser: which patchwork blanket of memories covered him in those final moments. Were any of them memories of the future, of spontaneous fires in spidersilk fields where blossom and grey-clotted fruit, scuttling arachnids, all homes buildings humans in the vicinity burst unexpected flames. Even of Hedayat.

Note that when Quincy brought Amun clinking chains to the site of the dirigible, the laws of nature hadn't yet settled into regular course in the unnameable country and were still competing with one another for prominence. Water flowed downhill in some places, uphill in others because the unnameable country was young, a yearling or younger, and hadn't yet been tamed: a child might throw a ball afloat for hours, maybe days, before it downed back into his hand. As for map appearances, explorers and geographers noted it was shaped like a foot stepping on the body's torso, with left hand rising north to squeeze throat, right hand moving south to clutch gonads, its wholeshape a hallucinated painting.

True to its name and as is clear to see, our country possesses an unfathomable geography. Unfathomable geography be damned, the unnameable country must be real because they're working invincible roundtheclock to invent it, depriving limbs lips ears, horsewhipping furiously for dream of curving and straight streets, edifices, architecture, yes, but also geography, whole rivers dammed and forded, pits dug, perished workers thrown into: let them cry out in joy, Quincy would yell, let them realize their place is here and nowhere else, planting spiders, cultivating webs, harvesting thread for wear or garrison.

A castle for the king: recall only Quincy could have ordered the construction of the Peacock Palace by first clearing a natural maze of sorghum at the riverhead near the SS *Nothingatall*'s first landing. Bemis, a first-rate mistri of Roman domestic architecture, right-hand gunman from the navy days, designed the house with urgent sands, all the necessary rubble and wood, allusions to conquest, with the roundtheclock labour of small strong hands fresh off the boat. Walls rose, doors multiplied, sandwiched base and entablature, while the surface of the house front filled with bay window fenestration and saw out onto water with beakhead mouldings of Quincy and Caroline again and again in decorated forms.

There he lived, John Quincy, perpetually dissatisfied, ordered one reconstruction project to another, from full to base to raised to jointed crucks, to enlarge the foundations of a large cottage to an ever-expanding edifice outfitted with abandoned rooms built for purposes long forgotten, hallways with the musty construction odour of plaster paints and pestle-goop, the wood smells of imported Southeast Asian evergreens, busy with hey you sounds of workmen, the buzz of noctilucent hives of insects indigenous to a house whose walls would suddenly give way to empty galleries that resounded the self-enclosed years of construction far from workmen, to arcades in which the sunlight would drizzle through rectangular apertures where the walls failed just to reach the ceiling.

Through this labyrinth house whose hallways the wind roars creature, in which the climate is icicle and pond freeze in some places against all reason, Quincy pulls Amun the one slave to mean many low and dirty past door immediately after door after door. It takes a long time to get outside. They pass a clinic room impossible to look at for all the odour of disinfectant and gauze, what are the wounds. The next chamber features a bureaucratic official searching an office of airborne papers for the right statement at the right time, with the right stamp. He shatters a violoncello. The slave moves on.

Will you look, Quincy points to an open door a room of the palace he had never seen where a young man paces, crying in the adjacent room the words fire in the unnameable country but I was born first, and before me my father, and before him and before him, before him, pacing, tracing rhythm through decay. The maw of the hallway opens wide into a roomful of rivers of dust and wind winding within walls far apart, governed by the most powerful incandescent bulb whose exact position on the ceiling is too high up to discern. It takes a long time to find the door to the garden and daylight, for the dirigible to appear in the distance.

Quincy was thirsty and though a dead snake dripped fluid disgusting viscera from the high branches of a tree, it was clear fluid to the ignorant eye. Quincy drank and, satisfied, he called for Amun, the greatest shit disturber of all: have him brought to me, he did a crooked smile. Nowtime is festal time, John Quincy smiled as they brought Amun shackled before him. And the auspicious air up there, he gestured broadly: wouldn't you like to feel the breeze on Jupiter, Amun, a right-sized planet for a man of your stature.

And when Amun suggested with silence he was home enough in an unnameable country on Earth, John Quincy threw in the heat on Venus, he suggested why not, hotter even than revolution. John Quincy smiled. Nowtime is festal time, he said again.

Why only me, Amun did eventually, why not all of us on loom and anvil, before donkey and scythe.

No, you, friend, because wouldn't you like to fly to the moon.

Amun did not know it would be impossible to breathe up where he would weigh one-sixth of earth weight, or that a handful of stars weighed more than the whole world, or that if he got into that growling dirigible several days later, he would find himself imprisoned some-where over the atmosphere. And yet. And then. If not for yourself for enjoyment, why not for the people, Amun: why not see if the unname-able country equals its mapshape. Amun had never seen the whole country on a single piece of paper. All he had seen were slices of forest and local landscape drawn by the Maroons, and he was curious.

BEN
JALOUN
BEN
JANOUN

On that same patch of earth for many years, people came to see the SS *Nothingatall*, great ship of excoriated dreams that housed raw living shackles and bondsmen, dry bread and brine for scalded throats, of such solid make and form it survived becoming wooden planks metal parts stationed in boxes for many years before being rebuilt and included in an exhibition of the unnameable country's deep past, which also featured John Quincy's pantaloons, his pipe, and smoking jacket.

For years, people have streamed into the Museum of Cultural History with gift bags and brochures, talking spiritedly about its dark history, did you know the slave Amun drank from a perfume vase that has survived all these years. Chic coffee pubs and bars sprang up long ago around the museum. Well-to-do jobbers, young up-and-comers have wheeled children in strollers and enjoyed afternoons gazing at a slave ship while cheerful attendants reported its functional parts, their builders, their histories.

Years ago, the neighbourhood sprouted grey government housing to accommodate employees of departments with ambiguous titles, imposing buildings with well-watered lawns and grocery service. In an apartment in one such building lived my grandfather Zachariah Ben Jaloun, son of Amun the Glossolalist, Maroon revolutionary, captor of the embalmed Caroline Quincy, Amun: victim first of a shoulder bullet wound before slaver John Quincy's machinations convinced him to get inside a hot-air balloon designed to whisk him stratosphere mesosphere ionosphere out of here prior to siring progeny, Amun, reading verses of E.E. Cummings in the nude while munching raw onions.

Glee and genuine tears from the eyes. Tears and mirthful laughter when the lines call for laughing and the sadder lines pressed into memory by the tears. Peel an onion, read a verse to no one. Disjecta membra: a ceiling fan better at spitting dust and droning on than cooling his small room spilling with books over around and within a little shelf, with a clean little cot in one corner and a pail for washing. The hunchback Aktar delivers a jar of milk each day to his doorstep and is always late to ask for his remuneration. A regular girl calls up, twists her hair round a finger, calls up from the street: you. Zachariah opens his window a yawning touch and hears: do you need your washing done today.

Zachariah Ben Jaloun, border guard between the unnameable country and Somalia and later transferred to La Maga during the British occupation, three hundred miles away from home on either side of things. Zachariah drinks half a thermos of black coffee throughout the morning as he checks the men and the boys for rifles pistols missiles shotguns under the jellabas and panjabis until the afternoon. Muslim women are to be unchecked until February 1944, after the orange harvest, and so the important stories must be put off until then. But he isn't impatient. Orange blossoms on the streets and the smell of the summer light hang on at the nose end of dusk. Only twenty-four years old, an abandoned University of La Maga literary studies major, but Zachariah Ben Jaloun is a minor poet among the café crowd. Just weeks after publication and already *Orange Blossoms* is a minor thrill among certain Victoria and La Maga readers. *Count me among them, a peeled onion / while orange blossoms fall wounded / from your tree.* Walks with long strides, passes a casual glance left-right, finds the place to sit with a slim volume of E.E. Cummings, munching an onion like an apple in his regular corner stall at the standalone café, weeping softly.

A grey-haired professor approaches, excuse me, are you Zachariah Ben Jaloun, may I have a word, and thanks him for writing verses on orange blossoms. He was lauded by his colleagues when he quoted several lines, and excuses himself for not acknowledging their author at the time.

Zachariah acts embarrassed, but is inwardly elated he has caused happiness in even a plagiarist, and for being recognized. Does he want to join a Marxist reading group, would he care to read some of his poems during a class. No, Zachariah softly declines the first offer, he is not a political man, but a writer in the style of certain modernists for whom poetry is a description of the effects of war on language.

Ah, but therein lies, Professor finds the political, self-evident and buried just beneath, he explains in detail qua qua qua qua, and Zachariah's recent departure from the academy burns bright in him, he rethinks his answer to the intellectual's second question, originally affirmative.

Let's continue with the unofficial biography of Zachariah Ben Jaloun. Their conversation is just one way of beginning, of course, and we were listening only to understand him a little better, to be able to empathize with his condition before we lose him to the maze of power. Be a little patient, but. One mild morning in February, four days after the British Council decreed women must be searched as well before boarding buses and all other public vehicles, someone stops at the train station after others and before more still. Arms out. She stares straight ahead. He looks at her eyes. Grey. Checks for any suspicious signs as he has been taught, runs his hands down her sides, her front, the lift of her lower back. Nothing. She leaves and he returns to the others, and to the stanza of blank verse that has been circulating his mind all morning. The momentary pause does not escape his notice, but when he turns around, confused, her shape has already dissolved into the crowd.

For the next few weeks, nothing much happens. Zachariah tries to forget those grey eyes and to stamp out the verses, already a few hundred stanzas pregnant in his mind, onto the page. But the blank sheet repulses him. On the one hand the lines feel unready to be written, on the other, the page is unworthy. He thinks, how strange, perhaps I unconsciously intend to spirit the Homeric idiom, or allude to some folkloric tongue. He continues to recite them at work while searching for weapons, quotes them while dragging down a youth carrying a large rifle under his dress onto the floor. He awakes feverish singing them and approaches the blank page with dread, he declares them naked aloud, in between the lines of *The Enormous Room*.

Not to worry, he tells himself, there is always time to write. Something a little meretricious about the near-total absence of his scrawl besides a few jottings in the diary, and his work suffers as he struggles with what might be the reasons, but the professor returns several times, brings friends to the café on occasion, and eventually Zachariah Ben Jaloun discovers himself, with slight embarrassment, reading his poems in front of a larger-than-expected audience.

What are you writing now, they are interested to know afterward at the professor's suburban flat, among clinking glasses of wine, plush cushions, long, thin imported cigarettes, hashish smoke, and American piquant jazz records. They move around him slowly in turn as Zachariah answers their questions calmly while standing next to a thin blue vase shaped like a young girl's throat. Have you considered an academic position. You would need to collect a master's degree but you seem like the type who could breeze by. And then there is the question of the political in your verses, as the voices drift energetically to the burgeoning independence movement, the growing damage to British colonial troops by radical, the idiot mawslem cows who will never have a hold on the common people's imagination in this unnameable country, and the secular giants will always walk with heavier steps, to the spot searches and the dehumanizing presence of the British military. You have the name of a poet, man. What do you do for a living.

Zachariah Ben Jaloun invents his daily routine as that of a humdrum office worker a paper sorter peon type, shrugs it off as a job. And nothing political about my verses, he withdraws into his shoulders, in fact they're little musings on human relationships and no more. I don't expect ever to take a political job in my life.

But the poet cannot help that, Professor's voice appears beside his ears, a little drunk tonight, flush in the cheeks, always ready in such conversations. Luckily, someone flips the vinyl and a three-fingered virtuoso blues guitarist draws up the crowd to a dance, but rather than accept a young sleepy-eyed woman's invitation, he laughs off her cool touch and retreats into the feint barking night of dogs and a paid-for taxi ride by the professor, who rests his arms on the hood overlooking the passenger seat.

I am sorry we did not get to talk further, but I have these gatherings on occasion; you must enliven them as you have done tonight with your company and your words. Zachariah Ben Jaloun cannot say he hasn't enjoyed the attention or the spot of wine or the cool touch of the sleepy-eyed woman for whose sake he already wishes he had not taken early leave, and promises to attend.

The following morning, he bounds out of bed at least an hour after the sun has shone all the way to the door of his room; he is late, and he is never late. Mahmoud has taken his spot and points nervously that way: the overseer calls him to the officers' den.

Ben Jaloun.

Zachariah's organs fail at the mention of his name: no, but some measure of concern must be cited for he is certain even a minor infraction could result in the loss of the only employment with which he has ever managed to support himself; a poet's income is hardly anything to count on, the small publisher that accepted his manuscript could not afford to advance him much beyond the milkman's uncollected monthly salary, and he pushes out a clambering blank verse from his mind as his superior talks.

Ben Jaloun, this job is not for you. The officer is writing something, and repeatedly pushes papers from his desk as a very small woman, no higher than a grown person's knee, catches them before they flutter to the floor, all the while balancing on her head a tray with several half-filled teacups. He lifts his eyes and catches Zachariah's curious gaze. You may help yourself to a cup, he says. And when Zachariah Ben Jaloun fails to reply or move, he coughs: I have received word you are to be transferred to the general infantry division as a junior troop leader. It is a more difficult position than that of a guard, but more respected, and the pay is higher. I don't believe you will refuse, he raises his eyebrows incredulously.

As if one has a choice in these matters. Refusal means an immediate sixty days' prison sentence and ineffable branding as unpatriotic by the British Council, among other hassles.

No, sir, I am delighted and surprised.

Yes, as I am surprised by your tardiness, you will not receive a cheque this week and you are henceforth relieved of your duties, he stamps loudly and tosses a paper, which floats high in the room, carried by the ceiling fan in a zigzag way.

How will I afford onions, Zachariah Ben Jaloun thinks, for the next two weeks, already feeling his eyelids shrink at the thought, his vitreous humour drained and with it all his emotions. A rattle of teacups. The miniature woman with the papers in one hand and the balancing tray on her head tracks its movement with short assured steps and deftly catches the page between her teeth.

Zachariah Ben Jaloun arrived at the steps of the imposing cathedral that was never a religious edifice, that was built only in the last twenty years in the style of old European Gothic churches to serve officious government, and whose outer walls bore many intricate carvings of inscrutable faces: gargoyles or saints, politicos or traitors, one could not be sure. He was told to arrive in the morning, but no one specified the hour, and so anxious was he about being late he spent the night sipping a full thermos of coffee and pacing, ready-dressed in a starched shirt and sharp-ironed pants, munching on raw onion after onion. He stayed from trying to write any lines of the blank verse just in case it interfered with his insomniac plan. On the past few occasions he had been seized with vomiting sessions when trying desperately to sketch out an outline of the poem that had grown into quite epic proportions in his mind, and it had become impossible to predict what effect writing would have on his body these days.

On the steps of the edifice lay several large sleeping dogs, and Zachariah Ben Jaloun could not tell whether these were strays or guard animals. They appeared to take no notice when he approached, but these were not ordinary dogs, he realized: they were striped like tigers and much larger than they had seemed at a distance, enormous, the size of nearly grown tigers, and with the faces of bullmastiffs. A small man with wizened white hair and a shrunken arm appeared before them and seemed to be their custodian.

Don't worry, they don't bite, they only prick up their heads to regard those exiting.

Those exiting.

Yes, to guard against theft.

Against theft.

Do you always repeat others like a fool.

Not always, no, I am merely thinking.

Of what.

Of nothing exactly, please go on.

Huh.

I mean, please could I have some description of what is inside this building of such value as to warrant theft.

Why, thoughtreels. Although, the reedy man lowered his voice, hushhushed with a finger to lips to indicate chupi-chupi. He beckoned with the same reedy finger comecloser, although, he said, even to speak of them causes a little urination in my pants, he said with a shudder of excitement or fear.

Zachariah Ben Jaloun took a step back and looked at the crooked nose, the strange white face of the man before him, his reedy figure and withered arm. What is this place, he looked up for a sign or some indication.

The Ministry of Radio and Communications, the little man spat, though Zachariah had not spoken the words, you really do have the jaws of a fool.

Oh, I must be at the wrong place, Zachariah took out the piece of paper where the overseer had written the address, I am here for a junior commanding position in the infantry, look here, he held it out to the man, who shook his head and refused even to glance at it.

I know what is written there, he said, you merely have to walk down the first hallway until the end, go up the stairs between the third and sixth floors, and you will find the station you are searching.

Station.

Yes, man, and don't go jawing about repeating their words, they'll take offence and then you will really be in trouble.

Zachariah Ben Jaloun stepped over the massive dogs. He had trouble pushing open the heavy door and felt embarrassed, pulled the handle, but that did no good either.

Here, let me, the little man said, and easily pushed it open with his good arm and hidden strength.

Zachariah Ben Jaloun muttered thanks and walked into an arid windy corridor that extended into the distance. In the far distance there was a faint light. There was no one else in the hallway and he walked alone in silence save for the sounds of his shoes against the floor, clutching his tie, which fluttered like a disembodied tongue. He walked and his steps echoed against the high ceilings. It took a long time for him to reach the stairs and then he had to decide whether to take the elevator adjacent to the stairwell. He decided against it, thinking it better to follow Withered Arm's instructions as closely as possible. He rose up the steps and decided on the third floor as where he should like to arrive. There he noticed only one other man, a young man like himself awaiting his turn in a mercilessly hot room with plastic chairs and a bespectacled woman seated behind a desk shuffling through papers. A caged mynah hung in the corner.

Zachariah took his seat after confirming the time of his appointment with the receptionist, taking little notice of the other man in the space. He was forced to wait a very long time. Hunger, thirst, the erratic predictable flight of a drosophila, the cries of the black bird, the itching of a welt on his right ankle from shoes of slightly incorrect size.

Ben Janoun, the woman called out, and Zachariah resisted the urge. Surely it was the other man who possessed that name and he would assume his spot, but since he did not, Zachariah wondered whether the woman was simply mispronouncing. Ben Janoun, she repeated.

Yes, I am he, Zachariah's mouth decided to take the chance, and his feet leapt up. Room 6119, she handed him a slip of paper on which there was written some inscrutable text beside the twisted number.

Zachariah Ben Jaloun focused unfocused his eyes, turned it upside down, but still the letters failed to reveal meaning. The more he tried the more he drowned in nausea. At first writing and now reading as well. Either I am going mad, he thought, or this is truly the loss of the written word. When he knocked on the indicated door, he received no reply. Though it was insensible to enter a room into which he was not invited, he tried the handle and found it locked. Without recourse he walked down the hallway and found to his surprise other doors also marked 6119. Well, which one, he laughed, and stopped in front of a random.

Yes, a voice from within.

At least something, he said softly, and went inside.

An ordinary moonfaced man with not a follicle of hair on his face or on the top of his skull, with long, feminine eyelashes, sat behind a large desk.

I'm Zachariah Ben Jaloun, and I've come here for a.

Ben Jaloun.

Yes, that's right.

No, we didn't call for a Ben Jaloun, you must mean Ben Janoun.

I see.

Are you Ben Janoun.

And Zachariah again had the opportunity to correct the mistake and save himself from the dispirited future that awaited him within the walls of this evil edifice, whose history he was not yet bound to shape. Once more, however, he chose to assume the mask of the other, this Ben Janoun. I am he, Zachariah said softly.

The man said good, then go down to the end of this hallway and make a left and knock on the second door of the second wing of the 6119 Department, in which you will find a man who looks like me, but who is, in fact, my brother. He will lead you through the rest of the interview process.

You mean the interview has already begun.

Yes, said the bald man with long eyelashes.

I am Zachariah Ben Janoun, he announced himself, and a man nearly identical to the one he had just encountered pointed him to the plush leather chair over there reminded him of the cushions in the professor's house, though these were a drab brown.

Would you like a hot drink, tea possibly. And without waiting for Zachariah's answer he muttered something imperceptible and a full-grown man sprang open the doors of a large chest of drawers behind the chair, barrelled and out, excuse me pardonsorrysir, nearly tripping over the long coattails of his jacket streaming behind him, with a steaming hot receptacle, handing Zachariah a saucer and a cup.

Zachariah held the cup and could not help but wince as several boiling droplets of fluid struck his hand as the man poured.

Manu, Ordinary Man Two shouted, and began rebuking the waiter with such ire.

Zachariah Ben Jaloun, or Ben Janoun shall we say, for we had better start getting used to this new name, better sooner than later, felt a great need to defend, my very fault, sir, I shifted position in my seat and so forth.

Very well, Ordinary Man Two glared, and sniffled di-dit, as if that were an indication for the servant to return to his wardrobe.

Does he live there, asked Zachariah.

In a manner of speaking, as a hermit crab lives in his shell. And no further speech passed regarding the waiter or the wardrobe. But throughout the interview, Zachariah Ben Janoun was forced to ignore a weeping whimpering scratching sound like a neglected dog emerging from inside the furniture.

Ordinary Man the Second began to read from a page before him. Zachariah Ben Janoun. Five years' experience in the infantry along the Somali border. Rise to Major in two years excellent. Associated with Black Organs in retrieving information through expert knowledge of Arabic, Amhari, and Quinceyenglish. Received the Order of New Jerusalem at age twenty-seven, Ordinary Man the Second looked up from the paper with an intense glare of respect.

At any point Zachariah could have interrupted, screamed out, no I am not these things, none of the individual facts and certainly not the composite hero you are describing, I am a minor poet only, no Ben Janoun but Zachariah Ben Jaloun, a quite happy man when reading E.E. Cummings naked alone and lying with a kindly washergirl several times a month, though I do not prefer her as much as the woman with the sleepy eyes I met once and more so another, whom also I have seen also on one occasion, a woman with grey eyes, who, though I have not thought of it until this moment, may be the source of a literary constipation the likes of which no human being should have to experience, and which brings me to my real question: why is orthography the source of nausea and vertigo for me now when it has always et cetera, and to continue I would say only that I am here for a job in the junior infantry position, hopefully one that allows me much time outdoors to think and to surreptitiously scrawl poems and marginalia into a notebook that may one day be transformed into another published slim volume, I know I will never be a great poet, but have you ever consumed a raw onion, there is no sweeter poetry than a cold unpeeled raw onion between one's teeth, Sir, I would only like to live inside the womb of language and to eat the light of dusk my whole life, indeed these are my true desires.

But Zachariah Ben Janoun said none of these things and assumed the mask of a valorous past, learned swiftly that as Zachariah Ben Janoun, he had never hunched his shoulders and had known how to defeat an enemy with a glare, to note slight changes in an enemy's psychological patterns, to destroy his familial ties and poison his friends against him, how to frame any words he has ever written in order to prevent him ever from writing again if he is a dissenting writer, and if he is a carpenter, how to turn his hands against him, how to make him feel his craft is ugly, his head is a shameful pot of lies, how to do these things and more to hammer to harm to harm to harm. Why, Zachariah Ben Jaloun. And yet no one would ever know himself.

Welcome to the Ministry of Radio and Communications, the ordinary man welcomed him with a clammy handshake. We are honoured to have such a decorated member join Department 6119. While as major you were no doubt informed of some of the inner workings of the Ministry of Radio and Communications, the affairs within these walls are of a deeply secret nature and much more complex; please allow me to give you a brief tour.

———————

While they turn onto another echoing hallway, which leads them to the correct room, allow me, friends and enemies, to provide you a brief history of Department 6119. What is Department 6119. And what do they say of Department 6119. Recall the untold history: many years earlier, John Quincy, oldhaggard and bedridden with boils all over his skin, not from some plague but a gruesome infection of lovesickness, is haunted by what he believes is the kidnapping of his wife, Caroline Margarita. In search of a palliative, he turns the dial of his bedside radio for some music or news or dramatic performance and lands on an in-between frequency only to discover strange electrostatic oscillations and the faint monomaniacal voice of a person speaking to himself: not an outer voice but an inner, a human mind, he is sure, and belonging to someone, no less, that he recognizes from the days of his military service. Recall, as it is said: he throws back the sheets and gathers his, rings the bedside bell, and then a wild cry Bovaire Bovaire, he calls, the British have landed.

The doctor is astonished: he himself is one of the few to know and was informed only an hour earlier, how on earth could Quincy have realized. Against the Maroons and during John Quincy's short rule following the insurgency the discovery of this alternate use of radio— which Bovaire called a natural extension of the instrument, since the mind, too, is merely the collection intersection interaction of waves— was not developed into systematic information gathering or intelligence. Quincy seemed the only one capable of manipulating an ordinary shortwave radio to pick up on the insights of a faraway unsuspecting mind. And even for him it was an inaccurate art, since most often he had no clue on whose thoughts he was trespassing. Others denounced the whole scientific basis of the endeavour and declared it as nothing more than the evanescent loony business of a pirate emperor who was fading day by day into the unreality of bhakti, of worshipping his dead mannequin wife.

Juan Baltazar, however, always fascinated by everything Quincy did, and who never lost faith in his predecessor, even when the other went mad and was said to have become a ghost, supposedly haunting the countryside of the continent, insisted on the recruitment of radio operators who would be able to spy on thoughts. Only one in every two thousand of those tested had some satisfactory ability to perform the operation, but slowly, during Baltazar's tenure as governor of the unnameable country, a small department furtively grew, and was eventually added as an arm of the British Intelligence Service in the Heart of Arabia (BISHA).

While the problem of whose thoughts exactly appeared over the airwaves on each occasion was never successfully solved, information sharing between the various branches of BISHA reduced it somewhat, and the clean smokeless rooms—Department 6119 always kept a pious atmosphere, and many activities, including cigarette-smoking, had been banned from the start—filled with keen, dog-eared radio operators that rose up to successfully defend against large drug trafficking attempts, coups d'état, and, once, even against an external invasion. Or so it was said. Arrests of suspects led inevitably to torture but often revealed nothing, or revealed the recorded thoughts as nothing more than a passing fancy or technological errors resulting in misinterpretation: no, a criminal would insist, even under great suffering, that thought interrupted by reel static is thought of film recollection plus conversation about recent plosive events with friend.

But the department was never abolished for an important reason. In fact, its Wall of Red is more important now since the fall of communism, more important than ever because now is terrorism and still features taped-up Polaroid faces of sports heroes, actors, directors, writers, schoolteachers, volunteers: could be anybody, your local anything. Do this: first discover cracks in a red life, what department hacks joke about as the AIDS Narrative (he has AIDS, he fucked his, stole from, was late for, never did his homework when) before driving this virus silent into the community with the instruction be quiet and very loud while saying it because there is more about him. Until: drive the infected individual running crying confused to motherfriend, incorporate him weakened shivering back into the folds of the unnameable country. Finally: pat yourself on the back with the knowledge you can defend yourself against any threat, movie star, terrorist, whatever, and even more important, that you can bristle all the backs of the unnameable country at once and coordinate everyone twenty-four hours and fearful proper. In short, Department 6119 was important because it knifestruck fear deep into the heart of the general populace of not only the unnameable country but throughout the continent and beyond, as rumours spread wildly and some claimed that 6119 now had the capacity to spy on everyone's thoughts and that it was impossible to know who was not 6119, who was or was not being targeted used for. A nimbus cloud settled over our mood and has since governed all our conversations and daily exchanges.

Down the hall and to the right, second room on the left. An enormous room divided and subdivided into cubicles. A deep hum in his intestines and the occasional squeal of a radio dial heard through the headphones of an operator. Hundreds, countless operators.

Is this all of them, Zachariah asked.

The bald man laughed, No, there are many other rooms. This is one room of Collections Subdivision, the largest of three sub-departments, whose purpose you know to some degree, though its functions are more nuanced as you will come to learn with time.

Then there is Assembly, his companion explained, in which the thoughtreels are cut and glued to order the thoughts of a single criminal (since one thoughtreel, due to the inaccuracy of the initial and subsequent locating processes, could contain impressions of the mind of more than a single individual, and, in fact, this was where mistakes were common, he did not reveal). After that authority passes on to Inspection, which edits and corrects any errors made by Assembly and decides whether to continue monitoring a suspect or to order an arrest. Ultimately, however, it is the executive council of the Governor's office that determines the length of interrogations after receiving a report from BISHA, whose hierarchies play decisive roles in determining the case outcomes.

Zachariah Ben Janoun shivered, recalled his volume of poetry and how it had inspired rebellious nationalist political debates among the professor and his friends, realized that if suspected, one was stripped of all possessions, and more than anything that meant the extraction and cauterization of memory itself; torture could do that, it was the point of torture to claw to penetrate so deeply inside. That his unwritten blank verses might contain dissident opinions, unbeknownst to the author, filled him with dread; he needed to forget them immediately but how. Equally, perhaps more important, he needed to retrieve all copies of *Orange Blossoms*, and decided at once he would contact the publisher, the small bookstores where they were sold, and track down each of their owners, smash rocks through windows, to steal them back if need be. Perhaps Department 6119 was simply teasing him, showing him the blade the night before the act of qurbanor ritual sacrifice. He had never heard of such a nefarious roundabout way of capturing a potential terrorist, but fear gnawed at his entrails and suddenly all the onions and coffee from the previous night twisted inside and he needed badly to shit. But he tightened his continence and silenced his crowding thoughts.

As they passed through the maze of cubicles he was met with the bedraggled sidereal glances of so many individuals that he lost count of their souls or what miseries might rule their daily lives. He had heard that the suicide rate of radio operators was very high, and could imagine many asphyxiating reasons. But then a gaze leapt out of that atmosphere. It was her, the woman with the grey eyes whom he had seen but once at a border crossing while wrapped up in his own song. She didn't look at him so much as through him, to some other time or distant location, and it was a quick glance before she returned to her dial. But as he and the man passed her cubicle, Zachariah Ben Janoun noted her posture, the curvature of her spine, the colour of her neck peering out of an ordinary cream-coloured blouse, and his curiosity was heightened, his blood rushed through vessels, and in an instant, he imagined several possible bright futures. He wondered if some operator or another, dialing through the infinite frequencies, was able to catch his mind at that moment, but he doubted it very much, and anyway what he felt was hardly a crime.

The other departments, the man was saying, as they turned around and followed a complex route out of Collections Subdivision 1, which did not involve a second encounter with the woman, who will be known to you in time, if you will excuse me, he said as they returned to the hallway, I have several important tasks to complete before tomorrow and I'll attend to them now, and he scurried away with surprising haste. The job begins tomorrow at eight-thirty sharp, he spoke over his shoulder, and his echo faded to a near whisper with the increasing distance, report to the Assembly Department on the ninth floor and they will show you to your workstation.

Zachariah Ben Janoun found himself alone in the hallway and without a way out. There had been no time to ask. The only directions he had noticed in the whole facility were located on a plaque that hung in the front foyer before the first hallway prior to the staircase adjacent to the elevator, useless to him presently. He was exhausted from the events of the day, and had not realized from all the excitement and novelty how much this building drained him of half his blood. He felt so weak he wanted to lie down in the deserted hallway for a moment, only a moment, and to close his eyes. The twists and turns and strange echoes. When he finally saw the front door at the far corner of the arid first corridor, he inwardly rejoiced. When he put a shoulder against its heavy body, however, he felt the impact of a large animal against the wood and a sound like a panther's growl. The bullmastiffs. They barked viciously. How could he have forgotten.

Now what. For more than a single reason, Zachariah Ben Janoun wanted to strip naked and weep, eating raw onion after onion and bury himself in the verses of E.E. Cummings. How did one leave this place. He stepped back and the walls fluttered in a slight breeze. His body did it everywhere, limbs chest head and all tiny tremors. He put his back against the wall near the door and sat utterly defeated. After a very long time, he heard a whistle in the distance and the animals, he heard, responded to it with their quick gait. It was safe to go, he imagined.

ASSEMBLERS
AND
COLLECTORS

Zachariah Ben Janoun watched the assembly of a magnetic tape of recorded thoughts. He had come prepared with a notebook and pen, but his supervisor insisted that junior members of Department 6119 never write anything; all employees were required to memorize, and to communicate in spoken language only.

Zachariah breathed a sigh of relief because he could barely read anymore; he had spent another restless night, this one roving from book to book, convincing himself he was reading *The Enormous Room* but knowing it was a delusion, as it was only because he knew all the verses by heart that the letters supplied meaning. Lesser-known works were more difficult to decipher, while the newspaper would have been impossible without looking at the photographs of presidents kissing babies, crowning pageant queens, or generals receiving orders of valour. He sighed as he bit into an onion, though he was far less lachrymose tonight, he noticed: one spends a lifetime gathering knowledge and is rendered an invalid in a day.

The supervisor showed him the tools of his new craft: a pair of scissors, a sharp putty knife, two reels, a tape machine that spun them, and large headphones, like those in Collections. One had to be careful and wear latex gloves when handling the magnetic tape, because the tiniest scratch could delete an important word or sound and jeopardize the case against a terror suspect. In the future, the supervisor informed, we will be able to tune in to images of the mind as well, but for the moment, we must be content simply to trespass on sounds. The job for novices like Zachariah Ben Janoun was to determine the primary speaking voice of a thoughtreel, the monologist or subject. Minds are extremely varied, heterogeneous within the same person depending on time and mood, he was told, sometimes secondary voices inter-cede, and with experience, one learns deftly to sift out the thoughts of a schizophrenic or the return of an old memory in a healthy mind, among other

Zachariah's mind left the conversation, wandered corymb-stalks of hallways he had caught whispers of on his way to the office with Supervisor. While Assembly is closer to the Governor's judgment, he tuned back to the speaker, thus higher up the bureaucratic staves, Supervisor was explaining, it is, in fact, a less challenging department in terms of the difficulty of individual tasks and the average length of time required for learning the required functions. Thus, it was not uncommon for employees of the Assembly Subdivision to be demoted, so to speak, to Collections if they were felt to excel at their work here. Zachariah Ben Janoun somehow preferred the darker atmosphere of this place to Collections, but the thought of those grey eyes released some scent into the air that intoxicated him. He must try to speak with her.

For the first hour while trying to identify key characteristics of the subject of a practice reel, he was in awe: could it be, he wondered, is this how far we have come in the black arts. It was at once a privilege and a godly perverse pleasure to experience another human being's thoughts so closely. How different a language, he gathered at once, than mere words. Many interruptions, he noted, rarely full sentences, buzzing and humming, impressions of what seemed like the person's surrounding environment, renditions of popular songs with incorrect lyrics, but he found it quite easy to identify the primary voice: male, thirties to early forties, educated, middle class in taste, a native Arabic speaker. On occasion, the dials slipped and the machines dug deeper, the Collections headphones caught cry and cackles inner screams of minds honed in to an unnameable suffering, the same vision of the future fire burning relentlessly backward in time.

Well, then, his supervisor peered over his shoulder from above, his shadow blocking sight of everything in the room, have we come to any conclusions.

Yes, Zachariah Ben Janoun reported his opinions with some hesitation. The supervisor listened, his face inscrutable in the darkness he cast. Soon, the darkness went away and Zachariah could see the room again, the back of his supervisor growing smaller, weaving among the workstations and into the dark back room.

There appeared before Zachariah several other reels, two, four, seven in total. Please review each of these, he was told, preferably before the day's end. What had he done, Zachariah Ben Janoun wondered, was this punishment or simply an extended portion of the interview. Since he was never informed whether his first day had begun, whether he had been hired at all, he realized he didn't know when it ended.

And there is still time, Zachariah Ben Jaloun, you can simply refuse to continue, walk through the arid outer corridor with a song in your throat instead, take a bite out of one of the guard dog bullmastiffs outside if need be and perhaps the written word will come back to you by the time you reach home. But our hero pays no mind, too busy deciphering the reels.

The second tape is more challenging because it is evident the collector had difficulty locating the correct frequency. Thoughts appear-disappear into-outof the maze of AM radio sports programs and news broadcasts, though it is a woman, he is sure, whom they are after, young, whose mind repeats melancholic phrases of loss, fearful worries, and indications she realizes they are listening.

He stops the reel and unhooks it from the set, rubs his temples. An onion right now would be the cure. Someone taps his shoulder and he jolts up with a start.

Lunch, she says, and Zachariah Ben Janoun follows the trail of ants toward the sugar. In a vast room like a church hall. A shapeless voiceless din. All are eating, no one speaks. All appear to be strangers and everyone is dressed in the same matte grey and blue. His white shirt, starched bright, shines out like an incandescent bulb, and he vows to replace it at the earliest convenience. He opens his sack and retrieves a roundmetal container of rice, vegetables, and a few bits of meat. An unpeeled onion stares at him from the bag bottom, but he knows its odour would be offensive to his colleagues, especially without his bottle of alcohol rinse. He picks at his food as time moves as it does.

A whole day passes and twenty-four hours later we find Zachariah Ben Janoun at a similar table, surrounded by strangers, on this occasion looking up from his meal from time to time in hopes of spotting the woman with the grey eyes, but in such a nameless vast crowd how can he find her. The weeks pass and the reels increase in difficulty, often he does not know when one person's thoughts end and another's begin, the voices, especially of friends or family members, he presumes, often bear similar frequencies and are difficult to set apart. Ill informed of the nuances of the craft, he interrupts his neighbour from time to time for his opinion and is greeted with hostility.

Can't you tell this is she daydreaming of her lover, and his voice is in fact her imagination.

But how can it be so exact, so extended, Zachariah asks, I thought it was a schizophrenic dialogue.

Don't be stupid, those are rarer than you think, and sometimes collectors will even tune in to one or two crazies just to make our jobs more difficult.

Really.

Who knows, his neighbour returns to his own workstation and resets his headphones. Zachariah Ben Janoun rewinds and listens and cuts and glues as best as he can, but since his efforts receive no feedback from the supervisor, he does not know whether his performance is satisfactory.

After work, he finds himself led along the same ant-trail out of the building, and at home he is anaesthetized by the silence, unable to write or to read, consuming onions, as usual, but gradually weeping less and less.

Despite changes in his life, Zachariah Ben Jaloun keeps some of his old habits, the small standalone café still reserves his spot at the corner table, and on some afternoons, by the dying light of day, he comes here with the same books and the new ones he can now buy with the added salary, in hopes of a miracle, but none finds him. His thoughts circumambulate the same grey eyes and he wonders if it would be possible to manufacture a chance encounter with their beholder.

Taps on the shoulder di-di-dit. You did not write or wire me, the professor says, and Zachariah must admit this is true, but provides no explanation.

Come tonight at least to my flat.

Another of your gatherings.

Yes, I've been singing your praises to every publisher in the country, some of them should be present this evening, so if you bring a sample of your most recent work.

Run, Zachariah Ben Janoun, out of the café and into your room, hide between the indecipherable pages until you are forgotten as Ben Jaloun the minor poet. Were you not wondering, just months ago, how to smash rocks through the windows of your few readers, to repossess your words; have you found a way out of danger so soon. And yet at the moment the author of *Orange Blossoms* feels nothing but pride for his minor success and a whetted appetite and loosened tongue.

Yes, I have been working on a, how should I put it, a rather epic poem; perhaps I'll recite a fragment sometime.

Professor is delighted and rebukes him again for having been out of touch, we had two contemporary poetry classes in my undergraduate seminar, you would have been a perfect guest. But tonight, he says, and they shake hands.

For a long time Zachariah Ben Jaloun wanders in his thoughts, dispirited, defeated. The Ben Janoun in him disapproves like a father or a shadow. Impossible, it undulates, interrupts, disturbs: recite it but no flying meter and skeleton, rhyme and sand to the typist, and besides, I am Zachariah Ben Janoun to Department 6119, and in the official records I am not Ben Jaloun, but they will find you anyway. Perhaps the double identity kissing teeth and mocking laugh, the difference of a single letter, is a sufficient shell under which to hide.

He is still wrestling with these shadows during the taxi ride to the professor's home, I have done nothing thus far in my new job, I have acted as a model employee, I have broken no laws, and to harbour minor literary ambitions is not a crime. And yet, he knew from experience, from friends who had suffered and those in the newspapers who had never returned once captured, whose names were mentioned in an advertisement in the back, perhaps, but never even in the opinions section let alone news articles, that one need not commit a crime to be twisted into an urn or blown into wreaths of smoke: the unnameable country did not take chances with its young, they were either institutionalized or vanquished. But there were more people at the gathering than the previous time. The professor greeted him joyously, with a ready wine glass, and Zachariah Ben Jaloun refilled it to the brim several times, making the rounds with his friend and fitting easily into the role of a rising star.

When the occasion arose to meet Benjamin Pasha, the owner of a prominent publishing house, with distribution capacity in Europe and Africa, Zachariah started with a terse, most difficult portion of the blank verses, one he had revised many times and for which he had suffered greatly, and did not realize when the room fell silent. He continued out of the sheer thrill of revealing the lines to human company, and when he stopped at the second stanza he was urged to continue. Shy in nature, he knew if he thought of anything now but the blue-throated vase in his line of sight, he would lose the poem, so he went on and on until he failed to remember what came next, at which point he invented a couplet to end the performance. The room stayed silent.

What do you call it, Benjamin Pasha asked.

Facsimile, Zachariah said without thinking.

It's very modern, elegant, the publisher noted, leave a fresh draft at the front desk and I'll see to it someone takes a look at the first opportunity.

For the remainder of the evening he swam in the delight of academic criticism from the professor's colleagues: watch your foot, young man, meter and rhyme, have you read Hart Crane, you would do well to study him, and blind appreciation what freshness, just what the movement and our generation needs.

The professor took him aside and spoke at length about the nature of the larger publishing houses, what he should be careful of and what to expect, but as Zachariah nodded thoughtfully he was thinking only that he had defeated Ben Janoun; the shadow had nothing further to say.

In the coming month, he was too wrought up in the task of completing the blank verses and ensuring their assiduous transcription to care for the particulars of his work. His neighbours noticed the change: he whistled as he cut magnetic tape, asked for directions less often, chomped on raw onions at lunch, sang as he gargled with alcohol rinse in the bathroom, accidentally wore bright shirts, looked this way and that as if searching for a face, and spoke with more confidence than usual when reporting his tapereel conclusions to the supervisor.

Fear, he decided, was their chief governing principle. It was meant to make you want less, to efface the past and to tether the imagination so no future but theirs could be loosened into the world. It taught you how to tighten your own rope so the neck would bear not marks. And censorship, though an official Lawful Publications Committee did exist, was more often self-censorship than the truncheon. True, abject violence and state terror did exist, but so forth.

The meaning of the magnetic tapes escaped him. He no longer thought of them as recorded minds but simply as sounds, puzzles to be deciphered. What mattered was to publish, to live as freely as one could, and eventually to die. That was all. But to die before dying, to live in one's throat like it was an unused rusted pipe, never truly to speak, was much worse.

Zachariah Ben Jaloun got by with maxims, but fear revisited him the day the supervisor stood over his desk, his face masked by his own shadow. He toyed with Zachariah's putty knife. You have been summoned by the deputy chief of the subdivision.

May I ask why.

One never asks why.

Hot lunar dust flew in his face and choked him as he passed several employees while travelling to the deputy chief's office on the sixth floor, for whom the wind blew in the opposite direction. A margay or an ocelot pounced by. The appropriate room never arrived. When it did, he was not ready. The man at the desk was overtaken with work. His face hung low with heavy jowls and Zachariah realized he was envious of all the papers before the deputy chief of the subdivision. If only he was able to read even a trite memorandum.

Zachariah Ben Janoun, the man spoke without looking up.

Yes, sir.

You are an assembler, is this correct.

Correct, sir.

Your supervisor tells me you have a penchant for the craft of recognizing voices, of separating meaningful dangerous iterations of the mind from nonsense.

Zachariah did not respond.

Is this correct.

I have not received any feedback on my work, sir, and could not say one way or another.

Good, the deputy chief looked up, for it had been the right response. We would like to offer you a junior supervisory role in Collections due to these bright spots in your résumé; we think you would do well to shepherd the flock.

Sir.

Yes, Ben Janoun.

I have no experience locating the correct frequencies of suspect minds. When I listen to the reels, I discover even a good collection will contain many errors and stray into the public broadcast stream. I am nervous to direct others in what appears to me a very difficult task.

The deputy chief sighed as one does when a bright child makes an asinine comment. Did you have any experience sorting the right voices and editing magnetic tapes into potential terror cases.

No, sir.

What makes you think we wouldn't provide you with sufficient training to perform your job in Collections.

Zachariah felt foolish, and dizzy from looking at all the papers on the large desk.

And another thing, Ben Janoun.

Yes, sir.

Watch your foot.

Sir. Zachariah's entrails froze: did he know.

There are loose tiles is what I mean, the construction crews have been making repairs all week, you have no doubt noticed all the dust in the hallway.

Yes, sir.

Good day, Ben Janoun.

Zachariah wanders the corridors, pulling on doorhandles, screaming high and grinding his bones into the walls, let me out I have been here for a century. He puts his head low to the ground and listens for a thread. Low voices. Vibrato. A beautiful chorus part in the distance. He lifts up his head just as a sword is about to lop off.

He awakes with a start. His bed is drenched with perspiration. The putrefaction of onionskin. The smell of burnt coffee beans. The dark shape of silent books. What happens if one wants to resign from the Ministry of Radio and Communications. Undoubtedly there results a complex bureaucratic process, several periods of interrogation and bullying, signatures on page after page confirming one will not reveal— no, that one is unaware of—departmental secrets if one gets so far, and probably then the intense surveillance for years after being granted dismissal. There is only one direction in the maze. Time only flows toward greater disorder. And yet there remained on Zachariah Ben Jaloun's bitter breath a lingering taste of the future, something beautifully grey that succoured all the alien dust and desert corridors, but he could not quite recall its name. Perhaps it had never possessed one.

So far she has only been referred to as the woman with the grey eyes. Time has come for us to set down Zachariah Ben Jaloun. Let us leave him to his solitude of the inscrutable page, to think through his decision to hatch the blank verses and to wonder about his future within the hallways and rooms of Department 6119. In his absence, and perhaps even in his presence, as time will tell, Grey Eyes, I claim, is the onetrue hero—or heroine if you prefer—of this story. (Her name, therefore, warrants revelation.) My father (or the man the story makes me call my father) would probably insist on the following version of things: the only reason to mention Zachariah Ben Jaloun at all is because he leads us to his mother, the woman with the grey eyes, my perhaps-grandmother. So many possible genealogies, birthparents, foster homes, prison wards, faulty endings, and halfway-voltefaces. Let's see, where to start, then: the tale of my young grandmother and her mistress of the many shoes is as fine a place as any.

SHOES
FOR
THE
SERVANT

Once upon a time, and this is true, in another country, lived a widow, a mistress of a palatial inheritance, who was old and whose house was dilapidated old, who burned for her youth through brocades and necklaces, long outmoded dresses dragged carpets behind the wearer, and above all, shoes: patent-leather pumps and high-angle heels, pyramidal shoes with long throats exposing much the wearer's feet, shoes from Continental Europe with sharp toes and thin cones for support, ballet shoes, aerobic dance shoes, tap shoes, long-lace black boots that augured glamour seven decades prior, opera shoes she had gathered before a singing performance during a recent visit to the boot island, singing baby slippers that jingle-jangled with the wearer's every step, suede shoes, cloth shoes, ankle wraps, monk straps, cross-straps, gladiator sandals, fashionable side-tie shoes, chappals for walking, cavalier shoes with the lace frills of a prior century, formal eveningwear shoes, shoes for cocktail luncheons not to be worn with incorrect saddlebags, bejewelled lachrymal shoes that seemed to weep in the light as they walked, shoes that bicycle pumps injected with cushions of air, cross-country ski boots and their alpine variety, shoes, shoes on the stairs and the landing, spotted on the dining room table and scattered in the drawing room, shoes for long outings, for quiet nights by the gramophone, abundant shoes, choice shoes for every occasion in an echo palace whose mistress hired costume artists and sports stars for in-house pageants featuring her clothes, especially her shoes. She changed shoes by the hour, and after draining a pair of freshness with wear, she handed it down to her servant. One could imagine why the girl might not take such care in the shoes' upkeep as she did the china and silverware, the rugs, teak coffeetables, and the expensive linen, since she would inherit them in due time. It was the single calculated failure in her job, and important to the story.

After six years of indentured service, roundtheclock rain-or-shine care of the palatial home, shared by the mistress with her several thousand doves, which must daily be fed, whose droppings must be cleared, who live in an aviary and sleep in spacious dovecotes, who exist for neither breeding nor consumption, who are bought at great expense and stationed in luxury until they die of natural causes, the girl commits a life-changing error. It happens on the day the mistress announces that the Archbishop of Bethlehem is coming.

While more often than not distinguished guests fail to keep their promises to come to dinner, there have been surprises: during an August sandstorm, Laurence Olivier had arrived as pledged, eaten a whole meal without speaking once or removing his hat, and with the solemnity of Death himself, had risen and toasted the mistress of the house. Then he had fallen asleep in the front hallway, inebriated and leaning against the coat-rack. One never knew for certain, is the point.

The chef has his hands full, and asks the girl to take care of the custard. She prepares the recipe and lets it cool. The floor shines after her mopping, so not even a small-minded Vatican clerk could discover fault. Though the curtains are washed and the carpets hoovered, the rats caught and roaches exterminated, the house still exudes its characteristic sulphuric odour. But this, she sighs, I cannot change, I have laid traps for the devil and he is smarter than any rat.

She looks to the aviary where the thousand doves await her arrival. Come on, she bangs on her pail and throws their fibrous seeds. Something seems different: most don't seem to be eating, and curious discomfited, she enters, leaving the latch behind her unloosened. The birds rush about her as if they had been planning this very mutiny, as hundreds peck at her skull and scratch at her body bloody senseless before every one of them escaping through the hatch ajar.

In her convalescent chamber—her bedroom with bandages around her face—she points eyes to the bedside lamp and the teak-wooden chair with its definite shadow, the calcified walls smell of flight near feathers still fluttering, to her pair after pair of hand-me-down shoes. Her bedside mirror has news: claws for her face and bird-implacable red. Her insides have new hungers biting clamouring for another place. She counts again her pair after pair of second-hand shoes leaning against the walls. Shoes, she thinks, for flight: a new beginning.

Her wounds heal, though she will always bear a scar above her right cheekbone. She wanders briefly, pawns the shoes pair by pair, which allows her to pay for board and room in various cities. She buys a crisp, recently owned dress, in which she interviews successfully for a typist's job at a telegraph company.

She is diligent and warm and charms her employer, gains the jealousy of her gossiping office neighbour, who threads news of his affections to others, and eventually his wife. To fend off his advances to retain her job suppress rumours and retain her stolid guard: these are irreconcilable desires. No other potential employment in sight, and she is reluctant to dip into her shoe savings. What can she do but sink into the hollow of his embrace, nocturnal dust of the shared bed where his arms snap like dead branches and his face turns into a scarecrow's, his pupilless eyes like coal and incapable of.

Some years pass. They carry on in front of others as if nothing at all, using a nearby flat where they meet regularly. She always feels the need to scrub the floors afterward. Eventually, he befriends a Portuguese woman poet, supposedly a friend of Victoria Ocampo, who suggests, as the three of them gather over tea one afternoon, that he should try the Mexican surrealists of their generation.

He pauses for a moment before proclaiming Mexico a lost nation of the world; Marxism, he says, is the reason Latin America will never produce great literature; it is a handicap, because any ideology or dogma cripples the imagination.

He does not look at the girl when he pours her tea, and she finds the steaming atmosphere intolerable, his arrogance reprehensible, the poetess's nose so sharp it could cut the thick scent of play between them. She leaves her cup while muttering an excuse or an apology.

She never returns to their flat or to her job. He sends her letters: she is the wife of a notary, her contact is invaluable for expansion of the company, and be reasonable, she is a friend. After several attempts, however, he informs her in a terse communiqué her typist's position has been replaced. Thereafter, he doesn't seek her out.

I suppose, she wonders one evening while staring at the everyday commotion outside her window, if this is how love ends: like a frail kitten, a litter-runt that dies on Christmas Eve, mewling and warm and close to the hearth.

On a map she finds in a bric-a-brac store, in a map of the world like none other, she locates a previously unknown country in the map of the world, its name crossed out with a pencil: an unnameable country.

Paradise, she thinks, beyond names. I will sell the remaining shoes and cut a ticket.

Paradise has its bureaucratic processes, however, its forms, psychological assessments, job applications. Through an agency, my grandmother manages at long last to find a customer service position at a shoe business, which sends her keys to an apartment in a company building and a membership at a local swimming pool.

The steam vessel of her journey sways across channels and oceans, hugs a continental coastline, rocks in strong winds bleak waves through which my grandmother keeps cool, endures chatter with fellow travellers, their sickness unexpected early births dizziness spells walk invisible through ship's hull into vast water return to night rest chattering teeth and doctor's order bedrest and fluids.

From docking ship to lock and key of her new front entrance, her new life's sole contents of clothes, travel documentation, and meat preserves secure safely in one suitcase through winding streets via taxi.

Baffled by all the cinema stuff on the streets, the cameras and people/ what's the show, she asked. The driver pointed at the spools of magnetic reel streaming from the staircase landings, at the boys carrying pails of clean drinking water for the staff. When the taxi stopped at an intersection she heard cameramen arguing about film formats and what had the Director said about each of them.

What's the movie called, my grandmother repeated her question.

They're all called *The Mirror*.

Why.

Beats me, he replied, but that's what they say about every godforsaken show.

Huh.

Longest movie in the world, he grinned.

She turns jammed lock presses whole weight against a door surrenders, gives way to her new home whose bed is a thin mattress, whose walls and ceiling and floor are mirrors, and whose electrical circuitry is crossed with its ventilation system so that turning a switch sometimes releases a gale-force via vents whole weightless apartment and belongings.

My grandmother paced around her house, grew thin and tall in a reflection, squashed and wide in another mirror. The lights in her home fell villainous shadows on her face, made her up to shine on other occasions. She laughed at her image, she gasped, this is me, she wondered aloud.

Cinema is in my home, she shouted. Already, my grandmother was beginning to understand the tenuous demarcation between meatlife and movie world in the unnameable country.

After cooking her first breakfast the next day in the communal kitchen, my grandmother travels to the address of her shoe company job to discover an edifice of trolleys of spilling tape reels, their wiry pushers with eight limbs' tasks to do at once rushed to reorder magnetic minds scattered on hallways, tumbling from storage shelves, classified for the wrong containers.

She reaches a desk with an employee furiously reciting a data sheet for the day's entries, figures upon pages pushing volume. Excuse me, my grandmother ventures. A clanging metal container and a pigeon's flight in the room add weight to her intrusion and the woman at the desk lifts her head. Your name is listed, my grandmother hears, but your job is not to sell shoes.

My grandmother hears descriptions of windy hallways, of the respective tasks of assemblers and collectors, appropriable mental functions of the average suspect mind, and for a moment considers returning to her servant's task of shoekeeping. But the mere thought of a return ocean journey defeats her surprise and indignation and she signs page after page of contractual agreements that lead finally to her first pair of peering headphones hearing people's thoughts.

In the Collections Subdivision, she is one of many employees one recognizes by face, but whose name is unknown. Surely there exists a dossier with all the painful details of her life, including descriptions of her voice, her cough, the angle of her neck when she leans forward to work the dial of her shortwave, her eating habits, her casual acquaintances, and, in all likelihood, one could probably locate her name there as well.

Through headphones, my grandmother hears tangles surfs of thoughts break crest in a pillow mind TRAVEL CARD TOMORROW, she hears loud and clear a man's dreaming plans to apply for the page that will unite two companions in the same unnameable country beyond thirsty light on congested road and car to car, nose to tail of cars in series. Permits for the same country, she learns.

She adjusts her headphones to catch the thoughts of a wandering thirsty caravan following tales of water floating flower petals poured directly from vase to beseeching hands. She learns that they're in a compound belonging to the heaving giant, twice a man's height, a people-eater with fart nostrils and all, called Murray who oversees the ungovernable region of the unnameable country. She hears a child Karim's disbelief as his home fills with dividing fences, megaphones, barking dogs, uniformed officials barking orders and directions from his nursery bedroom to the kitchen for a midnight raid of the pistachio jar. Where in hell's name have I arrived, she rubs her temples, removes her headphones.

Gradually, she adjusts, accustoms herself to the macabre connotations of her job by comparing its relative ease against the horrors of her previous life of indenture, though she remarks silently at the barking end of each day while gazing up at the sky as the mastiffs sniff her and the building guards rummage through her purse for tapereels that this is the final sky and she has consigned herself to this sky and none other. It fills her bones with dust.

But then this morning is like any other day, she thinks one morning, and orange in colour, she decides for no reason, not all days bear a colour, some are marked by a smell or tintinnabulation or some other sound, and today is orange. But look, she adjusts her headset and twists the dial resolutely: there is that man again.

Early on in his work, Zachariah Ben Jaloun was not supervising so much as questioning his employees on the particulars of tuning in to a mind. He would spend hours after his shift learning to manipulate the dial and discover the internecine transmissions. Eventually, he realized it was as much a trick of listening as it was of finding the right frequency, because an average radio drama could contain hidden minds chattering away. How many important facts he had edited out, he thought suddenly. Collectors were much more astute. They contained assembly as part of their job description. He learned slowly. And in other fields too he faltered.

His verses were finally complete, but since he could not read, he could not proofread them. Not wanting to submit an unedited draft to the publishing house, what he really wanted was for the professor to have a look at the lines, but the thought of the academic's pointed finger on a cipher and the question, here, Zachariah, what do you mean, drove a blade against that idea.

But lest we dig again into deep tenebrous soil, and since we have been waiting long enough, let us no longer delay the inevitable meeting of Zachariah Ben Jaloun and Grey Eyes, the revelation of her name especially, now that you realize the author was only designing another hoop-and-fire game for you to play, to jump through for his entertainment.

A cinematic forecast flight of a string orchestra: words are spoken in rain or fine weather: can you love an illiterate man, an illiterate writer.

Her unexpectedly husky laugh as the girl asks, what do you mean.

I mean simply that I have, in the course of the last several months, lost the ability to read.

That is a moment of surely high consequence if it ever occurs. And another, held within the cabbage-folds of a single cello prelude, though no, that one must be retained from even the slightest description. Order and logic prevail, sadly, and we must continue to exercise patience. If in fact these are the real developments between Zachariah Ben Jaloun and Grey Eyes there must be causal agents. Proximity is the first, of course; as you are aware, the two now work in the same subdivision of the same department. Yet it still takes three shrews of fate twenty-two long weeks to orchestrate a possible meeting.

The girl takes her usual spot under the large clock near one of the exits, its hands frozen supplicant together on six-thirty. She unpacks her cooked meal and that man again, sitting only two tables away, she notices. A shiver. Though on no occasion, she thinks, do his movements appear calculated. It may be that he simply happens to be in her vicinity, repetitions of sociality do occur, and friendships do arise among employees. On the other hand, supervisory staff never fraternize with collectors, and the nature of this job, and of this whole country, in fact, inspires fear in her. Not for the first time does she regret discovering that strange map, of closing her eyes and letting her fingers stop wherever they will. If he has taken interest in her then she is being surveilled even more closely than others. Why, fear gives way to anger, and she passes the stranger a glare while tightening her jaws.

At that moment, Zachariah Ben Jaloun happens to look up from his meal and notices her for the first time in weeks. He seals up his round-metal container and departs at the earliest opportunity. He suffers for the rest of the day from a debilitating stomach wound, and wonders if a mere glance can do all that. He hopes he will never have to speak to or to look again at that unkind face.

Eight days later, on her way out, the girl notices the same man sitting in a cubicle near the exit, turning the dial and listening carefully to a shortwave, as if unaware of the time of day. He doesn't seem interested in anything but his work, she realizes, and probably, like most male employees in Collections, is a lonely bachelor with a mother who lives two cities away whose death would not inspire in him the slightest feeling. She has read books about such men, and she is sure the Ministry of Radio and Communications produces scores of them. She does not think of him again.

B e n J a n o u n, the deputy chief of the subdivision looks down at his shivering frame from a great height. Papers flutter. Since their last meeting the deputy chief has grown a great deal taller and fatter. He takes up half the room now, or perhaps it is only that Zachariah has shrunk. A low wind picks up and moves papers off the desk and around the room.

Z a c h a r i a h, he speaks very slowly, breathing gasping deeply between words. Y o u k n o w I a m n o l o n g e r y o u r d i r e c t h e a d o f s t a f f, he blows all the papers pens notebooks and rattles the typewriter keys. Nevertheless, the deputy chief informs, he takes an interest in those who have been demoted-promoted to Collections, and is happy to announce that the subdivision is satisfied with Zachariah's progress thus far, and has chosen that he should undertake a deep survey of the collectors, and then to assemble an oral presentation on their strategies of locating mental frequencies for the purposes of increasing departmental efficiency.

This message takes over an hour to transfer, during which time the room becomes soiled with the deputy chief's perspiration and spittle, though the expenditure of all that energy returns him to a somewhat regular size. The positive nature of the message reassures Zachariah, the wind dies, and by the time he departs, the deputy chief is almost the height of a regular man, though not exactly. Out in the hallway, a loose tile gives way and Zachariah's left foot slips painfully all the way to the thigh. He struggles to restore it to the surface. Wincing, hopping on one foot, he wonders what the hell. Then through the opening he catches sight and dizzies him, of not the floor below but an infinite well.

The verses are coming along. He has the secretary recite them back and make corrections on the page. It is a slow and expensive process since the woman charges by the hour, but since she is patient and since Zachariah Ben Jaloun's costs have expanded only slightly in his new job, which is not at all new anymore, he doesn't mind. He has invested deeply in rhythm, but is worried he is sacrificing the narrative thread for the sake of sound.

The story is about a man who discovers his shadow moving about one evening on its own accord. The change is subtle at first, but eventually the shadow achieves a voice and declares independence from the protagonist's body. A struggle ensues. To keep the identity of the doppelgänger shadow hidden, the hero assumes the motions of his other the shadow, which extends into murder, among other evils. Eventually, he is tried for his crimes, and the story is told again, but in differing versions, by other characters, some of whom plead his innocence and advocate for his release. But the subtleties, Zachariah worries, and the others who provoke or assist or act as foils, are not yet clear.

Facsimile, he ran the word along his tongue, facsimile; it provided him an explanation of things, of what he didn't know: signification without signifier, conclusion without premise, though he knew it was right. Meanwhile, the minds he encounters on the shortwave multiply into identical similitude, many petals on the same bough. Not to say that as surveyor Zachariah Ben Janoun does not discover distinguishing characteristics of the minds he encounters. In the more recently employed, he notices a sharpness and desire for experimentation that older employees lose as they accustom themselves to common practices and set ways of functioning. He gathers admissions: they do not always know of the accuracy of their findings and rely on assemblers to edit their discoveries into stories. They are all self-enclosed and lonely, many of them frightened of speaking to him as they are to all super-visors, let alone so candidly about the functionality of their minds. He wanders from one to the next, there are thousands of cubicles branching into identical others and he will never finish. Thousands of names minds nuances locations he must how can he remember them all. He does not care where is she.

Fifty weeks pass this way in idle repetition. In Europe, the British have proclaimed victory over the fascist scourge, and the news leaks into the streets of the unnameable country, which is far away and where it means less, as half-hearted hurrahs, weak bursts of firecracker and Roman candle. The Governor, as they have begun calling Anwar, the man with the single name, has not yet launched his ultimately canni-balistic self-consuming revolution. The Black Organs are almost born. Then one day Zachariah Ben Janoun is shaken back into Ben Jaloun as he enters a cubicle and a pair of tired grey eyes stare back. He stifles a desire to weep and to be alone while eating a large onion, but gathers his senses and repeats what he has said to all the others, routine questions.

Be honest, he adds, believe me the way you handle the dial is beyond my capacity, and we—he assumes the form of the Department—are very interested in your.

How do you know my knowledge of the instrument is superior, she is incredulous, suspicious.

Ben Janoun retains his air of modest authority and assures her whatever he is doing is beyond my control, comes from higher offices of power, he is saying.

She nods, this much she understands, and takes a breath before telling him: Usually, I focus on the quieter sections between suchand-such a hertz and allow errant, more powerful thoughts to emerge as interferences in the static; these provide clues and I home in closer with the dial before the shapes begin to emerge.

Shapes.

Yes, shapes, she says, though more like colourshapes and patterns, she twists in her chair, very uncomfortable to continue, which is to say I see more than I hear.

What do you mean, Ben Janoun is puzzled. He has never received such an answer.

I mean I see the conversations people have with themselves, and sometimes I can catch glimpses of the contour of whole minds.

But do you hear what they are saying.

In fact, it is hearing, she insists.

Please forgive me, Zachariah is stunned, but I don't process.

She shrugs. I can't explain; it's simply the way I do my job.

For two long moments no words pass and they do not look at each other.

Can I have your name, please, Zachariah Ben Janoun says finally, I will have to report this.

Am I to be reprimanded, is this not the correct manner of proceeding, please understand I cannot lose this job.

Believe me, as far as I can help it you will not lose your job over what appears as an elegant and unique manner of collecting information on the minds of potential terror subjects.

She is visibly relieved. My name is Gita, she tells.

Ah, Gita. At last we discover. Gita or Geeta like geet any song or the song of arjunandkrishna.

I don't recall ever noticing your face, Gita says, were you recently hired or transferred.

The latter, yes, from Assembly, but not so recently, several years ago.

I see.

And yourself.

I work in Collections, I have been in the same cubicle for nearly five years.

They more or less know these preliminaries, they are not the most important questions, but necessary. He wanted to reveal they had encountered each other several times, and that one occasion she had inflicted him with a wounded stomach, that now he was delighted they were speaking, but what is the point of speaking on such things, and he asked instead: If you do not mind, just because of your accent, you are not from our country.

No, I'm originally from Cox's Bazaar.

And where is that.

The coast of the Bay of Bengal.

Ah.

And since in such situations all premeditated questions flee the scene for politeness, Zachariah Ben Jaloun stalls, and wonders whether Gita has anything else to add. Then unexpectedly she laughs, and the sound is bolder than he would have expected, and wrapped in a slight husk absent from her speaking voice. He does not join her but is content to enjoy the sound.

FIRE IN THE
ENDLESS
MOVIE STUDIO

A
VISIT
HOME

Time passes, stories lead us; when they feel fit, they call us back. To your knowledge, my grandparents met in a building where they listen inside people's skulls, a palace of ears that call eyes and limbs, truncheons, bullets, nightly kidnappings out into the world, a building of machines that make and multiply fear. Which wild eyes could spot love or a chance caress in such a place of ordered misery, of daily vortexes that suck you inside its walls because it's your time, for no other reason than because your number is called and time to die.

My grandparents lived. My grandfather died an ownbulleted death many years later (because he lost Gita, lost everything many years earlier). He was made into pieces, shipped eventually by Department 6119 to my grandmother, who emerged from her solitude at the sight of his eternal face in a duffle bag, carved into such thin slices the incisions were initially difficult to spot; only when Gita tried to raise him out of the bag did she realize what he had become, because Zachariah Ben Jaloun slipped as meat through her hands.

Years later, after watching her grandson Hedayat grow old enough

337

to dance gangster-steps with his friend Niramish, Grandmother Song would, with her daughter-in-law, my Mother Thankyou, warn us against our football-bag excesses, our solitary conversations behind closed doors, though neither we nor anyone in the unnameable country knew then what even Hedayat only suspected, what he would gather in a spontaneous gaze of total understanding exactly a moment too late: his friend was about to get his brains blown out. When Hedayat found a partner in grime and underworld after Niramish's death, he kept Masoud Rana and the Datsun out of his family's knowledge as much as possible for all the badnaam they might heap upon the unsuspecting.

Eventually, Hedayat did pay a visit home, hoping all was well and expecting to see it overrun like a seabed with the scuttling papers of his father's contract work. Recall my grandmother's home was an abandoned movie set, rented to immigrants at a time when cameras were large, clunky, expensive. By the time Hedayat became a man running guns and pepper through the Warren tunnels, cameras and microphones had miniaturized and multiplied ubiquitous.

All I heard when I entered my parents' home was a low ominous hum and could see no papers anywhere, nor any workmen. Changes: coloured markings on the floor, curious glass partitions, and a man seated at a chair before the first of these and right near the steps, holding a flat elongated grey instrument. He called me to halt and passed it around my body; it twittered like an electrical bird, all agitated, frenetic around my pockets. He had me show him my keys and all the coins and safety pins and whatever other metal objects before it became safe to pass. I recall he wore a nametag on his blue uniform with no name.

The small apartment had grown cavernous in my absence, seemingly much larger because much of the furniture had been removed since I last visited. There was no one, and the floor was covered in the grey shit clouds of perfumed mountain swallow chicks that were

338

cheeping and pecking at flaxen seeds scattered everywhere. My father appeared like an apparition out of a corner of the house that was unfamiliar to me, with an unrecognizable expression on his face. There were rooms and they were difficult to know.

Did you come back for long.

I am here now, I said. The house is a prison now, why are there perfumed chicks feeding everywhere on seeds, cheeping and befouling the floors. Where are the others, I asked when he didn't reply to the first question.

My father pointed to some forgotten corner of the universe, and it was a good thing the Quintuplets entered the room at that moment, because I could have sworn I was in the wrong house and with the opposite truth in mind I might have left with the intention never to return. They were the same, the four of them taller, though no less quiet, and the fifth, who was higher like the rest and still as silent, still swimming in an irrepressible inner world of which one caught glimpses. Without a salutation the Yeas threw down their schoolbags and bugled in unison some song they had learned in physical education or extracurricular that was about sweeping, what fun time is sweeping time, that was the refrain while the rest of the lyrics also had to do with cleaning, there was a line about the centipedes and the rats, which they sang with sweet diligence and these had to be swept, as well as notice the streets should be clean and one's house clean, the country and the heart unwell if not lathered up from time to time, a line about the mutinous grass also and why it should be cropped.

I might not have minded if the tune weren't so predictably repetitive, and it seemed odd to me that they would want to sing it instead of other possible songs; it was a good thing, anyway, Nehi was there to break the annoying number, which also featured a horse-galloping dance. She placed the quizzical have you seen. I hadn't and looked to the odd corner, where she pointed, where there was now a large elevator at the far end of the space that had once housed their cribs, their playthings, and later their desks.

So what do you do now, I asked.

Nothing until after six o'clock, when they've brought back all the furniture. She informed that the prison's budget had been mismanaged and the new penitentiary was leasing all the family's belongings until the Ministry of Profits could decide how to allocate the necessary funds; Nehi bore through the intimate procedural details, listed names of bureaucrats as well as dates and times and reasons provided, and they haven't paid us once, she concluded, looking at our father.

True but moreorless true, Mamun M was chewing the cud of his frustrations, rolling his tongue left and right cheek, hard to argue with the child when she's in her, one of those, though consider they leave us these perfumed mountain swallow chicks as collateral every morning, and I doubt it's a swindle since we also get it back.

True as his word, the largemetal doors opened promptly sometime around six o'clock and brawny musclebound warders, untalkative and greyclothed, shuffling and dragged out a whole apartment from within what looked less like an elevator and more like a submarine's interior. They had even set things up so there was a rug in place and lamps and the couch was pushed back against the wall of the dining area, and they gathered up all the cheeping swallows into the folds of their clothes and pushed them into their pockets, which left only their grey clouds and the beads of sunlight seeds across the floor.

I had meant to visit only for two nights at most, but when I tried to leave, the first gatekeeper, the one with the grey beeping instrument and his left twisted ear like a demented cauliflower, which was not like before, told me that, in fact, he was another man and didn't recognize me, I had no identification and he couldn't let me pass until the return of his superior, who was the first of the guards I had encountered.

When is that.

Unsure, could be tomorrow but no since the Friday is after and then the closesttime Monday following, but possibly not.

At first Hedayat busied himself with the mountain swallows, but there were so many of them, and though flightless, they had a way of evading touch with such ease that after a while he had to satisfy himself only with scattering their flaxen seeds and clearing their shit, which dissolved into dust putrefaction if left too long, because then we would be breathing it.

Restlessness clasped around his ankles and he dragged the whole musical heavy weight of it from one glass enclosure to another. In the mornings they came to take away the furniture, his father went off to the storage room of the local police division, where they had created a small workspace for him to gather and arrange the data of the city's latest gangs and kleptocrats, his mother and grandmother went downstairs to open the hosiery shop, and the Quintuplets went to school. By the hum and banging of the ever-expanding prison deep below, which had never been completed and which they would be building forever, he leafed through the explorers' magazines Mamun had bought for their precise high-resolution satellite images; eventually, he learned to identify every island of the Philippine archipelago, every urban centre town hamlet and road of the new world, before discovering a magnifying glass so powerful, it allowed him to explore the whole earth down to the details of the very hairs on the heads of the people as they walked frozen in their native streets or the smells of their meals at the time the pictures were taken. He inhaled with his boredom an agitation that found release only by singing the lowest registers of his range, and this way he rattled all the glass and brought the workmen deep below to curious pauses.

One day, two warders arrived, and a third. Not unlike the daily movers, but with crueller faces, they brought with them the music of loud jangle keys as they pushed in front of them a hooded man, whose legs were bound by real, not invisible, shackles; they paused before Hedayat to ask for directions to the elevator. All the mountain swallow chicks gathered cheeping around the three men, two of whom kicked nasty, while Hedayat pointed beyond several glass partitions. The birds followed the zigzag coloured markings on the floor, and when the hooded man faltered over a rough area on the floor, they beat him on his back and the back of his neck to disabuse him of failure until he was vomiting into his hood of stale socks and rotten colons, which was easy to smell all throughout the house. They halted for some time before the elevator without removing the hood, trampling on errant mountain swallow chicks, talking loudly about various things, whistling non-melodies, and never allowing the hooded man a moment's respite. Then they disappeared into the mineshaft of hell without turning a look around.

Each evening, at the changing of the guards, I would look for signs of differences in the twisted cauliflower ear, the moustache and gesticulations of the returning guard, but found none; he grew tired of asking are you the one and being told no, the other one, so that on the day things changed, Hedayat didn't notice until the differences in the pieces on the chessboard, which was also there before, though I did not mention; recall now: located on a low table in dramatic contrast with the very high chair of teetering daddy-long-legs for the guards.

Remember, I had passed a glance at the game, which had seemed in its advanced stages; now I saw that white had moved queen-side bishop to fianchetto in an angular defence against the black knight's advances on his castle-piece.

But your rook is still, I told him, and he bemoaned he knew of the danger. I watched as he thought about the move he had made, though it was clear he wouldn't make alterations, for that was what had been decided between he and his colleague, that they would not; and besides how could he while separated by such a distance from the low table while sitting on his very high metal chair with its teetering skinny legs.

After collecting my thoughts through our brief conversation about the game, I began to describe being marooned in my own home, including my inability to move freely between all the glass panes, the coloured markings that were transparent in meaning even to birds, daily disappearance of all the furniture, the odd appearance of two warders and a hooded man, as well as the ubiquitous presence of the cheeping mountain swifts and their habit of shitting on the floor of the house. While I related these absurd things, the guard would move chess pieces back and forth by bending over and extending a hand several feet beyond its actual length with surprising skill, and flatulate loudly at precise instances in my story. His wind had no odour but I grew concerned that the sounds were produced to censor critical moments of my narrative, a way for him to erase them from future possible recollection.

Are you listening, I shouted.

I am not only, in fact I was once a court stenographer and possess a ninety-five percent rate of recollection, he said, as if to counter my fears.

So what have I been telling.

A tale of eternal childish longing.

But I grew flustered that it was not, and in fact. The underlying message you cannot argue, old man, is one redolent of the theme. I was unprepared for his forked line of reasoning and told him I simply wanted to make the necessary arrangements to be able to leave and enter my own house at will.

That would be impossible without identification.

Which I have but which is elsewhere.

Where.

I cannot describe, would not tell you all the details of my life at once, but suffice it to say if I could leave I would return the next time with all my documents intact.

Impossible, he cut loose a furious fart not at all free of liquid or solid masses by the sound of it. He shifted in the very high chair on which he sat, which teetered on its thin insectmetal legs as if assailed by a formless draught.

So how do I then.

The guard yawned, he leaned back and nearly fell over as the chair teetered dangerously, he put his hands up to touch the ceiling because he was very close, and he looked at his watch. By that time, I realized many hours had passed, night had fallen, and in fact the whole family was bustling about the apartment now absent of the sound of its diurnal cheeping guests. The centuries had tarried on my behalf and now it was too late.

The guard made one final concession: there is one possibility, every second Tuesday of every third month a supervisor comes, and though he does not possess final say in the matter, he relays news of any unsolvable problems to the district director, who may push the matter up to a court order for you to leave the premises and gather your identity or else to have someone bring it here so that we may observe.

Are we finished here, Mamun interrupted then, I'm sure Salaam has other places he must

All but, I said, looking at one and then the other before retiring to the interior of the garrison. I had little faith in the turning gears of our state bureaucracy, but still one must.

In the meantime, one must grant a little attention toward the food in our home, which in times of trial had been inventive, and in the years of plenty consisted of scuttling daily self-deliveries from the Gulf of

Eden and Indian Ocean, as you know; let me extend brief description to eight curious meals as a way of suggesting their present-day mystery.

To begin, I discovered four-holed copper fasteners in my soup one day, and then an errant chicken's talon in the salad, feathers in the mutton curry, and once we had a whole dinner consisting of only capsicum candies and rum candies. On another occasion I arrived at the table to find only a single enormous egg situated at its centre, containing the steaming embryo of an unnameable bird that we carved up into small pieces and dipped into a communal bowl of raisin, fennel, and mint seasoning; the sixth notable meal was a feast of noodles as narrow as hair and which turned out to be entrails longer than human intestines; another dinner screamed on the plate; the last on the list had to be picked oozing out of an earthenware jar and was, according to Gita, from the thousand-year-earlier inhabitants of the region. Never a complainant of cuisine and the proud possessor of a cast-iron gut capable of variegated and difficult ingestion, Hedayat found himself wondering the meaning of it all, especially when one day he found himself spiralling into noisy expulsions of gas, belches if you will excuse, while knocking about against one glass partition after another and moaning in a way that sent the Yeas into ululating frenzy because they perceived it as a kind of game. They began singing the sweeping song again, what fun is sweeping time, what fun is sweeping time was the refrain, making horse-gallops with the placid glow of zombies in their eyes, while I teetered on my legs belching green gas from the deep, hissing and frothing, sticking claws into mouth in desperate attempts to invoke but nothing came out. The elevator rang in the distant reaches of the apartment, and not far away I could hear its doors opening but no one came out. They were singing and still on and on, galloping in unison while I teetered, mother father grandmother also gathered hollow pupilless and watching then as i suffered, and i saw no movement in their souls until a brute human instinct kicked Gita into

345

holding my neck like a nanny goat and feeding me a tablespoon of palliative broth. i numbed all over and lay on the floor as a hot spring gurgled inside me. When i awoke i realized our garrison home now not only contained glass pane separators, which prohibited free movement, but also that glass had ensconced our hearts to keep the pulse cold, and glass had sprouted walls upward and between the people who had lived here for decades in relative harmony. There were no explanations for the green belches and froth, i was provided no explanations; i ate like the others more or less, from my own plate as they ate from theirs. Yet the pains assaulted only me after every meal until i was certain the gaseous effusions were symptomatic of a deeper ailment, and i could garner no sympathy from the chess-playing guards. They disallowed me the effrontery of visiting a doctor since i would have to leave in order to, though they assured me the prison featured its own distinguished physicians, who would arrive in due course to clarify the matter, since all inmates are guaranteed quality care by the state. So i am an inmate now. Not officially, but officialdom has its many shades, the first one told me without looking up from the same fianchetto i saw him considering the last time. From then on, i decided never to eat again. Let me make clear it was neither a suicidal nor a fasting desire; instead, i made the only rational choice given the intolerable green belches and attendant ailments. i saw no reason why my body could not retain its present size and otherwise good health until the right and appetizing food came along, at which time i would make the necessary dietary changes, why not turn your attention, Hedayat, toward other facets of life in the apartment and try best to take interest in their nuances. Time passed and i grew accustomed to solitary wanderings through the repeating themes of glass and grey clouds and yellow seeds; i reasoned many ways but could never accept the daily alterations between barren moonscape and rug and home. Countless times i forgot the name of the guards, Salaam and Suleiman, mistaking one for another while discussing my case with either because it was difficult to keep the busted demarcating cauliflower ear in order, though it didn't matter because i was more interested in their chess match, which became intriguing in many dimensions. To recall from the fianchetto, bishop took black knight, black knight eventually took white rook, there were several other meaningful exchanges until the king of spades began to advance gallantly while the jack of diamonds showed his pluck but was lured by the spellbinding manoeuvres of the queen of hearts; two American F-16s fired four missiles into a home where a flank of students were gathered to study on the night before term finals where someone was overheard joking about the lottery's colonization of every letter of the alphabet and every number of every set of numbers, and there were many scattered pieces then. One day, while following a little bird that had stayed after all the others had been scooped up into warders' pockets and shirtfolds before being locked into cages deep in the mineshaft, and was cheeping about and moving on its own course outside the boundary of the chalk outlines, i stumbled upon a pair of strange feet. And who are you, i looked up to ask their owner. Brother, surely you know me. i looked at the dark face and the rain of hair which fell nearly to the floor and realized no, i had never encountered such a person. I am your sister, we are born of the same woman and hail from the same home. She tried explicitly when my vague face then: You don't remember me, Bhaiya, No as they are Yes, she asked explicitly. i tried to recall and realized the words bore certain resemblance to shapes from the swamp of some other time but whose meaning was now obfuscated by all the changes to our home. In any case, the bird: i cupped a hand to my ear to hear its cheeping, which was now distant; i placed the same ear to the floor to hear the fall of its feet and described my pursuit, which the girl listened to while wrinkling her brow. That bird is ours, she said, there is nothing mysterious about its wanderings, it was a gift from the penitentiary for leasing our furniture to them daily. Ours: there was another one that confounded in its plurality, and whose precise inclusive boundaries escaped me; was the bird mine also, or had i violated some licence by giving chase. Have you eaten, she asked. This question at least was straightforward enough: Not for a while, i answered; i have given up eating for now due to its hassles. From the distance there came a sound and my stomach lifted like a deep sunken anchor. My body swayed, i looked at my talons as if they were a stranger's and looked all around at the strange apartment whose floors were covered with unswept grey dust, which we were breathing, and then recall the edible yellow buttons everywhere. Then i began for all the confusion of shapes, the translucent glass squareshapes, the diaphanous darkness of the girl before me, who was all made of glass and whose spleen liver pancreas heart intestines lungbellows working pushing air were all visible and who claimed to know me. i began weeping then, i wept for every blade of grass and the animals who could not weep and for all the misers of the world whose tears had been stolen, and i was still weeping without the aid of onions or raisins or black pepper when she said, rise up, Hedayat, for it is not all misery and this misery is not the world. She pulled me up, and i realized at my full height i towered over her, which confused me because she had been a giant two seconds earlier. Come with me, she drove me expertly past one glass pane and another before stopping at an unfamiliar part of the apartment and asking if she could stand on my shoulders because it was too high. Unfortunately, i told her, i know that trick; it happened to a distant relative of mine or perhaps the story is all that remains; in any case, the imprisonment of the hunchback is not to be taken lightly, sorry but. She told me it was all right, she knew the story also though this was not the same. See up there, she pointed, and i followed the shape of a metal grating: That's the only way. i leapt up but even at my highest i couldn't and was forced to concede to her offer. i allowed this No to climb gingerly up my back and plant her soles on my shoulders; her weight was not so heavy, and she managed without great difficulty it seemed, as with a cantankerous sound the oldmetal square grating of the ventilation shaft fell down from her hands. She kept her word and descended from my shoulders. I suppose this is goodbye. Yes, i suppose, i said, but couldn't understand why her eyes had begun to moisten, we had barely been introduced, but i too had been weeping for unknown reasons and tears can be contagious. Now how do i, Hedayat asked, but No couldn't answer because he saw a curious encrustation of salt had gathered and shut up her eyelids, and she was rubbing but still it was impossible to see or think about anything else. Someone must have hit a switch then because i felt all my hairs lift, my shoulders began to lift as someone must have increased the intensity of the sucking wind that drew me upward so quickly there was no time for goodbyes. i travelled for hours, for so long i fell asleep and lost track of time in a dimensionless nightmare, and when i awoke i was still rushing through the vents, carried by the draught as knots and twists in the metal tube opened up according to an unrevealed logic. i landed on my back in an obscure corner of the warren tunnels where it was possible to breathe out but not in; it took me perhaps a whole month to correct the frightening error in that grave cave and to relearn how to breathe. Everywhere the smell of ash and though the tunnels had never presented a culdesac in my experience i saw black terminus; there was no forward after this. For fear of being buried alive i began to dig upward and loose tufts of soil covered my shoulders. For a long time i dug until my talons bled because i could not go back the way i came. How i rejoiced at the first grains of meagre light. Once on the surface, i removed my shoes and allowed my feet to taste the sands and waters of the Gulf of Eden. i wandered for a day or part of a day and encountered no one. i sang every note i could remember and reviewed the difficult lines of songs i liked to sing, though only their melodies returned; their lyrics seemed to have blown to oblivion. To amuse myself and to pass the time i gathered pebbles from the shallow waters and placed them into my mouth, first only one or two just to perceive the taste, but then whole mouthfuls. For hours i rolled pebbles around in my mouth and the melodies took new shape entombed in my mouth that way. They were so funny sometimes they provoked stone-scattering laughter that caused me to pluck new pebbles from the shore. At the failing light i still had not figured out where i was supposed to go and found myself in the streets, wandering through the souks from one stall to another and haggling with hawkers over items i had no intention of buying, invoking their wrath by overturning my pockets to show empty, laughing at the claws of loneliness and passing from one face to another while detecting not one flicker of recognition. i asked several people if there might be somewhere to spend the night, but revealing my impecunious state made them only laugh, and they sped me along my way. A man was sitting outside his home slurping from a bowl of froth, and he offered me part of this ambiguous meal. i told him no, though i sat with him awhile. i outstretched my talons and showed him the pebbles i had gathered that day at the shores of the Gulf of Eden, but he couldn't understand their importance, not even until after i placed them into my mouth and sang through them the sarcophagus-broken rendition of a popular tune. He looked at my face and my feathers and said either you are crazy or what is more likely is that you are dead. I suggest you hang a right, he pointed, after the end of this street. There are fewer mirrors there and you will come to a door separated from all the others by its lion's head knocker. Before i had a chance to consider, he retreated into the house and closed the door behind him. i stood up to take my first step and by the time i heard him fasten the lock i found myself in front of the door he had specified. i was led there by a deeper feeling than intuition, by a desire i didn't realize i had or which i had lost and had become unnameable, and i tell you it took no time at all to see the lion's head knocker before me. A woman answered my knocking and she was beautiful, her hair was a raven's dress and her face was full and shone the light of noon, and she didn't wait for me to speak, embraced me deeply and said my name many times while kissing my face, I searched for you, I sent after you and they could tell me nothing about you, she kissed me until the pebbles began to leak from my fisted talons, and with each leaking pebble the curtain of amnesia lifted a little. Where. Like the devil, without an abode in which to rest the back of my head, i answered, going and coming across the earth. How do you feel, she asked me as i looked around: the ghosts were shuffling, the television was its own monotony, the rooms were filled with undead guests, the empty frame hung in its place, blood was boiling on the stove and the kitchen was adrift in its usual shipwreck, and i wanted to tell her anything but it wouldn't leave my throat. It's okay, she said, and drew out a pin. She pricked her forefinger, bade me drink, and at the first red taste of ferrous salt I could already understand better.

BLOW
A
LITTLE
PEPPER

Months passed and Q and I wrote the odes to our limbs together, to gazes, to the nude passing hours that turned to days sprouted weeks. We clung to each other's prodigal words, which had drifted into odd corners of the world and refused to announce themselves as love until revived by bitefuls of custard cake or gulp after gulp of strawberry wine.

They were days devoted to none other than each other, to the geography of her breasts to her pubis, to cue or queue, the braid of her hair. Will you blow a little pepper with me, she asked one night.

To blow a little pepper requires concentration of the senses, because while the pepper is ordinary, the effects are hardly. Sneezing, yes, of course. But then. And also. Recall the raisins of Mamun Ben Jaloun, or the onions of his father, Zachariah, the latter by the way it allowed my grandfather to cry, with its powers of howcanwesayit literary cathexis, while the former gave the other his gifts of transformative memory, fabulism, and song. Recall the effects of black pepper, if used correctly/incorrectly depending on one's vantage point, is worse, or perhaps far more powerful, to be more precise. If you will trust in my

Gargantuan belch while I recollect Doubly Tea's greasy menu, in my Pantagruel appetite for exaggeration and largesse: this is the part of the story where Q and I fly.

It all began one night when Q and I were enshrouded in boredom. And what boredom. A glaze had fallen over the eyes of that exquisite lady who was not Hosanna, who would never accept an invisible diadem, who was not free, since the question is negated imprimis in the unnameable country. But at least hers was a laughter that jingled and wrenched on all our invisible manacles. Always certain mischief coded in her smile of score years, of Q among the ghosts and the bottler of human blood, of spirited speech and that mischievous smile going on and on until a threshold: and then nothing. This was the way with Q, for as much as Hedayat also fell into silence around her, he possessed no interrogative sonar with which to plumb the depths of her faraway gaze.

On that night it was just Q and I. Masoud Rana was not yet, though, scheduled to appear later. And El Doubly Tea was giving us the most of its usual crowned divebomb singers the zombie prattle of the working poor winded by hauling the sun across the arc of the sky and without a buzzing thought left in their concave. El Doubly Tea and its familiar odours of tar cigarettes and burnt soy from the kitchen's teriyaki grill; El Doubly Tea: twelve tables, at most, and sixty chairs when pushed to the maximum. Recall El Doubly Tea's greyslanted weak incandescent track lighting and the static disco ball hanging dusty unfit to scatter light from all the music videos filmed in the establishment. Also fit for mention: a stage left for the karaoke machine and one wrinkled regular who sat up there, a spinner, Tahir, of top forty singles, the usual; add soiled comic book pages littering the floor and a hapless old jukebox. A few changes, I suppose, and more or less the same since.

Have you ever visited El Doubly Tea of La Maga's crooked alleyways, near the Ministry of Education and Languages and ever since the days of the Screens some nearly four decades now: that historic establishment where Backslang was invented, and from where it was later lifted into the demonic realm of the lottery. Here, in the late hours or the very early, and for only the non-constabulary patrons working poor, mind you, cold tea still turned into a spot of bourbon or straight rye. A tap on the nose was sufficient cue for the waitress to perform the miraculous substitution. Once upon a time, tonight in fact, here and now in El Doubly Tea, the fad of blowing a little pepper would begin and eventually infect the whole country with fits of sneezing and its dogfighting, which would be just two fragments of the Re-Alphabet.

And what was I doing then. Nothing, mind you, except trying to tease out Q's impish smile. A game, why not, I clapped, and just how the light of her face. How so. Why take the pepper shaker, right or left hand is irrelevant, and place into the opposite hand, where the thumb meets the forefinger: and I poured out just a few grains, and like snuff, I raised it to my nostrils, you sniff. I had meant the funny, nothing more than to send her bubbling into laughter, and I had succeeded.

Again, she pleaded after both our tears subsided and I had finished mopping up the snot from my nostrils.

So I performed the trick again and this time her explosive laugh interrupted a karaoke artist's well-practised rendition of a popular tune that was breaking a lot of hearts at that time. Anger from the stage, of course, since the waves reverberated across three city blocks and continued hic for so hic long, with her intermittent addition of hiccups, that eventually it truncated the performance. But bemusement also, as the eavesdroppers' spotlight struck us from every other angle of the establishment. An odd applause found us, for her laughter, possibly, and for what I did to cause it.

I knew Q was speaking then, but I was sneezing and swimming in a mucoid and black pulmonary sea, and it was not good then. Deeply perturbing: surely you know the ordinary effects of black pepper from dinner accidents, but its effect on Hedayat was nothing short of revelatory. Understand that when black pepper is inhaled under certain conditions, the experience is not unlike that of hashish at first draw, with its racing heart and perspiring palms. But then one's tongue begins to drag like a hard drinker's two A.M., and the black pepper junky talk is anything but parrotspeech lingua mirari, its effect singular, individuated.

At that moment, no one dared karaoke, when what emerged out of Hedayat was an owlish woot. Q no doubt interpreted this as a continuation of my performance, and it signalled her continuation of thunderous laughter and I, too, was trying, hooting and cooing and doing all the screeching inimitable by human speech organs.

But know the animal transformation was exactly involuntary. The only glossolalist inspiration for the moment I can recall is having gazed at an early framed portrait of the Madam meeting with a high-level American dignitary in some far peripheral corner while snorting a little, and it splintered my thoughts. I slipped into a baffling avian tongue, which was trying desperately to explain, and fell deep into the earthquake of Q's laughter, which was far louder and bolder than mine had been during the spilling stones of Masoud Rana on the jetty, until her sounds became indistinguishable because the whole room was also laughing.

Here, let's, she grabbed hold of the shaker after I had stopped momentarily to drink whatever was in the glass before me. I'll see now, she did it, and disappeared into a grey cloud of dust from which she emerged with a bewildered scream; at first I was certain something vital in her had been destroyed. But after the confusion of the initial hit she sank into her nose and gave up a language of buzzing and clear crystalline nasal, and her throat was going so much then; I can recall it was the throat gristle and music then, not laughter. The more Q tried to refine her speech the more it resembled the beggar's cant of a common mosquito.

From across the table, I hooted back my replies as the Doubly crowd gathered around us, too curious a performance for anyone to miss. And what a performance. The cross-species pidgin of an owl and a mosquito cannot exactly be translated, but let me say it convinced them and they wanted to do it as well.

Then all the pepper shakers were dumping and the grey light of the tea bar shone weakly, and in the twisted light the people became like the sounds inspired in them by blowing a little pepper. The hair of the barber with his straight razor still in his pocket was now a kookaburra's crown, and for a time he strode from table to table on hidden wings, calling to this person and warbling to another, whatever hairs I cut are also sheared from my head and the whiskers on my face, he promised, but since he spoke in a pepper-inspired bird's babble, it was difficult for others to understand him.

Then a man's nose truncated, by which I mean the opposite, it stretched five aardvark times longer, in fact, and allowed him to search and suck up all the ants of the dirt underfoot. So solemnly he performed his task, as if he had been doing it all his life, with such little notice for his surroundings that when the kookaburra barber tripped over his ankles, he was glad to have been awakened, and yelled, enraged, how weary I am of this scuttling feast.

There were dogs then, how many so many dogs to emerge from the black cloud of sneezes and to meet the world with great barking and unyielding clamour, leashed dogs of the unnameable country, who played humans playing dogs in their muzzled everyday, but understand it was not only animals, for as well there were those who began humming and beeping like machines; there was an office lady who spoke only in alphanumeric configurations reminiscent of the lottery codes, and who after pronouncing each character would slap her own face, and another who chattered dit-dahs at the appropriate, repeated between grimaced teeth, not unlike John Quincy when he awoke from his great dream of Samuel Morse many years earlier.

It was difficult to know whether the hallucinations were theirs or belonged to us, whether we were peering into their minds or they were inside ours. The light twisted again and the jukebox started up on its own and spun a rousing dance number whose name had been lost in time.

That was when Hedayat stumbled into smoke, spun once, coughed a bunch as dells, torrents, flows and swift down both eyeballs cheeks flittering eyelids: a dense mist, another time, another light and heat: perspiring arms touched out of invisibility desiccated limbs levers or skeletons emerged, and hats, cloaks, ears, fluttering throats demanded attention/ Q, Hedayat cried out. Why, he asked the mist, but she was nowhere, remained nothing in only the mist. Fire in the unnameable country, what are you. Hedayat knew nothing about those pepper-inspired glossolalist visions and stumbled out of the struggling huddle into cooler streets. He turned a corner into a group of children crowded around, betting actual coinage on a chess match in which black had sent a knight errant to the furthest kingdoms of the board and white had just castled in front of an awaiting bishop. Excuse me, he asked one child, excuse me, he asked another, bouncing against one shoulder/ watch it/ against another/ where do you think you're going/ until he walked into the embrace of a beautiful woman. Hedayat tried to retrace the steps that nightmare. It's only the future, Q reassured, embraced tighter, recite. Only the future, Hedayat repeated after her, and when his face refused to abide and his thoughts remained close to the fire in the unnameable country, she tried lightening the moment: So pepper makes the crazy, Q sent up a froth of laughter, and I agreed with her then.

Eventually, the night dragged its feet, as do all great nights, and Q and Hedayat emerged from their pepper rush into the lunar dust and sublunary light of the curving alleyway where I kissed Q, her collarbones, her solar laugh that my mouth dampened. Accelerando: time rushed arteries flowed quick venal wait as seconds dragged loud minutes of silence. What are you doing, she asked when I paused, reached into my shirt's inner pocket for flight.

Once upon a time, I said as I gave her a bootlace stored in a velveteen pocket, once upon a time a no-good charlatan pretended to be my departed Niramish's friend's uncle. He gave me a gift I distrusted until it lifted me out of the darkest place. A bootlace, she looked at me incredulously. A bootlace, I affirmed. How does one, she began, and saw me tie it around my ankle. All right, she gave an impish grin and did as I did. That's when I took Q by the hand, raced alleyway skittered wall up onto rooftop. We leapt again and again until she whoa/ close to the edge of rooftop and deepest drop.

But we just scaled a building wall fearlessly, I reminded her, as she looked at me daft as if we'd taken the elevator. Come on, I coaxed, plucked the buzzing sky caught her a firefly fluttering noctilucent palm. And these, I pointed to the magic laces at our ankles, and she kissed me instead of speaking her disbelief. Hallowed her lips and tongue, hallowed the water of her mouth. Let's live to do it again tomorrow night, she said, as I stepped away from her embrace for one moment to look into the vast abyss before the next building, the between-space where one could see toy cars hundreds of metres below. Okay, I agreed.

Accelerando: time heightened its tempo. Fortissimo: the days became weeks became months so loud so quickly we hardly knew what to make of the changes. To blow a little pepper produced an unprecedented masquerade effect: El Doubly Tea began to overfill with nightly carnivals, which was not the lottery's prescribed revelry, and it was difficult not to sneeze at, once after entering, for the dark clouds of crushed smoke that hung perpetually in the air, or to pocket one's ears for all the din. In order to accommodate the overflow, all chairs and wooden tables were replaced with long metal counters, which housed lines of pepper shakers and glasses for the free jugs of sangria. Motley waitresses would pass in between and through the crowd, replacing the contents of each, and the only thing that wasn't free was the black pepper.

Something curious: the mutagenic effects of black pepper were conscribed to El Doubly Tea. No doubt other establishments tried to replicate such a lucrative venture, which increased the house revenue threefold, but they failed utterly, because it was not the pepper, as owners Hamida and Abdullah would proudly declare, though they never explained what was the key.

Then the Vulgarists arrived. Bete and Arachnae were the first, he with his extensive ball of yarn, which he kept with him at all times, which he would concatenate into knots he said allowed him to record any idea depending on the style of knot, of which he supposedly knew thousands—all thoughts recoverable at a later time by touch—and she with the flattest of faces, which allowed no light to escape, not for its colour but its ceaseless absent expression.

She was a painter of triptychs, only triptychs, she specified once, and offered no other explanations of her craft, though she would wear dresses of coarse lateen painted in broad solid colours, which one presumed were of her own design. As a counterpoint, he wore a goatee chin and mouth, which gave him the appearance of an off-duty sergeant of the armed forces, though his voice was placid and his eyes had the black drinking quickness of a lemur. What he actually did, aside from knotting balls of yarn, no one ever found out, but he belonged to the Vulgarists, and that gave him distinction.

Who were the Vulgarists. And what will they say about the Vulgarists once upon a time. How will posterity frame their projects vast tarpaulin sheets over richest neighbourhoods of Victoria Benediction La Maga with the words CARSANDHOUSES painted CARSANDHOUSES, CARSANDHOUSES repeated on top of actual cars and houses. The Vulgarists screamed when they wrote, painted, sculpted, made collage.

INSPIRED BY THE NAMELESS REBELS, THE VULGARISTS MADE A NAME THIEVING MOVING MIRRORS THROUGH THE WARREN TUNNELS AND USING THEM SMASHED IN ARTISTIC PORTRAYALS OF THIS REGIME'S GROTESQUERY: BILLBOARDS REPLACED WITH SMASHED MIRROR BLOODY TAIN AND BACK AND NEWS OF THE LOTTERY'S RECENT BETS, CHALK ON CAR ON HOUSE ON GRAVEL WITH THE COVERED OBJECTS' NAMES WRITTEN LAYERS OF PAINT MAGAZINE NEWSPAPER MIRROR: COLLAGE AND KALEIDOSCOPIC REFRACTIONS OF LIFE IN THE UNNAMEABLE COUNTRY. THE OCCUPYING ARMY BEGAN TARGETING AND FOLLOWING THE VULGARISTS. THOSE THAT GOT AWAY BEGAN PROPPING MIRRORS ON WOODEN CONSTRUCTIONS, CRACKED SHATTERED MIRROR-MIRRORS REFLECTING THE MIRROR-WALLS THAT *THE MIRROR* STARTED BUILDING LONG AGO AND WHICH, OVER THE YEARS, ENTIRELY COVERED THE STATE. THE VULGARISTS BUSTED BLOCKADE MIRRORS TO SHOW MIRRORS PREVENTED EASE OF TRAVEL AND MULTIPLIED NEEDLESS SUFFERING, REDESIGNED, RENAMED, REORDERED HOLLYWOOD SHIT MIRRORS, BUSTED MOVIE MIRRORS TO SHOW HOUSES BONES TEETH AND HAIR AND HOUSES AND A CAR IN EVERY DRIVEWAY, LAUGHED THE VULGARISTS BLACK SPUTUM.

During the day, the Vulgarists lived at El Doubly Tea. It became their home away from the La Maga Academy of the Arts, and Hamida and Abdullah were not only glad to donate the walls floors ceilings falling paint and chalk to their whims, but even to set up hammocks to accommodate their odd sleeping schedules.

Once, while they were spreading manure over a large bust of the Governor, Hedayat asked what they thought of contemporary art, and the room froze for one moment before issuing a sound like a ruptured gasline. Laughter out of little corners until let him, hush, Bete smiled and tried to thread his language through the still-hissing crowd.

In a single word: propaganda, he began. Every little. He stumbled. He smiled. He asked: Do you notice every film, H, or teleflicking advertising firm, and when every schoolboy doodle is the same hatred and identical. Ask this, H: Whence the spontaneity or ownmind ownlife.

Arachnae cleared her throat: Shit of rien de shit the shit to clog, she spat crystalline on the ceiling hung stalactite, and a little light shone from her mouth: to occlude all paths leading to any conclusion but the one: is this not the objective of propaganda.

Which one, Hedayat asked.

Total, the room tsk-tsked.

Surface-level topsoil totalshit, another laughed.

Farms and landfills, someone added.

Deep also, said the brushes and the foam churned inside Hedayat and his feathers rose up.

He shivered. And yet what are you: he pointed to the manure-laden bust: Is this not also propaganda in its own right.

The room laughed; there were hisses.

Bete merely shrugged; we are twenty-five of us Vulgarists on a bright day; twenty-five people cannot make propaganda. By definition, it is everyone eating ownflesh; by definition, it takes an entire perpetual beehive.

Despite his lack of a craft, Hedayat found a vocation at El Doubly Tea when he was not assisting Q at the Hospice, and he would carry paints and the utensils of the day's exercises and watch as they worked, while Bete knotted his ball of yarn into nodes for future reflection. Here were others in whose company it was possible to understand that the daily world shook deep vibration into bones, and that its smells were poison and that every apple in every marketplace was a lottery ticket to oblivion, systematically itemized, poisoned accordingly.

The margins in the unnameable country had become absolute: either in or out, tarrying to decide or to think had become dangerous, impossible, and contemplation criminal. Here were others who not only understood but who heaped onto the canvas and sculpted into shapes and pointed fingers.

Let it be known Q also preferred the company of the Vulgarists, but not the way Hedayat did. You and I, she would say, and others like those of the Vulgarists, and others like those of the original Eve, she would sniff a little pepper in the nighttime when we would still frequent, but not them, she would conclude: I have never observed a total transformation.

And this was true. It was something odd about the arthouse crowd, as if they understood but could not exactly perform the animal or machine. They coughed and they sneezed and blew an awful lot of pepper, they made motions toward either and yet one always knew these were incomplete trials, as if they were truly too human to change.

Not me, Q would say, I'm a mosquito, and I'll always be.

I loved her then, and truly it was good then. Between her and the ghosts and the Vulgarists on the other side, I was either with her or with them, my nights and days filled with laughter and contemplation, contented, in a word, until.

One day, while in between either place and shortcutting through the Warren tunnels, I found myself pressed up against a rockface, which gave like an oomph before my feet dangling and mouth cried uncle; but not actual uncle and a return, actually, of those Herculean words: child of clay and of clotted blood, born of woman, do you know me. I did not recognize the voice that was no longer spilling stones, which I had not heard once in the past two or three, during which I could have cared less because I was happy in the world, but he held me above the subterranean soil for so long I finally knew and cried out, mercy, Masoud, I have not forgotten. Then the rockface released me and exhaled. The tunnels' string of incandescent bulbs gave me his form and I saw it was indeed Masoud Rana, and I was happy because I remembered his illumined speech near the jetty on the morning I thought he was a friend.

Tell me, friend, he jingled his pockets, what are you worth these days. I thought of my once robust savings, which had dribbled through the holes in my pants like so many little pebbles and more of which I had scattered because I was certain there were many more where the ocean met the Gulf of Eden.

Come with me, he dragged me by the scruff of the neck, while dragging behind him our cart of daily wares.

That was how Hedayat returned to the courier's grind, and he did not like it then. Though slowly it replenished his depleted stock, he had little time for carousing with artists, and when he found himself back at the Hospice, the television gave out its stock colours and sounds, there were too many diaphanous shapes shuffling about like forgotten memories, it was difficult to remember who preferred rose oil with her blood or who liked yogurt and chopped parsley afterward because he didn't like the taste of blood at all, who were hunger striking and dancing skeletal with death beyond death, would anyone like to play dominoes, and all the tasks toward which he forwarded steps, though Q never asked. Nevertheless, a yellow ribbon of light would trail behind her when she was content, her gratitude and generosity were boundless, and her breath was an effusion that enriched the whole Hospice. For a long while, the mere company of each other was sufficient to mule the burden of work that drew deeply on their resolve and resilience.

Time passed. Since the lease renewal of the American air force base, the splintered religious groups gathered under the umbrella of the Islamic Justice Party, which was the largest political organization of its kind and situated in the Warren. Their divided understandings of the American military presence, exegeses of the lottery economy, the role of women in society, conflicting definitions of nationalism, of Islam, opinions on the Madam's regime, of *The Mirror*, whether reason and the soul were the same or separated, whether the ghosts of the mirrors were soulless vaporous images or the continuation of human beings, if there were such a thing as the ummah or the term was misleading, if it was forgivable to exchange the divinely ordained activities of the right and left hands, all seemed less relevant in light of a choking repression like none other in the unnameable country's history, and nowhere worse than in the Warren.

For a long time, the water there had become as saline as the Gulf of Eden; the turbid fluid that emerged from the taps came and went without warning. Darkness declared monopoly and engulfed the residents whenever it pleased as the electricity, gasoline, and natural gas were even more fickle than the water supply. Many people tried to leave, and often they were crushed in the tunnels, like families of rabbits by armoured bulldozers doing their grave work above ground. (Meanwhile, the courier's life grew riskier.) All the grains of sand seemed also to be trying to flee its cordoned premises, leaving the earth there smooth like a sun-polished whalebone.

Everywhere there floated the stench of rotted memories, and the future became mixed up with the present; out of nothing there bloomed the story of a little boy who kicked his soccer ball across the mirror-walls and found it several alleyways later, extending from the arms of a man with two weeping glass eyes who claimed to be his grandson. Volunteers from the United Front (as the umbrella organization became known) travelled from home to home carrying siphoned gasoline, firewood, baskets of bread fruits vegetables, schoolbooks and confectioneries for children, freshly built furniture, offers of zero-interest loans, with fingers pressed to tight lips, say nothing, you hear nothing, know nothing until the time.

When a world of young people from the Warren began trickling into El Doubly Tea, I had the premonition things were about to change in the unnameable country. At that time, the nightly carnivals had grown bolder and the carousing more urgent, as if there was no time to lose because the future could fail to arrive at any moment. The Vulgarists, who had never mastered the art of blowing a little pepper, sought to cover up their failure by accessorizing according to others' metamorphoses: beaks and canes became fashionable, ostentatious feathered boas and large plastic turtlebacks, even fur, despite the region's tremendous and perpetual hostile heat, not to mention letting off the scent of carrion: all these were preferable styles.

We knew the four newcomers were different because they stood out in those peacock proceedings as if covered by a dark lugubrious umbrella; their clothes did not befit an establishment that was becoming increasingly tailored to the likes of the young student crowd; they looked sad, though not pitiable poor, and their eyes were consuming everything, asking questions and acknowledging the responses their minds formulated in the next moment, and they didn't speak a word. They seemed to know why they had come and took their seats along the third row of the metal tables, where they began pouring onto the crook of their thumbs and forefingers without first having a drink of sangria, which was customary to do.

I didn't stop looking at them for an instant and was staring so much that Q took my elbow and quizzed me silently what's new with you. I couldn't say until they were well peppered and starting sneezing and blowing like a brass band about to start. Let me remind that among the four there was a tall and thick, a short and mangy, a box man, whose shoulders were wide, and an innocuous older woman, who played the cautious notes and who seemed familiar.

Who is she, Q floated into my thoughts.

Then they began: the four newcomers, after having inhaled their first tinctures of black pepper, began—listen to this—hear that blue buzzing from lips as if they are the striking midnight on twelve thousand trumpets: is that not the sound of Gabriel at beginning or unyielding clamour. Then whole bodies shaking and moving to the ground, recall as if you were there, a summit of dancers, limbs and heads piled high and thrown joyously and the idiosyncratic jukebox was going then, but it didn't matter because all the sound was everybody's. Every throat in El Doubly Tea was adding a noise, shaking tremulous into that transformation.

We followed them outside as they continued to blast their mouth instruments, the pied and so many singing rats and dogs behind them, panthers, standoffish prickly hedgehogs, bird-beaked humans wearing canes and with painted faces, spinning computer hardware, floating eyeballs, dragging the lyrical odours of garlic, black pepper, onions, raisins, and freshly baked bread, and recall from the footage the cameras were there, and that *The Mirror* continued to follow in vans and trucks what was for its crew no doubt a loud and impersonal clamour, and in the midst of that multitude I could hear Q's mosquito-buzz, because every so often I would press my ear close to her so I could add thirds or fifths to her song.

They found us, of course. The sirens scattered the crowd and the fear of truncheons, but when we broke apart, Q and I were not so far from the four and away enough from the coppers. We whistled at them and they waved back and smiled.

Fine performance, Hedayat extended, we don't ordinarily experience bands at El Doubly Tea.

We're not a band, said Tall and Thick.

But you were an oboe, if I remember, Q said.

We introduced, met hands, and that was when it became possible to know and not to have to weep with all mybody body later when I realized the truth about the unnameable country; the pieces may have fallen into place much sooner, is what I mean.

Hedayat, she spoke my name, and I wondered if, but the sound was not exactly right, the face not identical but it had been so long I blamed time for the errors and as I had done in the Warren tunnels when faced with the Herculean truth, I named, for what else.

Aunt Shadow, I pronounced on the interrogative.

She smiled and gave a soft hand as if the years had caused other changes, as well, and it was no longer appropriate to embrace.

Where, I said.

In the Warren.

And for how long.

Since forever or since leaving the hosiery shop.

And then.

I have a job.

Is that so.

Yes.

That's what the music was for, added Short and Mangy, clogging a nasal issue with fist and snort.

I didn't understand then, but they said they would be back, and lifted a patch of asphalt, which spread apart to reveal an abyss into which they descended one by one, each with a wave goodbye. Hedayat would not discover they were Black Organs until he would meet them again a long time afterward.

The buzzing of the brass band lingered for several weeks, peeking out from corners of the air all throughout the unnameable country, and causing strange disturbances in people's lives. One morning, Osman Yathrib, assistant to the vice president of an advertising and marketing firm invested in precisely locating trash in the streets and in the low atmosphere, as well as mapping corporate spies across the urban landscape for the purposes of hunting germinal desires, for capturing hearts and the hidden sighs of denizens, for seeding rumours and cultivating them into purchasing trends, the same Osman Yathrib who had barely known an ironed shirt out of his BCom, a company unknown until recently drafting a proposal for the novel appearance of holographic advertisements on the streets of La Maga and Benediction as a means of capitalizing on the everywhere mirror-walls, heard a sound like a loud blast on a piccolo trumpet, then twice again.

Osman Yathrib got up on tiptoes, abandoning the pageant queen with whom he had been temporarily sharing a palatial hotel bed, and saw a large wounded deer struggling on its feet in the vestibule leading to the kitchen.

He approached cautiously. The animal exhaled its pestilential breaths, and Osman discovered, in fact, it was not so much wounded as rotting away at the legs before his very eyes. Its hide gave off the odour of rotting seaweed. Before he could move or do a thing, however, he felt the knots in his stomach tightening and felt human hands lurching, clasping onto his shoulders while hearing a voice speaking clearly and terrified eyes that cried out please, I need a hairpin and a needle.

That was when Osman saw the tiger trap clasped around the intruder's legs. He ran into the bedroom to ask, but the pageant queen was very sleepy and turned to her side for another hour's rest. When he tried to explain the grave situation, his teeth chattered and got in the way of words.

He returned before sufficing a reply to her rising concern and try as he might, he couldn't pry open the trap. Osman Yathrib found himself knocking on every room on his floor, on the floor above and below, on all the rooms of all the floors of every building in the world but they all told him no, go away, it's Saturday, or they glared at him for interrupting until he was ashamed of what he was unsure. He found himself dialing a dead phone and then dousing the fly-infested wounds with alcohol and binding the stranger's leg with gauze, asking out of a desire to humanize the nightmare, where do you live.

In an unnameable country, the stranger answered definitively while shivering cold, oh they got me this time, and Osman noticed his skin had the egg-yolk tinge of a man who had been slowly poisoned.

He had no heart to ask what the other was doing in his hotel suite, knowing that the reasons he was here lay beyond a man dragging around a tiger trap; as well, he was unconvinced the scene was not a hallucination or a nightmare that would vanish with time. But as the day dragged on, he realized no nightmare he had ever had contained so many well-placed details, such as the diabetic hunger he experienced each morning at eleven o'clock for a slice of pound cake, or the heavy timbre of the front door slamming when the pageant queen departed through it with one scream and half a look at that unholy terror.

He knew it was not a nightmare when the deer that changed into a man died as a man, because from a few experiences in his own life, he could recall he died exactly the way men die. When Osman Yathrib stood up to wash his hands of caked blood, there was no blood. The hallway was filled with strangers, who tried frenetically to leave the hotel, and Osman Yathrib was looking for someone who would listen to the tragedy, but there was no one, because they were all concerned.

Did you not hear the great brass, all asked him; the fire alarm and public announcement systems had been disconnected by the culprits, they said, and the smell of black pepper hung in the air.

The incident sharpened Osman's intuitive understanding of the unnameable country, and he was unsurprised days later when Conception, Benediction, and La Maga were also hit by several explosions. The United Front took no responsibility and blamed the Madam's regime for fabricating the attacks in the crucial months before the first national elections in ten years. More explosions found the capital, the financial district was closed down for a week, high-level bankers and businessmen cried foul, hired paramilitaries, bought helicopters to prevent the kidnapping of their daughters and wives for ransom. Others suffered with the confused knowledge that other hidden organs of society

HUNGRY
GHOSTS

Then the hungriest ghosts found their way to the Ghost Hospice, skeletal thin and herded one grey evening by leaderman speaker predicant himself, Masoud Rana. No more, Q did not say, despite that some of the most diaphanous senile ghosts were so translucent four or five of them could have been superimposed on top of one another. Space was the issue; why, Masoud Rana, a high-ranking peregrine of the concrete jungle, obviously able to thisandthat place whenever at will and pulling in the notsobad bucks these days, would not move to a better than this singleroomflat and why he eventually did will be explained in due time. At the moment the new ghosts demand attention.

They are the thinnest apparitions, as I said, starving shivering nineteen of the sickliest, and incapable of gripping the teacups of their inaugural meal at the Hospice. Q and I had to assist with their drinking, to pre-chew their food like mother birds. Their ingested mash could be followed straight and winding through their digestive machinery, and when they urinated, what emerged was a stream that made them howl.

Their excretions (which they did into bedpans, which we later toileted) were a glassy and quivering colloid.

Q and I couldn't understand how these nineteen ghosts differed from the others so greatly until Masoud Rana plainly explained: read it in the newspapers like a schoolboy about the hunger strikers of Conception. Then I recalled I had indeed read it, and Masoud Rana had even predicted they would turn up at our doorsteps soon enough, and no doubt, they did.

You wouldn't believe it, Owl, but they all fit south of the Datsun, Masoud explained. I myself, he continued, was shitting firecrackers would the woowoos stop us for harbouring a dozen ex-cons and blow-up artists.

To clarify: there are a lot of ghosts then to port in the Datsun, self-immolators blackened skin stinking all charcoal or luminescent a thousand pinpoints per square centimetre, peaceniks: die-in sleepers rolled over by business business tanks; and of course the hunger strikers, who had wasted thin away in unnameable jail cells protesting identity cards for all ethnic groups that might be a nuisance or incendiary threat/ for everyone, government officials pointed out/ not for everyone to show upon request to an inquiring police officer, as we all knew. There were the ghosts who wanted to know the date because they had opened their morning curtains to a dimensionless sunlight through which they wandered, alone like all the others, for years in that visionless light through which we were forced navigated by touch, some of them insisted, for a thousand years, they informed, until we found our way to the Ghost Hospice. Some of the ghosts claimed to know Hedayat. One of them mentioned Niramish mentioned Hedayat.

Some of them were prepared to loosen their hold on life and vanished over time, eventually left the Halfway House to embrace the true nothingness of a death beyond death, while the remainder stayed with us as ghosts. To note: some of these members of the human tribe, such as the Friends of Conception, had forsaken eating in life, but in death, they had found the pleasures of food. Like all ghosts, however, they could not consume anything without a smattering of human blood, and at first we Ghost Hospice workers midwives of death tried to lessen their hissing urine pain among other ailments.

We're not doctors of the undead, Masoud Rana said, and can't treat afterlife's medical ailments. Leave them be, was the basic message.

But their screams terrified us, neighbours began door-banging talking pss-psst to themselves, and soon, we knew the popo would come. But the unspoken policy of the Halfway House remained: no ghost would be turned away or set out into the streets after being offered shelter. What to do but contain the problem, muffle the screams with towels. We offered but still the sounds and gaseous urine: an ammonia-rich fog contaminated the whole apartment. This is the way it was then. Room to room, let us. Inspect with a flashlight, shine a light at the translucent shapes lying limb to limb, head to toe, their hearts available for you to see through translucent flesh and to do it if you will. And always growing in number and variety.

That was around the time we started sucking hospitals of their throwaway blood, stealing bag after bag of the stuff, of jogging through the halls in tief-nurse uniforms and surgical masks: ma'am, ma'am, doctor sir, and we even had replica badges and education stuff made just in case. We used to do these gigs twice a week, a Saturday and Wednesday kind of thing, from one to four in the morning. We would trawl anywhere from twelve to twenty-six litres of blood, though our brightest tally was a whopping thirty-nine litres.

The blood did strange things to the ghosts, like loosen their tongues about their lives underground as well as above it once upon. As well, it helped with their health and created a great deal of ass effusions: flatulence I mean, and farting also. Q and I were not interested in challenging the Madam's Black Organs with its hundreds of thousands of civilian volunteers, who played the role of looksees or follow-follows in what was effectively the biggest street gang on the continent, funded and trained by the CIA, some of them without even demanding to be on any payroll, just out of the goodness of their hearts.

Live Social, declared the ads, Keep Community Alive, said another, when what they really meant: The most effective way to recruit the public, we realized, was to disappear the enemy so he is everywhere, lead-characters every story, so he is nowhere, defeated and always indefeasible. We did not want to be on any terror watch list or to waste the good years of our lovemaking in various nasty. Fuck that, we both conceded, lying with our fingers curled around, naked on the single-frame cot that sat us up or lay us down. We were interested only in feeding the ghosts.

And we worried for Masoud Rana and for the first time, and spoke of the future potential of the Halfway House what when we are notsoyoung, look how you have come already from seventeen to twenty-three, she would point out, when she was a ripe old thirty years of age. Of all the minor treasures of the tale, now is a good time to reveal the small booty I had kept apart from our daily peregrinations. So why not leave it all behind now, Hedayat. Already in my heart I knew it couldn't get any better, the narrative had achieved its nadir, whoever was penscratching my life had offered me this one passage.

Q, I called her back from the forest ahead, where I tried to laugh at this strange choice of scenery, why here before what inferno, and why at all. But no sound fled my mouth, while with my hands I harvested only thorns. I found her after all. When I found her mouth with my mouth my whole body issued with love for her. I opened my jaws again, but the spider had weaved a web there in the meantime, and it was all effusing then from my mouth, all the radii and signal threads, and the spider was swinging out of my open mouth and then from inside the funnel of my throat. That was when I wanted to kiss Q, but I couldn't.

There were other forms of pain then as an artificial famine struck the drugs-and-guns savanna we traversed, not a mere bust but a suppliers' strike, by the sounds of it, but there had been rough times before, Q reminded, and we haven't ever thought of closing down shop; the Halfway House won't go under for a few short dollars.

There was, of course, another way: traffic in blood, they will pay. And it was true, as we discovered: the multi-tier healthcare system was full of gaps, smaller clinics that served the unemployed and working poor, sometimes lacking licences or the basic units of medicine, empty shelves ranging from antibiotics to antileprotics stood sometimes on the same street as the well-stocked, well-staffed variety. No blood. Not enough donors, to say it simply. To explain further: we stole from the richer hospitals, who sucked out of whoknowswhere. We were the middlemen.

Our collective conscience was governed jealously by Q, who was already red in the face about our drug dealing still and why so, willyoutell, while also standing entirely against the idea of selling blood until we convinced her, in fact, we were helping two categories of individuals, ghosts and near-ghosts, that our markup was not so high, that all we were doing was moving blood from those who had more than enough to those who had less than enough.

She still didn't, but eventually she did. Just as soon, the most profound: Masoud Rana, the lager-wielding gallant, splish-sploshing it in belly on shirt and on face, emerged from a pub already in the midst of a story we have missed by following other threads, thumbing his gat in his pocket. He clicked it back, smooth, black metalheaving in his hand, pulled it out just as the copper turned backward and away from the oldtimers he had been speaking to, and found only a hole of blood where once his mouth had been.

BLACK
ORGANS

Who are Black Organs. And what do they say about Black Organs. The Black Organs came to pluck out our eyes, to blinddeafendisappear us. Your mailman turns out to be an Organ, or the toll booth collector true story says sir step out of the car please for one second and dig your own grave before you're buried. Stay on your toes, say Black Organs. We are winning but the enemy is everywhere and indefeasible.

True story: Libby Solkovitch, widow, aged fifty-seven, was approached one Sunday in '57 around the time of the Governor's reign when the unnameable country was sinking into the soft marl of totalitarianism, by a woman who looked like the grown-up rendition of her long-lost and longpresumedasdead daughter. She looked up into those watery pale blue eyes and concluded yes, the right age and shape, howled out of a long-abandoned hope, the idea that such a moment would arrive so deep in the redemptive future, out of a pain that had lingered inside her as some causeless shapeless ache.

Come, Ma, the young woman took her by the hand.

And that was how Libby Solkovitch disappeared for fifteen years.

Another now, this one about Kamal Bari, forty, father of a small boy, husband and machinist at a Toyota plant in the interior of the unnameable country: for months, Kamal complained about strangers who seemed to know too much about him, who laughed at the private moments of his life, howcouldtheyknow, echoed his suspicions of his wife's infidelity, and that they augured misfortune and illness. He felt strange tingles in his body, his mind was awash in confusion, he was sure his food was being poisoned, that his wife was one participant of a larger conspiracy to kill him so she could resume life with her secret lover. He found her weeping in another room and took her tears to mean guilt. Enraged and impotent, he could find no solution between suicide and flight. Kamal Bari withdrew his savings and made the necessary preparations.

At the airport, he was told his name matched another's and that he was to follow those gentlemen over there.

Dark teeming sweat, ten million maggots per second, hyperventilation, perspiration, inside his body hidden organs were making work, moving fluids from one part to another. They offered him water, and Kamal Bari accepted and drank without thinking. In the chair he sat in his private solitude. The torture within was something else, and his heart stopped beating for no prior medical reasons by the time they came to tell him it was all a misunderstanding, the other Kamal Bari also possessed Hussein as his middle name. Shall I go on interrogation point

In 1983, at the beginning of the Madam's regime, the Black Organs network expanded until there were two or three hidden cells under every subway station where the institutions of shiver your entrails and brick shitting could be rendered. Some people are eyeshut about it while others will go as far in the opposite direction as to write that the birth of crack cocaine abuse in the Palisades was fathered by Black Organs, but truthbetold, we all grew up thinking they could be anyone, your mustachioed uncle, your schoolteacher, your younger, bedwetting brother, your mother, the part-time mule, or your best friend, whose father one day screamed as they cut a hole through his ceiling and repelled from above costumed appropriately in dark, barking in an incomprehensible and eating the family's evening meal straight from the pot, rifling through the children's homework, inspecting the mother's eveningwear, before producing out of father's shirt, like sleight-of-hand tricksters, the apparent reason for it all: several bags of pure heroin.

Nowadays, since the incident in New York, it's the praying man, the mullah-man, Allahhissing serpent, oh spell it Islamic terrorist, who is the prime target of the Black Organs, is now potentially anyone. (They arrest Hedayat.) What are Black Organs. Why Black Organs. Black Organs, convince the private individual he wants public power over private lives: power over other human beings, power to see, to torture, to shame, to annihilate, power to tear a mind to repair however he likes. Give him that power in a soap ad, a car commercial, power with a certain number of snaps of one's fingers, with a lottery language a Re-Alphabet that does not exist: public power to accuse without saying a thing. (They arrest Hedayat.) Organs, who are not Black Organs. To the unbelievers, I ask: what did we hate before maybe communists. And did we hate as much and as well.

I mutter these things as I think. I call Q's name and find her, thankfully, sleeping peaceful next to me all is well. I drift off, still muttering under my breath. Until tomorrow morning, I grumble to myself, offered up to thoughtspies of Department 6119, are the following categories of Hedayat's thoughts: thoughts of twist and turning sheets in my bed, of a red blister from bum shoes need replacing, of rumble stomach and rumination of milk, of mealy wheat germ in the morning, offered up to their goddamn listening devices are thoughts of how do I fit this vegetable patch into the back seat of the Datsun today, thoughts of what is the shortest route through La Maga's mirror-labyrinths, of planning the fewest encounters with soldiers and checkpoints and guns and humiliation; surely they will hear my recollections, projections, I think, before remembering recent news reports, talk of Victoria's biggest mob bosses supposedly supplying arms to terrorists of undefined denomination, and oh yeah, I wanted to see that recent Nick Cage invasion film they're shooting with live ammunition. Who will listen. Why do they want all my mutter all the time. Fuck this unnameable country. I turn over, kiss Q's bare shoulder. I listen to her breezes for a minute or a peaceful hour.

The next day, Masoud Rana came home agitated pacing, what, bhai, I tried to tease it out of him, tell me, I pleaded, and still he said nothing. We sat on the couch for a long time until he rose up suddenly and with a great guffaw declared he had killed a man. Shit, brother, serious. Yeah, man, he said. Then he said it again, bam! pointed bam! a gat insisted he killed him blood funtoosh, could you do it, sucka. Since taking up residence at the Ghost Hospice I realized how different my friend and I had become, where our sights now lay. My owl eyes had begun, with Q's love, to understand my life and memories as longer than set to movie set of *The Mirror* staging gangster flick or domestic drama or science fiction scaffolds and wiring for the next edition of the longest film in the world, enclosing our country in a complex order of walls and floors and ladders and make-belief, turning it into dry ice dioxide, indiscernible movie mist.

When Masoud Rana deadpistolled Morris the cop, he did so in the throes of a passion that could only have been sustained by a member of our fatalistic youth that live between movie-set checkpoints governed by the same security forces that demand identification to travel between the rooms of your house if you're unlucky enough to experience such high-level surveillance: he knew his life was over long before he fired the shot, but since his heart continued to beat, why should it not do so forever. Despite the fog of youth, which hides death is always future death, he understood they would come for him, and that they would torture him and probably kill him, so why, then.

When Masoud Rana began to black vomit soon after the death of Morris the cop, Q presumed he was suffering an attack of listeriosis, a recent endemic in our country, and couldn't understand why he refused to seek medical treatment. Over the following weeks, he lost twenty pounds, and we were frightened it would infect us as well. But all we caught were mild headaches and a feverish sense of foreboding. We recovered soon enough and went about our business of thieving and selling blood, not knowing our friend had endangered the whole enterprise of the Halfway House and the task of survival.

The cardinal rule of the hustler: commit no unnecessary violence. That was, as Masoud Rana and I had always agreed, the way to move smoothly through the arteries of the other economy; why occlude the whole body and give everyone an aneurysm. No need for the gangster-front unnecessary and foolishness, we would say to each other in the Datsun, laughing while driving from one shitty deal to another.

———————

All the signs said the unnameable country insisted on tasting with your tongue, smelling the odours your lungs took in, crushing your life world, and my father's shoulderspy was one example of such Black Organ agenda. Not too long after Masoud said he performed his gun act, Q and I visited my family home. She had heard the stories of the shoulder-sitter who for the longest time in our family had been a joke, who hunched my father back-broken with years of the same misery of walk with brush with eat walk snooze and shit with that burden on your back.

Years earlier, when my father contacted the Ministry of Records and Sources, it told him there was no Mamun Ben Jaloun in the system before realizing it hadn't killed him yet. My father got a rise and shine phone call several mornings later. A purring female voice informed him that indeed a man-sized parasite had been scheduled to sit on his shoulders and that he was responsible for its upkeep. When asked why and what legal recourses he had to rejoin his life of relative comfort, Department 6119 resumed its primary position that until it could verify whether such stringent surveillance had in fact been implemented, it couldn't comment further.

Let's pry the sucker's mouth, Q dangled a packet of rum candy, sly smiling. Trust me, she insisted when I said I didn't understand.

Q and I entered my parents' home sweetmeats box and rum candies in hand, sweets for the fam and cane liquor concentrate for the surveillant. My parents got the game and my mother even played coy. Your stomach will churn for such gross trespass on God's law against alcohol, she warned, while my father, hearing each candy contained a single shot of rum, and wistful of his father's youthful flirtations with modernist poetry and attractions to late-nineteenth-century European bourgeois lifestyles, asked if he could have a taste.

My mother spun a dance single on vinyl that Aunt Shadow and Samir brought the last time they visited, on which occasion Chaya informed my mother she had aborted her pregnancy and she and Samir were debating the idea of expanding their record shop to include a practice space for bands. Amidst the sweetmeats, upbeat pop number, and alcohol candy, Hedayat and Q felt ready to join the fun.

The shoulder guard preferred the single the second time he heard it, and Hedayat pushed the next record in a series of songs that saw our house's dark windowpanes brighten with spirits rushing arteries without a drink in sight. His resistance lowered and for the first time in years, my father rolled, relaxed his shoulders. Rhythm pushed melody to crescendo, as Q bobbed sexy under dinnerlight, at the exact moment of the shoulderspy's drunk and tumble deep afterhours. He gave a fearful scream and Mamun Ben Jaloun ran as far from the fallen assailant as possible to the other side of the room while son defended father punches to the shoulder-sitter's head.

Since there are no explicit laws in the unnameable country governing the instatement of shoulder-sentinels, their deposition, naturally, meets a similar judicial lacuna. The warders guarding the doors of our apartment understood their limited roles against the house's inhabitants and watched as Hedayat fought argument retort counter-argument glossolalist for hours until the bow-legged scum was forced to leave our home. Q and I kissed a job well done as my father cried in relief and my mother thanked us with homemade jilapi.

———————————

On my shoulder, Q cried in a forest near the Halfway House after the incident.

Let's go, Hedayat.

Where, my love, I asked, recalling she had chosen to stay in the unnameable country for whose sake but mine years earlier after scoring the American dream in a lottery ticket. I remembered the holographic gleam of big-city lights on paper and wondered would she go today without me.

Anywhere, let's get out of this country.

We don't have passports, I searched for an appropriate counter, and we wouldn't get far with what I've got, I revealed my modest acorn stash for the first time. She was heartened by my efforts, my presence of mind, my lucidity, and that I would continue trying to convince her.

And Masoud, I asked.

We'll drag my brother black vomiting onto the plane. He doesn't know what a persuasive bitch his sister can be.

But the determination of the moment faded, because time in the

Palisades is a gyre. Because time is illmatic in the Palisades, which means the same lines on the same foreheads and same palms repeat across generations. A hot wind blows in the Palisades. Who killed Morris the cop, scream the headlines, Morris, Peaceable Policeman, whose life unnecessarily taken by a Warren rat. The Governor has taken the death of Morris the cop to mean an opportunity for a massive fly-swatting campaign. It signed the fire papers before he did.

Bullets fly miraculously. Three neighbourhood shops, several houses, an apartment complex, a pharmacy, the local doctor's office spontaneously combust. Six weeks later, the very day the UN Council on Internal Relations of the Unnameable Country delivers a report on the situation at the General Assembly, Claus Claude Van Damme, son of the action superstar Jean-Claude, fly-kicks a sugar-screen oriel window's ass in an action sequence for *The Mirror* that to film requires the closure of a well whose drinking water is key for Palisades residents. The UN report, by the way, lists the number of disappeared or dead in the retaliatory campaign to be as high as six hundred, but numbers speak as well as corpses. Finally, scholars scouring La Maga police records from that time never discover the existence of such a character as Morris the cop. Nevertheless, all the fieldmice of the Palisades scatter across the flathouses and through the fire-streets, but we can call them cats or dogs or snakes or rats if we like. Whatever the term, lead is indiscriminate.

The matter reached a head during a Die for Peace theatre assembly, a monumental act of civil disobedience: over one hundred thousand grandmotherschildrenwomenmenyoungandold lay down on the busiest highways in the unnameable country, spaced lengthwise head to toe for one hundred miles with white sheets placed over their bodies, corpses for a day. General Morganson, commander-in-chief and direct descendant of Admiral Mulligan, called in the tanks. What exactly occurred next is contested, though the available footage speaks clearly. The army claims public mischief and potential threat of terrorism prompted the retaliation, but one thing is clear: for a long time, no one moved, as if already/ they were screaming they're killing us killing us, and the tanks began trampling unarmed bodies the horror.

Several days later, the first suicide attack in the unnameable country: a young woman equipped with a semi-automatic and half-dozen clips entered the head office of Barclays, the first British bank to settle in the unnameable country. She bulleted twenty employees, waited until the feds gathered below, took the elevator down, and with arms upheld in a deferential pose of surrender she walked outside to the awaiting militarymen and shit, in her hand, a copper screamed but too late. A hot wind overturned Jeeps and police cruisers and scorched fourteen soldiers. Of her body, there remained a few charred organs.

Today in the Palisades they are doing it not just with the military police but also with the ambulance worker, who after taking your son's pulse shows you his red card, offside, sir. They search and sniff all your pockets and belongings while barbs nettles in your lungs and your silence, sheared voice/

Or they might insist you hurry, you, the young woman, while they poke through your underwear drawer as you bite your lips. Won't find anything there, you say, while your mother stands tearing from the eyes, pleading for an exchange, meinsteadofshewouldbefrightened.

You would be frightened too, the handsome officer replies in even syllables, and for a moment the mother reconsiders, whowouldn't, as another actual dog pushes in with front paws and on hind legs, out of the way, he says, talking language barking sniffing ravenously under bedsheets, he smells something. Terror and shame as they thumb through your bookshelf, underwear drawer, intimate thoughts. They read the pages and they watch. Hurry, they insist, and push you doors open into a car you don't say a word. Not a word as they lead you among the trees marking graves.

Black Organs generally pump harder through hidden arteries

of the unnameable country after catastrophe, accusing haranguing capturing bodies for blame and reprimand for spontaneous fires. The recently appointed government of our nation featured representatives of large defence contractors, an American general, and the head of the largest spidersilk corporation in the world, Joshimuddin Khan Jr., son of Nasiruddin Khan; it imposed curfews, thumbprint identification and payment devices that allowed you to pass checkpoints if your records were clear, if you were allowed, and let you make purchases at gas stations and department stores simply by scanning your hands, revealed intimate details of your life and body to Black Organs. They heightened army and paramilitary governance of the streets and people's homes, where they set up stations as they did to monitor my father Mamun Ben Jaloun, making our home into hell for many years.

What kept me owl-eyed, focused on understanding our country's unnameable past, was Q, who told me once upon a time before she left we have never been a nation, Hedayat, we have never been ourselves. I don't understand. We are the world, she said. What do you mean. Sometimes I forget our name, she shrugged.

For her sake, though she had never spoken of children of her own, because I had never seen her happier, I was glad when there emerged a living child among the ghosts, one with a shell in his hand. He walked right up to Q as if he knew her, the child with coal-bright eyes who never releases his grip on his backward shell.

THE
BOY
WITH
THE
BACKWARD
CONCH

When the boy with the backward conch came to the Hospice, everything changed because the damp ash smoke of a hundred apparitions trailed behind him. We couldn't figure out why until Masoud told us he had read in newspapers that spontaneous fires fall on spiderfields, on village residents. It's as if an asteroid fucked the hinterland, Masoud said about pictures of a moonscape. Where did it happen. Benediction, he showed me the page. Shit, I looked at the photo. Q, who subscribed to a magazine called *Unnameable Earth*, relayed that it was the largest spontaneous fire recorded in years, and showed us another shot of the region high above the city's corolla tossing petals three-sixty, all plant animal machine become one flower. The number of reported dead increased daily after that while thousands of ghosts wandered blood-hungry, wailed Re-Employment Office corridors seeking recognition rebirth remuneration for their losses.

That a hundred of them eventually made it to the Hospice surprised us, we expected more, would have welcomed all of them, obviously, but with apprehensions about enough blood. Something was happening: our facility, which had originally been constructed to care for the dying dead before they disappeared from even a faded existence, was becoming a treatment centre for ghosts that wanted to rejoin the world of the living. Benediction's spontaneous massacre was proving to Q that we were like a United Nations workspace, under-staffed, underfunded. As with the multiplying walls and ceiling for sky that now characterized our ensconced unnameable country, she began to become agitated, frustrated. I will stay here and build it nevertheless, I said of the Hospice, because it was respite for me, outside all the shit in my mind. Q didn't reply.

Fire. We know you. Ever since I can remember, since an ill-gotten, forgotten time long before my birth, fire has been the motif of the unnameable country, exploding hospitals to hell, schools, buildings, machines building machines all collapse and catafalque, gravebound spontaneously without warning.

We had never had to deal with such a large party of undead. They were so translucent we could direct all of them to a single room where their mouths moved soundless, and their faces emerged chest legs torso for mere moments one hundred pale screams. These were ghosts that huddled together, a hundred of them, according to newspaper numbers, in a room, stunned. Like the boy, they didn't speak.

Like them, he blinked his answers to our questions. We had encountered such spectral tap tap shit, such dit-dahed rise from grave into world another visit, but they had belonged to Chance Game victims who once upon a time had bet more than gallbladders, appen-dixes, liver sections, or single-centimetre patches of skin removed. We had watched how with their eyes the lottery ghosts reiterated the alphanumeric combinations of tickets they had received accidentally, bought and wagered, had traded for, the pathways from lottery bet to acquired housing debt to lottery-directed removed organs from those whose homes had been destroyed by spontaneous fires, as Hedayat learned from a ghost who in his life had bled to death during a requisite midsection operation and awakened Re-Alphabet in the morgue, speaking the language of his lottery demise ticket number by ticket bloody number, blinking Re-Alphabet for all time thereafter. But the boy and his ghosts were subjects of spontaneous fires, reports of which made peripheral mention on occasion of the hornet hum and unidentifiable aerial motion over a spidersilk region before a blanket of fire but never the direct causes of sound and heat and light.

Suddenly, we had to take care of one hundred more ghosts and the boy. We didn't know what to do with them at first, but as for the boy, a glow came over Q as soon as she saw him, all love as she was, and he immediately nestled in her crook, hardly whimpering, never for a moment relinquishing the backward shell he held close like a disembodied organ, which he would place at his ear, pause, before turning around to exchange rapid blinks with the ghosts that followed him constantly. Who was the boy with the backward conch and what do they say of the boy.

Recall, if you can, the time of street water that followed, which was a new thing, a Director's choice, a thing belonging to an imbroglio whose image we had no idea of, so mysterious was he, and who had a handle on all four elements of the periodic table. While we worked, Masoud would tune a transistor radio high volume to an international news station that described how the Director had recently placed enormous heating rods in the Gulf of Eden to create dense humid updraughts for a storm scene of *The Mirror*; brine collected into cumulus clouds rich with sea fauna. It rained crustaceans in La Maga; schools of albula and barracuda fell from the sky as did pipefish with red posterior lateral lines, which splashed in neighbourhood waters alongside shrimp, crayfish, mussels, lockets belonging to maidens prior to their mermaid transformations, which they had taken with them into deep waters. The wheels and gears of heavy industrial machinery splash-landed. Household and industrial waste seeped into new swimming areas, while hammerhead sharks swam outside our doors with eels that opened demonic mouths containing more incisors than one hundred healthy full-grown men. As the rains grew heavier, trucks got stuck and had to climb out of the mud on long flat rectangles of wood placed before their wheels. The streets flooded up to ankles to knees to thighs in some neighbourhoods, and children waded in between cars, netting, spearing, basketing enough live seafood for weeks of roasted fried boiled marine meals served with rice with lentils with couscous and vegetables.

On Monday, Hedayat waded in the streets and speared minnow with the boy, who carried his conch with him, of course, for the expedition. Tuesday Wednesday featured sardines, and on Thursday they were eating manta meat that Q grilled butane gas cookery, simmered to juice every bite. I gambolled word to word to evoke him speak but my glossolalia yielded no response. Meanwhile, the other room blinked a sea of switches, hundreds of eyes frozen masks moving eyes.

There were human mouths and ghost mouths to feed. Hedayat speared cuttlefish and koi in the streetwater and tried to include the kid in these activities but he wouldn't leave Q's nest, her crook of arm, her lap.

Does he speak to you, I asked her.

No.

Does he laugh.

He howls.

Who was the boy with the backward conch, and what do they say of the boy.

Why did the ghosts follow him here, I wondered aloud. How the hell do we feed them, I asked her look, pointed at them flickering light-nightflash, starving. Food, I paced the Hospice, right index at chin, but these were such unordinary apparitions; our ghost encounters were usually with flesh and bloodless types, the dead but still visible, and these creatures couldn't handle intravenous or eats, so far as we could tell. It was Q who figured it first, let's try, she said when I asked her bustling room to room what are you doing. Sublimation, she replied finally, and handed Masoud, the boy, and me surgical masks and goggles from the equipment room before melting a solid ice blood pack from the fridge with steam machine, vaporizing red gas. A purr and rumble through the Hospice when the ghosts breathed their fill.

Among the hundred ghosts grew clearer outlines after ingesting blood, I recognized the face of a man anxious fidget for a nic-fix, a face like mine but weathered older from life in the grave, who demanded onions, said he missed eating onions most in the grave, so we got him a bag and he chomped them like apples, streaming tears down his face, this Zachariah Ben Jaloun, my paternal grandfather, who had already been dead boulder in a coffin by the time I was born. I recognized him from my grandmother's pictures as the man who undressed minds with her in Department 6119 before they were wrenched apart by Black Organs. He motioned for a light and I passed him my butane flame. He peeled an onion, blinked words with his eyes, but I couldn't hear. How frustrating, I thought, to meet a ghost with a once upon a time that truly interested me/ what was the stone carapace that your dead body became, Dada, I wanted to ask/ but who I couldn't understand. I tried some rudimentary blinks whose meaning Masoud and I debated, asked him to tell us how he got here, but my grandfather spoke too quick and difficult with his eyes.

That's when I felt a tug on my shirt and the boy's gesture extending, offering me the conch with backward grooves whose regional meaning, according to Q who knew and loved the ocean, brought fortune to its beholder. I couldn't understand what he wanted until he put it up to his ear, absorbed by sounds I couldn't detect. I took it from him and heard Zachariah Ben Jaloun say the universe was shaking when the bullet entered my skull through the roof of my mouth, as I caught my grandfather describing his death.

So that's the meaning of the conch, I said aloud, as I listened with it pressed against my ear; how in that moonscape did the boy find such a thing. Zachariah Ben Jaloun smoked his cigarette. Why did you follow the boy, I asked. My grandfather ignored my question and instead blinked dust, lunar landscape after fire burned silk fields, after a blaze in village acres first covered with thick clotted spiderclouds. The living and most materially composed living dead sifted rubble for hours of rescue, he said, until even wispy ghosts barely bodies began rising dust to live another day, but they still didn't find the boy buried in the muck and fire.

Rather, Zachariah smoked as he said it, the kid found himself trapped in between fallen walls in open window room of his family home, where he was learning character plus character make a word. When walls fell flaming around him, neighbours rushed buckets of water, and after the blaze retreated showed its rubble, they could find no trace of the kid because in a moment of luck and wisdom, he had managed to find the cellar hatch. Hedayat bummed a cigarette as his grandfather continued.

The boy travelled hours through spidersilk stores and pantry chambers in the rabbit warrens that connected all the houses of his village, lost, but calm walk one hand in found jam jar and the other with conch at his ear. So he already had it with him. It was on his desk; it's how he heard us wispy ghost types standing in an underground potato storage room, rejoicing lamenting after blast after blast above ground, blinking furious can you believe we're alive after death. How does it work, I removed the shell from my ear and looked at it mollusc and groove, how do I hear your voice clear in my head while you blink.

Zachariah Ben Jaloun drew a deep breath of foul smoke and said it's a simple magic, really, found in uncommon shells in beaches of our region. Farmers usually find them in the same environment as minnow lizards that warn of spontaneous fires and keep them as household showpieces. Mind you, backward shells are rare, Zachariah's ghost informed between bites as the air of the Hospice became sad from onion fumes, and children have always noted something unordinary about such conches, he continued; they use them in echo games because they say backward shells can amplify distant sounds. We think the boy used the conch in the past as a means of hearing a spider farmer acres away named Amir gunned down by paramilitaries belonging to the largest spidersilk retailer, that he used to listen to the old man wandering seized spiderfield heavy flat feet low moaning in graveyard and blinking thoughts of life after death, Zachariah peeled an onion. That's why the boy was able to recognize our blinking many rooms away underground as whispers, he concluded.

Who was the boy with the backward conch and what do they say of the boy. His region had been recent explosion and gravemounds, so we contacted an adoption agency through which Q filed to continue keeping custody and to induce the organization to try and find his living relatives. He stayed with us in the Halfway House after that. Cot or hammock, I offered; he chose both, hammock for the fly-swatting daytime and cot for night rest. Masoud and I tried to determine requisite meal amounts of blood for the ghosts while Q grew closer to the boy. What will you call him, I asked, and she said she would know when the authorities informed her, but time passed, the agency could find no record of such an individual, and reported it would continue searching for anyone who did. Q said she would invent his name when it came to her; for the moment, he would be her Boy.

That night, the three of us sat in the kitchen ate seasoned tuna can entrees with pita bread. We needed to write entries in our files and report to government agencies the nature of our most recent arrivals, but if the boy couldn't speak and the ghosts merely blinked. Masoud's transistor radio told us the Director's recent storm experiments had been aided by a gust of westerly winds and the movie's design engineers' recommendation that the settings of the underwater rods near the coast of the Gulf of Eden be changed for the occasion. The intended result was fog, mist blown into La Maga everyone walk sheets of stratus. By the following afternoon, residents of the city made it home through stumble streets still knee high water and swimming marine life. They found day-old food items in full health of just prepared, fruit pits restored to flesh in their kitchens, calendars marked dates earlier than conflicts with friends, co-workers, colleagues. Time was moving toward greater disorder no longer, it seemed, because of the mist. Though the temporal effects of the fog were initially positive, and though it hadn't reached the Hospice, the transistor radio recommended higher ground to La Maga residents because of its uncertain nature. We heard voices in the streets grow louder. Let's go, Q prompted us when the boy began tugging at her sleeve, his conch held up to his right ear. We decided to leave the vaporizer breathing blood for the ghosts to continue eating in our absence, but they wanted to go with us, they followed.

Where, I asked Q. Maroon Peak, she announced, highest point in the city, she said, as we walked Hospice to alleyways, wended shortest route until reaching high mountain trail where the trees cast light shadows above the Director's fogscape, where you could see all of La Maga and beyond. Fog rose up on the road ahead of us, and I felt cold light move through my body take shape ahead with the others as the ghosts walked through us around us toward that ether. One of them paused near Q, knelt beside the boy. I saw Zachariah's ghost blinking talking to the boy backward conch up to ear. I saw him hand the kid an onion as a parting gift after hearing words. Then he walked into the mist with the other ghosts. After Q and the boy finished exchanging furious whispers, I asked her, what does he say. He wants to eat an onion like an apple, Q laughed.

RING
AROUND
THE
ROSIE

Ring Around the Rosie: why mention that Abol Tabol macabre rhyme behind whose trochaic sweet-step hides death and the plague. Why drag Albion Britannia, cobbled streets, and the fourteenth century to an epoch of the unnameable country's history marred by its own mass pathologies and black deaths. Handkerchiefs and crushed flowers. Hasha hasha. We all fall down. No: the rhyme is important, most of all because the Yea and Nay Quintuplets loved it so much. Portentous children with inclusion-exclusion principles as groove-worn as grown-up society; thumb-sucking children who cast faraway stares into the future or engage in blinking telegraphic communication with ghosts. Even such unusual children need to play.

Recall, as if you were there, soon after the arrival of the Boy with the Backward Conch, Q's breaths fell shorter when I held her, pensively, anxiously, as if she foresaw. I knew she was applying for jobs with Oxfam, Amnesty International, and the United Nations, and she asked me would I like to do the same. Wait, I told her, let me think, I said, and I thought, I considered every moment of the past my owl eyes could see, from John Quincy's black sputum ship of infections and cattle-whips that was the actual story of the journey from the unnameable country, of its travels to the Caribbean port that secretly still admitted African slaves in the early twentieth century, to Quincy's discovery of the ability of shortwave radios to hear the human mind, his institution and development of Department 6119 its rows upon rows of thought-spies that greatly contributed to the hundred-year transformation of our country into corridors and hallways.

Wait, I told her, let me think. I thought about Masoud Rana and how he was still drug dealing, about my owl's suspicions of Black Organs rounding every street corner behind me making every shadow in every alleyway, of being arrested. Does he need to keep doing this, I lamented to her. Does he need to come home night after night a sick and booger-dripping fee fi giant eat all our provisions, I thought, hungry after his desert drug dealing, about which we never ask but which makes a purse sound night after night spill coins onto kitchen table, I paced, gnashing teeth, and after which he falls into a sternutatory nap of sneeze afternoon to sneezing evening unto nighttime, sneezing and coughing and sleeping and sneezing that disturbed the Hospice's bubbling atmosphere of love so much I couldn't stand Masoud Rana's congested thoughtlessness that left Q and me to tackle all the everyday tasks of running the place, and I got up one morning to go to my parents' home for a few days for a break, and without even a goodbye to Q, tiptoed into the mirror streets, stepped into a strange house for shortcut purposes, and crossed two rooms with high wooden ceilings. The first contained a boy labouring to teach an older man to read, the man who was cringing and pulling out hair.

Stop, it's impossible; these are not the sesame words.

The second contained a porcelain tub in the middle, and a woman drenched in suds from top to toe, reaching up into the high notes of her bathing song.

Oh will you, she sang.

Pardon, I responded in key and in the baritone register, but I couldn't help but pause before moving on because the room, I realized, was surrounded by high rising panoramic stands, and a deeply immersed crowd was enjoying the woman's private aria, though it didn't seem as if she was aware or cared about their presence.

A requisite cameraman of *The Mirror*, still ongoing, who caught everything, moved closer to the centre of action, a grumble passed through the audience for my interruption, and still I couldn't move: in the corner a man was whipping and all the shadows were longer than his cat o' nine. A woman was bent over canine, naked from the waist down; a bag of spilled pears before her as she struggled to gather them, and she cried out for the ghost of my father, salt of my wounds, I know nothing.

The bathing woman was singing again and I cringed as she rose from the tub and extended a hand in my direction while running a sponge across the naked hulk of her behind. At the highest note of her register I looked for crevices in the air, and finding no place to hide I was happy to discover an opening in the opposite wall of the room. Though it was small, I managed to crawl through it, and there was a tumble then for Hedayat as he fell upward, because the wind was sucking him up through a ventilation shaft almost as powerful as the one in the hallway of the Ministry of Records and Sources, if you'll recall.

For a long time I travelled swiftly through metal tubing and heard only the whirring of fans as I was dragged through the air until flung somewhere in the midst of the Warren tunnels. When I recovered from my terrifying journey, I limped through the passageways instinctively. It had been so long, I almost missed their pungent ammonium odour, and every so often I would hear a whistle or a come on you from one porter to another, but I encountered no one in the flesh. At last, I pushed aside a wooden wall and found myself no more than one hundred steps from my home, but I was barred from going there. Between me and my door, five thousand people stood crammed together, screaming as if they were all being bereaved of their organs.

A large machine was destroying everything, digging into the ground and gouging at the sky, and when the people came too close it would rush toward them, and when satisfied it had thwarted the people it would return to its task of digging and destroying walls and ceilings of the homes in our street. In this way, many people were deterred by a single machine.

Who were they, what did they want. Who are you. Why are they wounding the houses. I asked these things and members of the crowd only showed their placards on whose hard surfaces were written the meaning of their presence.

They are building the largest prison, said a young woman. Her forehead was beaded with perspiration. She exhaled like a workhorse and spoke the words absentmindedly as if I were a child and would never understand. She said more: they are in-between enemies, in-between sources, and boot-hopping across the continent, she tried again, measuring randoms with tongue dispensers and meat calipers from north Nilo-Saharan all the way to Khoisan south, trying to find the right things to eat.

I knew about the prison; however, the country was a prison, and although I felt indignant, I didn't correct her, and instead weaved my way slowly through the mass in hopes that what they all hadn't managed to do I would be able to accomplish through skill or by chance: to bypass the machine that was destroying everything. I needed to go home because it was too late to turn around and return to the Ghost Hospice. Besides, *Masoud Rana* was still there sneezing and cynicism and I wanted nothing to do with him while he was sleeping and sneezing and blowing all the dirt of his desert travels and befouling everything.

At that moment, my thoughts became bisected: first, I thought of Q, how I had abandoned her to a stranger, who was my responsibility because over time he had become my business associate more than her brother. Then I thought of my father. Is this the theatre of his fateful descent during which Mamun M is trampled. Is he among us. The sky was a merciless vulture that day; I recall wishing for a drizzle that was still some months away.

Is that your house, a man beside me pointed, and I saw that he had identified it correctly, and that it had been spared thus far.

How did you, I asked.

Of course that's his house, an old woman beside him said, it's his house, she said again and smiled at me in such a way that I knew it was good, and that to be here was right. Still, I looked at my home with such yearning and wished I could go there and I also wished it was not so hot, because being in the crowd was making everything hotter, though it was not the fault of the people to have gathered in such a large number, the machine was at fault and the commander of the machine more so.

My thoughts came to a close exactly at the moment one man rose above the others. Without a sound he stepped up onto the nose of the bulldozer and though I was not close to him, I could see his green uniform of an American officer and knew that his eyes were blue. He looked at all of us and passed through us like a mute swarm of bees that was sucking all the nectar and leaving colours and numbers at will, gathering and deciphering, and I tried to hide my mind from this man who prevaricated by showing us a singular body and coming after us with so many minds at once.

Something stirred in the crowd as if it had waited to encounter exactly this person, as if he was the day's reckoning or Death himself. He must have been a great man because when he breathed in, we were all forced to exhale because he was sucking it out, and when he breathed out we could not inhale because he would release a wind-storm that threw up all the dirt of the road. Were it not asphyxiating to stand in his presence, I would have thought it a great trick for a pair of lungs to need so much air. And then he began to speak and his voice was moving round and round. He told us to remain calm, but this only agitated the crowd and brought it to reiterate through slogans what it had been shouting all day, which by the parsimonious way of sloganeering it meant only to say that homes should not be exchanged for prisons, and we are prepared to meet metal with flesh if need be to stop you.

Even from the distance, I could identify that the man was the same tourist we had encountered in the forest. He warned us as his subordinates crept up from behind and shadowed him; his voice was calm and it pervaded through all space without the aid of a megaphone; it was not loud, and arrived at our ears several seconds after he moved his lips as if he was very far away. But we understood him over the hum of the bulldozer engine. He said that he was a notable general in the American armed forces, and that we should believe him because he had served in Vietnam once upon a time, and that he had the authority to use everything at his disposal, including fire and earthquake against us, if we continued to interfere with the lawful destruction of buildings in this area.

At that moment the crowd bubbled up with great laughter, for though he had displayed evidence with his great heaving breaths and his beehive mind, at that moment we forgot; he appeared human like any of us, and there were so many of us and he was threatening all of us as with a divine cataclysmic hand, which was invisible. Without passing a clue that he was agitated by our reaction, just as quietly as he rose up onto the bulldozer, he descended, and the engine of the beast began to turn.

The universe was shaking as the armoured bulldozer advanced through the narrow corridor of our street on which houses stand closely packed together on each side, and the bravest of us tried to keep our word of meeting the metal and attempted to climb onto it; some were crushed beneath its treads, while others managed to get as far up as where the general had been standing, and they were defeated by its inertia, by bullets or by other means. Much of the great crowd, however, could do nothing but retreat some five hundred metres to the souks. There, Jeeps and armoured vehicles were already waiting, and they broke its back and its tail and legs and entrapped it.

When a frightened animal/ but no, that isn't enough, for there was great fury in the moment also for all the senseless wounded houses, and agitation for all the heat, the sand, as well as graver, wooden, mirthless sentiments, which belong not to any individual but to the centuries. Let it be known that the feeling in the crowd must have hardened his throat because Hedayat found himself singing a curious melody in a slow tempo while everything was moving so fast. Everywhere, the sounds were going when Hedayat's throat began fluttering, not loudly, but in tune and in onetwothree-onetwothree waltztime, and as the rubber bullets stung, the real bullets felled, and the gas was searing, he found himself in the throes of a mournful ballad with his talons deep sunken into the neck of the closest soldier who dared, amidst a cacophony that Hedayat's song almost overmastered.

The force of the crowd tore the rifle from the American soldier's hand and Hedayat continued providing the music as the two of them danced death's dance, round and round, each with hands pressed to the other's throat. The talons sank deeper, while the other tried to choke the sounds, and then the soldier's feet began to move involuntarily because Hedayat was still singing, and to the rhythm, because the crowd was also moving, while the melody wound into the guttural quarries of his deepest basso range. It was not unlike Mamun Ben Jaloun as he dashed across the continent, the Indian Ocean, up the Subcontinent, across China, when his father was singing Siberia to the Chukchi Sea, across the miniature world of the endless film studio; yes, it was like that in a way as Hedayat continued balladeering and hanging on for dear life with his legs up on the chest of the soldier like a very large owl, while the crowd swayed in one direction and in the opposite, until finally he lost the thread, when the other could no longer produce his cry of a slaughtered calf and was only able to weep with his whole body. Then Hedayat released him.

The great crowd dragged the gravely wounded man round and round, so closely packed were we that he did not even sink from the upright, and Hedayat realized the waltz was no longer his and the melody now undulated through the thousands, that all and sundry were swaying to the ballad, and if we were dying it was not for the melody, and if we were falling down at least there was the song.

It was then that I returned to my senses and realized I was close to home amidst the carnage, and that the eggplant and cauliflower vendor Hamid's stall was ruined; Amina, who beaded jewellery, would not have a place to display her wares tomorrow; all the garlands of Abdel-Nasir's flower shop had been shredded; and overhead there now precipitated a cool rain of violets, hyacinths, red roses, and orange blossoms, though the army had diced them into such small shards they were indistinguishable in colour, and they hurt us because we thought of them as glass and shrapnel. The ground was slippery with the blood of so many because the large treaded machines were singing a similar song as Hedayat's, but louder and far more efficiently; for the one near casualty, which would be trumpeted throughout the world, there were five hundred fifty-five to balance the scale, ignoble theirfault people, unmentionables: Adam the woodcarver, flattened by an armoured bull-dozer. Belayat Mujumdar, rifled through the forehead by a clean shot. Thirteen others, each with an identical earlier arm wound, not unlike that of Amunji, if you'll recall. Almost near the end of this selected list, and to my father's great consternation, Xasan Sierra, the cigarette vendor, who had tried to remain neutral through the whole proceedings and was doing nothing but smoking his regular half-carton in his shop. Then the bulldozers were doing another job and the ambulances theirs as Hedayat fled through one narrow street and another while the arrests, beatings, and desertion of friends, family, home, country continued. At dusk, several hundred members of local unions and others of the most committed and the damned were still cordoned into a narrow strip of space, walled in by mirrors, tanks, and bulldozers and pleading for water and mercy in three-four time.

What of Hedayat then. Did they know whose talons. Were there other owls in the crowd that day. Recall he had nearly done the thing for which God identified Cain, despite his best efforts to hide his brother under the earth, the worst and nearly first of all things done in the world. Did Hedayat feel something akin to Raskolnikov's earthly guilt; was he weighted with a hunchback-rendering remorse like his father; what did Niramish feel when.

Hedayat's feet were moving and he realized he was still singing the saddest ballad without the aid of instrumentation or a chorus. It was hurting his throat to go on, but when he stopped his bones continued vibrating to the marrow. The ashes of the day's gruesome carnival lingered on his palate and he spat into the mist, which rose up all around from the remains of the fires. Hark unto: the early dead are already beginning to make the right turns to the Ghost Hospice.

When Hedayat came home, he passed by a group of workmen sitting on the steps up to the apartment, taking a late-afternoon break; their jackhammers and other high-powered equipment blockaded the way. He excused himself, since they peered at him as if he were an intruder, and didn't even ask why they were there.

Upstairs, he was greeted by Gita's cry of terror; he had no idea about his appearance, though he knew his clothes were ruined and his feathers exposed in various places. They asked him where he was wounded and when he replied it was not his blood, they would not believe him and continued searching. Then, despite his annoyance and abhorrence of its taste, his mother held his neck like a billy goat and fed him a wretched spoonful of castor oil. When Hedayat arrived home, his sisters were playing Ring Around the Rosie/ correction, the Yeas were playing, Nay was sucking her thumb and watching. This was how it had always been, the four of them together and the one by herself.

To say Nehi was torn by or reconciled with her observer's status would be wrong. She had a way of noting the necessary facts, which Hedayat had always found more endearing. The girls spun around in a circle, they fell down at the appropriate moment in the rhyme; truly they loved Ring Around the Rosie. They asked Hedayat to join, but he was exhausted from his own circular motions and encounters that day, with its many hands and bodies; besides, the Yeas had a grazed look of another kind of crowd that was not the one he had been in today.

Nehi appeared beside him. They're knocking down the walls, she pointed before Hedayat had had a chance to see for himself. You're right, he craned his neck to peer at the astonishing disappearance of the storage room–nursery and the appearance of an abyss in its place. The weeks vanished before his eyes as workmen came went through a hole in the universe, or just the front door that remained unlocked the entire time. He stood baffled, unable to do a thing to stop the mineshaft they were building right in their home, which had been zoned by the city to contain an elevator leading directly to the new prison, and which therefore meant that in the future, judge advocate generals, warders, and whoever else who needed access to the penitentiary would have a key to the house and freedom to wander through any of its rooms at any hour.

There were also other worries. Recall, by that time, the reinvigorated love of Mamun M and Shukriah was long over, and cuisine at our home no longer featured the bountiful fruits of the Indian Ocean or the Gulf of Eden, which, due to my father's dismissal from his job as an Archives clerk and five new mouths (albeit minus one, that of Aunt Shadow) of the Quintuplets, created a tense atmosphere despite Hedayat's furtive material contributions. When he thought about the decline of their second romantic turn, Mamun M threw up his hands with the casual remark that even ghosts die a second death. Unfortunately for him and Shukriah, the deterioration of their passions also indicated an enlarging gulf of understanding; they would grow entangled over the slightest disagreements; she would trip over his feet and instead of the patience she showed in earlier years for his grotesque form, which became even more stooped with the years, she would snap at him mercilessly. When he grumbled under his breath, she would twist the near-inscrutable sounds into reasons for full-blown arguments.

With the years, Mamun M lost much of the humour and grace with which he had seduced her heart; smoking too many cigarettes had destroyed his tenor's voice and prevented him from lightening any situation with a song; and when he ventured outside, he experienced such pain in his liver and in other hidden organs for the passing of Xasan Sierra, whom the machinery that day had wiped clean from the earth without leaving a trace of him even in the mirrors, that Mamun sought the cure of friendship from every vagrant and birdcaller of the souks.

Since the Black Organs had been watching him for many years and knew his vulnerabilities well, the reappearance of Imran of the Screens at this stage is not so surprising from Hedayat's illuminated prison vantage point. Imran returned with the goodbuddy gestures that fitted a madman tramp. From his pockets and sleeves he removed freshly hatched and perfumed mountain swallow chicks, and one by one he dropped them onto my baffled father's lap.

You don't recognize, he pinched his cheeks, but who was the one that stole my girl. And still Mamun M could not guess, for the swallows were cheeping and fluttering uselessly and they had both grown so old by then that even the memories had decayed. My father looked closer: the aged voice and the moving shapes before him when compared with those features belonging to one of the toughest toughs of decades earlier were incongruent, but he sought after the name in the cobwebs of all the dead memories.

Imran, he threw it out.

A great guffaw, broad sounds and gestures of victorious affirmation, here let me take these, the stranger lifted the odorous birds and pushed them back into his sleeves and the pockets of his shirt.

You are he.

I am he.

What brings you from going and coming across the earth.

And yourself.

I am just sitting, my father pointed to the other coffee patrons around him at the open-air bar, pointed to the empty seat beside him.

Imran drank a half-dozen cups of bitter coffee and then ordered a pot of mint tea, which he insisted Ben Jaloun, Scooter, Noob share with him, for those were how he used to identify my father. Afterward, twisting in pain from a full bladder, he excused himself, disappeared into the vaporous mirage of noon, and when he returned he wanted to drink anisette. They went to a garage bar that had evaded destruction by the zoning laws that had ordered for the purposes of upholding public morals, and that now spun the same lugubrious bop records and through whose casement streamed the identical sunlight of years past and better days.

For every anisette the hunchback drank, Imran drank four, and by dusk they had lifted out of an ocean of endless time two skeletons of their lives apart. Then they paused at a reef to order more anisettes and gazed at each other with the laughter of the living dead as the little mountain swift chicks continued cheeping and kept wanting to come out of Imran's sleeves and his pockets. It was a good time for which my father, bereaved of his wife's goodwill and the company of his best friend, was truly thankful.

Would you like a job, Imran spoke now as Gorbachev, because despite the dipsomania he had managed to keep a clear head.

I need a job.

Then you can have a job, friend.

And that was how my father found employment in the constabulary as a record-keeper of the city's complex kleptocratic network in an office in downtown La Maga. The job was difficult, despite his experience in the Archives, because the dead kept piling up so high and mixing with the living. At that time, it had become customary for members of gangs in the city to take the names of their dead comrades, so that Hassan Mahmoud would become Hasan Ratrace Elvis Mahmoud, which often meant not only that he had inherited some of the others' wealth but also, because taking the names of the dead sometimes meant he assumed their characters (often with surprising accuracy), he might even be continuing to live out parts of their lives as well as his own.

Mamun M worked out of the house, which equalled the acquisition of an expansive table and two metal filing cabinets, and these left even less space for others, including the Quintuplets, though, granted they had begun attending school during the days. The presence of so much paper in the home, so much paper floating like cobwebs through the rooms or crabwalking across the floor or slithering like slugs, boiled Shukriah's blood and increased her fury to heights that frightened even Gita, who recalled her own days of whipping her son with renewed contrition. But the hunchback would not relent, and only pointed to the constant presence of the workmen, whose noise of jackhammers and slathered stink of onions, coffee, and halitosis were ubiquitous, and who were still digging the same mineshaft for the prison, though now they claimed they had attached a wire-system of pulleys crucial to the elevator's functionality.

Throw them out first, my father would say.

But the workmen came and went, immune to Shukriah's wrath, while the papers concerning the dead, living, and living-dead klepto-crats mounted everywhere and so high that our home became a sort of archives; one could detect pauses in daylight as it devised courses around all the obstructions in our apartment.

These children poorfive kids, Shukriah complained one day, when Hedayat happened to be present. That was the moment Hedayat burned with oversight, suggested how about I take them for a time.

You, uttered the incredulous voice.

Yes, I, why not after all.

Absolutely not, you would take them through some tunnel place and they would godknowswhat.

No, I said, I know a place, a very good place. Nothing would have occurred had Gita not argued on my behalf. Primary and secondary schools were going to close soon because of nationwide demonstra-tions organized by the Madam's regime in support of renewing the twenty-year leasing agreement with the Americans over their hinterland air force base, due to expire at the end of the year.

The ersatz vacation would be perfect, she declared, for Hedayat to introduce them to other spaces in the city than home, neighbours' homes, swimming club, and school. But just where exactly, she asked.

A good place, I repeated, and imbued in my descriptions of Q and the Hospice an ambiguous dignity, by which I mean I named neither.

After the paper tower of reports she had been leaning on collapsed and nearly crushed Shukriah, she became convinced I was describing a clean edifice free of satanic revelry and assented. The Quintuplets responded to the offer of elsewhere with the stampede of free herd animals, even Nehi.

I had not warned Q; so many characters passed through that house of the damned that to add a few more would not alter the balance too much; I trusted her generous nature and knew she would enjoy the surprise.

It was quiet when the six of us came to the Hospice that day. The television was spewing the silent ashes of an in-between channel. The ghosts were moving pieces on the chessboard from Staunton to various gambits and back again to the start, sipping red from the glass or staring with mouths agape at the silent television. None of them noticed us. I tried to introduce but gained no sympathetic response. I wondered where she was, and then noticed the brewing odour; once detected it replaced all other smells and through curiosity it transformed into a ribbon of light that possessed a colour that could almost be touched.

Let me find her, I told the five, stay.

I followed the light past the empty sleeping chambers of the ghosts, with their square perfect bedsheets without a crinkle or cottonwisp of dust, and it pulled me whispers closer until revealing its soundshapes the truth of the mewling, which was climbing into a howl behind the only closed door in the whole house, and which in no time grew into the first pangs of relentless torment before another and another. The full effect of that cataclysm would not occur immediately; at first it was only a palsy of the hands, which was to last two hours. It was also noticeable that the floorboards of the house had become a turbid swamp, through which any feet, but especially mine, would have found navigation diffi-cult and into which my left and right sank to their fetid bones. Recall, though you cannot know, it was painful to swallow the burning coals in my mouth.

In the kitchen, preparing sandwiches for the Quintuplets took me nearly an hour, though it was a life-affirming task that gave me strength to oversee the fate of the ghosts and whether their fill of blood this late afternoon. When finally she emerged, and he also/ who might these darlings: she was radiant, and a healthy fawn's glow burned on her cheeks.

The Quintuplets occupied a whole couch, blinking at every item of worn-out furniture and every ghost in sight. They remained silent and blinked at her, as I urged them to speak.

But you never, her lips flashed brightly, he never told me a thing, and, damn, five of you, too. One by one, she quizzed them on all various topics until, by virtue of her ability to understand the inner world of any human being, living or undead, by a manner of interrogative sonar that relied not on the responses of the individual but on the way her voice reverberated inside the other, she clapped hands very good, satisfied with her primary assessment that these were five exquisite specimens of Hedayat's kin.

There was a man who did not introduce himself, and he stood there, neither introducing himself nor being introduced. We've brought hammocks and we're staying, declared the Yea Quintuplet Hum.

Is that right, Q meditated on logistics for three moments before berating me on my culinary choice. Sandwiches letssee, she peered in between the bread; hardly, Hedayat, come look, she drew me up from the carpet by the hands.

Her mere touch crossed all the wires and I withdrew as she was a naked electrical. She followed me with her eyes to the kitchen, and there her eyes shrank and her lips moved to ask a hidden question, but no sounds emerged.

From that day on, all eight of us camped together in the bedroom adjacent to the lounge, and there was so much spontaneity in those hours, and the Quintuplets eased the tension and incorporated the three of us into their ceaseless merriment so easily that my ears began to forget and my liver detoxified the nightmare of the brewing odour that became a ribbon of light that turned into the mewling and howling that still echoed through the house if you paused to listen.

It was difficult to grow accustomed to Q's fleeting touches, concili-
atory gestures in darkness, an errant hand lingers, or a foot touches foot
extended under the other's blanket, because the perpetual hieroglyphics
of my mind rearranged them into shapes that gave rise to another theme
of palsy of the hands. For several days after, she rested her chin on
my shoulder as I stared into the distant reaches of the lounge wall on
which hung a large empty frame for no more than two minutes, and
while speaking, seventeen commonplace words punctuated end stop
by her explosive laughter, I was assailed by an abdominal illness that
was painful and whose symptom was florid shit: hyacinths floated in
the bowl, not unlike the Governor after first gazing upon the ageless
beautiful corpse of Caroline Margarita, the digested petals of birds of
paradise, which I had never consumed, and a whole lotus flower with
its water roots still intact.

What had meant to be an overnight vacation extended into a week,
and then three weeks, while outside, the protests against the renewal
of the air force base raged, and we could hear the strikers and understood from the television the violence was escalating and the papers
had been signed already and the real strikers were outnumbering the
Madam's propagandists four to one, because the American air force
base was due to remain in the unnameable country for another fifty-six
years, it had been decided.

We stayed at the Ghost Hospice, and my sisters accustomed to Q's
presence better than I did. One day, I was listening to the radio while
kneading dough when Q stole up, leaned close, dipped finger into a
bowl of batter what's this/ don't, I exclaimed, it's for them, for shit's
sake. I had never shown anger in her presence but at that moment her
face arms legs near me were fucking hell. I fled to the interior of the
Hospice where a sad thread of smoke lifted from my cigarette. We live
in a halfway house, I thought, a place of recovery and the chance for
life after death for some and the interval between death and a deeper

death for others. I heard Q's quiet motions mixing measuring fluids, battering flour and blood for the ghosts. How reassuring the sound of her breathing, her presence in the world. I wanted something magnificent with her for one moment, to fulfill with her the dream she had balked at the night we scuttled up walls and leapt on rooftops almost to our deaths. She and I had broken for a time when Masoud Rana convinced me to include black pepper on the side as part of our daily dealings. I was initially against the idea but he cajoled so sweet minimal investment so strongly I found myself moving swift pound bags larger than ever. Our old contacts touched us good for dough and for a bit I felt enlivened walking our old Warren haunts.

Q pretended not to notice or care when I rolled into bed at three in the morning, and absence makes fond reunions, I thought, but one night, I awoke to find sheets pillows blanket made crags and gullies between us. I flattened the impositions with my hand, thinking I'd find her underneath it all, flung them away from me, but only my bed stared back.

It was dark in the room when I thumped onto the floor, and that's when a thoughtless tack fuck it got right up there. I howled knife wounded as morning wind blew bedroom through window. Foul odour drifted open sewer tributaries. The Hospice's location in a piss-and-orchard La Maga neighbourhood meant we could afford to rent our apartment turned care facility, but also that it came with few light switches. Solid shapes prohibited me abrupt sounds. I stumbled in the dark. Liquid flecks of fallen glass from a table.

I got as far as the joint of our room meets hallway, which featured a standing fan we sometimes hung clothes on, but in the darkness it felt like coarse trunk of tree. Owl-eyed, I looked ahead and beside and finally turned my head around a hundred and eighty to inspect all the shifted bedroom shapes. Frightened, I hurried back into bed, bumping into boughs, trunks, knotted roots, nameless objects along the way, confused about where had she gone, shivering, motherless child, until I felt her body sneak back under the sheet with prodigal caresses, kisses on face shoulder arms, I just went to get a drink of water, she said.

How long it's been since we've spoken intimately, I thought at the end of my cigarette alone in an interior room of the Ghost Hospice while recalling that moment long ago, how long I've trespassed on those moving images, regions of our bed together, how long it's been since Q and I separated. I thought these things as I withdrew bootlaces from my velveteen packet and tied them around my ankles. I thought of how we had fought over my decision to return to black pepper with Masoud to pay bills, thought about how she'd said screw it, we'll hop from grant to NGO grant, Hedayat, leave that shit, love, I/ I wanted to repair those fissures now with a test flight.

It had been a long time since Masoud Rana and I had leapt deep underground archive of magnetic reels onto a road near my parents' place, if you'll recall our banquet with the animals many stages earlier. I hadn't tested the bootlaces since and the opportunity arose at the sound of Q calling Hedayat through the afternoon sunlight.

At the sound of my name from the kitchen, I flew to her side. How did you, she began couldn't finish for my lips against her lips as I jumped up while embracing her. Our feet flapped so high we lost our breaths floating above the kitchen cabinet dirty dishes fennel broth chickpea salad and blood pudding for the ghosts.

I stayed because I wanted to be near Q and also because of the good time the Quintuplets were having, especially during their games of checkers with the ghosts, whom they thought of as old talking prunes and ensouled oranges, whose citric fluids required daily replenishment. Nehi had the patience to learn the rudiments of chess, though she insisted on playing with the ghosts only if the pieces moved according to her rules, which they allowed. The Yeas had begun to include her in their games, and she even participated in rounds of Ring Around the

Rosie, though not always, and hardly with their volatile ambition to fall down great theatrics, or to repeat the dizzying motions so often that she was left muddy thinking the rest of her day. Then everything changed because the ghosts of the skeletal hunger strikers.

We didn't know at that time why Masoud Rana's great frame was wasting away, but it would grow clear in the scene that began when I called after his immense land porpoise's gait, hard to catch up to those swimming arms that propelled him from one step to step through folds of the cloak of beforedawn. The ocean breezed and the water was talking, but at that moment I felt only the buzz of anguish inside me because I realized Masoud Rana was my friend, because he too had suffered, was suffering. Many years later, when we would become mortal enemies in my mind and play opposites in a great game/ but at that moment he was my friend and I strode across the sands to meet him.

I reached him before the first stone fell from his mouth, when he was just sucking stones. He had them in his hands and he was putting them into his mouth one by one, and I was laughing while he spilled rocks from his mouth for the tears he couldn't cry, I presumed, for he once told me he had never cried, not even while he was being born; I recall responding I was also born tearless, but that I had cried on occasion.

What now, I asked, when he was stopped for a moment. Who hell, I kidded, but there were still only mouthstones falling and falling. Is it her then, I asked outright because it was better to say it simply. Is it for her and me that you, I repeated; because you needn't, I said, but his face.

She, his fingers coursed over the word before he broke down totally as everywhere the Law, he cried without warning, and of course pebbles from the mouth. He continued and spoke of many things at once, I felt his thoughts meandering in his mind blinked from one to the next idea passing through fluttering eyelids, and I saw them falling out with the stones. He included in his soliloquy the blood we funnelled into bottles for the ghosts, the blinkers, the hunger strikers, the phosphorescent ghosts, and all the others, the strikers, the strike, the Madam who drove three fire hoses to flush out His shit from the stables that had become the Presidential Palace, but only to roost her own anda of oblivion mutatis mutandis, the American air force base that would stand for a century or part of one century, and then he genuflected to raise the beach sand that was for his forehead, and he poured a handful there, and the rocks, recall, that were falling from his mouth as he wailed. When the beshitting Law that plays all-knowing God/ and they are always doing it, he wailed.

Difficult to distinguish what were stones and what were words, and I was laughing because I didn't remember him storing so many pebbles in his mouth, yet they continued to fall, one by two or more down the front of his shirt, and we were walking very far from the car then. In the distance, I could see that Q and the Quintuplets had emerged from the vehicle, and they were advancing toward us, though they were still far away. I said tell me, do you drink the blood that is meant for the ghosts, Masoud. And for as long as it took for the darkness to break and for the dawn to reveal that he had been trailing blood in the sand for a hundred metres from a netted cracked glass gash in his right foot, he buzzed between closed lips and would have continued deliberating like a wild honeybee had I not/ will you give me already, Masoud: what of the blood, man, do you drink it or not.

But only the beshitting Law interested him then, and he began to wail anew: Which peels our fruited hide, Hedayat.

So I met him at that plateau, said yes, friend, for the nectar, and then we are husked.

We had discovered the language that mattered and now I listened as he spoke: what would prevaricate and break itself, the Law above the law, again and endlessly in order to prove its bewildering strength. He did not speak of the forced volunteer blood drive that he had. He stopped. The wind had picked up by then, and the rocks were still falling from his mouth, but I no longer noticed how many, or perhaps he was swallowing them too.

I wasn't with Masoud when he shot Morris the cop, but he said he killed him; that's what he said in the tsetse fly heat, in the days before Black Organs trailed us cold shadow in every corner and jokes could be passed, I killed a man, he could tell us, and because of his powerful stature, his voice that echoed long after he'd spoken, we believed him murder. But where the body, dead cop, and blood. Masoud Rana would never go to jail, I would, and he would be the source, as I would blame, for four years suffering in prison cell, as I will tell you.

Do you drink the blood, I pleaded his mouthstones anguish in the sand. Maybe Masoud believes he's like a ghost, I thought when he didn't reply, neither living, neither dead. Maybe, I thought, he drinks blood to understand the burden of a cannibal life known to the residents of the Hospice.

Masoud the Generous, Masoud the Wise. And yet I would blame him one day for killing me. Years later, Masoud Rana would claim he had nothing to do with my prison stint a spill blood and cell deep underground. Organs, he would shake his head, Black Organs, brother; today, they're rounding us up on sidewalks in sidewalk cafés, late night busting doors, haven't you heard. Masoud the Great, friend and enemy, teller of tales once upon a time, street storyteller of the Palisades until he settled down and became a Hospice worker forever. Why did he black vomit. Did he drink blood meant for the ghosts, maybe as a vampiric act of empathy for the dead.

Then it happened, for the first time, and another of my transformative firsts, because there was a pause in our conversation and I was thinking where is Q: Hedayat turned his head backward all the way around like an owl, and his eyes covered more than metres of beach sand, saw beyond the present dimensions of space. All at once there arose many images of the past: the first was of Q and the Quintuplets advancing across the sands that ended at the Gulf of Eden never ended, which was already memory, already in the past, and which belonged to all the weeks, years earlier, each day clear and simultaneous. He was gouging with talons again and this time he was dancing as well, and he felt the heaviness of another emotion, rarefied and black mirthless, which began on the ship of infections and cattlewhips, cast-iron leggings, of slaves with their game of limbo and that demented trip to a secret Caribbean slave harbour in the early twentieth century. Hedayat gambolled across all the years of the unnameable country with his body facing forward and his head turned backward like an owl until he could feel the century vibrating in every hidden organ of his body.

Raskolnikov's terror and his earthly weight were there then, but the other voices were very different and forgave him seething cold, writhing, insisting it was good to do what you did, Hedayat, to have sunk your talons so deeply. I heard them say these things in waves of heated indignation, as together they completed the melody and dance that was the mournful ballad and the waltz.

Was Hedayat's wounded waltz partner the Law. And if so, who was Hamza Alif, clockmaker of La Maga, trampled by a treaded great machine. Or Yahyah Samater, once employed as an Archives clerk, disappeared the same day, vaporized, funtoosh, into invisible air. Who will give the Law unto them. Eventually, there was pitter-patter in the sand as Q and the Quintuplets after all; the girls bounded the final steps with a good clamour that belied their exhaustion. By that time, Masoud Rana's maddened speech was gone and there were no more stones to hatch from between his lips.

But your foot, Q bent to examine.

A scratch, he gave her a laugh.

Nevertheless, she bent closer, she winced, and took into her the pain of that starburst smeared with dried blood and sand.

The Yeas seized upon the moment as soon as the medical assessment was complete, a remaining shard of glass removed, a game, they cried, and would not relent. Their voices bore the collective cry of a far larger crowd.

He can't play, said one and pointed at Masoud Rana.

He has to play, said another.

Of course, added a third before the final fourth voice affirmed with a knowing hum.

Masoud Rana played lame, Q reasoned let us at least wash his feet in the ocean, Nehi sucked her thumb, and I too tried my best to yield to their demand let's play, but it was impossible. Come-all-you, they grabbed our hands and formed an unbreakable circle, and then we were spinning round and round.

HOSANNA

Today I saw a man murdered in the street. How did they kill the man. This is how they killed the man. A bullet kicked up his hair and he bit the grey asphalt as if it was his bread. Hosanna, as they say, and as she was.

Though I didn't know him, I wept for something for the nameless man murdered in our unnameable country. At a man's death they take everything; at a man's death they take nothing, for he finds the singularity of origin and eternal rest. I dug into a nearby bus shelter into the sky and wondered if the bullet had been an Organ's. You didn't hear so much about the Organs these days except that they were everywhere. Closed-circuit television is the most watched station in the country, and some people laugh that we watch ourselves better than they watch us. Tell us, if you can, what we are in that case.

Things changed in four years and I no longer grieve for the past, not for Q or for anyone. I grieved for everyone in that boxhole apportioned space because it was given to me to do. After four prison years, centuries, I watched a man bite the grey asphalt as if it was his bread.

Things happened while I was away. My mother awoke one day to find the guards in our home muttering to one another about schedules and dates and conferring together in the kitchen. It wasn't unusual to find them fraternizing; she had got up earlier than usual and though she wasn't in the habit of speaking to them, their quizzical expressions demanded explanation. We're leaving, they said simply, and by noon, they had packed up all their belongings into trunks large enough to house even the insect-legged chairs on which they had guarded the rooms of our home for so many years Shukriah couldn't remember what it was like before they arrived. She looked at her house without glass partitions, without metal detectors between washroom and kitchen; no more internal security checks, she thought, mystified by the new freedom.

Later that day, my father exited the Ministry of Records and Sources stinking magnetic shit. After so many years of thoughtreels, he thought, I pore it from my balls. He always felt an agoraphobic pang when leaving the barbed wire compound and emerging outdoors after the world got huge in the nine-to-five interregnum, miles of sidewalks such lively children their hopscotch games and companion animals, all the vendors hawking eats sweets and colourful acrobatic toys on the sidewalk. In between indoor and free street feelings, a man emerged from a tinted-window coupe, gripped pistol to my father's right temple and inside the car, please, Mr. Ben Jaloun.

My mother's repeated unanswered requests to the government for an explanation prompted her to join a widows' group, and on weekends, she circumambulated the Presidential Palace with them, beat ladles against pots with them demanding whereabouts and lives returned unharmed. Had her husband not suffered a lifetime already answering to guards in his home who demanded identification to travel between rooms; and what of our suffering, she thought in rage about her bereaved children and her mother. What is a thoughtreel; she too had listened to Zachariah Ben Jaloun's mind. When would she disappear. Who would beat ladle against pot for her, she wondered.

When my aunt Reshma heard the news, she immediately invited my mother and grandmother to Berlin with the promise she would pay the ticket money. My grandmother, who had never taken a plane, agreed as much for the thrill of flight as for the need to be in a world where her daughter wasn't digging eyes out with fists all her waking hours. You go, Amma, Shukriah wiped boogers tears with tissue, I'll manage the hosiery shop while you're gone. Are you sure, Gita asked, and when my mother returned to weeping streams, my grandmother started packing her bags.

Recall that many years earlier, Gita worked in a government department where they peered into people's thoughts with shortwave radios, and more than once in her years she had wondered whether the experience of serving innocents up to butchers' knives desensitized her to the sanctity of human life; she wept with rage, thinking about putting on a fresh dress dark orange pair of sunglasses after her late husband's death, and starting her life again the very day he arrived at her doorstep heavy as a boulder, coffined. Hell, she gnashed teeth at her tote bag's busted zipper, and yelled for my mother.

My father never came home after my grandmother left, and Shukriah searched for him in every calling bell call and on the face of each customer that walked into her hosiery shop every day of the rest of her life.

At that time, the Quintuplets were sprouting quick adolescence without a father and sought shelter in Samir and Chaya's record shop. Under Aunt Shadow's gothful gaze they began touching black makeup to eyes lips, dangling metal piercings from creative incisions, and they began building pop music collections; Nehi gathered noise albums she blasted into headphones while her sisters went to the lottery. When Hum came home one day with a centimetre patch over a fleck of her nose removed as dictated by her ticket, Nehi buried herself in news broadcasts of the most recent spontaneous fire in a spidersilk refining plant, which had been accused of refining spidersilk for antiballistic army wear.

Four years changed me too.

It happened without warning. I left Masoud at the Halfway House one evening and went to cigarette shop for a soft drink. I was dazed, had been feeling utterly bereaved since a recent trip to the airport whose events I couldn't recall but which left my stomach and chest full of shards of broken glass. It hurt to breathe, I wore a bandage around my midsection to curb the profuse bleeding, eating was an impossible task, I was constipated shat goat pellets diarrhea rush, fled from room to room of the Hospice and sought comfort among ghosts resigned to a deeper death, and it was Masoud who said to me go, bhai, get yourself some fresh air and a Fanta, and get me one too. A shadow fell across Masoud Rana's face when he spoke these words, and he shivered in the balmy equatorial June weather. What's up. Nothing, he said, and get me some rock candy, he added, as I shrugged off his strange demeanour before travelling streets and alleys, crossed quite a few intersections to reach Xasan Sierra's cigarette shop because I wanted to clear my head, needed the walk, and because I wanted to visit with his daughter Vera, to sit and have a Fanta at her store, see how she was getting along since the army shot up the street and killed her father among hundreds of others when the people protested fifty-six more years of American occupation.

I recognized the landmarks fall friendly shadows late afternoon, and knew the cigarette shop was near. That's when shimmer and heat peeled my eyes, lifted my skin cooked shrimp in a place where tapering streets required travellers to pass through them sideways, where the walls bled into one another, and that's where I felt the flutter of a bird insect or bat moving around my body, and when I slapped the sound I brought blood to my right palm and crouched in pain as a car careened into view. A man opened the door held unrecognizable instrument to my skull before shouting loud words into my ears. The universe was shaking when they bundled me into the back seat muffled scream.

Hedayat awoke on a cold concrete floor in a room where walls pressed against his body from all sides. In dim light, he saw that his hands and feet were shackled. He rejoiced when all five walls began gliding soundlessly apart into invisible horizons, when the ceiling continued climbing, when the room's grey light let him plumb the increasing depths of its length width height, but when he tried to get up he realized either he had grown very large or they had really fucked up his brain with the fuzz pedal to his head, because he remained in place. If it was dusk when they brought him here, the artificial light, which seemed to emerge from the walls, which were opaque if you looked close, turned night black. Crawl centipedes flight of birds/ blade sounds of a string orchestra sustained one million rubble cries/ the breathing of a stranger whose breathing paused when his did, who didn't answer when he asked who are you. Time passed and to care for himself, Hedayat began once upon a time and halt, cried a voice. Hello, Hedayat tried to address the interruption, but met only silence. Once upon a time, he tried again/ at the bottom of a deep well, he continued despite the interruption, yet halt the voice cried halt in his grave. Again and again he tried to think of his present state of affairs halt and to thread past present future halt but halt was always the forceful response. Glossolalia, Hedayat cried, you have always been with me. Mutter and reason, I've trusted in you to part all the shadows, clear a path through the worst times. Was it there when you were with the underground animals, asked a big voice vibrated my skull, or when bigshot Hedayat announced the black economy also has its slavers and supplicants, the voice chided piquant, nasal, unsettled the boundary between outside skull and in my head. Where and who, I looked at the tight walls. Fear, a glacial breath rose up from the soles of my feet how did he know these things about me. What amazes me, said the voice, is that you know we know and that we have always known. Hedayat said nothing. When his thoughts resumed, he remembered his sleight of tongue, that he knew the stories of others who knew. He had thought about them, mumbled their stories to himself of his grand-parents knob-twiddling, listening headphones in Department 6119/ there's a movie about that, the walls shook as they said it. But Hedayat held his ground: my story, my owl's eyes on my head turned hundred and eighty/ loud laughter scraping glass: the film features a man with two tongues. Hedayat said nothing. Your grandfather, I presume. Fuck you. The voice subsided and for a moment, I felt victorious. I slept in patches of fake nightfall, peculiar daylight, pissed and shat in my pants. I tried to count the days with the revolutions of light and dark but I was convinced they were extending the intervals of each. Day and night occurred for increasingly longer periods, for so long I lost sense of dimension or direction, and the hot box they had put me in started expanding walls again. It continued growing until suddenly, I was sitting on its floor became a plane of sand, seemed suddenly like John Quincy's enormous room governed by an incandescent sun. How surprised I was when I could get up and stretch finally, when the walls expanded miraculously and the cage became a desert chamber. I heard nothing, didn't know why, what had happened to the voice or why the walls were running, and I ran at first to get as far away from the big voice as possible, and later, exhausted, I walked in the insufferable heat in the room's fetid breath electric sunlight, in the damn heat, for miles of dry throat. I finally stopped, removed and wrung my shirt under the high azure ceiling for a drink. Walking the thirsty sands gave me camel dreams. Caravans carrying sheikhs or sultans walked ant lines along the horizon under Oriental skies. I found no shelter except in hot rocks' shade. I walked for so long in such hot weather that the very name

Hedayat became a scattered remnant, grain of sand without memory or longing. Somewhere in the distance, I, if the term is correct, saw a grey rock in the sky and dust. I walked towards the colour and its shape broadened into a brick wall marked veins to mean years of weather-beating, in front of which stood a lone faucet, metal vegetation rising out of the ground. Like a thief, I searched quickly in all directions, and finding no one, drank greedily from an unknown source. The pressure of the tap suddenly increased violently as I drank, gurgling, bubbling water in my mouth and down my throat, choking me, and when I tried to jerk my head away, I was held in place by the stream. Huge hands adjusted the nozzle while another, gloved pair of hands stretched my eyelids and directed instrumental light into my eyes. The oasis image of wall and faucet disappeared, the sky vanished, while the earth under me waited a second until my body realized it was horizontal, not vertical. Machine squeal a barren room slightly larger than the box I was interned in appeared in its place. I could feel a hard plastic rigour level with my spine, forcefeeding tubes in my mouth, as well as wires, instruments in the room beeping, detecting my vitals. I heard the voice that had hitherto emerged from the walls of my box cell say it's been a long time, son, it'll be over soon. He's going to a dual cell, confirmed the second voice. My last thought was of my mother's cheek on my cheek while she comforted me during the tsetse fly plague after I told her about the fever dream animals, when she said, your father calls it glossolalia but I think it's just kid's stuff, and you'll get over it as you grow older.

Time passed. When they brought me to the second room, I had been reduced to an item of description, mere diagram, stick figure on a stretcher that for weeks couldn't move without an intravenous. Slowly,

I regained the ability to turn my neck to sound and light, changes in temperature, movement, to the thin sand streaming conical pile on the floor, and to identify the possibility of other human life in the vicinity. I was probably introduced formally to Habib in the months I relearned how to walk and to remember, but I don't recall the exact occasion anymore. What I do remember about the cell an hourglass is how the sand fell soft through a precise bullet-hole in the ceiling. Every day, the sand would stream through the hole. The conical pile was always already chest high at its centre and spreading, growing higher. From where I sat, I could see that prepared for the inevitable, my fellow prisoner was standing in a corner, smoking, watching the soft drizzle, desert precipitation in the cell, which belonged to a cell block of the prison consigned to silence.

Since I would reside with him in the same room for four years, allow me to introduce Habib, whose three characteristics of note include his quietude, his tobacco addiction, and his curious dice game, which he played constantly, rolling it in his hand in response to the slightest sound in our cell block, closing his eyes, and muttering to himself and smoking as sand rose in our room.

I've never seen anyone smoke as much as Habib. He had formed trade relations with the guards, and bartered keenly for slather-grey tobacco and foolscap for rolling paper. He smoked in a corner of the cell, farthest distance from the sands, and buzzed smoke and melody through lips while standing stiff upright with arms folded as guards moved past us, as delirious men were forced to enter adjacent holding rooms, as every day the sands piled higher.

He taught me to sleep standing up like barnyard animals as slaughter prisoners shouted abattoir sounds around us despite the tight laws in this section of the prison against noise, as their minds testified against them from thoughtreels. The agoraphobic claustrophobic horrors of the first room gave way to other sufferings in the second, though interrogations continued. They would haul me out of my cell by the scruff of my jumpsuit collar each day, several times a day when their reasons demanded, and, blindfolded, lead me down dark hallways in soft velvet shoes, as silent years passed by on either side of me, this one five, another one eight, ten years of imprisonment without trial or *habeas corpus* in one case. Four years for me. Four years of enter vast room shackled while loud disembodied voice demands answers to questions about times lives memories all suddenly suspects in fires in the unnameable country. The same brawny same bawdy interrogator appeared with his scalene pointy face, his humour of drink this, brother, thought I heard you wandered a desert in a coffin cell. This time, he came prepared with questions of whether I had participated in any meetings of the Islamic Justice Party, of what training Niramish had given me in the way of electronics, whether I had funnelled my drug money to any of a list of terror groups more populous than words in a dictionary, as well as with the constant query when had I last seen the Banquet Animals. Do you recognize these, he held up Niramish's uncle's bootlaces, the magic that had flown my friend and I out of an underground cavern. No, I lied. So be it, he said, and took out a lighter. Don't. Why ever not, he teased with a twinkle in his eye. Just don't. For a pair of laces, he taunted.

In the light of the halogen lamp shone bright, I remembered clearly how Q and I/ I said nothing. Our image together that night burned among lobster shadows, plumbing pipes, bloodstains, excretions. The interrogator swivelled the arm of the lamp away from me and I suddenly sat in the cold, in a dark expanse. My eyes adjusted. He was talking, I noticed, listening closely, murmuring secrets into a mirror that filled the entire back wall. An outside light entered the room. A corner door I noticed just then opened, and a man entered pushing a trolley containing a flat box and a television set.

Our country is filled with false stories, said the interrogator, of people who imagine the things they see in *The Mirror* are real life. My heart fumbled a beat. The light on TV flickered blue before a moving image. My face appeared on-screen; not my face exactly but enough of me to call it a *Mirror* reflection. Then I saw her face and I fell down in my chair. Of all the methods, I thought, and the pained expression on my face signalled to my captor the method was working. He hummed quietly and with a remote drove the television to another scene, an action sequence. A boy and a girl held hands and laughing fun fun ran up a wall like ants or animé; they hit the rooftop running. I knew what would happen next, of course, and could have narrated the/

You cried, said Habib.

Not then but later in the scene, I told him in our cell an hourglass.

They burned your chest.

And my arms, my throat, I said as the sand poured steady from the hole in the ceiling, as a red metal taste and shiver and I crumpled onto my bed. I thought about the terror.

They changed scenes.

They played another part of the film.

Then you cried.

Yes.

They burned you again.

No, they clamped my mouth open

Then what, he asked softly after a long time.

They pulled my tongue out of my mouth with forceps.

Shit, Habib drew from a foul and nasty cigarette.

Knives, he asked.

Scissors, I said.

Lucky sonofabitch.

No shit, I said, and I said nothing while remembering the most frightening part of the movie, of Hedayatesque on-screen waking up deserted, to the male protagonist's unanswered howl before descending

427

into an unlit path, to string orchestral cries at his gymnastic leap at a car-horn blast and his log-roll onto the sidewalk. I watched him walk for another minute until they did a close-up of a nearby vagabond, pestilential shape, man in cloth, grey, worm-eaten, whose face under lamplight was five hundred years old, judging by appearances, and too much to bear. Hedayat knew what the film would show next as he clenched teeth and fist, directed his double back to bed in his mind along the straight street until the camera caught Hedayatesque in bed right in his kisser, his bewildered face crawling under sheets, shivering for a whole minute of what the hell until her naked figure, moist sepals, her tongue doused, warm. Where did you go. To get a drink of water, where did you go, she asked, as the scene ended with arms legs entwined embrace. Now I realize the leap from life into *Mirror*, Hedayat thought as they showed him the film, the robbery of one's very mind, love and all.

They burned the bootlaces, asked Habib.

I sighed. If the contest was glossolalia versus *The Mirror*, Black Organs was insisting *The Mirror* had already eaten everything, even your thoughts, your desires, and that all the magic in the world, every inexplicable feeling image or event was on a Hollywood reel.

———————

Imprisonment. Privation. Loss. Suffering. Over the years, my busted insides became a central point of comparison between more suffering or less suffering, and how my prison pains compared with the break and shards that happened at the airport, in the coldest room in the world just before my arrest. In all our years pissing in the same toilet and sleeping in the same room that filled up to the neck each day with sand through a precise bullet-hole in the ceiling before they vacuumed it up so it could fill again tomorrow. I seldom told Habib of my life and learned little about his apart from the fact that he had once been in business with two men named Yasin and Kabir, spidersilk salesmen that had retired and now owned and operated a brothel in La Maga. The three of them had been accused of hiding weapons-grade spidersilk for antiballistic garb somewhere underground, which is to say such materials were never discovered to verify the accusations, and Habib was still serving time. He had grown children, he told me, and said that I reminded him of his eldest son, Raul, who had studied ergonomics in Germany and was designing the most comfortable chairs in Europe for a furniture manufacturer. You both have the same beaking lips, Habib said. It's just that you have eyes like an owl and fucked-up hands.

Confined men dream, they predict the future, play cards, smoke, and talk of women or angels. One day, during the hour each day when we were allowed to talk, when the guards pacing silk shoes weren't counting decibels with the most sensitive audiometers, my cellmate narrated once upon a time, there lived a woman in a house to which sand water and the Gulf of Eden were all accessible from a Blue Lagoon Room, where indoors were your own private outdoors the moment you agreed to the night's wages of the most appeasing woman in the world. What was her name. Laila. Where did you meet her. In the nightingale street where children and birds are often mistaken for one another due to the accuracy of the water whistles sold there. Vague directions, Habib. Best I can do under the circumstances, I'm afraid, he drew huge from a foul cigarette. Unfortunate, I said.

Habib tried again, recommended a boardinghouse a shared rent space near Laila's brothel, and gave directions, recognizable street names. Look her up, he recommended, and I humoured him, yeah, when she's my grandmama's age, I'll get out of here enough to lower her jeans. Habib rolled dice in his hands, he frowned, muttered under his breath, rolled again and said you'll be there sooner than you think, sly winking, rolling dice in the associative manner he said allowed him to relate sounds in the environment with dice numbers with correct predictions of the future. He got so good, he claimed, that he could tell from thumps in the adjacent room and two dice rolls whether the inmate three cells away was going to make it through the night, whether they were going to be on time with our dinner trays, and whether the rumours of a listeriosis epidemic were true or not. I told him how afraid I was of never feeling the sun at my back again, but he told me after a secret roll of dice and peer into his right palm not to worry, that I was about to be assisted by some heavy-duty hardware. Prison breaks were rare, they did occur on occasion, one major incident at another prison splashed international headlines when they reared a bread truck full of bombs, when they ruptured wall motor oil fumes, brick and twisted metal for the release of several Taints serving time after a simple jewel-thieving hustle in the 1970s, but I wondered who would pull a stunt like that on my behalf. I didn't ask Habib how he knew any of the things he claimed to know, his predictions were often correct so I encouraged him to speak his mind in the one hour of each day we were allowed to speak. The rest of the time, I usually thought alone in my corner of the cell, breathed heavy behind neckerchief sand filter read tawdry magazines, and, because our cell block was a silent region of the prison, I didn't say anything. Sometimes, I smoked Habib's shit cigarettes in a corner to try and avoid the constant trickle of sand in our hourglass cell.

One Monday night, while I was deep sleeping, a fee fi giant squeezed into our prison room and hauled me out of bed with enormous pliers. His partner, a rotund creature several feet high, conked Habib with a hammer on the head thin stream of blood and out cold. Flashes of doors light and shadow, they led me down dim-lit hallways overflow latrines, row upon row of salt-and-water-accustomed occupation prisoners, silent corridors, softscream soundproof walls until a courtyard where wandered an eminent vizier from centuries earlier, muttering, bubbling under breath release me sultan, I wasn't the one that stole your flying carpet, it was Alauddin.

There, the giant who caught me huge pliers made me stand under a baobab branch in the courtyard the vizier's eternal prison. His accomplice found the shovel eats earth mounds, dug deeper until space enough to store a man. The unceremonious scenario of my life's end brought me chortling choking tears, laughing as pale blood circled my body, hard to breathe even before they noosed me up to treebranch. Stand before the grave, they ordered, and I disobeyed them shrank to the size of a grain of sand to avoid them. Unsurprised at my struggle, my strategy to defy death, they pawed the earth, searching for my shape in the dust, tossed tufts of grass, dug mountains, struck deserts in frustration as I ran without a thought in my mind, hid in the shadows of one blade of grass after another until the morning sun beat me exhausted back into a man's size and found me drinking from a shallow fountain at the edge of the courtyard farthest from the entrance.

Then what, Hedayat. Did you die. No, the simple truth is, I lived. Deus ex machina: as unnatural as it sounds for all their efforts against me as a man a speck of dust, when they found me a thirsty animal lapping water with my hands at the fountain near the courtyard's edge, they caught me gotcha to tell me I was free to go. Sometimes, they let you go to catch you again, I thought nervously about the records of such arrests; sometimes, however, I thought the opposite truth, Habib's predictions actually came true. Astonished at the wind in my hair, the early sun at my back, I wondered what else he was right about.

I travelled intuitively through La Maga's streets twisting into alleyways where kids busted bottles with bottlecaps in opposing teams of threes and fours. In an avenue that clanged the sound of every bird in the world water whistling warbling ululating though there wasn't a feather in sight, just schoolkids, two men played chess in front of a row of smoke-stained houses. One of them clutched a wand of bread under his armpit while the other man opened a valise in which was stored a vase of red wine.

I paused to watch them negotiate a complicated arrangement on the chessboard; they exchanged a knight and a rook after long deliberation, and because of my interest in their game, divided the bread and shared the wine with me. Curious of Habib's stories and of the fact that my feet found their way exactly here, I conversed with the men, called Yasin and Kabir, who shared their lives' stories with me, which culminated in seventeen children whose precise genealogy has grown inscrutable over the years, they said.

They all live inside, Yasin reminds between mouthfuls, and says that all the boys, as far as he can remember, all called Victor, while all the girls are known as Laila. They play chess until the sun goes and the noises inside go louder and the voices become hoarse from all the shouting. Then matrons with expanded waists emerge from within, and soon there emerge, with the realization of there sits a nameless guest, various appetizing dishes that answer the question of what's for dinner tonight.

Eventually, we enter the house. And what cacophony then, strange men seated on chairs, delivered single-bite mouth amusers by uniformed servers, salmon roe and basil canapés, stuffed mushrooms, among other eats one might find in a hotel lounge or an abode of ill repute. Then we are covered by the shadows of guitarists, moth-eaten, blue painted, sitting waiting like the rest of us, while behind closed doors play vowels between the tongues of strangers. The red wine is now a thousand pinpricks on my skin, and these commingle until there emerges a girl in a dusty dress made of what appears like actual butterfly wings moving lapping chatting their many private languages, whose owner is Laila, which we already know from my mention, and who calls a number that means me.

Then I go with her, my Galapagos girl in her living dress her glossolalist butterfly garment, up the stairs and down a hallway, which recedes in width and height but not in length, through which we crawl and which could easily be called a crawlspace, until she stops at the right tiny door and pulls a latch that opens a tiny aperture. There she loves me, my Galapagos girl, on a fishnet island raised above the actual seawater so that it would appear the whole continent was enjoying with us our mouths for meals for hungry senses.

The chess players, I venture, shift my position because her weight increases every minute, is either of them your father.

She answers with a glint in her teeth, which shines the yes of her profession.

You were just breaking bread with my father.

Yes.

And you are from prison.

I shifted her weight uncomfortably on top of me. Where do you live, she pressed her thighs against my chest, and I lost my breath in darkness. The shimmer, light flickering water in the room made her a giantess when I awoke. I'm looking for a place, I told her when she asked again where I lived; she looked at me a moment more, suspicious, before relaxing, becoming lighter, easier to bear on the knotted-rope hammock; her skin glistened, her kisses simmered, and an inviting musk overwhelmed me. Time passed. You're one of Habib's men, she said, and I didn't respond.

When we were finished, she ferried me on her back broad strokes on water to the small door, and instructed me to crawl through the tight hallway until the space grew large enough to let me stand. If you walk a left, two rights thereafter, she said, you reach a hallway you should follow until the canal near the boardinghouse Habib spoke of. Mention Laila, she urged.

I moved on all fours at first. During my prison years, the unnameable country had sprouted so many venal pathways and become one jumble-map, you didn't need to leave your roof in the morning anymore to start work at the spidersilk factory, you just walked hallways or crawled there if the corridors demanded. Pathways changed daily with all the construction, so it didn't surprise me that Laila's directions were different from the actual road to Habib's boardinghouse. Hedayat tried to follow but wound up walking excuse me straight through someone's kitchen stewing fish in boiling pot while baby wailing. He cut through the room until the living room labyrinth of mirrors constructed at the Director's order many years earlier to make a movie set so complicated the Director himself was unable to navigate it. It took him a whole day to travel upstairs landing to front hallway, during which he was forced to follow a young camera assistant with a clipboard directed him past the guard tower, past guard dogs behind the sofa silenced with a whistle, and threaded him carefully through the barbed wire brought indoors for the desert firefight sequence in the film before the domestic scene near the dining room table.

Hedayat gazed around him at *The Mirror* in a home, recalled his father's shoulder imprisonment, the guards that demanded identification before allowing the family to move from one room in their home to another, and thought how homogenous time and space had become in the unnameable country: everywhere was indoors with sentinels sat our shoulders. I thought of a glimmer of difference in all the sameness, thought of Q, who told me the past is a haunted house, Hedayat, when I awoke beside her one morning from a terrifying nightmare: I saw you leave forever, I said, and she sighed, smiled while holding my hand to her cheek before informing me of her exit kit, her job, a plan to flee the unnameable country.

Four years later, I awoke from my recollection when a mirror on my right bent light and image into my left eye, and a mirror on my left shot a picture into my right eye. Fog and shimmer of a 3-D stereogram image made the face of none other than the man I had accused in my prison years of handing me to the cops after careful induction from every word and silence in the time we knew each other. So fragile my belief in his very existence, he flickered as all the mirrorlight teasing question object or image. But he was no less wiry with the years, and quick to pull me into jovial tones, disappearing puffffff of smoke returning lickety-split with laddoos and sweet swears, all bhai-bhai and shit as if we were in the days of the '66 Datsun.

I'm looking for a boardinghouse, Masoud, I said, and he, arms outstretched, said welcome home. Must be a mistake, I wondered Habib's prophecy and intention. Stay, please, Masoud seemed serious at my frowning volteface, called a name loudly into mirror-mirrors. You're here for the room, he bade me follow when she didn't appear. Turn after turn through the passageways, Hedayat saw himself growing shrinking in size, fat or string-bean skinny depending on the reflection suddenly little Hedayat's candy face in Confectionarayan's shop with a school friend, gorging on chocolate. The image of Narayan Khandakar's tin-metal receptacle appeared in my mind's eye suddenly because all the reflections around me stirred the most beguiling memories of the distant past, and I was tempted to ask Masoud if he had thought of its meaning in all the years, before remembering the event belonged to the story of Niramish.

You'll love it here, Masoud Rana pointed at the ceiling: the room is upstairs, he said, before inquiring how I earned a living. I'm clean now, he told me when I didn't respond, quit the pepper dealing soon after you started your prison stint. What do you do now, I asked. I run the place, man, he told me of recent changes to the Ghost Hospice, of the increased number of ghosts walked through doors due to proliferation of spontaneous fires in spidersilk fields, even hired our first undead staff recently.

Masoud, I shifted my tone, embarrassed to ask the man I was sure betrayed me for help. I'm clinking remains, man, what they gave me when I left jail, I said.

You want a job.

Yes, man.

We've been short-handed for a while, I'll cut you a deal on rent. I'll come by after you've settled in to talk to you ropes and literature about Ghost Hospices; I should also

What.

Hosanna, he exclaimed, and paused at a mirror without reflection unlike all the others, knocked against its surface, strange, he said. Wait here, he motioned with a hand, and pushed the glass, before disappearing behind it.

For a long time, no one appeared, and I was unable to persuade Masoud's mirror-door to open sesame. I tried to retrace the paths we walked by remembering their reflections and images, and wandered hours alone looking for stairs upstairs. Exhausted, I rested against a concave surface and fell asleep. I woke when roused by hands, questioned by a mouth are you lost, and gazed upon by disembodied eyes, by a face every child knows from gradeschool from museum trips to see slaver John Quincy's embalmed statue of his dead wife Caroline, captured by *The Mirror* in every role from charwoman to Cleopatra. Hosanna, I stammered, and the dislocated items joined into a woman's shape. How did you know my name, she smiled as I gathered my senses.

I told her about Habib, and Laila sends her greetings, I said. I told her about my encounter with Masoud Rana and his disappearance behind an unreflective mirror. He and I run this boardinghouse; he just walked an unusual mirror malfunction but he'll turn up; I'll show you the room myself in the meantime, she pointed ahead.

THE
RE-EMPLOYMENT
OFFICE

What ambiguous torments. What nameless interrogations assailed me soon after. And why.

Recall, though I haven't told you, it had been four years since Q accepted a job at the United Nations Relief and Works Agency in Mogadishu and that the Boy with the Backward Conch went with her crowded airport concourse still gripping his backward shell smiling at the side-selling juice and snacks salesmen loud hawking wares watch them walk into hollow metal fuselage. I remember shivering T-shirt in air conditioning light antiseptic odour fresh washed floors wonder walking distance to Mogadishu. I remember recalling at that time how, years earlier, Q had showed me a DV winning lottery ticket, a Diversity Visa with date and time and air travel information above a holographic New York City landscape, and how she had brushed that forever aside for my embrace that evening and many evenings since, how with my hesitation before responding to her request will you come/ wait let me think, wait because New York from an unnameable country is tricky gangster-steps/ wait because Mogadishu is a fresh bucking horse, as

I said to her when she asked me follow, differently, years later/ I had lost her to the in-between oblivion of an airplane hangar. I wished her departure was a dream from which I would wake up to even the painful reality of her breathing into my lungs on the Hospice floor, wake up, Hedayat, death is a dream, always in the future. I'll visit you, I yelled through the fog window reflection shattered glass insides. I stepped back to look at my right hand at belly weeping blood.

There was no explosion no visible wound, but it crunched glass when I walked and hurt like hell to sit down or to dream. I wore gauze and a tensor bandage around my stomach to tie the bleeding, and when I convinced the bloodstream abate, I wore it anyway as a precaution. The air of the Ghost Hospice became unbreathable without Q. By games of chess with the most senile ghosts, I began a life after death that lasted a pawn's move, knight's gallop, at most a bishop's far diagonal extension across tabletop. Game after game, the ghosts helped narrate a desert existence until I acclimatized to life without her until the day they hauled me face-first into car and jailed me in a room with one fibreglass window that let only the most temeritous light clamber in.

Time passes.

Year and year and year and year: I think of the hourglass trickle of sand behind heavy metal door. I lie in bed eat an onion weep quietly counting time with thumb and the lines of my forefinger: four years and another woman lives in my blood, I realize, astonished: Hosanna, she rattles and stones, daggers, penumbra, parched throat arterial flow, many cigarettes in one night in search of her, Hosanna. Hosanna, Masoud's girlfriend, my brother's wife, runs the Ghost Hospice with him and co-owns the boardinghouse where as a newly freed inmate I've taken up residence despite its mirror-labyrinth. Why did I choose this place. Apart from my cellmate's prophetic dice roll, recall such houses aren't unusual, initially having served as movie sets in *The Mirror* before being auctioned to the public. Though expensive, they're often converted into international hotels and hostels and are major tourist attractions in the unnameable country. I look around at wall hanging painting, a bookshelf, and a bedside table with its ornate crystalware, the room's posh carpet drags and I think of the mirror-passages I just crossed to arrive here. This is a drug dealer's estate, I think to myself. I wonder how Masoud made the money to build a palace; we were small time when Black Organs picked me up fuzz pedal to my brain and back seat of a sedan.

I lie awake thinking and casting Hosanna's shadow into the grey mist of my room where the light refuses to penetrate, making there the image of Hosanna and Masoud, of Masoud and Hosanna in their various, and does she ever call on me at that time to lie together this way or that way. I roll on my side and think of the coincidence of Masoud after all these years, I think of Hosanna, her face an exact mirror-cut of Caroline Quincy's glacial visage that from history textbooks television programs and toothpaste commercials all the kids know. Where did he pick her up, I wonder. In the coming days, I see him with kitchenware at feeding hours, in the equipment room grabbing balance balls for the undead, I see Masoud with Hosanna. How strange to work beside her wax museum, her television figure, beside Caroline Margarita mixing blood bags or serum with eggs parsley flour. Strange to return to the Halfway House, and stranger to inhabit it without Q.

What ambiguous torments until Hosanna asks me whether she can accompany me to the Public Records Department to inquire about procedures of hiring ghosts at halfway house establishments. Ghosts have recently joined our staff and I realized we should gather official assent for their continued employment. Hosanna had heard of our recent increase of blood bags from hospital raids and donations, of pistil and stamen flower foliage, coriander and fennel smells efflorescence and spice that now radiated house atmosphere the buzz excitement of new hires.

A ghost named Gibreel wide-eyed watched us bottle blood and wanted help us, keen, young, very much alive despite death. Gibreel of the swift hands punk plumose hair, of few but precise words measured blood portions new clients, wrote names on sheets changed clothes from corpsecloth to streetwear, an important volunteer before we decided to make him a salary man.

There was also Surayya, whose tears wouldn't curb even after doctors pronounced her hearthalted, dead. Unmoving as a tombstone she kept weeping for so long her family postponed her burial until her body began to smell. Rise from death without a thought of pastfuture, for a bloody drink. If it wasn't for a Halfway House team making cemetery rounds waft platelet odours through window to draw attention, to guide her to bath after death, registration, rest, she probably would have wandered indefinitely. Surayya's luck: her blinding thirst guiding to car, bottle of red to lips from my own hands as sit, I bid, sit, I asked, until she sat, got inside the vehicle, and Masoud Rana and I could drive her to the house where ghosts arrived singly, daily, on their own accord or in droves at our bidding.

Masoud asked Surayya about her sadness, and she couldn't speak, he asked/ leave her alone, I argued, but Masoud insisted official sheets, resisted, Halfway House rules, he reiterated as always in such cases until I demanded enough or the ghost in question declaimed, as with Surayya: my husband disappeared, my neighbour also left vanish as only remainder. Bring a mirror, she said, and showed us a bullet wound still weeping neck, secret to the unreflected image.

Dark night quiet steps, she explained how her house slept a cabaletta of muzzled shots. Celerity and mysterious indemnity reign as this government's night motions, no one said.

We gave her a nametag and a blood ration card, she stayed until we adjusted to the idea she wanted to make the Halfway House her home. Salt and yogurt, she demanded, took cloves and pepper, turned blood drinks for sustenance into cuisine art, as our shelter became a restaurant for the undead, as the Halfway House resumed an atmosphere we knew when Q was still here. Music filled the rooms, and Surayya's weeping turned into an admixture of emotions punctuated by plosive laughter manic tears. Though a difficult case, we thought the job would help busy her through life after death.

The Halfway House is a shelter, however, and has few posts for hire. We direct the majority of ambulant ghosts to the Re-Employment Office because it carries lists of jobs at institutions willing to hire the walking dead and ads for apartments around the country. I myself need to go there today because many new ghosts have arrived at the Re-Employment Office and by law we have to register them all, especially ghosts that we think can co-exist with the living so as to make room for others bound to appear due to an increase in the rise in spontaneous fires.

The events of the most recent such example were difficult to separate from cinema, but Journalists without Borders reported that a faction of the Islamic Justice Party, pinned in a neighbourhood languishing under an American blockade that hadn't allowed basic amenities to flow for weeks, accepted a surprise *Mirror* role as Hollywood villains for food. Cameras arrived in a convoy of trucks that also brought milk bread and fruit all fun fun for the gawking kids and their relieved guardians, arms outstretched. Then a flock of Justice Party terrorists who were probably terrorists were ambushed among the freeloaders by occupation army brush fire, and there were a lot of civilians there too. All the sounds turned militant and the bodies that could fled indoors. Within hours, after hundreds of magazines loaded reloaded, the entire region erupted without warning into a petrochemical blaze arising from an unspecified source. Luckily, *The Mirror* caught all the action.

At the appointed hour, I walk by Hosanna's door because she agreed to go with me to the Re-Employment Office that day. While I

sing a song under my breath, I think of the fire events in nearby neighbourhoods blaring television talk everywhere, and wonder how to make
them sound conversational while imagining us dancing hand in hand
through a government building's hallway and maze chambers whose
diagrams are historically known as being unable to guide visitors, and
who by word-of-mouth are advised to carry packed meals and sleeping
bags because they might spend days for a simple excursion to the
Re-Employment Office. But since I hear no human reply from behind
her door, I walk corridors that were once open-air streets to the address
everyone in our unnameable country knows, covered now by movie
ceiling for sky, and I pass crowded visage and tremulous aquaria fish
markets, marketers dancing chassé after reedy cries buy my wares.

The Re-Employment Office is located in the Ministry of Records
and Sources, a sarcophagous building of filing cabinets and papers,
whose archives we already know as caverns subdivided into quadrants
of shelves storing human thoughts, a building of doors and offices
behind whose doors appointed and hired officials pace while reciting
transcribed tortured minds ex cathedra.

Its front hallway extends into the empty distance. Door after door
forces our hero to closely follow a pocketed map from a table near
the entrance wonders location of the Re-Employment Office. From
the crinkle sheet diagram, at a point where the hall inclines, the lights
disappear. That's when Hedayat feels bodies appear suddenly, breathing
onto bodies making fetid smells. From the commotion, he senses a
crowd gather ex nihilo in the dark place as he tries to gather his senses.

He feels a shoulder, a neck, parcels, wheeled luggage, before he
remembers he has a lighter. With that butane flicker only light in all
the world he forays between shadows: workers hunchbacks giants bend
against the ceiling as dwarves and huddled women comfort children.
Hedayat asks a lady with her child in a cesta basket mere flickers in a
hallway: Do you know where the Re-Employment Office is. The woman's

reply is lost to tug on her hair cascades to her hips, to the child's cry, its ear-rending wail for another mealbite from her hands, you are looking for the Re-Employment Office, says the woman lifts hand from child. She turns her gaze from the cesta basket and allows me to see her old face its fissures, her mirror eyes designed by successive generations of hallway pilgrims to catch all the meagre light of the dark indoors.

Everyone hears stories in our unnameable country of weatherblown travellers journeying hallways and concourses and escalators elevators, and this woman is surprised I don't know the names. She looks into my lighter's light; her eyes reflect its flame. Find the assistant supervisor, of course, she says, before tilting her head back and laughing: we are all looking for the assistant supervisor. Others around her laugh with her at the old joke, and before I can ask who is/ the woman rude eyes suddenly shadows, believe it, indistinguishable as my lighter's flame stalls.

My lighter's momentary respite, its revelation of a heterogeneous world of people and locations, the perimeters of walls, floors, ceilings, disappears into indiscernible coarse cloth, expletives and pushes, groans as I am carried in that dark sway for hours or days until thirst swallows hunger as the greater need, until trickles down my pant legs, I am adding to the odours, I think. Somehow in the waves of motion, for step after endless step of momentum provided by my legs on auto, I fall asleep.

In my moving bed upright stiff-necked, I dream of a game of running and touching opponents in turn. Every playground contact makes red geranium follicles burst arms torso ribs and gullet, from everywhere on my body. I jerk awake to so many visible hallway shapes of crowd and walls I pat the inner pocket of the inner pocket of my shirt where the velveteen package, wonder for a moment whether to wear one of the bootlaces for flight gifted to me by the sorcerer who claimed to be Niramish's uncle, and leap over all the shapes, and realized the interrogators had burned that magic. Suddenly the moving crowd comes to a stop, single file in front of a door ajar, and around them stand tents and sleeping bags, the miserable, sick, the geriatric and hallway-born young who have made a campground in front of the bureau.

Quickly, I find my way near the front of the line, to an area of slight reprieve around the door because I see light, actual light, light despite bodies and obstructions believe it, light from the ceiling or a lamp behind a door, delightful light after all the darkness, yet no one enters. Is there an official inside who's going to come and see us, I ask. Minutes become hours and I decide to honour my curiosity, break from the line, and walk toward the door. A man with a bowtie notices my discomfort and tries to dissuade me cautiously, kindly: he points to the concourse of intersecting pathways nearby and tells me this office is the locus of many journeys; soothsayers have sworn by this door for many years, which they claim is the Re-Employment Office. The door is ajar, Hedayat points, why hasn't anyone tried to find the truth.

We have made important discoveries, the man nodded to his hallway friends, who hummed in compliance.

Has he ever addressed your concerns, I pointed to the tents, the gas ovens cooking midday meals in the hallway. Near the tents, an old man tasted from a pot of boiled fluid, smiled as he lifted it to his lips. The smell of lentils and onions invited whiffs and grumbling stomachs.

The Ministry of Records and Sources is a vast civil and economic enterprise and Department officials are known to grant meetings to hallway refugees on rare occasions. But I'm alive, I protested. Do I have to wait with the refugees.

The Department takes advocates and caregivers to be the same as the ghosts they serve, informed the bowtie conversant.

444

How often does he see you, Hedayat asked.

The bowtie conversant laughed: Though no one has seen the assistant supervisor, voices have been known to emerge from inside the bureau. Phone calls, one presumes. How the assistant supervisor comes and goes is also a mystery. We believe in an inner door linking the office to other parts of the building via passageways accessible only to Department employees, and have tried to listen by stethoscope provided by aid workers for creaking hinges inside, but no one has ever heard such sounds. However, just today, I myself witnessed a hand inside push the door for fresh air, though we travellers can attest, he laughed, to the asphyxiating atmosphere on this side.

If the Re-Employment Office might lie behind this door, why not just open it and find the truth, I asked, and the two men began giggling, gesturing to the people around them, who joined in the fun.

What are you waiting for, Hedayat raised his voice, and they laughed harder.

Has anyone entered this room, he finally yelled.

Have they entered, the bowtie conversant exploded onto his friend's face, apologized, wiped the spit away before the pair began laughing together, each egged on by the other until they had to hold their aching sides.

I don't get the joke, said Hedayat.

Have they entered, began the second conversant before bubbling again, quivering, quieted this time by his friend's gentle hand.

The door is open. I am merely asking if you've gone inside.

People have died trying to exit, exclaimed the man with the bowtie finally.

For a moment, Hedayat weighed his options. So much time had passed, he had nearly forgotten why he ventured underground today, and he wished he could see both directions in the hallway before deciding the shortest route back to the Halfway House. But the crowd began to simmer around him suddenly and the air became too hot and too foul to breathe. Bodies drew closer together, clotted the hallway, while, because Hedayat was close enough to the door, he could feel a refreshing breeze blow from inside the room. Time passed and so many minutes dragged shouts, infants' cries, grown men and women in a sweating crowd churning muddy water, sediments, immeasurable wait, that a chink of hope, a door with the slightest opening, despite Bowtie Man's mortal warning, seemed like Hedayat's only plausible option.

––––––––––––––––

Hedayat pushed the door open and the others who were flung into the room with him ran out immediately, crying anxiously, accursed place. Inexplicably, the heavy metal door slammed shut. When he found his feet again, he walked slowly because he had to part the dense shadows with his hands before he could see the first wall twenty feet away with its grey spines adjacent to one another like books until the next crowded wall of rectangular shapes separated by an indentation, walkways through which one could see walls coming and going, intersecting perpendicular in soft light. Dead light in the distance, rested ancient thoughts. Fluorescent lights high above.

Soft pebbly light fell onto the floor. Rough steps, Hedayat stumbled in a narrow passage. Clangour as he stepped foot over foot tripping foot, and something fell onto the floor. He stared at the rows of nocturnal shelves on either side of him. Then another sound, a syllable or rock hurled somewhere behind him against a metal case. Where am I, he thinks. Where is Hedayat.

I am in a dead world, I mused, without corpses, only coffins and tombstones. If there is life after death here, it is hidden and much bigger than the living world, a collection of all the minds on magnetic reel. *The Mirror* wants to be this place, Hedayat shivered, it wants every thought in every jar. Hedayat recalled how when they tortured him they showed him his life's most intimate moments. He thought how his heart fumbled when he saw the male protagonist, Hedayatesque, on television patting sheets in an empty bed in the middle of the dark. Recall his rage and confusion at how could they know and take my deepest fears of being deserted by her. *The Mirror* wants moments like that, he thought, to multiply a billion times bigger by ingesting all the realities that were and are, might have been and could be in the unnameable country, where traces of histories my glossolalist tongue never ventured to describe exist somewhere in this haunted library, where even traces of non-lives must exist on thoughtreel.

What would have happened, I ask, if my grandmother had never surrendered her shoe servant's job and migrated to the unnameable country. Would her bejewelled grey eyes have haunted Zachariah Ben Jaloun. Imagine, even after arriving at our shores, my grandmother finds her first weeks of life in the Ministry of Records and Sources so stifling she chooses to apply at the Bata department store near her home, and that after repeated visits to insist upon the strength of her footwear credentials, she earns a salesperson's job.

As this version of the story goes, she never ends up meeting Zachariah Ben Jaloun's border crossing, never goes to his standalone café either, where instead of drowning in onion-tears, in this version of things, he decides not to break things off with one Marjane B, theatre reviewer for the *Victoria Star, Benediction Post,* and assorted literary magazines, his fling directly prior to our story, a relationship unsettled by squabbles of the working poor, and which, it must be noted, was the cause of his hallucinogenic poetry in his volume *Orange Blossoms.*

In this version of the story, Marjane's work in literature, her publicist's charm, helps the book catch lucky break after lucky break and become a national and international hit. Zachariah files for temporary leave from his border guard's post and starts writing fiction and poetry full-time, furiously. Marjane and Zachariah move into an intimate, clean little flat where, soon, along comes a baby in swaddling clothes. Barely minutes newly born, still wet with mother water, what shall we call him, Marjane asks. Zachariah disappears into the recesses of some parallel consciousness: Mamun, he says.

What if my grandmother and grandfather never met is what Hedayat means. Hedayat spins glossolalist in the airless Archives, lets himself feel the eeriness for one moment of having never been born, unruly free, unhindered by even the prison walls of the human heart or body.

I, if that is the proper term, wander thinking, hunting Ariadne thread for a clue out of this labyrinth of thoughts, its door shut firmly behind me, the Assistant Supervisor or his superior nowhere to be found, and its future of wandering twisting miles, millennia in search of my beginning, as I think and hope that though Zachariah might have biting onions into verses better with Marjane and Zachariah's détente, his border guard boss would probably one day have ordered him into Department 6119's dungeon due to reasons beyond them both, that Gita with the grey eyes and my grandfather would surely eventually have made Mamun out of kisses and kismet. I rest my hand against a shelf of metal receptacles: and we have another generation to go before Hedayat, I think, before Hedayat's big bang, years' out of gestation in an unnameable sky that still sets fire to millions of people below, before the involuntary contractions of my mother's body shiver and ache on a flying carpet that Alauddin the magician drives, as you know, before her howl with eyes poised above at the airless oblivion, as

ACKNOWLEDGMENTS

The author would like to thank friends, family, teachers, warm restaurants, welcoming homes, a half-dozen laptops desktops personal computers, my mother, without whose moral guidance and financial support I would have withered at the basement stage of creativity, my father's uncanny endurance, the encouragement of an octogenarian great-uncle who declared immortality to my face, Margaret Atwood, Jonathan Garfinkel, a tremendous writer and true friend, and Nicole Winstanley.

e universe is shaking.the universe is Shaking.th
 shaking.the universe is shakinG.the universe is
rse is shAking.the universe is shaking.the unive
aking.the universe is shaking.tHe universe is sh
 sHaking.the universe is shaking.the unIverse is
rse is shakiNg.the uniVerse is shaking.the unive
iverse is shaking.the universe is shakinG.the un
e universe is shAking.the universe is shaking.Th
g.the universe is shaking.the universe is shakin
aking.the universe is sHaking.the universe is sh
 shaking.the uniVerse is shaking.The universe is
rse is shaking.the universe is shakinG.the unive
iverse is shAking.the universe is shaking.the un
e universe is shaking.the uniVerse is shaking.th
g.the univErse is shaking.the universe is sHakin
aking.the uniVerse is shaking.the universe is Sh
 shaking.the universe is shakinG.the universe is
rse is shAking.the universe is shaking.the unive
iverse is shaking.the universE is shaking.tHe un
e universe is shaking.the universe is shaking.th
g.the uniVerse is shaking.the universe is Shakin
aking.the universe is shAkinG.the universe is sh
 shAking.the universe is shaking.the uniVerse is
rse is sHaking.the universe is shaking.the unive
iverse is shaking.the universe is shakinG.the un
e uniVerse is shaking.the universe is Shaking.th
g.the universe is shakinG. the universe is shaki
Aking.the universe is shaking.the universe is sh
 shaking.the universE is shaking.the universe is
rSe is shaking.the universe is shaking.the unive
iVerse is shaking.the universe is Shaking.the un
e universe is shakinG.the universe is shaking.th
g.the universe is shaking.the uNiverse is shakin
aking.the universe is shaking.the universe is sh
 shaking.the univErse is shAking.the universe is
rse is shaking.the universe is Shaking.the unive
iverse is shakinG.the universe is shaking.the uN
 universe is shaking.the universe is shaking.th